HO

A

Than Fiction

A Truth Stranger Than Fiction

A DAKOTA STEVENS MYSTERY

CHRIS ORCUTT

A Truth Stranger Than Fiction

A Dakota Stevens Mystery Novel

by

Chris Orcutt

First Print Edition: 2015

ISBN-13: 978-0692352571 (Have Pen, Will Travel)

The photograph on the cover, "MacBook Pro backlit keyboard," is by photographer Remko van Dokkum on Flickr. The original design for the Dakota Stevens Mystery Series covers is by Elisabeth Pinio, a graphic designer based in the Silicon Valley. The cover artist and ebook formatter for this novel is EBook Converting|High Quality Ebook Conversion: ebookconverting.com

Also by Chris Orcutt:

A Real Piece of Work (Dakota Stevens #1)
The Rich Are Different (Dakota Stevens #2)
The Man, The Myth, The Legend (Short Stories)
One Hundred Miles from Manhattan (A Novel)

www.orcutt.net
www.dakotastevens.com

For Alexas:

My Véra, My Hadley, My Muse

'I'll love you, dear, I'll love you
Till China and Africa meet,
And the river jumps over the mountain
And the salmon sing in the street,
. . . . .

— W.H. Auden

"Truth is stranger than fiction, but it is because Fiction is obliged to stick to possibilities. Truth isn't."

— Mark Twain

1

She Sounded Blonde

At nine o'clock in the morning I stood at the windows of my new office overlooking Madison Square Park. I was sipping Jamaican Blue Mountain coffee, admiring the early October foliage, and exchanging naughty text messages with a 30-year-old divorcée on the Upper East Side.

Texting was a new skill for me, but apparently I was a natural. My latest message caused its recipient, Clarissa, to message back, *"OMG Dakota! I almost fell off the damn treadmill!"*

I fired another salvo, a steamy text guaranteed to knock her on her berry-ripe backside for good this time, then turned my attention to the moving boxes. Svetlana had agreed to handle most of the unpacking, but she was in Connecticut at a speed-chess tournament and book signing. In all, since our last case a couple of months ago, Svetlana had managed to win four tournaments and write a second chess book. Meanwhile, I hadn't even dropped off my dry-cleaning yet.

Standing there in the stillness, three floors above rush-hour traffic, for perhaps a minute I was at peace with the world and my place in it. Then my cell phone rang. With its new ringtone—the theme from the 1970s TV show *The Rockford Files*—I usually reveled in the theme, letting it play for a while. But today the music was ominous. Today it shattered the silence in the room and foretold trouble on the other end of the line.

And if I'd known how *much* trouble, I might not have answered it.

The ringtone played insistently. Soon the phone would go to voicemail. I didn't want any trouble today, but too bad. Like the title of the Raymond Chandler story goes, *trouble is my business.*

I put down my coffee, took a seat and answered the call.

"Dakota speaking."

"Mr. Stevens?" It was a woman's voice. "Where are you? Your office is closed."

I leaned back in my chair and looked down Fifth Avenue, as if I could see all the way down and across town to East 10th Street. *Dumbass.*

"I'm at my new office. The directions should be on the door."

"There they are," she said. "You really need to update your website, Mr. Stevens."

"I'll get my I-T department right on that."

"Madison Square Park?" she said.

"Yes. My building is the ancient one with the bay windows. Third floor."

"I'll be up in fifteen minutes. Please be there. I think someone is following me."

"Do you want me to—"

She hung up. I stared at my phone. Most likely, no one was following her. New clients, enamored with the novelty of hiring a PI, often imagined they were being followed. I got up and freshened my coffee at the credenza.

The new office lacked a break room, not to mention the old one's slick glass walls and hi-tech conference room. One could say the new office was retro. *Very* retro. It had been occupied for decades by an ancient pair of accountants, then had lain empty for years after the second partner died. They left behind two elephantine oak desks, frosted glass doors and about an inch of dust. The walls, probably eggshell white 40 years ago, were now the color of a paper bag. And the dozens of moving boxes strewn everywhere only underscored the shabby feel of the place.

Svetlana had decorating plans though, and what the office temporarily lacked in creature comforts was made up for by its address—an address I wasn't sure we could afford: Fifth Avenue.

I went to the window and looked down at the street. Traffic was at a standstill. The sidewalks teemed with jostling people late for work. I sipped some coffee and thought about the woman on the phone. The woman had sounded attractive. Attractive and confident. I wondered what color her hair was and decided she sounded blonde. Blonde and tall. I scanned the heads of tall blonde women walking past the park, and waited for one of them to cross the street to my office. None did.

After a couple of minutes I realized I couldn't put off unpacking any longer. Surveying the sea of boxes, I saw one labeled "Dakota Desk," and, with a leaden sigh, started to unpack it.

Out in the hallway the elevator grate banged, followed by a knock at the door. The glass rattled.

"Enter," I said.

The door swung open and a bobbed head of hair—cotton candy pink and blue hair with Cleopatra bangs—entered the room. She was a petite woman—early 20s, I surmised—dressed in a short black leather jacket, white tank top, denim shorts, and Doc Martens boots with black knee-high socks. A canvas messenger bag dangled from her shoulder.

"Mr. Stevens?"

"Are you the one who just called?"

"Yes."

So much for my deductions based on the woman's voice. She shut the door.

"Here, take a seat." I nodded at the two client chairs in front of the desk.

She sat down, pinching her knees together. Now that she was closer and I could see details, I knew she was younger than I'd thought. Her skin was porcelain, her eyes cobalt blue. There were circles under her eyes, which she had attempted to cover with heavy eye makeup. A small diamond stud adorned the side of her nose. And tattooed on the inside of her left wrist was a single word: "TRUTH."

She looked nothing like my usual client. Not that her personal style mattered to me. As long as she was old enough to hire me and her case didn't require me to go undercover in a high school, I would take it. I got my digital recorder out of the desk drawer, hit the record button and set it down facing her.

"Before we get started," I said, "how old are you?"

"Why does that matter?"

"Because if you're not an adult, I'll have to talk to your parents first."

"My parents are dead, Mr. Stevens," she said. "They have been for a long time. And I'm eighteen. Satisfied?"

"I'm sorry about your parents. Can you show me some ID?"

With a huff she rummaged through her messenger bag, produced a wallet and casually tossed it to me. Inside was a New York State ID card. Her hair was just cotton candy pink in the photo; the blue, it seemed, was a later inspiration. Her name was Kelsey Wright and she was 18 years old.

"You don't drive?" I said.

"Nope."

My cell phone chirped. A new text from Clarissa had come in, but I didn't have time to amuse her right now. I tossed the wallet back.

"Thank you, Miss Wright."

"Kelsey."

"Okay...Kelsey. How can I help you?"

"My brother's disappeared, and I'm being followed."

I leaned forward in my chair. "All right, let's take this one step at a time. When was the last time you saw your brother?"

"Six days ago. He left the apartment in the morning and never came back. I've been staying in hotels since then. I'm too scared to stay alone."

"You live with your brother?"

"I do, on Riverside," she said. "How'd you know?"

"You said, 'He left *the* apartment,' not '*his* apartment.' What's your brother's name?"

"E. Conover Wright. He's a sci-fi writer. A famous one, in fact. Maybe you've heard of him."

"Sorry, I haven't."

"What about the TV series *Earth 2.0*—heard of that?" she asked.

"No, but I don't watch much TV."

"What *do* you do?"

"I read a lot," I said. "Just not science fiction."

My phone chirped again.

"Anyway, *Earth 2.0* is incredibly popular and it made Conover rich, really fast."

"That could be significant."

"How?"

"Blackmail possibly, but never mind that," I said. "What does the 'E' stand for?"

"Edwin," she said. "But he goes by Conover."

"I assume he isn't married, because if he were, I'd be talking to his wife right now."

"Correct. Conover isn't married, and never has been."

"Does he have a girlfriend?" I asked.

"I don't know if they're exclusive, but yes."

"Did you see him leave that morning?"

"No. I woke up and he was gone. So was his laptop. That's how I know he left. He never goes anywhere without it."

"You said it's been six days. Did you report this to the police?"

"A couple days ago," she said. "*Huge* waste of time."

"What did they do?"

"I don't know. They took a report and checked some stuff—his credit cards, the airlines, stuff like that—and then they said that"—she made air quotes—"'there were no indications he'd been abducted.'"

"And?"

"And...there's been no activity on his credit cards and he hasn't flown anywhere. The thing is, Conover's gone on last-minute trips before, so the cops aren't taking this seriously. But he's always left a note. This time he didn't. Don't you think that's suspicious?"

"I don't know enough yet," I said. "What else did the detective say?"

"Nothing helpful. She said I should call them in a week if I haven't heard from him. In the meantime, she said I should contact you."

My phone chirped twice in a row. I grinned thinking of Clarissa, hot and sweaty, frantically texting me.

"She?" I said. "Her name wouldn't be Ellis Carter by any chance?"

"I think so." Kelsey reached in her jacket and pulled out a business card. She yawned. "Yeah, that's her. Why, you know her?"

"I do. She sends me cases sometimes."

She was also a single and aloof strawberry blonde who had resisted all of my advances. I resolved to keep trying. Kelsey nodded at the credenza.

"Can I have some coffee? I've haven't slept much lately."

"Help yourself."

She wended through the boxes and poured herself some. When she sat down again, her hands were curled around the mug.

"I have more questions," I said.

"Go ahead."

"You mentioned you've been staying in hotels."

"Yes," she said. "The Waldorf, the St. Regis, and the Pierre."

I whistled. "Nice hotels."

"I wanted to be safe. Anyway, what difference does it make?"

"Well, have you been back to your apartment at all?" I asked.

"No."

"Then how do you know your brother hasn't returned?"

"Because I've been calling him and calling him, and he doesn't answer, and he hasn't tried to call me."

"What if he lost his phone?"

She looked at me like I'd said something legendarily stupid.

"He never has before."

"Fair enough," I said. "Does your brother have any reason to want to disappear? Is it possible he did something illegal and he's avoiding the law?"

"No and no," she said.

I leaned back in my chair and tapped a finger on my lips. "What about vices? Gambling? Booze? Women?"

"What, like he's off partying someplace?"

"Yes."

She rested her mug on the armrest and looked at me without blinking.

"He doesn't gamble, he doesn't drink, and I'm positive he doesn't chase women."

"How old is he?" I asked.

"Thirty. Does it matter?"

"I don't know yet. It might."

In a span of ten seconds, my phone chirped three more times. Kelsey scowled at me.

"Maybe you should, like, *answer* that? You seem to be getting a lot of texts."

I picked up my phone with a jaunty swagger. Then I started to read Clarissa's messages. I was knocked back in my chair with the wind taken out of me.

"What's wrong?" Kelsey asked.

I shut it off before her words fried the circuitry.

"Nothing. Just a friend in need," I said with a smile. "She'll be fine."

I stood and gazed out the window. Rush hour was over and the stopped traffic on Fifth had cleared out. So had most of the pedestrians. A few stragglers shambled along the sidewalk beside the park.

"So," Kelsey said behind me, "what do you think?"

"Before your brother disappeared, what was his behavior like?"

"What do you mean?"

I turned around. "I mean, was he acting like his usual self, or did he do anything strange, out of the ordinary?"

"Definitely out of the ordinary."

"How?"

"I don't know, it's hard to explain," she said. "He's raised me since I was seven and we're super-close, so I know when he's not acting normal, all right?"

"Tell me something specific that's different."

"Well, he was leaving the apartment at odd hours, and he was talking on his phone in his bedroom with the door closed."

"The phone—that's unusual for him?" I asked.

"Yes. Conover hates talking on the phone. I handle his calls."

I stooped over and checked the desk drawers for my tennis ball. Bouncing it always helped me think, but I couldn't find it. Must be buried in one of the boxes. I sat down and put my feet up.

"Why do you handle his calls?"

"I'm his assistant. I handle all his business—and I'm his first reader. That's another thing: he hasn't shared *any* of his new book with me, which tells me something's up."

"Do you have any idea what the book is about?"

"The moon, I think." She sipped her coffee. "A few weeks ago, he left his laptop open and I saw the words 'the moon' in several places on the screen."

"But isn't the moon a standard topic for a sci-fi author?" I asked.

"Sure, but this didn't look like fiction. It was dense, like nonfiction, and he's never written a book of nonfiction before."

"Maybe he's not confident about it. Maybe that's why he doesn't want to share it."

She shook her head. "He shares everything with me. I've asked him about it, but all he says is, 'Not this one, Kelsey'—like there's something to hide."

I stroked my face. I needed a shave.

"What?" she said.

"Honestly? It's sounding like he was working on a difficult project and needed to get away for a while. Someplace alone where he could finish his book."

"But that doesn't explain the people following me."

"Who's following you?" I asked. "A man, a group of men? A vehicle? Can you describe any of them?"

"No, it's not like that. Haven't you ever felt like you're being watched—like, followed?"

I had, but I didn't want to play into her possible paranoia. She sighed and stared at the floor.

"All right, so never mind about people following me. You don't believe me. Fine. But will you take the case? Will you find my brother for me?"

I was thinking it over, wondering how Svetlana would feel about it, when the elevator grate banged in the hallway. The office door opened and two tall men in forgettable suits walked in.

2

THE CHA-CHA

One of the men wore a gray pinstripe suit, the other solid charcoal. They looked fresh out of the law school oven, and their hair was cut close. Their movements were self-conscious and deliberate, as if they had recently learned how to handle themselves and were still adjusting to it. I shut off the digital recorder and slipped it in my pocket.

"Gentlemen," I said. "You're with the Bureau, I presume?"

With a glance at each other, they pulled out their badges and showed them to Kelsey and me. This was my first time on the receiving end of the FBI badge-flash. It was weird.

"I'm Special Agent Lewis," Pinstripe said, "and this is Special Agent Gallagher. We need to ask Miss Wright a few questions."

"I don't understand," she said. "What's this about?"

"You *are* Kelsey Wright, sister of E. Conover Wright, the novelist, are you not?" Gallagher asked.

"I am."

"We need to know where he is," Lewis said.

"I don't know," Kelsey said. "Why do you think I'm here? So *he*"—she gestured toward me—"can find him."

"When was the last time you saw him?" Gallagher asked.

Kelsey was about to answer when I signaled her to stop talking.

"Six days ago," I said. "Guys, she doesn't know anything. It would help if we knew why you're looking for him. It might give us a lead on his whereabouts."

"Mr. Stevens," Lewis said, "you know we're prohibited from discussing open investigations with the public."

"Yeah, but I thought I'd try anyway." I turned my phone on again.

"Who are you calling, sir?" Gallagher asked.

"Friend of mine. Assistant Director Craig Hanson. Perhaps you've heard of him?"

They studied me impassively. I had hoped that upon hearing his name, they'd spill everything they knew about Conover. They didn't. They just stood there like a pair of wedding cake grooms.

I got Hanson's secretary. She put me on hold, then came back on the line and said Hanson would return my call soon.

"What is this regarding?" she asked.

"The two agents in my office," I said. "Thank you."

I hung up. Kelsey was trembling. Adrenaline. Had the sudden appearance of the agents scared her, or was she hiding something?

"Are you okay?" I asked.

"My brother is wanted by the FBI, Mr. Stevens," she said. "What do you think?"

"Well, I believe you now."

"Believe me?"

"That you were being followed," I said.

"Told you."

The *Rockford Files* theme played. I smiled and answered the phone.

"Stevens," Hanson said, "what's this about? I'm late for a meeting."

"Two agents are in my office looking for a writer named E. Conover Wright. Why?"

"You know I can't tell you that," he said.

"Not even a hint? After I helped you make assistant director? Come on."

"Yeah, thanks. Now my days are eighteen hours instead of twelve." He groaned. "It involves national security. I've got a dozen agents on it and I'm under a lot of pressure, so if you find anything, tell Lewis and Gallagher. Goodbye, Stevens." The line clicked off.

I put the phone away and came out from behind the desk to face the agents. Kelsey was trembling even harder now. I put a hand on her shoulder.

"Guys, she doesn't know anything. That's why she's hiring me. Leave your card, and if we learn anything, we'll call."

Agent Lewis handed me a card. "We'll expect to hear from you."

"Soon," Gallagher said.

"If we learn anything," I said.

"No, even if you don't," Lewis said. "We need a list of Mr. Wright's known associates. Call and set up a time when she can come in. She's welcome to bring a lawyer if she wants."

They headed to the door and paused.

"You know," Gallagher said, "you ought to get a painter in here before you unpack. The place is pretty dingy."

"Any other decorating tips?" I said.

He thrust his hands in his pockets and looked around. "A plant or two wouldn't kill you."

They left and closed the door. The second the elevator grate banged shut, I sat down in the other client chair. Kelsey was staring at the floor. I lifted her chin.

"Hi there."

"Hi yourself," she said.

"That was the FBI."

"I know," she said.

"We need to talk."

"Okay."

"What is your brother mixed up in? If you know *anything*, you need to tell me."

"I have no idea," she said. "Honest. I'm in shock."

The elevator grate banged in the hall again. Kelsey jumped in her chair.

"Relax," I said. "Probably the agents. Forgot their personalities."

She nodded.

The door opened and two sides of beef clomped into the room. They were in their mid-20s and wore jeans and boots. They were twins: about 5'10", dark brown hair, dark eyes. In fact, the only way to tell them apart was by the brand of work coats each wore—a Dickies and a Carhartt. They shut the door and stared at Kelsey.

"We wanna talk to you," Carhartt said.

"Where's your brother?" Dickies said.

I stood, pulled Kelsey out of the chair and got in front of her.

"She's not talking to anyone right now," I said.

"Yeah?" Dickies said. "We'll see about that."

"Kelsey," I said. "Get behind my desk and sit in the chair."

I kept my eyes on the men while she moved. Behind me, the chair springs twanged in the quiet room. The men approached flexing their hands—huge, gnarled hands.

Habitually I reached for my gun, but it wasn't there. It was in the desk drawer. I'd removed my hip holster intending to transfer the gun to a shoulder holster, and never got around to it. They stepped toward me. Carhartt was closer, but I couldn't believe how wide open he was leaving himself. Neither one was protecting his chin, which meant I could knock out either of them with one solid punch to the jaw. These guys were brawlers, not professional fighters. Relieved, I took a breath and assumed a defensive stance.

Carhartt lunged to tackle me, but I was ready. I sidestepped and shoved him. He tripped on a box and fell head-first into the steam radiator—so hard, it made the pipes sing. By the time I turned around, Dickies was already on top of me. He swung a haymaker at my head. I ducked as his big arm whooshed past, then spun inside and smashed him twice in the face with my elbow. I felt him stagger—I might have even broken some of his teeth—but he got his composure back and followed up with a punch to my stomach that doubled me over. Grabbing me by the belt, he slung all 200 pounds of me into a tower of moving boxes. The boxes toppled, and I struggled to get back on my feet. My gut was screaming from that punch. One thing was for certain: I couldn't take another one of those.

I faced Dickies again. He charged at me with those menacing hands extended. When he was six feet away, I feinted left, then right, like a football wide receiver. He tried to match my shifts in direction, but they put him off balance, and I nailed him with a left hook to the jaw on his way by. He stumbled forward and hit the wall. Solid plaster. It took him a second to shake it off, and when he stood up, he was holding a big hunting knife. Kelsey called out behind me.

"Mr. Stevens, he has a knife!"

"I see it."

I looked around for a weapon. In the meantime, Carhartt began to stir. My eyes darted around the room until I saw a box near me labeled in Svetlana's precise handwriting: "Dakota's Toys." Dickies moved in again, extending the knife. I punched through the tape on top of the box and groped around inside. A plastic rectangular object: a stun gun. No good. Then my fingers fell upon a cold length of metal with a foam handle on the end, and I knew what it was: an ASP collapsible baton. I yanked it out and extended it with a flick of the wrist. I now had two feet of striking steel at my disposal. If Dickies had known anything about hand-to-hand combat, his face would have fallen at the sight of the baton—it was that devastating a weapon. Instead he waved the knife and kept coming.

Over by the radiator, Carhartt was almost on his feet. I needed to end this before they got smart and coordinated their efforts. If they rushed me together, I'd be in trouble. When Dickies got close enough I crouched and lashed out with the baton at his knee.

"Ah, Jesus!"

His leg buckled, and as he tried to regain his footing, his arm with the knife dropped. I whipped the baton across his wrist. He yelled and the knife clattered to the floor. To put him down for good, I dodged his flailing arm and kicked him behind the knee. He fell, knocking over a stack of boxes.

I collapsed the baton and put it in my back pocket, then went to the desk and got my new gun. A sleek, black Sig Sauer .45 ACP with an 11-shot capacity, it was guaranteed to punch big holes and break bones—even in sides of beef. I switched off the safety and pointed it at them.

"All right, fellas—game over."

I glanced at Kelsey. She was shaking harder now, and her eyes were enormous.

"It's the adrenaline, Kelsey," I said. "You'll be okay. Take slow, steady breaths."

I went over to the twins. They were sitting next to each other against the wall. Dickies held his smashed wrist while Carhartt rubbed his noggin.

"Your wallets." I snapped my fingers.

Carhartt reached in his jacket and handed me his.

"His, too," I said.

When he had given me both wallets, I took them to the desk and opened them: James and Luke Bishop of Bismarck, North Dakota.

North Dakota? What the hell was Conover Wright into? Keeping the gun on them, I wrote down their information in my pocket notebook.

"I don't know who is who." I tossed them each a wallet. "Now, who are you working for?"

No answer. I looked at Kelsey. She was trembling.

"Who...who...are they?"

"They're from North Dakota, that's all I know."

The elevator grate banged in the hallway again. I'd been considering asking the building super to fix that noise, but now? Not a chance.

"Get under the desk, Kelsey," I said.

While she crawled into the space underneath, I came out from behind the desk with the gun leveled at the doorway. The door opened.

A pair of Italian men in their 20s who could have been models for Armani walked in wearing belted black leather coats and ribbed black turtlenecks. They had that fashionably unshaved look and enough styling product in their hair to be a fire hazard. With a glance at James and Luke, they took a step forward, saw me pointing the gun, and immediately stepped backward in sync, like they were dancing the cha-cha. They raised their hands and started to retreat out the doorway.

"Stick around, guys," I said. "And close the door."

They did.

"See that big couch? Sit down."

They sat and crossed their arms and legs.

"Now," I said, "what brings you to my humble agency?"

They declined to answer.

"Let me guess. You're looking for Conover Wright, and you were hoping to ask his sister where he is. Well, get in line, fellas. Get in line."

"We don't want to hurt her," said the one on the left. "Just talk to her."

"Sorry, but you won't be doing either. Who sent you?"

They laughed.

"You kidding, buddy? You think we're gonna tell you that?"

"Well, you two look pretty vacuous, so I thought I'd give it a shot. Your wallets." I snapped my fingers. "Let's have 'em."

The one on the right smirked. "We're not carrying any. We never do."

"Right," I said, nodding at them. "So in case you get caught or end up dead someplace, you can't be identified right away. You're smarter than you look." I wagged a finger at James and Luke. "See, guys—*that's* how the pros do it. You learned a valuable lesson today."

"Screw you," Dickies said.

I smiled and turned back to the Italian guys.

"My instincts tell me you're working for Francis Falcone."

They didn't say anything.

"You must at least know who he is."

Not a twitch from either of them.

"I'm curious," I said to the Italian models. "How long does it take you two to get ready in the morning? And do you text each other first to coordinate outfits?"

One of them brushed the back of his hand against the underside of his chin in reply.

Out in the hallway the elevator grate banged again. The door opened and two Asian men in smart navy suits walked in clasping their hands behind their backs. They left the door open. One was in his 30s, the other his 50s. They looked like a couple of generals surveying a battlefield after the carnage. They zigzagged between the boxes and stood in front of me. I was now surrounded on three sides.

"Show me your hands," I said. "Slowly."

They did. Their palms were empty.

"Mister Stevens," the older one said. "If you would allow it, we wish to have a conversation with Miss Wright."

"I will not allow it. If you're looking for her brother, she has no idea where he is."

They nodded to each other.

"Very well," the older one said to me.

They turned in unison, put their hands behind their backs again, and started for the door.

"Hey," I said, "who are you working for?"

They ignored me. Although I held a powerful handgun, I was feeling rather impotent, and I didn't like it. As the two of them walked out, the younger one gave me what I'm sure he thought was a stern look.

"We be back," he said.

"Come on," I said, "if you're going to use tough-guy lines, at least get them right. You mean, '*I'll* be back.' Beat it, sonny."

He paused in the doorjamb. "Sonny?"

"Google it. Now get lost."

He left. I heard the grate clank shut and the elevator start down. One of the Italian models jutted his chin at me from the couch.

"*Sonny*? Who the fuck says 'sonny' except old coots?"

"I do."

I looked at the four men on opposite sides of the room. I'd had enough of this sideshow.

"We're done here." I pointed the gun at each of them. "Get out."

"*I'll* be back," one of the Italians said.

"Great. Looking forward to it."

While the Italians sauntered out, James and Luke got shakily to their feet.

"Guys," I said to the twins, "let's be clear. If you come near Kelsey again, I *will* shoot you. Nod if you understand."

They nodded and shuffled toward the door. Dickies clutched his wrist and limped on the bad knee.

"Hey, one more thing." I waited until they were facing me and the gun. "Welcome to *Noo Yauk*!"

Carhartt, still holding his head, gave me the finger.

"Shut the door on your way out," I said.

He slammed it. I waited until I heard the elevator start down again before locking the door. When I went back to my desk, Kelsey was hunched over in the chair, clutching her stomach.

"It's safe now," I said.

She looked up at me. "You're sure? What if more of them come?"

"They won't," I said.

"I feel sick."

"Bathroom's right over there."

While she went in the bathroom, I put the Sig Sauer in the shoulder holster and strapped it on. A couple minutes later, the toilet flushed, the sink ran, and Kelsey came out blowing her nose. Her eye makeup was smeared.

"I need to make a call," I said, "and then we'll talk some more, okay?"

"Sure."

I dialed Falcone's number and sat behind my desk. Francis Falcone was Bizarro Superman to my Superman—a "finder," or PI of sorts, for the New York Mob. I suspected the two Italian men worked for him. He picked up on the first ring, which was surprising. Often I got his voicemail.

"Ah…if it isn't my favorite PI douchebag," he said. "To what do I owe the pleasure?"

"Cut the crap, Falcone. A couple of your guys just paid me a visit."

"What? Who?"

An air wrench, like you'd hear in an auto shop, squealed on the other end of the line.

"Couple of male model types," I said. "What are they, new guys on your crew?"

"Look, Stevens, I don't know who you're talking about. What did they want?"

"They wanted to talk to my client about her missing brother."

"Who's her brother?" Falcone asked.

"Wait, you're telling me you're really not behind this?"

"That's what I'm telling you. Who's the brother?"

"E. Conover Wright, famous science-fiction author. Besides them I've had the FBI, two Asians and a couple of tough guys from North Dakota in here looking for him."

"A writer? What's this guy into?"

"Tell me about it," I said.

"Did they get to her? Talk to your client, I mean?"

I gazed at her. She and her cotton candy hair had grown on me.

"No, they didn't."

"Look," Falcone said, "the FBI, Asians and North Dakota dudes—all after a friggen sci-fi writer? It's messed up, I gotta admit. But all I care about is this rival crew. I want to know who hired them to work in *my* territory."

"If you find out, will you let me know?"

"Normally I'd tell you to screw, Stevens, but I'm pissed about this one. Tell you what—as long as the information flows both ways..."

"A *quid pro quo*?"

"I prefer 'tit for tat,' but yeah, okay," Falcone said. "Look, my car's almost done, so I gotta go. Just one more question for you."

"What?"

"Your new place on Fifth. You sure you can afford that? I mean, what's your nut over there? Six, seven grand a month?"

I hung up.

3

Take It On the Lam

I spaced out at my desk for a few seconds, then checked my watch. My phone made the thing superfluous, but it was a vintage Omega that had belonged to my grandfather, so I still wore it every day. Here it was, only ten thirty, and I was spent.

An hour and a half ago, my life had made perfect sense. I'd had a great day to look forward to: gorgeous fall weather, a burger at the Shake Shack, and a stroll through Central Park to the Guggenheim, where I would meet Clarissa, and from there to her cavernous apartment on 89th Street, where we would exchange naughty messages face-to-face beneath 1200-thread count sheets. But that was all shot to hell now. Now I had the FBI, the Mob, a pair of enigmatic Asians, and two North Dakota thugs to worry about. I hadn't even officially taken the case yet, and already I was working for a teenage girl with cotton candy hair whose sci-fi author brother was into God knows what.

"Is everything okay?" Kelsey asked.

"Yeah, fine. Just give me a minute to think. I'll be right out."

In the bathroom I ran the water until it was good and cold, then splashed my face about ten times. The shock of the water began to clear my head, so by the time I patted my face dry with a paper towel, I was able to form a plan.

First, Kelsey wasn't safe. She would have to stick with me, whether she liked it or not. Second, her hair had to go; with it, she could be spotted half a mile away. Next, my car—a rakish black Cadillac—was also a dead give-away; I'd have to leave it in the parking garage uptown and contrive some other way out of the city. Obviously, staying in Manhattan—either at my apartment or Svet-lana's—wasn't an option. We needed to get upstate to my place in Millbrook, pick up some heavier artillery, and continue to the Indian casino in Connecticut where Svet-lana was. With her at my side, I could turn my attention to Kelsey's brother. I threw out the paper towel.

It was time to get Kelsey on board with the plan. I went out to the office.

"Mr. Stevens, what are we going to do?" Kelsey asked.

"At this point, I think you can call me Dakota."

"Okay, Dakota, why are all of these people after my brother?"

"I have no idea, but that's not important right now," I said. "What's important is getting you safe."

"And just how do you propose we do that? The FBI's following me, remember?"

"It's like the old bank robbers used to say: 'We've gotta take it on the lam.'"

"What's that mean?"

"Means 'get out of town.'"

"Okay," she said, "and go where?"

"Upstate, to my place in Millbrook."

"Then what?"

"One step at a time, Kelsey. First we have to get out of this building."

"But what about my hotel? I need to get my stuff. My laptop's there."

I shook my head. "It's too dangerous."

"But I haven't checked out yet. The bill's gonna be enormous."

"You can call and tell them you've had an emergency. Ask hotel security to store your stuff."

"What about my apartment then?" she said. "I *have to* get some things."

"Your apartment's too hot right now. Kelsey, there are four different groups of men looking for your brother. I would bet good money that they're camped out in your apartment this very second, waiting for you."

"But I have nothing." She shook the messenger bag. "No clothes. No makeup. Nothing."

"We'll buy whatever you need."

She crossed her arms and planted a boot.

"So you're saying this is our only option. There's no way we can stay in the city."

"Correct."

"Don't you have an apartment in the city?" she said.

"I do."

"Why can't we stay there?"

"You aren't getting it." I took a breath and counted to three. "I need you to understand, Kelsey—some of these people looking for your brother are bad news. If they have to hurt you to find him, they will. You saw what happened earlier, right? We can't stay in the city because they'll have people everywhere. I can't protect you here. But I can in the country."

"What are you saying? Like, I can never come back here?"

"No, this is temporary," I said. "Maybe in a few days. But first we need to get you safe, and then we need to find your brother. Because none of this goes away until we find him."

"Do you think he might have been kidnapped?" she asked.

"There will be plenty of time for speculation later. Something I didn't ask you—don't you have a job you need to call into?"

"No. Taking care of Conover *is* my full-time job."

"You mean you're not in school either?" I said.

She shook her head. "I graduated from high school a year early. Conover doesn't have anyone else to look after him. I told you before—I'm his assistant."

"All right, it's time to get out of here."

There was a blue ski cap on the coat stand across the room. I got it and tossed it to her.

"Make sure it covers all of your hair," I said.

"Oh, that's right. I am pretty obvious, aren't I?"

"Obvious, no. Conspicuous, yes."

"And a girl wearing a ski cap on a beautiful fall day *isn't* conspicuous?" she said.

"Just do it. Now, do you have access to cash?"

"Sure. Like what, five hundred dollars?"

"Try like ten thousand," I said.

"What? Why so much?"

"Because we're going to be on the run, we could be for a while, and we can't use credit cards, either of us."

"Oh, I get it," she said. "They'd trace us."

"Exactly. So, can you get the money?"

"I should be able to. I'm on all my brother's accounts."

"Is there a branch of your bank nearby?" I asked.

"There's one in Herald Square."

"Perfect. That's only about ten blocks from here. Make sure you get small bills, okay? Like twenties."

"Why?" she asked.

"Large bills draw too much attention."

Which reminded me: we couldn't bring our cell phones—we'd be tracked. I'd buy disposable ones later, contact Svetlana and let her know what was going on. I sent Clarissa a quick text apologizing for having to cancel our plans, then dropped my phone in the bottom desk drawer.

"Kelsey, your phone."

"But what if Conover tries to contact me?"

"I'm leaving mine, too," I said. "We have to. GPS. As long as we have the phones on us, people can follow our every move. Especially the FBI."

Her shoulders slumped, and she dropped her phone in the drawer. I put my laptop in the desk, too, and locked it up. A lot of good that would do.

I looked around the office. I wouldn't be back for a while, so what should I take? My eyes fell upon the box labeled "Dakota's Toys." I cut it open with my penknife and took a magnetic GPS tracking unit, a can of grizzly repellent (a holdover from the Montana case), and my trusty stun gun.

"Open your bag, please," I said.

She did, and I dumped everything in, including the ASP baton in my back pocket.

"Can I use the bathroom first?" she asked. "I want to get cleaned up."

"Go ahead."

While waiting for her to come out, I went to the windows and looked down at the street. One of the Italian models sat on a bench against the park fence with his legs crossed. He was holding what annoyingly appeared to be a shake from the Shake Shack. He stared at the door of my building. I didn't see his buddy, but he might be covering the alley in back. No sign of the Bishop brothers, the Asians, or the FBI, but that didn't mean they weren't out there. They could be better hidden.

Wherever they were, they'd be expecting us to come out the front or back door. What they wouldn't be expecting was us exiting half a block down the street, from a different *building*.

It was a dangerous risk, but a risk we had to take.

4

Rope

Kelsey emerged from the bathroom with her eye makeup scrubbed off. She patted her head in the hat. "What do you think? Incognito enough for you?"

I squinted one eye. "I wish you had a pair of pants. Those shorts…"

"Sorry, no pants. I *could* just wear my Hello Kitty underwear. But I think that would probably draw more attention."

"Probably?"

The hat wasn't much, but it covered her hair, and the key to good disguises is to not overdo it. For myself, I put on a pair of square-framed aviator sunglasses (which I rarely wore because they made me look too damn good) and a New York Yankees cap. I wasn't a baseball fan, but I kept the cap around because it enabled me to hide in plain sight in Manhattan—especially during the postseason, when all of the fair-weather Yankees fans wore one.

"All right," I said. "Ready?"

"So, what's the deal? How are we getting out of here, Dakota?"

I'd been giving this some thought. When Svetlana and I were looking for offices, we saw that the three buildings next door to this one shared a huge common basement. The trick would be getting into the building next door, which wasn't connected to this one.

"I have a plan." I put on my leather jacket, drew my gun and went to the door. "Unless I say otherwise, I want you two feet away from me at all times, got it?"

"I'm not sleeping in the same bed as you," she said.

"That's what you think."

"What?!"

"Gotcha!" I yanked the ski cap down over her eyes. "Let's go."

I went into the hallway first, made sure it was clear, then waved for her to join me. Once I locked the office door, I led us down the back stairs to the basement. Her heavy boots echoed in the stairwell, and I was relieved when we reached the bottom. Relieved, that is, until I peeked around the corner and saw the other Italian model standing near the recycling bins, about 20 feet away. I held out a hand and whispered to Kelsey.

"Stun gun, please." I holstered the .45 and took it from her. "Stay here."

Steeling myself with a deep breath, I swung around the corner and sprinted for the man. He was facing away from me and didn't turn around until the last second, when I rammed the stun gun into his neck and pressed the button.

Nothing happened.

He swung wildly at me, striking me in the neck below the ear. My ear rang. I dropped the stun gun and hit him with three fast jabs in the nose. Blood ran down his face. By the time he got a hand inside his coat, it was too late.

I threw a straight right with all of my weight behind it, and connected with the point of his jaw—the knockout button. His head snapped back and recoiled like a Pez dispenser. Good night. He crumpled to the floor against the recycling bins.

The gun he'd been reaching for was a .38 snub nose. Nothing to scoff at. I opened the cylinder, dumped the cartridges and threw the gun away. I wiped my hand on his pant leg.

"Kelsey, you can come out now."

She peeked out from behind the corner. I led us to the superintendent's office. The door was open.

"Earl?" I said.

No answer.

I went inside and grabbed a crowbar and a big coil of heavy nylon rope. I rifled through drawers until I found a pair of leather work gloves. I put them in my back pocket. Kelsey said something, but my ear was still ringing.

"What?" I said.

"What's that stuff for?" she said loudly.

"You'll see."

"I got the stun gun." She patted the messenger bag.

"Good. Follow me."

We returned to the stairs and climbed all the way to the roof access door. Fortunately the door wasn't alarmed. I pushed the latch bar, and we went outside. Crisp and bright, the weather was some of the best I'd ever seen for October in Manhattan.

"Kelsey," I called over my shoulder, "don't let the door"—the automatic hinge creaked, and the latch clicked—"shut."

She tried the handle. "Locked. Sorry."

"Well, my dear, we just crossed the Rubicon."

"*Rubicon?* What?" She reached into her pocket, presumably for her smart phone, and frowned when she discovered her pocket was empty.

I shook my head. "You kids and your dependence on the interwebs. I'll explain later."

Svetlana and I had only been in the building for a week, so I hadn't had a chance or a reason to come out here. In keeping with the antediluvian character of the building, the roof was an old-fashioned tar one with chimneys and vent pipes scattered around.

"Why are we up here again?" Kelsey asked.

I walked past a chimney and a couple of vent hoods, to the brick and cement parapet on the north edge of the roof. I put down the crowbar and looked over the side. This building abutted the one next door, but it was—*I counted the windows*—one, two, three stories higher. To get to the next building, we would have to rappel down. I waved Kelsey over.

"You haven't done any rappelling by any chance?" I asked her.

She gaped at the rope in my hands, then over the side.

"Oh, no. Screw this."

"Look, it's either this or we go out the front or back of the building, where I know they'll be waiting for us. It's not as bad as it looks. Honest. Have you ever done any rock climbing?"

She crossed her arms. "A little."

"Excellent. Where?"

"Chelsea Piers. You know, the sports center over there?"

"Not exactly what I had in mind," I said, "but it'll do."

"Yeah, well at least over there, they harness you in and give you a damn helmet."

"You'll be fine."

About six and twelve feet from the parapet were two steel vent pipes with elbows on the ends. I went to the more distant pipe and cinched one end of the rope to it with a constrictor knot. I pulled on the rope with all my strength. Once I was certain it would hold, I uncoiled the rest of the rope, walked it toward the parapet, and threw it over the side. It landed on the rooftop below with length to spare.

"Good, it's long enough," I said, pulling it back up. "We're in business."

"Wonderful."

When I got it all back up, I estimated how big around Kelsey was at the armpits and tied a bowline on the end a little larger than that.

"Here," I said, handing her the loop, "put this over your head and under your arms."

"I've changed my mind, Dakota." She gazed up at me. "I…I don't want to do this."

"Neither do I. But we have to." I removed her messenger bag. "I'll send this down after you."

I put the bag aside and threaded the loop over her arm and head. After a pleading look, she pulled her other arm through. I patted her shoulder.

"You're going to be fine, I promise. Keep the loop under your arms, and there's no way you can fall. In a second, when I tell you, you're going to put one leg over the side at a time. Once you're a ways down, try to put your boots flat against the wall and walk backward. And keep looking up, okay?"

"Oh yeah, piece of cake." She trembled a little.

"Take a few deep breaths. You'll be down there before you know it."

She nodded.

I took off my leather jacket and draped it across the parapet, putting the satin lining face-up so the rope could slide across it while the leather gripped the cement. Then I walked backward with the coil of rope, letting out slack as I went. I looped the rope around the second pipe—the one closer to the roof edge—to act as a braking mechanism. I laid the rest of the coil behind me so it wouldn't snag on anything, then slipped on the work gloves. With the rope against my backside, I braced my foot on the braking pipe.

"Ready?" I said.

"No."

"You can do this. I'm going to lower you slowly. When you reach the bottom, yank fast on the rope until I come to the edge. Whatever you do, don't shout. They could hear you down on the street."

"Okay," she said.

"Now, get on the wall and put one leg over at a time. Look up, and keep a tight grip on the rope." I gave her a reassuring nod. "Go."

She crawled onto the jacket and put one knee over the side. "I'm going to kill you, Conover." She put her other knee over and slid backward on her belly. Just before she dipped below the roof edge, she closed her eyes.

For the first few feet, there was a lot of jerking on the rope as Kelsey tried to plant her feet against the wall. I heard her boots scraping against the brick. After ten feet or so, the rope went out more smoothly; she must have gotten her footing. I fed the rope from the coil behind me and across my backside, and it snaked around the second pipe, across my jacket on the parapet, and over the side. I was sweating, but so far, so good.

When I'd fed out half of the rope, I heard the roof door creak. I stopped lowering Kelsey for a second and looked over my shoulder. It was the other Italian model. He stood holding the door open with one hand, and a gun in the other. He scanned the roof. Still bracing my leg against the pipe, I eased myself down and hid behind a vent housing. I kept an eye on the model and carefully started feeding out rope again; if I waited any longer, Kelsey might panic and start to shout. The model swept his gaze across the roofline. Sweat ran down my scalp, into my eye. I kept feeding out rope, and the pipe made faint metallic noises as the rope rubbed against it. Then I noticed Kelsey's messenger bag. It was in the open. I couldn't tell if the model would be able to see it. I prayed he wouldn't, because there was no way I'd be able to hold the rope *and* remove a glove *and* draw my gun. As he turned, I continued to feed the rope. When he paused, I paused.

Then, as suddenly as he had appeared, he left. Once I was sure he was gone, I fed out the rope until there were several quick yanks on it, then I got up and looked over the side. Below, Kelsey shielded her eyes and gave me a thumbs-up. I hauled the rope back up, tied the messenger bag, crowbar and my jacket to the end, and lowered them down. Once Kelsey had removed them, I waved her away from the wall. I pulled the rope taut and eased myself over the side.

Unlike Kelsey, I wasn't wearing boots. I was wearing a pair of European walking shoes, which were great for walking upright on city pavement, but not so great for walking backward down brick walls. My feet kept slipping, and my already fatigued arms did 90 percent of the work. I lowered myself hand-under-hand until my feet were level with the second-story windowsill, and then my arms gave out. I loosened my grip and slid down to the bottom. My palms burned from the friction. I peeled off the gloves.

"That was crazy," Kelsey said.

"Maybe, but it's going to work." I put on my jacket.

"What was the holdup? I was like halfway down when you just stopped."

I glanced at my shoes. They were a favorite pair and I'd scuffed the toes on them.

"Shoot," I said. "Tell you later. Let's go."

At the roof door, I started to shove the crowbar in the crack when she grabbed the handle and opened it.

"Or we could just do *this*," she said.

"Smartass."

I left the crowbar behind and we went downstairs. At the next floor, we boarded the elevator and rode it to the basement, where I led us through the labyrinthine corridors. When we had reached the basement of the last connected building, we went upstairs to the entryway. There was no doorman.

"Here's the deal," I said. "They'll be looking for the two of us together, so I'll go out first. Count to sixty, then you come out. The second you're out the door, turn hard left and look straight up the sidewalk. Do *not* look at any of the parked cars. They might have bad guys in them, watching my building down the street. From here, it's about fifty yards to the corner of Twenty-Sixth and Fifth. I'll meet you there. Okay?"

Her eyes were an iridescent cobalt blue, and I liked seeing them big and alert as she processed my instructions.

"Hard left when I get outside," she said, "and don't look at the cars."

"Correct." I held her by the shoulders. "It's going to be fine. Count to sixty, then come out."

She nodded. "Okay."

I smiled and walked out.

As soon as I stepped outside, I spotted the two Asians, idling in a cherry red Range Rover on the park side of Fifth Avenue. They were staring down the street at my building entrance. There was another car behind them, so I couldn't see their license plate. I strolled up to the corner of 26th and looked back. Kelsey exited the building, and at precisely that moment the older Asian got out of the Range Rover. He lit a cigarette and stood near the front bumper sweeping his gaze along the street. I held my breath as he swept right past her. He must have been looking for the cotton candy hair.

When she reached the corner, I guided her behind the building so we were out of sight from Fifth Avenue.

"Well, here's the good news," I said. "I think that was the worst of it. Ready for part two?"

"Yeah, I can't *wait.*"

"Do I detect a bit of sarcasm?"

"Yes."

5

The Narrow Margin

We crossed 26th Street, went over to Broadway and headed uptown, toward Herald Square. Along the way we popped into an electronics store, where I paid cash for three disposable cell phones and fresh batteries for the stun gun. I also got us a couple of bottled waters at a bodega. Once we'd had a drink (and I'd cleaned the blood off my hand), we continued uptown.

Kelsey's bank was on 35th Street, across from the miniature Herald Square Park and catty-corner to Macy's. I waited at the bank entrance while she went inside to make a withdrawal. I scanned along 35th and down Broadway, and as far as I could tell, no one was following us. Shoppers streamed in and out of Macy's. People chatted at cafe tables in the park. The sun was shining, the air was crisp, the sky a crystalline blue. I thought of the line by John Cheever: *"...and who, after all these centuries, can describe the fineness of an autumn day?"* Looking around at everyone enjoying the pristine weather, it seemed impossible that Kelsey and I were in danger. Pedestrians hustled by at New Yorker pace, yammering on cell phones, oblivious to our plight.

The cell phones reminded me—I needed to activate the burners. Using my penknife, I cut open the plastic armor on two of them, fished out the phones and threw away the plastic. I activated the phones and called each one with the other. By the time I finished, Kelsey had been inside the bank for fifteen minutes. I began to worry. *Should I have gone in with her?* I started for the revolving door. She was just coming out.

"So we've got our ten grand," she said. "Where to?"

"Penn Station. Here's a phone. Don't call any of your friends. These are only for us."

"No problem. I don't have any friends." She put it in her pocket.

"Give me some of the money, would you?"

She handed me two bundles.

As we walked over to Seventh Avenue, I explained to Kelsey that while in the station we needed to stay apart. It couldn't be obvious we were traveling together. By now, the Italian guy I'd punched in the face had surely reported back to his boss that we'd escaped. If the boss was smart, he'd send some guys to Penn and Grand Central Terminal to watch for us. I didn't entirely trust Falcone when he said the models weren't working for him, so I would keep my eyes open for familiar members of his crew.

"All right," I said, "we have to move separately from here, and we can't talk again until we get upstate, so a couple of things. Are you listening?"

"Yeah."

"I want you to buy a one-way ticket to Poughkeepsie for the next train. I think it's at a few minutes past noon."

"Next train to Poughkeepsie, got it," she said.

"Good. Board the car, and sit near the rear of the car. And don't look at anybody. Just stare out the window or read a magazine, okay?"

"Rear of the car, and don't look at anybody," she said. "You've got me nervous with all this stuff."

"I'll be near you the whole time."

We entered the station at the 32nd Street entrance and rode the escalator down, Kelsey staying about ten feet ahead of me. I had always loathed Penn Station. With its low ceilings and endless maze of third-tier shops and eateries, the place looked—and smelled—like a failed 1980s mall. Close to noon on a weekday, it was crowded, too, and as we wove through the chaotic crush of travelers—everyone heading in different directions, everyone cutting in front of everyone else—I lost sight of Kelsey.

I spotted her again at the ticket windows. We got in separate lines, and it was then that I noticed the first man. He was standing off to the side, near a trash bin, eating a Boston Creme donut and watching the lines. He was an Italian man in his 50s with salt-and-pepper hair and a gut that gave him a sizable head start toward a job as a mall Santa. I knew he was looking for somebody because his dark eyes were darting all over the place. Fat donut-eater or not, he stood with a solidity that made me want to avoid tangling with him.

The situation was beginning to remind me of an old noir movie, *The Narrow Margin*, in which a Chicago cop escorts a woman witness to Los Angeles on the train. Hopefully things wouldn't end the way they did in the movie.

Kelsey bought her ticket before I could buy mine, and then she walked away, unknowingly passing within six feet of the donut-eater. He happened to be looking in the other direction when she went by. It took me a minute to get my ticket, and in the meantime I lost her. Blood pounded in my throat as I headed for the train platforms, walking fast and scanning everywhere for a blue ski cap. I caught sight of her again at the electronic departures board. She was about 20 feet away. A pair of Amtrak cops, including one with a German shepherd, walked by. I tried to study the faces of travelers, but the crowd was too large. Instead I looked off to the sides for people who weren't watching the board—the ones who were either watching the travelers or ignoring the scene altogether.

There was a man near the escalator reading a *Daily News*, but with a computer bag at his feet, he looked like an ordinary commuter. Maybe a dozen men were hanging around not carrying any luggage, but all of them gazed up at the departures board or were with other passengers. None of them looked to be carrying a gun either.

In the entire departures area that I could see, there was only one guy who concerned me. He was an Italian man in his early 30s, 6'6" tall and built like a linebacker. He had closely cropped jet black hair and stood with his arms in front of himself like a club bouncer.

Kelsey glanced at me every so often, and I could tell she was afraid. I gave her a tiny nod to assuage her worry, but it did nothing to help me.

The board updated and our train's gate number appeared. I made sure my jacket was zipped up and my gun hidden before looking at Kelsey. As soon as I had her attention, I gestured with my eyes for her to follow me. I started walking.

Our gate was behind us, but I went in the opposite direction at first. Somebody might be watching to see who headed for our train. I led us around the throng of waiting passengers, walked the entire perimeter of the hall, and got in line for our gate. Kelsey was three passengers behind me. I made sure to stand sideways so I could keep an eye on her.

The line inched forward. Ahead, an Amtrak employee scanned tickets at the gate. Standing ten feet behind her, against the wall, was the Linebacker. He was perfectly positioned to study the faces of everyone before they could get on the escalator down to the platforms. If I didn't act—and fast—he'd spot us.

An Amtrak cop approached. I gestured to him.

"Can I help you, sir?" he asked.

"Yeah," I said, removing my sunglasses. "I know when we see something, we're supposed to say something."

"What did you see?"

I feigned a gulp. "There's a suspicious guy standing behind the woman taking tickets. Is he supposed to be there?"

"Probably not." He turned around. "No, definitely not. Thank you, sir."

I put my sunglasses back on. "Glad to help, officer."

The cop walked over to an information booth, where some other cops were, and then four of them went over to the Linebacker. There was a brief argument, but he soon followed them over to the booth. The line moved ahead.

Once my ticket was scanned, I paused near the escalator to wait for Kelsey to catch up. Between the hat, her petite build, and her porcelain skin, she looked like a scared

14-year-old girl. I let her and another passenger step onto the escalator ahead of me, and rode down behind her.

We boarded the train without incident. Kelsey sat at the rear of the car, in the second-to-last row. When I passed her, she appeared to be on the verge of tears. I thought I heard her sniffling, but I couldn't say or do anything to comfort her. I sat in the row behind her.

At 12:20 p.m., the train eased out of the station, and by 12:35 we were zipping along the Hudson River. Barges plowed upstream. The foliage on the far riverbank sparkled in the bright sun. I glanced down the car, saw that no one was looking in this direction, and peered over the seat back to check on Kelsey. She was against the window, staring out at the view. I sat back down. I could only imagine how she felt. Her brother was missing, and she had to trust a man she'd just met.

The conductor passed, heading toward the front of the train, followed by an elderly woman, who came unsteadily out of the bathroom behind me. In a little over an hour, we would reach Poughkeepsie. In the meantime, I needed to contact some people.

First I texted Johnny Quinn, my teenage neighbor and caretaker in Millbrook, asking him to pick me up at the station. "It's important," I added. He texted back that he was in school, but he'd cut class to do it. It's nice being a positive influence on young people.

Then I texted Sherilyn Jones, an occasional companion of mine, and the owner of The Pretty Filly in the village. I told her I needed to bring in my niece at 3:30 this afternoon for an emergency hair coloring. She replied, "Dakota honey…4 U…*anything* ;) <3."

The train slowed and pulled into Yonkers station. No one got off or boarded this car, and as the train began to move again, I sent my final text message—this one to Svetlana. I would be there sometime that evening, I said. I didn't mention that I had a teenage girl in tow. I put my phone away and gazed out at the shimmering Hudson.

Now that I had time to think, one question repeated in my mind: *Why are four dramatically different groups looking for Conover Wright?* Hanson said the Bureau wanted him on a matter of national security. All I knew about the other groups was that one was made up of Italians, another one Asians, and the last one husky white guys from North Dakota. However none of this told me what happened to Conover. Was it possible he'd been kidnapped, as Kelsey suggested? If so, who was the fifth party? And if not, where was he, and why had he abandoned his little sister without a word? What kind of trouble was he in? Meanwhile, I had no idea what this guy even looked like. I would need a photo of him eventually.

After checking on Kelsey again, I glanced down the aisle and noticed the fat guy from the ticket lines entering the car at the far end.

Damn it.

He popped something in his mouth—the last bite of another donut—and plodded up the aisle looking side to side at each passenger. I pulled out my phone and dialed Kelsey's.

"I don't get it," she said when she picked up. "I thought we weren't—"

"Quiet. Listen to me. Keep staring out the window and pretend you're talking to one of your girlfriends. Do it right now. I'm going to hang up, but you keep talking. Got it?"

"Why, what's going—"

"Just do it."

"Fine, Maya, I'll do it."

I hung up and put my phone away. In front of me, Kelsey talked about the new exhibit at the Met. Meanwhile, the fat man had reached the middle of the car. An announcement came over the PA saying we would be arriving at our next stop, Croton–Harmon, in a few minutes.

Down the aisle, a shaggy-haired young man stood up and pulled a backpack off the overhead rack. While he was blocking the donut-eater's path, I tossed my Yankees cap on the seat, went in the bathroom, and left the sliding door open a slit to peek out. From here I could see Kelsey's seat.

The young man with the backpack went by first. I heard the automatic car door open, the loud train noise outside, and the door slide shut again. The fat man approached next. He paused at Kelsey's seat and looked at her. I started to unzip my jacket to pull my gun, but he moved on. He waddled past the bathroom and went out the car door.

I waited five seconds, then came out of the bathroom. There was no one behind the fat man. Time for a calculated risk. I went to the car door to exit, and caught a glimpse of myself in the window. I looked great in the sunglasses, but at the moment being able to see trumped style. I put them in my coat, pressed the button on the car door and stepped out. I expected to find the fat man in the vestibule between the cars, but only the young backpacker was there, leaning against the wall with an unlit cigarette in his mouth.

The vestibule was deafening with the clacking of the wheels and the groaning of the floor plate where the cars were coupled. The fat man wasn't on the other side of the vestibule. He must have continued into the next car. I peered through the window and, sure enough, he was already halfway down the aisle, staring at passengers' faces. As he neared the end of the car, I pushed the button on the door and went inside. I was marching down the aisle when he exited at the other end.

This was a huge guy that I was about to confront, and I needed some advantage short of double-tapping him in the chest. At the end of the aisle was a large open space with heavy luggage lined up against the wall. Checking over my shoulder first, I grabbed somebody's medium-sized, hard shell suitcase and followed the fat man outside.

I crept into the noisy vestibule, holding the suitcase in front of myself. Every conceivable sound that metal could make was out here: scraping, squeaking, screeching, rattling, clanging, clattering, clunking. *In case you forgot*, the racket seemed to say, *this is the most dangerous place on the train.*

Again I had expected the fat man to be here, but he wasn't. Wobbling across the shifting floor plate, I glanced through the window into the next car. He was there. It was a cafe car, the last car. I ducked into the exit alcove on the side of the car door and waited, suitcase at the ready. I would be facing his side when he came out.

The wait was interminable. My mouth was dry. Sweat gathered on my lower back. And then the door opened and he emerged—stomach-first. I let him take one step outside before thrusting the suitcase at his leg. I was aiming for his knee, but at the last second the train lurched, I fell forward, and the suitcase glanced off his thigh. He grunted and stumbled sideways into the opposite alcove. Then the train sharply braked, causing me to trip on the suitcase and land on the floor plate. Half a second later the train accelerated again. The car coupler jolted beneath me, the floor plate shifted, and my fingers slipped into a crack between the sheets of steel.

I yanked them out just as the floor plate snapped back into place like a guillotine.

I flushed. My heart pounded. I pushed myself up by my fists.

As I was getting to my feet, I was shoved in the back and went headlong into the door across the vestibule. I righted myself and faced him. For a fat guy, he moved lightly and fast, and before I could react he got off a decent punch. It only grazed my ribs, but it still felt as though I'd been hit by an 80 mph fastball. In reply I thrust from my legs and put a stiff convincer into his gut—a blow that would have buckled a smaller man and heaved him off the ground—but in this case my fist felt as though it was sucked into Swedish memory foam. The train slowed. The fat man spread his legs to balance himself.

"Gonna have to do better than that," he said.

"Okay," I said, "try this."

In such tight quarters, I had to keep my punches compact. Pivoting with my hips, I pasted him below the eye with a blistering right hook. It was another punch that would have leveled a smaller man, but in his case it was as though I'd just patted aftershave on his cheek. I followed up with a quick jab, then a hard elbow directed at his jaw, which he blocked handily.

A wave of dread came over me, a sensation that I might be over my head with this guy. Things could get ugly. I might have to break his knee or shoot him.

"My turn," he said.

He was in the middle of a chuckle when the train pitched forward again. As he stumbled toward me, chuckling and groping for something to catch his balance, I braced myself against the car door and plowed my knee deep into his open groin.

This made him a lot less jolly in a hurry.

While he was stooped over, clutching his groin and second-guessing his choices in life, I gritted my teeth and slammed an uppercut into his solar plexus, putting every fiber of my muscle behind it. His other hand flew to his chest, and even with the deafening noise in the vestibule, I heard him wheezing for air. The train slowed and stopped. I fished in his coat pockets and got his cell phone. The exit doors opened.

I couldn't believe my luck. All my adult life I'd waited for a chance to use a certain line from the Clint Eastwood movie *Dirty Harry*. Now I had my chance. Grabbing him by the coat, I hauled him past me toward the open door.

"Go on out and get some air, Fatso!"

I shoved him in the ass with my foot. He landed hard on the cement platform, rolled halfway over and lay still. The conductor stepped inside the doorway.

"What happened to him?" he asked.

"He didn't watch the gap."

As the doors closed and the train began to move, I returned the suitcase I'd borrowed, cleaned up in the bathroom and went back to my seat. Kelsey was still talking on her phone. I spoke to her over the seat back.

"You can stop now. The coast is clear."

"Good," she said. "I felt like an idiot."

"Why don't you call the hotel about your stuff?"

"Okay."

I leaned back in my seat and took out Fatso's cell phone. It was a cheap flip-phone, and I redialed the last number that had called him. A man answered. His voice was grating.

"Tell me you fucking got her, Vito."

"Not Vito," I said. "And no, he didn't get her. Who is this?"

"Fuck you."

"Hello, Mr. You. I'm the guy protecting Kelsey Wright. Why are you looking for her brother?"

"Go fuck yourself."

"You know," I said, "you really shouldn't use the F-word so much. Dulls the effect."

"Fuh…" He stopped himself.

"There you go. You're learning."

"Screw you." He hung up.

I checked the phone for other information, but it seemed that the only thing Vito had used it for was calling, not email, texting or contacts. None of the numbers had names associated with them. These guys all used burners, I bet. I wrote down the number of the guy I'd just spoken with, along with a couple of others, and then I went in the bathroom and flushed the phone down the toilet.

6

Fire Superiority

When we walked through the Poughkeepsie train station, I half-expected to encounter another group of bad guys. Maybe the Asians this time. Or, considering the vintage details of the place—the tall arched windows and high granite walls, the long chestnut benches and brass chandeliers—maybe fedora-wearing gangsters out of *The Untouchables*. While Kelsey used the bathroom, I stood guard by the door and studied the waiting passengers. There were a few seniors, mothers with children, and college kids, but unless they were also ninja assassins, I'd be okay. Nobody like Fatso to deal with.

When we walked outside, Johnny Quinn was waiting with his pickup. It was a four-door king cab. This gave me an idea.

As Kelsey neared the truck, Johnny's eyes dilated. This was understandable. She might have been wearing a ski cap, but she was also wearing saucy denim shorts and knee-high socks. And she had an exquisite profile. We rode in silence for a few minutes, Kelsey in the back seat, before I told him the gist of the situation: people were after us, and I needed to borrow his truck for a while.

"Borrow it?" Johnny said. "For how long?"

"Not borrow," I said. "Rent. As in I pay you. And I'm not sure how long. Could be a few days, could be as long as a month."

"Why can't you rent a car?"

"Duh," Kelsey said, poking her head between the seats. "Because we can't use credit cards."

"What do I tell my parents?" he said. "They just got this for me in June."

"Tell them the truth," I said. "Mr. Stevens needed to borrow it."

"Why can't you use *your* pickup? The one I plow your driveway with."

"Because it's registered to me, so the people looking for us will know to look for the truck."

"But I can use it, right?"

"Absolutely not," I said. "Again, people will be looking for it, and most of them are bad news."

Johnny was silent. His hands tightened on the steering wheel. Kelsey reached over the seat and touched his shoulder.

"Come on, Johnny, what do you say? *Please*?"

"All right."

When we reached the Clove Valley near Brush Hill Road, I dropped Johnny at his house. I gave him $500 for use of the truck, shook his hand and drove away.

"A pickup truck, though?" Kelsey said. "I don't know anything about the PI business, but don't we want something faster, like to outrun people?"

"Ordinarily I'd say yes. But right now it's more important we keep a low profile."

I went past my driveway to the old Middlemiss place. As we turned in, a run of wild turkeys exploded out of the trees and flew into the overgrown pasture on the other side.

"What the hell is that?" Kelsey said.

"Relax. Wild turkeys. Have you *ever* been in the country?"

"Hey, I walk around Central Park sometimes," she said.

We got out. Kelsey nodded at the boarded-up house.

"Wow, this is your place? Sweet."

"No, we're going in the back way, wiseass," I said. "In case anybody's there waiting for us."

She squinted at me. "You are *smart*, Dakota, you know that?"

"Yup."

A pretty brook separated this property from mine, and an old footbridge was still intact. Once across the bridge, we walked down a path beneath the trees. Canary yellow leaves rained down in a light wind.

"What kind of tree is this?" she asked.

"A maple."

She pointed. "How about that one?"

"Shagbark hickory," I said. "Come on."

We emerged from the trees near my pool, which had been drained and covered. I glanced up the hill at the main house and drew my gun.

"I'm going up to look around," I said. "I'll call you if it's clear."

"Wait, what's the signal?"

"Signal?"

"The code word," Kelsey said. "For if it's clear."

"How about, 'All clear'?"

"You're no fun."

"I'm lots of fun," I said. "But I'm working. Now wait here and be still."

I had a choice: I could go up the lawn to the driveway, or up the stairs in the hillside to the deck. I chose the stairs. They were flanked on both sides by undergrowth, giving me cover. I bounded up. At the top I walked along the side of the house with my gun ready, to the deck. Empty. Just the slate table and some leaf-covered Adirondack chairs. The door was locked and none of the windows had been tampered with. I circled the house. The alarm I'd installed over the summer hadn't been tripped, and the outside box was undisturbed. Back at the stairs, I called down to Kelsey.

"All clear."

She stomped up in her Doc Martens. Her hands were in her jacket pockets as she looked around.

"Nice," she said. "The detective business must be good."

"Actually, the place costs me money. But it belonged to my grandparents, so I can't bring myself to sell it."

"Sentimental attachment?"

"I suppose."

Inside the house, I did a quick sweep alone, making sure there were no bad guys lurking, then grabbed my go-bag from the closet by the back door. I unzipped it, took out the folding Buck knife, and zipped it closed again.

"What's this?" Kelsey asked, kicking the bag.

"A go-bag," I said.

She looked confused.

"Clothes, cash, survival gear, toiletries, first aid kit, passport, and some other stuff," I said.

"I don't even have clothes, and you've got all this," she said.

"We're going to buy everything you need later today. Follow me."

I led her through the living room. As we passed through the library, she stopped and looked at the shelves.

"Wow, have you read all of these?" she asked.

"Pretty much."

We went into my office. At the sight of the pool table in the center, Kelsey's face lit up.

"Awesome," she said. "I love pool."

She grabbed a cue stick from the rack on the wall, tossed a few balls on the table and started to shoot. She was pretty good, too, sinking the 14-ball with a two-cushion shot.

"Impressive," I said.

"Yeah, I'm pretty awesome."

She sank a few more, then put everything away and wandered around the room, inspecting the photographs, the hi-fi, my desk. While Kelsey was occupied, I went to the gun safe and opened it.

Although I had the Sig Sauer under my arm, I needed a concealable backup weapon. I strapped on an ankle holster under my pant leg and slipped in a Ruger LCRx .357 Magnum. It was a 5-shot, snub-nosed revolver that looked like a toy in my large hands. Still, I wouldn't want to be shot by it.

For fire superiority, I grabbed my Colt AR-15 M4 carbine with a 30-round magazine. This was a semi-automatic version of the rifle used by the U.S. military and law enforcement. For close-quarters defense, I wanted devastating power. I chose my Benelli 12-gauge pump shotgun. Flat black like the AR-15, it was a scary weapon just to look at. Finally, for long-range shooting, I brought my stainless Remington 700 SPS chambered in .308 Winchester. This beauty had served me well in the past, during one shootout in particular.

I pulled out a large tactical soft case and put all of the guns inside. I added extra magazines for the AR-15 and a few boxes of each type of ammunition, and zipped up the case. I was locking up the gun safe again when Kelsey murmured behind me. I turned around.

"What?"

"I said, 'Nice *porn* collection you've got here, Dakota.'"

Facing me were Shay's two nude self-portraits—one of her on a lake dock, the other of her in a movie theater. The paintings had been covered and left in the corner facing the wall so I wouldn't see them. Dizziness washed over me. I lashed out before I had a chance to process any of this.

"Put them back!" I stormed over to the paintings. "Did I say you could touch those? And they aren't porn either. They're art, done by a great artist."

I put the paintings back in the corner and covered them with the bed sheet. The next thing I knew, Kelsey's head was bowed and she was crying.

"I'm sorry," she said. "I didn't know."

I looked at her crying and was ashamed. The poor girl was already anxious and afraid, and I'd yelled at her.

Nice job, Dakota.

"No, I'm sorry," I said.

I hugged her. She responded by burying her head in my chest and sobbing. We stood in the light of the window that looked out on the woods for at least a minute, until I couldn't tell who was comforting whom. Outside, a fox crept warily out of the undergrowth, loped across the clearing and disappeared into the woods again. For some reason, the fox made me acutely aware of how isolated we were, and how dangerous it was to stay here.

"We have to keep moving," I said.

She nodded into my chest. I reached behind myself and uncoupled her hands.

"Go use the bathroom," I said. "It's outside to the left."

"Okay."

As I watched her leave, I had an odd sensation of vulnerability. It came and went with a shiver. The last time I'd felt like this was with Shay, and I worried about what it might portend.

7

GRAND THEFT AUTO

In retrospect, going into Millbrook was a mistake. If Kelsey were any other client, I would have bought a hair dye kit and made her color it in my kitchen sink. Admittedly, I let the fact that she was a teenage girl cloud my thinking.

It was three o'clock when Kelsey and I sat down in the diner for a late lunch. Kenny took our orders, and when he walked away, I broached the topic of Kelsey's hair.

"I made an appointment for you at a salon up the street. Sorry, girl, but the cotton candy hair has to go."

"Does it have to?"

"Yes."

She sighed. "Guess I can't wear the hat forever."

"Nope."

"What color should I do?"

"I don't know," I said. "Just no tangerine, lime-green or fuchsia. No offense."

She reached under her cap, pulled out some strands of pink and blue, and regarded them wistfully.

"I'll miss it. But it has to be done."

Afterwards we strolled up to The Pretty Filly. Danielle was hanging Halloween decorations in the front window. As we went inside, she got off the step stool.

"So, Dakota, this must be your niece."

"Yes. Danielle, this is Stacy. Stacy, Danielle."

"I didn't know you had a niece," Danielle said.

"She's from California. I don't see her much."

Danielle nodded. "So what's this about an emergency coloring?"

I plucked the ski cap off Kelsey's head. Her pink and blue hair ballooned to twice its size.

"I see." Danielle looked at Kelsey. "Well, we'd better get started."

The curtain to the back room snapped open and Sherilyn appeared barefoot in the doorway. She wore black yoga pants and a form-fitting grape tank top that showed her hair to its fullest effect. Sherilyn was that rarest of redheads—a wavy auburn red—and all it took was one toss, one quiver, of those thick tresses to make me shove Reason into an oncoming truck. On paper she was six years older than I, but her yoga-fit body and radiant skin thought otherwise.

"My, my—Dakota Stevens," she said in a faint Southern accent. "It has been a *while*."

Danielle led Kelsey over to the sinks.

"Come on back here, darlin'." Sherilyn beckoned me with a forefinger. "Wanna show you my new yoga and meditation area."

"I don't know, Sherilyn. I'm in kind of a hurry today."

"Relax," she said. "Your niece's hair is gonna be at least an hour. Come on back here and take a load off, hmm?"

She tilted her head and regarded me with a pout. For a luscious instant, her hair heaped on her bare shoulder before sluicing off. I stopped breathing.

"Okay," I said.

She smiled. Two of Sherilyn's lower teeth were crooked, but you'd never catch me complaining.

The second I stepped into the back room, she drew the curtain shut. Meditation music played softly from an iPod dock on the supply shelf. The track lighting was dimmed, and where her desk used to be, there was now a thick yoga mat and a tall glass indoor waterfall. I thought the bit about the yoga and meditation area was code, but it seemed she really did the stuff back here. An old leather club chair sat stiffly in the corner, like it knew it was out of place among the New Age décor.

"Nice club chair," I said.

"Picked her up at an estate sale." She took me by the hand. "Get in her—she's *real* comfy."

She eased me into the chair. I have to admit, after a day that included three fistfights and rappelling down the side of a building, it felt nice to unwind a bit. The music and the waterfall sounds were also soothing.

"Why don't you show me some poses?" I said. "That's what they're called, right?"

"Another time maybe."

Slowly she reached out with her foot, pinched the yoga mat between her toes and dragged it to the base of the chair.

"*Sherilyn*...what are you doing?"

Looking me straight in the eyes, she got on her knees in front of the chair.

"Oh," I said.

She put her hands on my inner thighs. Her hair covered my lap.

"With you," she said, "this is my favorite yoga pose."

My breath was ragged, my entire body ached. I felt poisoned. I was reeling with desire for this woman, but I was also working. Kelsey was in a lot of danger and protecting her needed to be my top priority. I lifted Sherilyn's hands off my thighs and stood up with her.

"Sher...I'm on the job right now."

"I thought that was your niece out there."

"No, she's a client," I said. "And she's in a lot of trouble."

Sherilyn put her palms on my chest. She and her hair and her form-fitting tank top were inches away. She leaned toward my ear.

"Stay, Sugar. I'll be fast and quiet—I promise."

At moments like this when she was proving impossible to resist, Sherilyn reminded me of the redheaded seductress and assassin, Fiona Volpe, in the James Bond movie *Thunderball.* Indeed, she bore a striking resemblance to the character, especially when she wasn't getting what she wanted, like now, and her dark eyes glinted with flashes of rapaciousness. I swaddled my hand in her hair, jerked her head back and squeezed. Her eyes fluttered shut.

"Mmmm, that's nice."

"You are positively the devil, you know that?" I said.

She opened her eyes and gave me her crooked little smile again, and I kissed her. I kissed her hard and then I tugged her aside by the hair and opened the curtain.

Kelsey was seated at the mirror, while Danielle held hair color swatches against Kelsey's face. They glanced at me.

"A wonderful yoga area, Sherilyn," I said. "Thanks."

Sherilyn smiled furtively in the dim light. I walked over to Danielle's station and touched Kelsey on the shoulder.

"Going out for a short walk," I said. "Be right back."

"Okay."

Kelsey would be safe for ten minutes while I got some air and let my blood cool from its current temperature, which was somewhere in the vicinity of magma. Besides, the tell-tale cotton candy colors were out of Kelsey's hair now, so she looked like any other young woman getting her hair done. I opened the door and started up Franklin Avenue beneath the golden albizia trees. The village was busier than usual for a weekday afternoon. Most of the window-shoppers wore riding clothes, and a poster on a streetlamp explained why: the Millbrook Hunt, a 100-year-old fox hunt tradition, was this weekend.

When I reached the library, I turned around and headed back toward the salon. At the village's lone stoplight, I was about to cross the street when a gold Cadillac sedan pulled up to the curb a hundred yards away. Fatso, the two models and the Linebacker got out. They started up the street toward me.

They hadn't spotted me, but if I didn't act quickly, they would. My best option was to lure them out of town, away from Kelsey. But I didn't want to use the pickup to do it.

And that's when I got a different idea.

I jogged down the alley between the paint store and the gourmet coffee shop, climbed over a fence and ran through a couple backyards to the village hall. I went inside and hustled upstairs. The village court and the police were both on the second floor, but since they operated part-time, neither office was open today, and the hallway was empty.

At the end of the hall, I stopped in front of the police department door and pulled out my lock-picking set. There were no cameras around. I was prepared to pick the lock, but decided to give the knob a try. It opened. The keys to the department SUV (labeled "SUV") were on a hook inside the door. I grabbed them, shut the door and went back downstairs.

Recently they had begun parking the SUV behind the building, which was good because no one would see me. As I pulled away, I remarked to myself that I'd never committed grand theft auto before. I ignored the worries that cropped up and took a circuitous route through the village to the pickup truck. I'd parked it out of sight behind the funeral home. There I got the AR-15 and an extra magazine, went around the block and crept up Franklin Avenue. As I approached the gold Cadillac, I slowed the SUV to a crawl and jotted down the license plate number. It was a New Jersey plate. With any luck, Svetlana would be able to trace it to someone later.

I caught up to the four men in front of the deli. The Linebacker and Fatso were holding cups of coffee, Fatso with his ubiquitous donut. I rolled down the window and waved. One of the models pointed and shouted, "Hey, it's him!" They ran back to the Cadillac. I continued up Franklin, watching in the rear-view. As soon as the four of them jumped in the car, I accelerated past the decaying Thorne Building and roared out of town.

The trick was keeping them at a distance, but not such a distance that I lost them. At Route 44, I turned left. Then, at Stanford Road, I turned right. My plan was to lure them down Woodstock Road, a narrow and twisty dirt lane that ran through the woods, and ambush them. On the asphalt, they gained on me, but the second I took a left onto Woodstock, which was heavily rutted, they had to slow down.

I zoomed over the twisting hills, kicking up a dust cloud behind the SUV, until I reached a cornfield below the gun club. No one would think twice about gunshots around here. I backed into the tractor path, grabbed the AR-15, and jumped out. Jogging to the corner of the field, I racked a round into the chamber and switched off the safety, then got down on one knee. With the dried corn stalks rustling at my shoulder, I peered down the sights and aimed at the turn below.

I heard the car before I saw it, and then it emerged from the dust cloud, exposing its side to me. The ideal outcome here was a one-sided shootout like those in the 1980s TV show *The A-Team*: where a whole lot of bullets got fired, but no one got hurt. Aiming just ahead of the front tire, I fired six shots in quick succession. The tire blew and the car slowed. I shot out the rear tire next, and when the car skidded to a stop, I put six rounds into the front grill, then emptied the rest of the magazine over the car roof to keep them pinned down. With my final gunshot echoing in the dell, I ran back to the SUV and sped away. There were the pops of pistol shots in the distance, but by then I was long gone.

Back at the village hall, I wiped down the SUV for prints, returned the keys, and went back to The Pretty Filly. Sherilyn and Danielle were at their stations, cutting clients' hair. Sherilyn still wore the salivatory yoga outfit. She gave me a broad wink, a wink that promised a mind-blowing assignation between us in the not-too-distant future. I narrowed my eyes at her.

"That was more than a short walk," Danielle said. "We've been done for almost an hour. What've you been doing?"

"Oh, you know—just shooting the breeze with people."

Kelsey was sitting in the waiting area with her elbows on her knees and her chin in her hands, staring at a newspaper on the coffee table. Her hair was still bobbed, with the Cleopatra bangs, but now instead of cotton candy-colored, it was a lustrous raven black. She wore bright red lipstick that, with her pale complexion, brought out the blue in her eyes.

"Wow," I said. "Gorgeous."

Kelsey beamed. "Yeah?"

"Yeah."

"So you didn't like my hair before?" she said.

"No, I liked it. But I really like this. Makes you look more mature."

"Thanks."

"Did you pay Danielle?" I asked.

"Yes, sir." She saluted me. We went to the door.

"Goodbye, ladies."

"Bye, Dakota," Danielle said.

Sherilyn glanced in my direction with a faint smile on her lips.

"Y'all take care of yourself, Dakota Stevens. I expect to see you soon. *Real* soon."

"Yes, ma'am," I said.

We went back to the truck and headed south out of town. Kelsey gazed at golfers on the country club course as we drove by.

"Where are we going now?" she asked.

"Connecticut."

"Why? What's in Connecticut?"

"An Indian casino," I said, "where we'll meet up with my associate."

"Associate? Like another detective?"

"Yes." I turned left onto Route 343.

"What's his name?" Kelsey asked.

"Not he. She."

"Your associate is a woman? Cool."

"No," I said. "Not *a* woman, my dear Kelsey. *The* woman."

8

Svetlana Krüsh

It was quarter past ten, fully thirteen hours after Kelsey had entered my office and my life, when we reached the Indian casino in Connecticut. For many reasons the 2½-hour drive had taken us more than twice that. First, we stuck to the back roads, which were slower and more meandering. Second, we made stops for gas and the bathroom. Third, we had a layover at a department store in the Hartford suburbs to assemble Kelsey's go-bag. There, I got a painfully slow education about all of the *stuff* a teenage girl requires.

Then, dinner, somewhere in the Connecticut sticks. The name of the place alone—The Country Grille—should have told me to drive on, but we were starved and hadn't seen another place to eat for 25 miles. The second my headlights swung into a cratered parking lot and raked across bleached aluminum siding, I knew the kind of restaurant we were in for: the kind that serves dispirited coffee in brown, hourglass-shaped mugs and that spells plurals on the menu using apostrophes (e.g., "burger's"). Regrettably, I was right on both counts. We choked down the food and got back on the road.

After dinner, Kelsey curled up and fell asleep. I had hoped the long drive would give us a chance to talk, but we were both exhausted and said little during the trip. This, I supposed, was for the best. Kelsey was in a lot of danger and I needed to stay alert. Outside the department store dressing room, I had scanned the area for suspicious characters. On the road, I checked for tails every few minutes, and at the top of every hour I took three right turns in a row to see if anybody was following us. So far, we were clean, but the Mob guys had managed to find us upstate in no time, and I had to assume Kelsey's other pursuers were capable of the same.

With nothing to do but drive and think, I once again asked myself, *"Why are four dramatically different groups looking for Conover Wright?"* What was he into? Hanson said it "involves national security," but what could an author do that would make it a national security issue? Expose state secrets in one of his books? Possibly. Or maybe this had to do with his current book, which Kelsey believed was about the moon.

But how would a book about the moon involve the Mob, a pair of Asians and two thugs from Bismarck, North Dakota? Then again, maybe it didn't. Maybe the four groups were after Conover for different reasons and their showing up at my office the same morning was just a coincidence.

I was considering all of this when I reached the Indian casino parking lot. I shut off the truck and shook Kelsey awake.

"We're here," I said.

She sat up and blinked.

"Tell me I've been dreaming, Dakota. Tell me my brother isn't missing and a bunch of scary people aren't after me."

"Sorry, I wish I could, but that's the reality." I took off the Yankees cap and tossed it in the back. "Let's go inside. You'll feel better once you shower and get into a soft bed."

"I guess."

I decided to leave the bags for now, and we went into the hotel. In the lobby, I picked up a house phone and asked for Svetlana's room. It rang several times and went to voicemail. I left a message. I tried her cell phone but that also went to voicemail. I hung up. Beeping and clanging wafted out of the casino entrance.

"I know where she is," I said. "Act like you're twenty-one, okay? It's illegal for minors to be on the gambling floor."

"And just how do I act like I'm twenty-one?"

"I don't know. Stand up straight. Raise your chin, look haughty. Act like you belong."

"I can do all of those things," she said, and before my eyes she became a solipsistic young heiress.

We passed the slot machines, and the craps and roulette tables, before we reached the blackjack tables. If Svetlana was in the casino, this is where she'd be. We strode past the tables, studying the players at each one. There were lots of men in bowling shirts smoking cheap cigars, and women in risqué blouses drinking white wine, but nobody who even remotely resembled Svetlana.

"Not here, huh?" Kelsey said.

"No."

"I bet *she'll* know."

A cocktail waitress approached with a tray of drinks. She was a middle-aged blonde with aftermarket features and a hypnotic sashay that wasn't learned at Wellesley.

"Good idea." I pulled out a $20 bill and held it up to the waitress.

"Oh, hon," she said, "can I get you on the way back?"

"We don't need drinks." I tossed the bill on the tray. "I'm looking for a friend. Ukrainian woman. Tall, trim, exotic looking. She's a special guest of the hotel, and she plays a lot of blackjack."

"Oh, yes…I know who you're talking about." She pointed at a room across the casino floor. "The high rollers lounge. Can't miss her."

"Thank you."

We crossed the floor, and as Kelsey and I went inside, I ignored the fact that the other men were in suits, a few even in dinner jackets. Meanwhile, I looked like a character out of a Jack London novel. A throng of people—mostly men—surrounded the center table, and were concentrated around one seat in particular. Although I couldn't see the person, I already knew who it was. Tugging on Kelsey's arm, I pardoned my way to the front and stood at the side of the blackjack table with an unobstructed view of the scene.

Svetlana Krüsh, in a little black dress, sat facing the dealer, while elegant, sour-faced women stood in the back, clutching cocktails and looking daggers at her. On the green baize in front of Svetlana was a small city of chips, a red drink in a martini glass, and an iPhone. She was staring down the dealer. I didn't envy him; as a chess grandmaster with the eyes of a jungle predator, she had the most formidable stare I'd ever seen. One of her cards was face-down, and the second was the Seven of Clubs. She tapped the baize with a fire engine red fingernail, the dealer placed the Seven of Diamonds in front of her, and she made a tiny waving motion over her cards. The dealer continued past her, and when the cards were all revealed, Svetlana had three sevens and won the hand.

There were two things I knew about blackjack: that the goal was to get to 21, and that Svetlana Krüsh had the game down to an evil art.

Her hair was down, grazing her smooth shoulders. I admired her regal posture, her graceful neck and lissome hands—once again marveling at how I ever got anything done working with her. Svetlana was one of those rare women so stunning and brilliant, she excited the very air molecules around her. Kelsey tapped me on the arm.

"Wow, that's her? *That's* your associate? You work with her?"

"Yes, yes, and yes," I said.

"She doesn't look like a detective. What does she do?"

I smiled because I knew what Svetlana's answer would be.

"You should ask her."

Svetlana won the next hand with the Queen and Ace of Hearts. She turned and winked at me. Apparently she'd been aware of my presence all along. She tossed a pair of $100 chips in front of the dealer and put the rest in a black purse with a gold chain. With a final sip of her drink, she stood up, the crowd of men attentively parted, and she strode over to us. If she was surprised by the presence of Kelsey, she didn't show it.

As we walked out of the lounge, I leaned into her shoulder.

"Counting cards again?"

She made a sexy little movement in which she closed her eyes and shrugged minutely.

"One loses skills if one does not use them from time to time," she said.

"But the high rollers table?" I said. "A little risky with your own money."

"I did not bet my own money. I was comped five thousand dollars."

"Why?"

"They consider me a draw," she said. "You would not know because you do not play, but there were several whales at that table."

"How much did you smoke them for?" I asked.

"Enough."

She shook her handbag. The chips inside rattled.

"Nice." I gestured at Kelsey. "Svetlana, this is our new client, Kelsey Wright. Kelsey, this is Svetlana Krüsh, my associate and the former U.S. women's chess champion."

"Nice to meet you." Kelsey shook her hand.

"By the way," I said to Svetlana. "The speed chess tournament. I take it you won today."

"Of course."

"But I don't get it," Kelsey said. "If Dakota's the detective, what do you do?"

"I solve the crimes and handle the money," Svetlana said.

I winked at Kelsey.

"So, Champ," I said to Svetlana, "how about we go someplace and talk?"

"I would suggest the bar upstairs, but Kelsey looks very young."

"That's because she is young."

"I'm eighteen," Kelsey said.

"I see." Svetlana raised an eyebrow at me. "And where are her parents?"

"They're dead," Kelsey said. "And I'm right here. You can ask me."

"Look, let's not discuss this here," I said. "Svetlana, you have a suite, right?"

"I do."

"With extra beds?"

"Yes, two," she said.

"Good. We need to stay with you if it's okay."

"If you must. But why?"

"Because we can't use credit cards," I said. "I don't even want our driver's license info in their system. I'll explain later."

"Okay, we will go upstairs," she said. "Let me cash out first."

"We'll meet you in the lobby, by the elevators."

"Fine."

Once she had walked away, Kelsey and I wove through the gaming tables, out of the casino. At the elevators, she made a face.

"What's wrong?" I said.

"Nothing."

"No, what is it?"

"It's...why was Svetlana such a bitch to me a minute ago?"

I took a deep breath and formed my words judiciously.

"It's not that she was being a bitch," I said. "It's that... like a lot of geniuses—and she *is* a genius at chess—she's temperamental. She heard you were only eighteen, and that your parents aren't around, and she's thinking about how we've never taken a case for somebody so young. It's different than what we're used to. She's also thinking that since you're a teenager, you're going to be a spoiled pain in the ass. But she doesn't know you yet like I do."

"So I'm *not* a spoiled pain in the ass?" Kelsey said.

"Not yet."

She punched me on the arm. I looked around the corner for Svetlana, didn't see her, and turned back to Kelsey.

"Hey, I'm sorry you lost your parents."

"That's okay," she said. "I shouldn't have said that to Svetlana. Not so bitchy anyway."

"I know what it's like, that's all. I lost mine as a kid, too."

"Really?"

I nodded. "I was raised by my grandparents."

"Mine were in a car accident," she said. "Yours?"

"Disappeared on a sailboat and presumed dead."

She stared at the floor. "It sucks, doesn't it? And now with Conover...I don't know what I'm going to do."

"We're going to find him," I said.

She leaned into me, and I put a hand on her shoulder. Svetlana rounded the corner. She gave me a disapproving look.

"Get your money?" I asked.

"Yes."

"I'm sorry I was snippy before," Kelsey said.

"And I am sorry if I was callous," Svetlana said.

"I think everyone's tired," I said.

A bellboy went to the elevator towing a luggage cart heaped with bags. He was followed by a couple in their silver years. Kelsey pointed at a bathroom across the lobby.

"Is it okay if I go?"

I scanned the lobby. It was quiet and there were no suspicious people hanging around.

"Sure, go ahead," I said.

I watched her until she entered the bathroom, and kept one eye on the door.

"You two seem familiar," Svetlana said. "Are you sure that is a good idea?"

"I like her, she's a good kid," I said. "Besides, we've been through a lot today. We bonded, I guess."

"You need to be careful, Dakota."

"What are you talking about?"

"Getting too close to the client. It may cloud your judgment."

"I'm fine, Svetlana, I swear. It's just my protective side coming through." I glanced at my watch. It was almost eleven. "It's been a long day. I think we should all hit the sack and discuss the case tomorrow morning—when everyone is fresh and thinking clearly."

"That sounds like a good idea."

I glanced at the bathroom door. It had been a while and Kelsey still hadn't come out. I was beginning to worry.

"What are you not telling me, Dakota?"

"She's in a lot of danger."

"Danger? Your message said nothing about this."

"Sorry, it's been a busy day."

I gave her a quick rundown: Kelsey hiring me to find her brother. The four groups of men showing up. The fistfights, the rappelling adventure, the shootout in the Millbrook woods.

"Excuse me," she said. "You stole a *police car*?"

"I'll admit—not my finest hour."

"And what about payment for the case? I assume she isn't in a position to pay us."

"She gave us a retainer—ten grand. Well, now it's nine thousand and change."

"That might cover our expenses," she said. "But not if we have to go underground for long."

"Kelsey's brother is a bestselling author. According to her, he's loaded, and she has access to all of his accounts. Getting paid isn't going to be an issue."

"I hope not," Svetlana said.

"One other thing," I said. "Two, in fact. We need to leave early. It's only a matter of time before they figure out we're here. Also, you need to destroy your phone. The people after us will—"

She dropped her iPhone on the marble floor and crushed it under her stiletto heel.

"Scary," I said. "Yet, oddly sexy."

"Thank you."

Across the lobby, Kelsey exited the bathroom, and I almost didn't recognize her with the shimmering black bob. I had become accustomed to the cotton candy hair, then the ski cap. She glanced at the shattered phone on the floor and yawned.

"So, are we going to sleep or what?" she said.

Svetlana smirked at me.

"We need to get our bags," I said to Kelsey.

"Can't you get them?" she said. "I'm exhausted."

"Don't be a spoiled pain in the ass. Come on."

She rolled her eyes and followed me out to the truck.

9

Where is Conover?

We reconvened in the morning at the hotel breakfast buffet. It was seven thirty. Kelsey had woken up and gotten ready in minutes, but I had trouble with Svetlana, a notoriously late riser. As for me, now that I'd had some rest and the three of us were safe, I was eager to shift from bodyguard to investigator, and find Conover Wright.

Kelsey and I had piled our plates high with scrambled eggs, sausages, hash browns, pancakes and fruit salad, while Svetlana sipped a cup of chai and picked at a pumpkin muffin.

"I can't believe how hungry I am," Kelsey said.

"Eat up and get ready to talk," I said. "Svetlana and I need to ask you a lot of questions."

"What kind of questions?"

"Eat. Then we'll talk."

Svetlana put down her cup. "So, what progress did you make with the unpacking yesterday?"

"Yeah," I said. "About that."

Between bites, I explained that playing host to the FBI and three other groups of callers had left me with little time for unpacking.

"One box."

She said this to me with no inflection whatsoever.

"Well," I said, "half a box."

"Half a box."

"I didn't have a lot of time. Kelsey got there at nine-fifteen."

"Sure, blame me," Kelsey said.

The waitress came by and refilled our cups. Kelsey stabbed a strawberry and some melon onto her fork.

"Hey, why'd you guys move offices anyway?" she said. "I peeked in the window of the one downtown, and I've gotta be honest, it's much nicer than that place you're in now."

"We had a conflict with the landlord." I sliced a sausage in half and glanced at Svetlana.

"The building belonged to my father," she said, "and I did not wish to be beholden to him any longer."

"Why?" Kelsey asked.

"She has her reasons," I said. "Look, if you're going to be talking instead of eating, you're going to answer *our* questions, not the other way around."

"Fine, I'll eat," she said.

Across the restaurant, a group of college boys ogled Svetlana. They were hunched over their table, clearly nursing hangovers. I gave them a look and they turned away. Sometimes Svetlana's ability to attract attention was an asset, but right now we needed to be invisible, and her outfit for today made that impossible: a short, belted chocolate dress with orange trim, and brown knee-high boots. She wore a pair of spangly gold earrings, and her bouffant hair was flipped up at the ends

60s-style so it flounced on her shoulders. The autumnal go-go girl look.

"Excuse me, Miss Krüsh," I said. "It seems somebody didn't get the memo about us being on the lam. Don't you have anything less...*stunning* you can wear?"

"No. I left all of my fugitive wear at home."

"We'll stop someplace so you can buy some things."

We finished our breakfast in silence. Svetlana signed the check, and we went upstairs to her suite. The curtains were open, giving a fantastic view of the fall color. The woods surrounding the casino stretched for miles into the distance.

The three of us sat around a meeting table near the window. Svetlana placed her laptop in front of her and a digital recorder in the center of the table.

"Okay," I said. "First, let's define what we want to get out of this conversation."

"What do you mean?" Kelsey asked.

"If I may," Svetlana said.

"Please," I said.

"Kelsey, since people are after you to get to your brother, and since that threat does not go away until your brother is found, the most important question is, 'Where is Conover?'"

"Correct," I said. "Continue, Svetlana."

"A related question, but one more difficult to answer at this juncture is, '*Why* are these different groups of people after him?'"

"Right again."

"So," Svetlana said, "for now it seems we should focus our energies on the where and not the why."

"Agreed," I said.

"Excuse me a sec," Kelsey said. "But why *are* all of these people after him? It makes no sense."

"We can't answer that right now," I said. "Only the groups looking for him know why, and they're not going to tell us squat. Instead of why they're looking for him, a better question is, 'How will they look for him?'"

"I don't understand," Kelsey said.

Svetlana looked up from the laptop. "Dakota means, 'What methods will the various groups use to find your brother?'"

"Exactly," I said. "For example, I'm sure they've all looked for some kind of electronic trail—credit card transactions, electronic bridge tolls, reservations, that sort of thing. But NYPD said there's been no activity on your brother's credit cards, and the FBI showing up at our office tells me they didn't find anything either. Which means they've shifted to the next two lines of inquiry."

"Which are?" Kelsey asked.

"One, places Conover has frequented or to which he has an attachment. And two, his known associates."

"Just a moment." Svetlana adjusted her laptop screen and looked at Kelsey. "Do you have access to your brother's social security number, perhaps passwords to websites?"

"Sure, all of it. I handle all of Conover's business and life stuff."

"Such as?" I said.

"Such as...dealing with his agent and publicist. Managing his calendar. Paying the bills, meeting with the accountant. Blogging, Facebooking, and tweeting as him." She leaned back in her chair and stared at the ceiling. "All of the social media stuff, now that I think about it. What else? Hmm…the shopping. Laundry. Laying out his clothes."

"His clothes?" I said. "Seriously?"

"Yeah. I also do the cooking, but not the cleaning. We have a woman who does that, thank God. But pretty much everything else."

"So what the hell does your brother do?" I asked.

"He writes," Kelsey said. "And does publicity stuff—you know, like TV, radio, cons, speaking engagements."

Svetlana gave her a rare smile.

"I am impressed."

"Thanks," Kelsey said.

"Pretty remarkable for eighteen," I said.

"Since she knows his personal information," Svetlana said, "I will do some electronic searching of my own."

"Good. While you're at it…" I pulled out my pocket notebook, opened it to yesterday's page and handed it to her. "Some other things to look into. The little bit of information I have on the North Dakota twins. A New Jersey license plate number for a late model gold Cadillac. And a few cell phone numbers. I think they're for burners, but I was hoping you could do reverse lookups, or whatever it is you do."

"I will handle it." She typed in the information and tossed back my notebook.

"Can I help?" Kelsey asked.

"Are you skilled with computers?" Svetlana said.

"Uh, *yeah*."

"Okay. You may help."

"Thanks. I don't like feeling *totally* lame."

I got up and returned with three bottles of water from the mini-bar.

"All right, next topic." I sat down again. "Places to which Conover has a connection or an attachment. Kelsey, I want you to free-associate. Tell us about places he goes regularly, but also ones he might have gone to a long time ago and wanted to return to."

"This is tough," Kelsey said, opening the water bottle.

"Relax," I said. "Let's start with a typical day. What does Conover do, and where does he go?"

"My brother writes. That's what he does."

"Surely he doesn't write twenty-four hours a day," I said.

"You'd be surprised."

"Walk us through his day, please," Svetlana said.

"Okay," Kelsey said. "He gets up around five and writes until noon. Then he eats lunch while he reads—*Scientific American* or the *New York Times* science section. Then he goes out for a long walk. He's gone until five or six."

"Where does he go?"

"Depends," she said. "Sometimes over to Columbia to use the library. He's an alum. Once in a while, a bookstore." She pursed her lips. "He's only let me come with him a couple times, so I can't tell you every place he's gone. All I can say for certain is, in the last few months he's been getting home later and later."

Svetlana typed away on her keyboard.

"Keep going," I said.

"When he gets back, he writes for a while, then we eat dinner. Afterwards, if he has an engagement that night—like a signing or a reading—I'll sometimes go with him. Once in a while there's a swanky benefit-type event and we have to get dressed up. But most of the time it's basic stuff, and we're back by eleven. He goes to sleep, wakes at five and starts all over again." She drank some water. "But there's one other thing."

"What?"

"Lately when I've asked him where he went, he's snapped at me and said it was none of my business. He comes home irritated about everything."

"Interesting," I said. "And he never mentioned the people he saw or what he was doing?"

"Nope."

"Okay. Now, tell us about places he's been—places to which he has an attachment."

"I'll try." She drummed her fingers on the tabletop. "Well, he took me to Paris a couple years ago. The International Sci-Fi Authors Conference. I loved Paris, but he hated the place. *Hated* it. Vowed he'd never go back, so I doubt he went there."

"I agree," I said. "Unless he went to Canada, I doubt he left the country. Maybe if he had access to a forged passport, but I don't think your brother knows where to get such things."

"You're right," Kelsey said.

"Where else?" I asked.

"We've been to Vermont a couple times."

"Can you remember which town?" Svetlana asked.

"No. It was a cabin in the woods, and there was a covered bridge nearby."

"That narrows it down," I said.

"He hated it anyway," Kelsey said. "He likes places on the water. You know, the ocean."

"Any specific place?"

"Let's see…we've been to the Cape, but it was too crowded for him. We rented a condo on Maui last winter, but that was also too crowded. He likes quiet places on the water. I'd say the coast of Maine is his favorite place."

"Where on the coast?" I asked.

"Camden," she said. "It's like an eight-hour drive from New York."

"I am very familiar with Camden."

My throat got tight. I was just a little boy when my parents sailed out of Camden harbor after lunch on a crystal-clear day, never to be seen again. I hadn't had a crab salad sandwich since then. I took a deep breath and brought my thoughts back to the case.

"Anyplace else within driving distance of Manhattan?"

"The tip of Long Island. Way out there. What's it called?"

"Montauk," Svetlana said.

"Says the Queen of the Hamptons," I said.

Svetlana glanced at me as she typed. "Quite."

"Anywhere else?" I asked.

"No," Kelsey said. "That's it."

"Good job."

"Known associates," Svetlana said, tapping the RETURN key on the computer. "*Une liste, s'il vous plaît.*"

"This is totally random." Kelsey picked at the label on the water bottle. "Okay, there's Conover's agent, Stoddart Prince. Then there's the sort-of girlfriend I told you about yesterday. Her name is Jennifer Lin. She's a model,

I guess. Let's see…there's a freelance editor that works on all of Conover's books. His name is Kyle Foster. The two of us see Conover's work before anybody else."

"Any chance Kyle's seen what he's working on now?" I asked.

"Well, I haven't, so I doubt it." She pulled her feet up and hugged her knees to her chest. "But I don't know… maybe."

"Anybody else?"

"Not that I can think of."

"What about his friends?"

"What friends?" she said. "His work is his life."

"Okay, that's enough," I said.

Svetlana finished typing and closed the laptop. She opened her bottle of water.

"So, what is our next move?"

"Beats me," I said. "She only gave us about fifty leads. I need time to think."

I stood, chugged the rest of my water and threw the bottle away. I gazed out at the sea of foliage until I suddenly became aware of the time. My watch said it was a few minutes after nine.

"We need to go," I said. "Let's get packed and be ready to leave in ten minutes."

"It will take me that long to freshen and pack my makeup," Svetlana said.

"Yeah," Kelsey said, "and I might want to change my blouse."

"Fine. Twenty minutes. But not one second longer."

10

Where is the Nearest Exit?

The night before, I'd snuck in the shotgun wrapped in a blanket. Fortunately for my lower back, I'd left the rest of my arsenal in the truck, which meant this morning I had only the shotgun and my go-bag to carry. Kelsey carried her bag, and Svetlana had packed shockingly light: one large Rollaboard, her Louis Vuitton train case, and her magical Gucci handbag. I say her handbag was magical because it somehow always contained exactly what we needed during our investigations. We took the elevator to the lobby and stopped at the front desk.

"I will check out," Svetlana said. "Would you take my things out to the car?"

She handed me everything but her handbag.

"Actually…it's a pickup truck," I said.

Her face was deadpan. "A pickup truck."

"We have to keep a low profile," I said.

"Surely not *that* low," she said.

"Hey, don't knock it. It's a king cab."

Svetlana frowned. As the belle of the chess world, she was used to first class transportation and accommodations—always. Confident she'd get into the spirit of being on the lam, I ignored her objections.

"We'll meet you out front in ten minutes," I said.

Kelsey and I exited through the automatic revolving doors and followed a walkway into the parking lot. Somehow I managed to balance my go-bag, the wrapped shotgun and Svetlana's train case on top of her Rollaboard.

The lot had been full when we'd arrived, so I'd parked on the farthest end, abutting the woods. It was another picture-perfect fall day—bright, colorful and crisp. I had no idea where we were going from the casino; I'd decide once we were on the road.

"Are you thinking about what I told you?" Kelsey asked. "Was it helpful?"

"Yes." We passed between two cars. "Wait, stop."

"What's wrong?"

A few rows ahead, two large sedans pulled in and parked beside each other. One of them was the gold Cadillac I'd seen yesterday. Eight men wearing sunglasses got out of the cars. Among them were the Linebacker, Fatso, and the two models. I didn't recognize the other four.

"Kelsey, turn around slowly and walk beside me. We're going back inside."

"Why, what's—"

"Do it. Walk normally."

We turned around and started walking. The casino was more than a hundred yards away.

"They're here, aren't they?"

"Yes, but don't panic. We'll be fine." Suddenly I wished I were carrying the arsenal. "Put your arm around me and get close. Like we're boyfriend and girlfriend."

She did it. I could feel her trembling against me.

"Hang in there, you're doing fine."

I desperately wanted to look back and see how far away they were, but if I did, they might see my face, and then it would be all over. Kelsey tugged at my waist.

"Let's run," she said.

"No, we can't run. Do *not* run, Kelsey."

I put my arm around her and held her tight. We kept walking. We passed the last row of cars and neared the entrance.

"Almost there," I said.

The glass of the casino was reflective so I could see behind us now. At first all I saw was the row of cars nearest the building. But as we drew closer to the doors, eight heads appeared over the roofs of the cars, and then their full bodies appeared. They were fifty yards behind us at the most.

I let go of Kelsey, guided her into the oversized revolving door, and followed her into the compartment. The door revolved at a turtle's pace.

"The second we're inside," I said, "head for the front desk."

I had no idea how close they were now. If they had jogged any of the remaining distance, we were screwed. When the doorway opened, Kelsey sprang out and started for the front desk. I followed closely behind. Svetlana was walking toward us.

"They're here," I said to her. "We have to go. Right now."

She hitched up her purse, and we started across the lobby. With all of the luggage, we were about as nimble as Noah's Ark.

"Where should we go?" Svetlana said.

"Can you get us to the loading dock?" I asked. "Like through the kitchen?"

"Yes."

At the corner before the elevators, I ventured a glance over my shoulder. Fatso and the Linebacker were in the revolving door, with the other six men queued up outside.

"Svetlana, I hope you know where you're going," I said. "They're right behind us."

She led us into an alcove off the lobby, to a service elevator. While we waited for it, I peeked out. The men had gathered near the front desk. The Linebacker was talking and pointing around the lobby. They were about to split up and search.

"We don't have much time, Svetlana."

"It's coming." Her voice was icily calm.

I unwrapped the shotgun enough to get my hands underneath the blanket. I pumped a round into the chamber, switched off the safety, and rewrapped it so I was clutching the stock with one hand. I kept my forefinger on the trigger guard. Kelsey was shaking.

"Kelsey, we'll be out of here in a second," I said.

The doors opened and the women slipped inside. I walked in backward dragging the luggage and steadying the shotgun. Svetlana punched the button for the basement. We started down.

"Where do we go at the bottom?" I asked.

"We'll find out," she said.

"You mean you don't know?"

"I am not in the habit of wandering around hotel basements, Dakota," she said.

The elevator belched us into a wide hallway full of laundry bins. Svetlana clip-clopped ahead. There were voices coming from the next room. She stopped at the doorway.

"*Perdón, señoras,*" she said. "*¿Dónde está la salida más cercana?*"

Kelsey and I looked inside. A group of Latina women were folding laundry. They looked at each other and chattered in rapid Spanish, then one of them spoke to Svetlana.

"*Gracias,*" Svetlana said.

We continued down the hall.

"What'd you ask them?" I said.

"'Where is the nearest exit?'"

I tapped Kelsey on the arm. "Svetlana knows seven languages."

"Uh, okay," Kelsey said.

The hallway brought us to the kitchen. Workers stopped what they were doing to watch Svetlana pass by. A sous chef whistled. Svetlana marched ahead.

After a series of turns, we ended up at the loading dock. Svetlana led us out a side door. We were standing next to a dumpster.

"You two stay here," I said. "I'll get the truck."

"Shouldn't we all go together?" Svetlana said.

"No. If they have someone watching the parking lot, a man and two women would be too obvious. Do you want my pistol?"

"No."

"Okay, then wait behind the dumpster. I'll be right back."

I took the shotgun still wrapped in the blanket, went around the building and crossed the parking lot. Even walking briskly it took me five minutes to reach the truck. When I got back to the loading area, I didn't see them.

A tingling sensation crept down my neck. I parked and got out.

"Svetlana? Kelsey?"

They were gone.

11

Grace Under Pressure

I looked around the dumpster. There was no sign of them, but the luggage was gone. If they'd been caught, the Mob guys would have left their bags behind. I jumped in the truck and started around the building, looking for the other exits. There were several—too many to count—and I had to creep so I didn't miss any.

I couldn't believe I had been so stupid. Svetlana was right: the three of us should have stayed together. I pounded the steering wheel. If anything happened to either of them, I would never forgive myself. I circled the building again. Workers stood outside a second loading dock, smoking. I kept going.

On my third lap around the building, I spotted them hiding behind a pine tree. I closed my eyes and gave thanks, then pulled up to the curb. Svetlana and Kelsey ran across the grass with the bags. Once we were all in the truck, I drove straight to the casino exit. I wasn't sure whether to turn right or left, so I chose left. I touched Svetlana's arm.

"Hey," I said. "You okay?"

"I will admit to being scared," she said. "We both were."

"What happened? One of them showed up?"

"That is precisely what happened," she said. "He came from around the building. Fortunately I saw him first, and we went back through the kitchen to the exit where you met us."

"Grace under pressure," I said.

"What's that?" Kelsey asked from the back seat.

"It's how Hemingway defined guts, or courage."

"She was totally like that, Dakota. You should have seen it."

I ribbed Svetlana. "Must have been your maternal instinct kicking in."

"Ha." She examined her nails on one hand. "Good—I thought I chipped a nail."

"I'm glad you're both all right," I said.

"Sure," Kelsey said, "I'm *great*."

I turned down a county road and accelerated. I wanted to put some distance between us and the casino. Svetlana looked around the truck cab.

"Charming."

"Hey, it's perfect for keeping a low profile."

"Perhaps. But do I look like someone at home in a pickup truck?" She gestured at her outfit.

"You're right," I said. "Time to do something about that."

Twenty miles up the road, we entered a formerly prosperous mill town. We drove along a river, passing abandoned textile mills with most of the windows shattered. As we continued into the town, brick storefronts loomed over a narrow main drag. We rolled past a bank, a bookstore, an old movie theater, a diner and a Chinese restaurant (somehow they're everywhere) before serendipity struck.

We found a rarity nowadays: a small-town department store. I parked at a meter and faced Svetlana.

"Time for a new look," I said. "Nothing glam, okay? No offense, but you have a tendency to attract attention, and that's exactly what we don't want right now."

"If I must." She held out her hand. "Our retainer?"

"Kelsey, give her the money, would you?"

Kelsey dug into her messenger bag and handed forward the bundles of $20 bills, which Svetlana dropped into her bottomless handbag.

"Ahem," I said.

Svetlana pulled out one bundle and tossed it in my lap. As she grabbed the door handle, she looked at the pathetic window displays and heaved out a lingering sigh.

"I know," I said, "they're hardly the Christmas windows at Bergdorf's. Think of this like a Band-Aid. You just have to *rip* it off."

In one swift motion, she got out and slammed the door with spirit.

Half an hour later, she emerged from the store wearing a sweater, down vest, close-fitting jeans and boots. The spangly earrings were gone, and her hair was now in simple braids. She looked like a model in an L.L. Bean catalog, but fifty times hotter. So much for not drawing attention.

"Wow," Kelsey said, peering between the seats. "It's like one woman went in and a different one came out."

"That's Svetlana," I said. "A chameleon."

Svetlana put the shopping bags in the back seat. Once back in the truck, she pulled down the visor mirror and applied lipstick.

"So, what is next, Holmes?" she said.

I smiled.

"As in Sherlock?" Kelsey said.

"Yes," Svetlana said. "He likes it when I call him that."

"We need to find a place to regroup, my dear Watson," I said.

"Like a motel?" Kelsey said.

"I'm not sure."

I pulled back onto the road and cruised down the rest of the main drag. A mile outside of town I saw a cinder block building with a mural on the side showing a bowling ball and pins. "BOWL!" it read in huge letters.

"Perfect," I said.

There were cars in the parking lot. I pulled in.

"Bowling?" Kelsey said. "Awesome, I love bowling!"

Svetlana gave me her signature "You Have to Be Kidding Me" face.

"I refuse to bowl," she said. "But I will keep score."

We parked and went inside. All of the lanes were empty but one, where a group of male retirees bowled and sipped late-morning beers. They froze watching us walk in, paying particular attention, I noticed, to the fit of Svetlana's jeans. We paid for a lane, got shoes, picked out balls. Even though the scoring was electronic, Svetlana sat in the scorekeeper's seat and watched. I wanted a beer, but it was too early, and besides, I had a rule of not drinking while on a case. Instead I got a cup of the tar they called coffee, bowled with Kelsey, and thought about the case.

We bowled a complete game, and with me distracted and throwing gutter ball after gutter ball, Kelsey won easily. Afterwards I sat beside Svetlana and we watched Kelsey play a game alone. Every now and then, she waved or made faces at us.

"She seems to have relaxed," Svetlana said. "I stand corrected. This was a good idea."

"It was more for me," I said. "I needed to think."

"And what conclusions have you reached?" Svetlana asked.

I sipped some coffee. It was now lukewarm tar, but it was caffeine, so I drank it.

"We have to go back to the city," I said.

"Hmm."

"What?"

"That seems like the last place we should go," she said.

"I know, but we have to. Kelsey gave us those leads on places Conover might be, and we need a clue to narrow things down. And the only place I can think of where we might find one is their apartment."

"And they would not be watching it?" Svetlana said. "The four groups you spoke of."

Kelsey went to the line and rolled the ball down the alley granny-style. She made a strike and danced around.

"I don't know," I said. "The Mob guys were up here in force, so I think they've abandoned the place. I haven't seen the Asians or the North Dakota boys at all since we left. It's possible they're hanging around there, but even if they are, I doubt anybody expects us to come back. If I were them, I'd think we left the city entirely."

Svetlana nodded. "And Conover's known associates are another reason to go back."

"Right. I'm thinking we do a *blitzkrieg* attack. Hit them all in twenty-four hours and high-tail it out of town again."

"Then we should leave." She glanced at my watch and held up my wrist. "Now."

12

Rome After the Visigoths

When we reached Kelsey's apartment building, I parked the truck on 116th Street, around the corner from the main entrance on Riverside Drive. Svetlana got out and checked the street for suspicious cars, and when she gave us the all-clear, the three of us entered the building from a little-used side entrance. Kelsey led us upstairs to the third floor. The hallway was dim.

"Here we are," she said. "It's at the end. Three-A."

As we walked down the hall, I pulled out my Sig Sauer and flicked off the safety.

"All right," I said at the door, "give me the keys."

"Bossy," Kelsey said.

She slapped them into my hand. I unlocked the door and opened it with my jacket sleeve.

"You two wait here. I'll be right back."

I crept down a short hallway and continued into an expansive living room. The place was beyond ransacked; it looked like Rome after the Visigoths. There were holes in the walls. Floorboards ripped up. Sofas gutted. Picture frames shattered. Drawers smashed. Books tossed on the floor. Light fixtures detached. Even the electrical outlet covers had been removed. It didn't take a person with advanced skills of ratiocination to know that somebody had been frantically searching for something. Something small.

Without touching anything, I took a quick tour through the rest of the apartment and discovered that some of other rooms were also in shambles. I holstered my gun and returned to the outside hallway. Kelsey was leaning against the wall. Svetlana produced three pairs of latex gloves from her bag and handed Kelsey and me a pair.

"So?" Kelsey said.

I slipped the gloves on. "Come in first." When they were inside, I shut the apartment door. "Now, Kelsey, what you're about to see is going to be upsetting. I need you to keep it together, okay?"

"What is it?"

I led them down the hallway.

"Ohmigod!" Kelsey gasped. "Who…who did this?"

"I'm guessing one of the groups looking for your brother," I said. "By the looks of it, maybe all of them."

"Are you insured?" Svetlana asked.

Kelsey was in a daze. "Yeah…homeowner's…"

"The good news is," I said, "this amount of destruction tells us something."

"Tells us what?" Kelsey asked. "I can't wait to hear it."

Svetlana looked at her. "Whoever did this was not solely looking for your brother."

"Right," I said. "They were looking for a *thing*, a thing that could be hidden in small spaces."

"Like what?"

"Your guess is as good as mine," I said. "A key. Diamonds. Who knows?"

"Could it be a flash drive?" Kelsey said.

"Sure, why?"

"Because Conover's paranoid about losing his work. He always keeps a copy of his work on him."

"Good to know," I said.

"Shall we get started?" Svetlana asked.

"Yeah."

I took a deep breath and gathered myself for what came next: searching through the rubble.

"Let's split up and take different rooms," I said. "My focus will be the living room and office. Kelsey, you check your bedroom and clean up the kitchen. They made a big mess in there searching through food. Also Kelsey, try to find some recent photos of your brother. And Svetlana, you take Conover's bedroom and the bathrooms."

"And what are we looking for?" Svetlana asked.

"First and foremost," I said, "any clues about where Conover went. Second, any signs of who did the ransacking." I looked at Kelsey. The shock was wearing off. "We need to be fast. And stay away from the windows. Somebody might still be watching the place from the street. All right, let's go."

"This way, Svetlana," Kelsey said.

I started by giving the living room a cursory search: reaching into sofa cushions, inspecting the bookcases, picking up books and fanning the pages. I hadn't expected to find anything, so I wasn't disappointed when I didn't. I moved on to the office.

This room had borne the brunt of the searching, so I decided to work my way around the perimeter. Inside the doorway were the dust outlines of two filing cabinets.

A painting leaned against the baseboard with its back cut open. Like the living room, some of the floorboards were ripped up, and the electrical outlet covers had been removed. A heap of books lay on the floor. Among them were several science fiction titles, books about the moon, and reference books.

Next I found a floor safe with its door left open. Of course with my luck, it was empty. However, I wondered if Conover might have cleaned it out before he disappeared.

Continuing around the room, I finally reached the desk. As Kelsey had already mentioned, there was no laptop. A document scanner and a small printer sat on either side of the desktop. But what made the desk curious was the complete absence of writing materials. Every writer I'd ever heard about was notorious for having stacks of manuscripts, notebooks, newspapers, magazines and other research materials lying around. Except for a small tray of notepaper, his desk was bare.

I switched on my new tactical flashlight and rummaged through the drawers, hoping to find a key, an address book, anything resembling a clue, but there was just the usual junk. I put the light away. Then, on the floor in the corner, buried under some books, was a paper-cutter. I squatted and worked the handle a couple of times, wondering what the heck Conover had a paper-cutter for, and then I looked back at the desk.

The notepaper.

I grabbed the paper out of its tray. There were maybe 50 sheets. The top few sheets were blank on both sides, but the rest had computer printing on the back. They were sheets of 8½" x 11" paper cut into quadrants. I zipped through the stack. At first glance, a few of the sheets seemed to be email messages. They might contain a clue.

It made sense that the ransackers had ignored the notepaper, because the blank top sheets covered the ones with writing on the back, making them all appear blank. The stack looked like standard office supplies. I pocketed the stack, took a roll of tape from the desk, and gave the room a final glance. One thing seemed clear: whoever had searched the place was after Conover's work.

I went out to the kitchen, where Kelsey was cleaning up. It was a large kitchen for a Manhattan apartment. Containers of liquids had been dumped into the sink, and loose sugar, flour, oatmeal and other dry goods covered the table and countertops. Kelsey was sweeping the piles into a garbage can.

"Find anything?" I asked.

"Yeah, a mess."

"Well, clean it up the best you can. We have to go in a minute."

"Almost done," she said.

Out of habit, I looked in the refrigerator. We detectives always look in here and never find anything. In this case, all of the condiments were now in the sink, and anything boxed had been ripped open.

"What about your bedroom?" I asked.

"I found photos of Conover."

"Good. Let me see."

She handed me two photos. In one, Conover was alone, sitting in his office with the bookcases behind him. In the other he and Kelsey were standing at the Delacorte

Theater ticket window in Central Park. Conover was not a good-looking guy: average height, at least 30 pounds overweight, brown hair, small brown eyes, and a scraggly beard. I put the photos in my pocket.

"Was anything missing?" I asked.

"No, I don't think so."

"What about the safe in Conover's office? It's empty. Do you know what he kept in there?"

"The usual stuff," Kelsey said. "Some emergency cash, his passport, legal documents..."

"Was it open when Conover disappeared?"

"Not that I noticed," Kelsey said.

Svetlana walked into the kitchen.

"How'd you make out?" I asked.

"Nothing," she said. "I found one of those novelty shaving cream cans with a false bottom, but it was empty."

"Anything else?"

"His toothbrush is gone, along with some other toiletries."

"That was the first thing I noticed." Kelsey dumped the dustpan into the garbage can.

"Anything else missing from the bedroom?" I asked.

"A couple of sweaters, I think," Svetlana said. "The piles in his wardrobe are uneven. What did you find?"

"These slips of paper. A little puzzle project for us."

I handed her the stack, along with the tape. She put everything into a Ziploc inside her handbag. Kelsey threw out all of the opened condiments and packages of food and cinched the trash bag shut.

"At least the kitchen is clean now, so we won't have an infestation," she said. "What were they looking for anyway? Do you know?"

"Your brother's work," I said.

"How do you know?" Svetlana asked.

"Because they took it all. Everything."

"*All* of it?" Kelsey said.

"Just about every scrap of paper. Anything your brother left behind. Whoever ransacked this place either wanted to figure out what he's working on, or they already knew and wanted to stop him from working on it. I'm not sure who did this, but I don't think it was the FBI."

"Why not?" Kelsey asked.

"Because it's too sloppy, the apartment wasn't sealed, and there was no notice on the door."

We went into the living room, Kelsey carrying the trash bag to throw out. I took a final look around. My eyes stopped on the coat closet door.

"Hey, did either of you check in there?"

The women glanced at each other. I opened the door and shone the tactical flashlight inside. Next to Svetlana's closets, it was the most organized one I'd ever seen. Two hangers were empty.

"Kelsey," I said, waving her over. "Is this where you hang your coats?"

"No, this is Conover's closet. I've got my own walk-in."

"Can you remember what he had on these hangers? This could be important. Think hard."

"Okay. Well, there's his overcoat…it's brown… he wears that a lot in the fall…and"—she closed her eyes—"a bright yellow one, like a jacket you'd wear on a sailboat."

"You mean foul weather gear?"

"Yeah."

"Svetlana, are you thinking what I'm thinking?"

"Yes," she said. "If sweaters and a foul weather jacket are missing, he might have gone somewhere on the ocean."

"Right, and cold water ocean, not Maui. But we can discuss—hold it."

"What's wrong?"

"Listen."

Footsteps echoed out in the hallway, along with what sounded like two women talking to each other.

"Relax," Kelsey said. "Those are the Weinberg sisters. They live down the hall. They're like ninety-eight. I think you could take them, Dakota."

"Hilarious," I said. "All right, one last thing. I'd like a few small objects your brother has touched. DVD and CD cases would be ideal. Does he have any?"

"Are you kidding? An entire cabinetful. Why do you want them?"

"To get a baseline of his fingerprints," I said. "This way, when we show up someplace, we can know if he's been there or not."

"Cool. How many do you want?"

"Say three of each. But make sure only he's touched them."

"He doesn't let anybody touch his media. Not even me."

Svetlana snapped a quart-sized Ziploc from her handbag. "Put them in this."

"And be quick," I said.

She hurried down the hall.

"It seems you have a junior investigator on your hands," Svetlana said.

"Maybe," I said, "but I'm still waiting for the other shoe to drop."

"What do you mean?"

"I mean she's a teenage girl, so I'm expecting her to turn into a bratty, spoiled pain in the ass any second."

"I cannot argue with you on this," Svetlana said.

Kelsey jogged back into the room and handed the sealed Ziploc to Svetlana, who dropped it in her handbag.

"I also got the deck of cards Conover uses for solitaire."

"Smart. Good job."

"Where to next?" Kelsey asked.

"You tell me," I said. "Who's closest—the literary agent, the editor, or the girlfriend?"

"The girlfriend lives down on 83rd, but I doubt she's home right now."

"What about the agent?"

"He's in Midtown," she said.

"And the editor?" Svetlana asked.

"He's close—up Broadway like ten blocks. It's a walk-up in Harlem. He works at home, so I'm sure he'll be there."

"Then it's the editor," I said. "Let's roll."

13

Just a Little Existential Angst

Given the mess we'd found at Kelsey's apartment, when we knocked on Kyle Foster's door and no one answered, I got concerned. Without a word, Svetlana slapped a new pair of latex gloves into my hand. I put them on and tried the knob. It was unlocked. My intuition told me we were about to walk into another major ransacking. I sighed.

"What's wrong, Dakota?" Kelsey asked.

"Nothing. Just a little existential angst."

"Huh?"

The door opened into a long, dark hallway. We went inside and shut the door.

"Mr. Foster?" I said loudly.

No answer. I drew my gun.

"Let me guess," Kelsey said. "You want us to wait here."

"I'll check it out and be right back," I said. "Don't touch anything."

Svetlana raised her chin haughtily. "Oh, you mean we should *not* smear our fingerprints on the walls."

Kelsey giggled.

"Two against one," I said. "Wonderful."

I crept down the hall toward a lit doorway, but when I turned into the room, I didn't see the God-awful mess I'd expected. In fact, the living room was pin-neat. The kitchen, bathroom and bedroom were also untouched. I felt a twinge of hope. Hope, that is, until I reached a den at the back.

The floor was a swamp of ankle-deep paper from the doorway to the opposite closet. Manuscript stacks had been swept off the desk and side table. On the desk, a banker's lamp was lit, and more papers—all manuscript pages as far as I could tell—covered the desktop. There was a large laser printer on the table and a printer cable that reached to the desk, but no computer. I holstered my gun, got down on my knees and rummaged through the paper, but with every page being from a different manuscript, I decided it was a fruitless exercise. I stood up again.

Like with Conover and Kelsey's apartment, since the place wasn't sealed and the searching was sloppy, I doubted this was the Bureau's handiwork. Whoever did this had been looking for something specific and was in a rush to find it. I decided to check the closet before I left to see if they had searched in there.

I opened the door and something heavy shoved against it from the inside. The force of it knocked my feet out from under me on the loose paper. I fell on my stomach, the door flew open, and a body rolled on its side in front of me.

I was face-to-face with a dead man.

He was a man in his early 40s. His eyes were open, and his mouth was parted as if he were about to speak.

There was no smell yet, which told me he had died recently. I checked for a pulse even though I knew there wouldn't be any, and was taken aback to find his skin was still warm. It wasn't 98.6°F, but it was discernibly higher than room temperature. Body temperature falls after death at about 1.5°F per hour. This meant he was killed only hours ago.

One at a time, I picked up his arms and legs and maneuvered them. His muscles were still displaying considerable flexibility. *Rigor mortis*, or a stiffening of the body, tends to set in between two and six hours after death, so the fact that it hadn't set in yet corroborated my reasoning about the body temperature. Although I couldn't know exactly when, I knew this: the man had been killed sometime earlier today.

As for cause of death, there were no signs of strangulation—no bruising on the throat, no blood-staining around the nose and mouth, and no vomit—and he wore a white Oxford dress shirt, so if he'd been shot in the chest, I would have noticed it immediately. I wanted to examine his head for signs of blunt force trauma. Having watched my medical examiner friend Wendy Hamilton do this a dozen times, I knew what to look for.

Gently, I lifted his head and found the cause. There was considerable bleeding where the base of his skull and his spine met, and now that the papers had been shoved away from the door, I saw a pool of blood on the closet floor. It was difficult to be certain because of the amount of blood, but it looked to me like he had been shot in the medulla with a small-caliber gun, like a .22, and the bullet had pinged around inside his skull. The hole had an abrasion collar on the edges and some tattooing caused by the hot gases. And…ah, a second bullet hole. The killing had all the marks of a professional. He never knew what hit him. His murderer had then stuffed him in the closet and kicked the papers up against the door cracks.

There was no ID on the body, so I checked the desk and even his bedroom, but couldn't find one. I needed to know for certain this was Kyle Foster. I went back out to the hallway, where the ladies were waiting.

"What did you find?" Svetlana asked.

"More ransacking," I said. "Kelsey, I need to borrow you for a second."

"You don't want me?" Svetlana said.

I shook my head. "One of those things you didn't sign on for."

"Ah."

"What's that mean?" Kelsey asked.

I led Kelsey toward the den. "Now don't freak out. I need you to look at this man's face and tell me if it's Kyle Foster."

"You mean he's dead?"

"Someone is." We went into the room. "There, on the floor. Look closely at the face."

"Ohmigod!" She looked away. "Yes, that's Kyle Foster."

"Easy, settle down. You're sure?"

"Yes."

"You're not going to be sick, are you?"

"No, I'll be okay."

"Time to go," I said.

Using a phone on the desk, I called the police, reported finding a body at this address, and we hurried out of the apartment. We drove back down Broadway, past Columbia University and Kelsey's apartment. I stopped next to a trash bin, and Svetlana threw my gloves away. As I pulled back into traffic, I noticed a cherry red Range Rover idling half a block behind. It was the same color and model as the one I'd seen the Asians in the day before. I couldn't see the vehicle's occupants, but I was sure it was them.

"Dakota?" Kelsey said. "Why do you think Kyle was killed?"

"Well, clearly somebody was looking for information," I said. "They rifled through all of the manuscripts in that room. But as for killing him, he might have had information somebody didn't want getting out."

"Or they *thought* he had information," Svetlana said.

"Right."

After three more blocks, the Range Rover was still back there.

"What now?" Kelsey said.

"We talk to the agent," I said. "Hopefully he'll be able to tell us something."

As we neared 107th Street, the traffic light ahead turned yellow. I waited until the last second to swerve into the right turn lane, and when the light turned red, I was in the front position at the crosswalk. The Range Rover was stuck behind two cars in the center lane. I still couldn't make out the license plate, but the vehicle was close enough now that the occupants' faces were distinguishable through the windshield. It was the Asians all right, the older one smoking a cigarette, just as he'd been doing yesterday.

Unconsciously I thought aloud, "Who are those guys?"

"Who?" Svetlana said.

"The red Range Rover back there," I said. "Center lane."

While they glanced out the back window, I watched the crosswalks for an opening. Pedestrians crowded both the Broadway and the 107th Street crosswalks. I couldn't do anything yet.

"The Asians that visited the office yesterday were driving that exact vehicle," I said. "I'm ninety percent sure it's them."

"So we're being followed?" Kelsey said.

I glanced at her in the rear-view mirror. "Not for long. Are you belted in back there?"

"Yes."

"And hold on," Svetlana said. "Trust me on this."

"But...how did they find us?"

"I have no idea," I said. "They must have picked us up outside Kyle's apartment."

Although it's illegal to make a right on red in New York City, I wanted to lose them, and I knew this might be my only chance. A man being led by a service dog finished crossing Broadway, and then both crosswalks were clear. I floored the truck through the opening and roared down 107th Street. I blitzed across West End Avenue through a yellow light and got up to 60 mph on the double-parked street. When I reached Riverside Drive, I turned right on red again, right at the next block, and sped down 108th Street. Now I was heading east, toward Central Park.

"Wow," Kelsey said, grabbing my shoulder from the back seat. "Can we do that again?"

"Dakota is an excellent driver," Svetlana said. "And in a pickup no less."

"I'm embarrassed they ever made us," I said. "It was sloppy of me."

Svetlana looked out the rear window. "You appear to have lost them."

I stayed on 108th until I reached Columbus Avenue, where I sped downtown, accelerating through the yellow lights with the taxicabs. I followed Columbus down to 77th Street. The Museum of Natural History was on my left. I turned right.

"Are you…?" Svetlana said. "Are you trading in this travesty of a vehicle for the Dakotamobile? I hope."

"Maybe," I said coyly.

"Dakotamobile?" Kelsey said. "What the…?"

"You will see," Svetlana said.

I knew trading the pickup for my Cadillac might be a mistake, but at this point the Asians had made the pickup truck. If I was going to have to evade people in high-speed pursuits, I preferred to do it with a car that had proven itself in similar situations before.

"We'll get the car," I said, "and then we'll go see the agent."

14

INTERNATIONAL LITERARY TALENT

Stoddart Prince, Conover's agent, worked for International Literary Talent (ILT) in a Sixth Avenue high-rise a few blocks north of Bryant Park. By the time we signed in, it was almost five o'clock. Everyone was leaving the building, while we seemed to be the only ones entering it.

"Hope he hasn't left for the day," I said.

"Not a chance." Kelsey waited for Svetlana to get in the elevator, then hit the button for the 31st floor. "Stoddart's always in. He's all about making money."

If seeing a dead body earlier had spooked Kelsey, she didn't show it. She watched the buttons light up floor by floor as the elevator rose.

"We don't get along," she said. "He resents having to work with me, because he thinks I'm just a kid. Don't be surprised if we get in an argument."

When the doors parted, my eyes were treated to a brightly lit glass room with marble floors. High on the opposite wall hung three giant-sized capital letters:

I L T

The reception desk was made of dark marble. It was chest-high, curved and bare of any computer or telephone. It looked less like a reception desk and more like the bar in a trendy SoHo nightclub Svetlana had dragged me to recently.

A young woman sat on a barstool behind the desk. She had butter blonde hair pulled back in a smart updo, and the sheen of it at certain angles was blinding. In contrast to the hair—as if she were deliberately de-prettifying herself—she wore large black-framed glasses. I think the look was called "hipster." I didn't care for it. I also didn't care for the Bluetooth headset she wore. I stepped up to the bar and put my elbow on the counter.

"Make mine a Macallan eighteen-year, miss. A double."

She gave me a cold stare.

"Is he in, Blair?" Kelsey asked.

"Of course he is, Kelsey. And it's a good thing you're here. He hasn't heard from Conover in days. He's been going nuts."

She pulled out a tablet computer and tapped on it. After a pause, she said, "Stoddart, Kelsey Wright is here. And she has a man and a woman with—yes…yes, okay. I'll send her in." She pushed the tablet aside and folded her hands together. "You can go in, Kelsey. Just you."

"Thanks." Kelsey opened and held the door. "Come on, guys."

"Hey!" Blair said.

We followed Kelsey inside. We walked around a bullpen of cubicles, then down a long hallway adorned with oversized author photos and covers of bestselling books, to a large glass office. My first view was of piles of manuscripts on a credenza, then, across the room, a bald man in his 30s pacing behind a desk.

The Midtown skyline, including the Empire State Building, loomed in the windows behind him. A guy could develop a Master of the Universe mentality with this view. He wore the vest and trousers of a navy pin-stripe suit—Brooks Brothers, I think—and black-framed glasses like Blair's, although on him the glasses seemed necessary, and not an ironic hipster affectation. He appeared to be talking to himself until he did an about-face and I saw a Bluetooth earpiece in his other ear. Svetlana, who knew about my disdain for Bluetooth people, raised an amused eyebrow at me.

"Hold on a minute, Richard, would you?" He touched the earpiece. "Kelsey, I said just you. Who are these people?"

"They're detectives I hired to find Conover," she said. "Remember when I called you the other day, asking if you'd heard from him? Well, he's still missing. I thought you might care, considering he's one of your biggest moneymakers."

"I should call security and have them thrown out," Stoddart said.

"I wouldn't do that," I said.

"Excuse me?"

"I'm not easily thrown out."

"Who the hell are you?" Stoddart said.

"Dakota Stevens, private detective." I flashed my license. "This is my associate, Svetlana Krüsh."

"Well, excuse me if I don't offer you tea and cucumber sandwiches," he said. "I'm in the middle of a major deal right now."

"We'll wait."

He rolled his eyes and walked to the window, where he tapped his earpiece again and gazed across Midtown.

"Richard? Sorry, but I have to cut this short. Tell the pub board that Drake House bid half a mil, and they're going to have to top it if they want this property. And they have to take the midlist thriller I mentioned, too." He paced to the other window. "Yeah, I know, Richard, but that's the deal. I'll call you back in twenty. Bye." He tapped the earpiece and blinked at me.

"All right, you have ten minutes."

"But you just told Richard twenty," I said.

"Ugh, whatever. Sit down." He collapsed into a high-backed leather chair.

As we sat, I noticed him checking out Svetlana. Here she was—in a lady lumberjack outfit in the middle of urbane Manhattan—and she was still hypnotizing. I snapped my fingers and Stoddart's head jerked in my direction.

"We're looking for Conover," I said. "Have you seen or heard from him recently?"

"No." He picked up his smart phone and typed.

"I know you're busy," I said, "but could you give us your attention for a few minutes? This is important."

"Fine." He typed a few more characters and placed the phone on the corner of his desk.

"Thank you," I said. "So, how long has it been?"

"Weeks ago. Two or three at least."

"Did he come here?" I asked. "Or was this on the phone?"

"He came here. Unannounced. Stormed in like you three just did."

Svetlana leaned forward in her chair and put her chin on her fist.

"And what, pray tell, did you two talk about?"

"If it were anyone else, I wouldn't say. But since you're doing the asking…" Stoddart mirrored Svetlana by leaning forward in his chair. "We argued, that's what we did. As Kelsey knows—or should know—Conover has a December deadline for the next book in his Zanclus series. If he misses the deadline, the publisher can break the contract."

"What are the terms of the contract?" I asked.

"It's a five-book deal, and this one is number three. Anyway, there's a lot at stake. So, what's Conover tell me? He tells me that he's working on a nonfiction book instead, which is crazy because the last thing readers want from him is nonfiction."

"This other book," Svetlana said. "Do you know what it was about?"

"He kept going on and on about a conspiracy involving the moon," he said.

"The moon?" I glanced at Kelsey. "Can you remember anything else about it?"

"No, except that it wasn't about the moon landing being a hoax," Stoddart said. "It was something else. He was talking so fast, I couldn't follow half of what he was saying. Frankly, I thought he was having a nervous breakdown."

"Stoddart," Kelsey said, "why didn't you tell me this when I called?"

"Look, what do you want from me?" He leaned back in his chair. "I had work to do. Besides, Conover's always been a little crazy. That's what makes him such a great sci-fi writer—his odd fantasies."

"Don't tell me about my brother." Kelsey jabbed a finger at him. "I know him a lot better than you do."

Stoddart smiled at her outburst. I wanted to leap over the desk and power-slap him about thirty times in the face for that, but I was here to get information and had to keep my cool.

"How did you leave things with him?" I asked.

"Not great," he said, adjusting his glasses. "I told him to stick to fiction because I could sell it, and he told me to screw. He said he didn't know why he even brought it up to me, because he planned on indie pubbing anyway."

"Indie pubbing?" I said.

"Indie publishing, as in independent. Like an indie filmmaker. He'd do it as a print book and/or e-book."

"Which would cut you out of your percentage, right?" I asked.

He paused, glanced at his phone. "Yes, it would."

"Let's change the subject," I said. "Do you have any idea where he is?"

"No, I don't. It's Kelsey's job to babysit him, not mine."

"Screw you, Stoddart," she said. "If it was up to me—"

I held up a hand for her to stop, and looked at Stoddart.

"Can you think of where he might be? Maybe there's a hideaway you've sent him to in the past to finish a book?"

"Kelsey would know better than I," he said. "There's no place I've sent him to, but I do remember his mentioning Vermont."

"Do you know where in Vermont?" I asked. "Which town, or the general area at least?"

"No, I don't."

"What about places on the ocean? Can you think of any?"

"No." Stoddart glanced at his phone. "I'm going to have to cut this off soon."

"A couple more questions. When Conover talked about his moon conspiracy project, did he mention any people?"

"What do you mean?"

"Well," I said, "did he mention anybody who might be helping him? Maybe his editor came up—Kyle Foster?"

"No, Kyle never came up. Although…"

"Yes?"

"He did say something about having"—he made air quotes—"*inside sources.*"

"About the moon conspiracy?" I asked.

"Right. He used a plural, but I got the impression he was talking about one person."

"What gave you that impression?"

He tilted his head back and looked at the ceiling. "Conover was mumbling at one point—he does that a lot—and it was like, 'I need to call Terence.'"

"Terence? Is that a first or last name?" I asked.

"How should I know? I'm not the white pages over here."

Svetlana took off her down vest, revealing a snug and fuzzy sweater. In trying to get a better look, Stoddart leaned forward so far that his elbow slipped off the armrest. Svetlana crossed her legs.

"Did Conover say whether or not these inside sources were from NASA?" she asked.

"No, he didn't." Stoddart took off his glasses and laid them on the desk. "I'm afraid that's all I know, and I need to get back to work. If I learn anything else, I'll get in touch." He looked at Svetlana. "But I'll need your number."

"My phone is broken," she said.

I scribbled the number to my disposable cell phone on a business card and tossed it on Stoddart's desk.

"Stay in touch," I said.

We left. Out in the reception area, I waved to Blair the receptionist.

"Have a good night. Love your hair by the way."

"Hmmph," she said.

I pressed the button for the elevator and we waited.

"The girlfriend now?" I asked.

"After dinner," Svetlana said. "I am famished."

"So am I," Kelsey said.

"We haven't discussed where we'll stay tonight," I said. "Much less dinner."

The elevator doors opened, and as we started to step inside the car, Lewis and Gallagher, the two FBI agents, stepped out.

15

National Security Stuff

An hour later, Svetlana and I sat alone in a conference room at the FBI office in Federal Plaza, waiting for Kelsey to emerge from an interview with Agents Lewis and Gallagher.

To protect her interests, Svetlana had called Jefferson Barnes, a savvy African-American defense attorney we sometimes worked with. While the interview was technically voluntary, it also cleared Kelsey from any suspicion and further pressure from the FBI. To the best of my knowledge, however, we still had three groups after us, so Kelsey remained in danger. And now with the Bureau out of the picture, she might be in even more danger. I had to stay sharp.

Svetlana was playing chess on her laptop. I, meanwhile, had nothing to do. There were the sheets of notepaper in Svetlana's handbag to be assembled, but here, in the FBI office, where the walls had eyes, was not the place to do it. The walls likely had ears, too, which was why we couldn't discuss the case either. I had to think it through alone.

Two days. A lot had happened in two days. Kelsey comes to the office and hires me to find her brother. Four groups show up looking for him. We go on the lam and meet up with Svetlana. The Mob comes for Kelsey again and we have to leave. We search her ransacked apartment and find the notepaper as a possible clue, and in Harlem we find a dead man—Conover's editor—killed by a professional.

Then we talk to Conover's literary agent, who gives us actual clues. One, Conover was working on a nonfiction book about a conspiracy involving the moon. Two, a man named Terence might be Conover's source. We go to leave, and the Bureau brings us downtown. Which led to my standing here, at a conference room window with my hands in my pockets, gazing upon the glowing high-rises of Lower Manhattan.

Why do offices keep so many lights on at night? Seems so wasteful.

If I was honest with myself, I was on this case for one reason: Kelsey. I had grown to like her and didn't want anything to happen to her. And finding her brother was the best way to eliminate the threat to her. Naturally I was also curious about what Conover was into, but that was secondary to watching over Kelsey.

I walked around the table to the glass wall that looked out on the bullpen. The cubicles brimmed with male and female agents—on computers, on phones, consulting with each other, poring over documents, talking in small groups. I recognized a handful of faces, but for the life of me I couldn't remember any of their names.

Did I miss it? Sometimes. The camaraderie, the rush when we made a big bust. I didn't miss the paperwork, the strict adherence to procedure, or the Bureau's fondness for moving agents around—especially the single ones like me.

"Traveling down memory lane?" Svetlana said behind me.

"Yeah," I said, "something like that."

Pairs of male agents began to walk by the glass, glancing in at Svetlana. Still playing chess, she was oblivious to them. The chessboard on her computer screen reflected in the dark window behind her.

There were two raps on the glass beside me, and the door opened. A dark-haired agent stuck his head in.

"Stevens, is that you? I thought it was you."

We shook hands. I couldn't remember his name.

"Nice to see you," I said.

"It's Harper," he said. "I know it's been a while."

"Of course. Sorry."

"So you're private now," he said. "How's that going?"

"No complaints." I waved like a magician in Svetlana's direction. "This is my associate, Svetlana Krüsh."

The two of them exchanged nods. When Svetlana went back to her game, Harper shook his head imperceptibly, as if to say, "You lucky dog."

"Same old, same old around here," he said. "Excellent job security, though. World's not running out of criminals anytime soon, right?"

"True," I said.

"Got married." He held up his left hand. A wedding band glinted. "You married yet?"

Behind me, Svetlana sniggered.

"Not even close," I said. "I barely have time to date."

"Yeah, I remember that. Thought I'd always be a bachelor. Now I can't imagine my life without her. It's nice to go home after a long day and know there's at least one other person who cares about me, you know?"

I didn't know, but I nodded anyway.

"Well, I'll let you go," he said. "Heading home soon. Why're you here anyway?"

"My client's being questioned," I said. "In fact, here she is now."

"Bye then," Harper said.

"Take care."

Harper left as Kelsey came in. She looked much more at ease now.

"How are you?" I asked.

She rubbed her wrist where the small "TRUTH" tattoo was.

"The agents said I'm free to go. They asked me—"

"Not here," I said. "Later."

Jefferson Barnes was walking by outside the conference room. I got his attention and went to the door.

"Be right back, guys," I said.

Jefferson put down his briefcase and shook my hand. Leaning back against an empty cubicle, he crossed his legs at the ankles so an expensive-looking chestnut loafer stood on its toe.

"Looking good, Barnes." I nodded first at his suit, a rich brown three-piece, then at his shoes. "Nice. Bruno Magli?"

"Ferragamo," he said. "O.J. ruined Brunos for black men."

"You come straight from court?"

He straightened his tie. "Nope. Peter Luger's. Was just slicing into a beautiful porterhouse when you called."

"Well, thanks for coming over. Sorry we ruined your dinner."

"Don't worry, I'll bill you for it."

He smiled. Jefferson's teeth were surreally white, and I was convinced the reason he won so many cases was that he mesmerized juries with that smile. He looked me up and down.

"Gotta say, Stevens—*you've* looked better. Pretty scruffy, my man."

I ran a hand over my beard. I hadn't shaved in four days. I was also wearing my leather jacket, British SAS commando sweater, jeans and Under Armour mid tactical boots. Standing next to Jefferson, I looked like a military Humvee parked next to a Maserati. A pair of agents walked by carrying evidence bags.

"It's a tough case," I said. "This is my second day, and it feels like it's been a week."

"Oughta go home and chill."

"Can't go home. Didn't Kelsey say anything about being chased by four groups of people?"

"You know I can't tell you anything she said."

"Listen, Barnes, I'm desperate. I need some idea of why the Bureau wants Conover."

"I understand, but I've got attorney–client privilege to honor."

He glanced at his watch—a platinum Rolex that cost more than my Cadillac.

"Time is money, Stevens, and in this case it's your money. Anything else?"

"No. Thanks for helping out Kelsey. She's a good kid."

"Don't thank me. It'll be on your bill." He pulled a notebook and Montblanc pen out of his inside pocket and started to write. "I'm giving you the name of my tailor. You need a new suit, my man."

"I have nice suits," I said. "I'm just not wearing them now."

"Trust me, you want to see this guy." He tore off the page, folded it and handed it to me. He put the notebook and pen away, and picked up his briefcase.

"Don't show that to anyone else," he said. "This guy's very exclusive."

With a final smile that froze me in my tracks, he brushed by and swaggered down the corridor. I unfolded the note. It read, *"Her brother's in some serious shit. National security stuff. Some guy named Terence Dalton came up a few times. From their questions it sounds like they think Conover's spying."*

I went into the bathroom and flushed the note down the toilet. When I returned to the conference room, Svetlana slipped her laptop into her purse and put on her vest.

"It is time to eat," she said.

"Yes it is," I said.

"I'm starved," Kelsey said.

"We can't go out to a restaurant," I said to Svetlana. "And we need to think about where to stay tonight. Someplace nobody would know to look for us."

"Lazar is out of town," Svetlana said. "Perhaps his apartment."

"Right next door to the Marshall, where you play chess every day? I don't think so."

I gazed out the window at the Brooklyn Bridge.

"Brooklyn," I said. "Frank Roma's."

"*Yes,*" Svetlana said. "I love Frank."

"Who's Frank?" Kelsey asked.

Svetlana picked up her handbag and stood next to Kelsey.

"A lovely man Dakota used to work with. I met him at my chess club years before I met Dakota and never knew about the two of them. He is quite charming."

I dialed Frank's number. He answered on the second ring.

"Roma," he said.

"Frank, it's Stevens."

"Dakota? How are you? How's Svetlana? I haven't been to the club in months."

"She's fine. Listen, Frank, we need a place to stay tonight. Three beds and two squares—can you do it?"

"Course I can," he said. "Are you coming in hot?"

"Yes."

"All right. I'll leave the garage open. Park on the left side."

"We'll be there in forty minutes," I said.

"Take the Battery and the Belt Parkway, not the bridge."

"I know how to get there, Frank. Thanks."

"I'll open a bottle of wine," he said.

"No wine. I'm on a case."

"Like I was saying, I'll put on coffee. See you soon."

He hung up.

16

Take a Thompson at Least

Frank Roma lived on an oak-lined street in Dyker Heights. The house was a five-bedroom Victorian with a view of the Verrazano–Narrows Bridge. The windows glowed warmly as we pulled in.

We parked in the garage in back and went inside the house. Frank greeted me in the kitchen with an iron handshake, and Svetlana and Kelsey with kisses on the cheek.

"It is wonderful to see you, Frank," Svetlana said.

"Mr. Roma," Kelsey said, "I hope this doesn't cause you any trouble."

Frank waved a hand. "Are you kidding? What else does a ninety-year-old widower have to do?"

"I cannot believe you are ninety, Frank," Svetlana said. "You look terrific."

He did. Despite his age, he stood solid and tall, and although he wore a thick cardigan sweater, I could tell he still had muscle tone (and a gun) underneath. He also had most of his hair. I hoped to look as good at seventy as he did at ninety.

"Well," Frank said to Svetlana, "you'll see I'm ninety later on—when we play chess."

Svetlana pointed at the counter. "Are those steaks I see?"

"They are, Princess. How's everyone like their beef, by the way?"

Kelsey and I said, "Medium," but Svetlana said, "*Rare*. Simply coax the cow into a warm room."

Frank laughed.

"She's not kidding," I said.

I brought in the luggage while the women made a salad. Actually, Kelsey made the salad while Svetlana gingerly handed her vegetables out of the refrigerator. After I finished with the bags, I got the fingerprint kit from the CSI case in the car trunk and brushed and lifted a dozen good prints from the DVD cases and playing cards. The prints were all tented arches—an extremely rare ridge pattern, possessed by less than five percent of the population. I clenched a fist.

Pleased that I had a unique set of baseline prints for Conover, I put the lifted prints in a Ziploc, poured myself a cup of coffee and joined Frank in the backyard. The yard lights were on. Frank stood at a stainless Weber gas grill the size of Rhode Island, flipping the steaks with tongs.

"So, tell me what's going on," he said.

While the steaks cooked, I gave him a high-speed recap of everything that had happened over the past two days. I finished just as he placed the steaks on a clean platter and shut off the gas.

"Finding Kelsey's brother is the priority," Frank said. "He's the key."

"I know."

"The literary agent was a good start. Maybe the girlfriend will have more. As for the three bands of mystery men, you need to figure out the common link between them."

"Yeah, I'm working it," I said, "but I don't have much to go on."

Over dinner, I stayed silent while Frank, the master investigator, questioned Kelsey about her interview with the FBI. It was fun to watch him work: the methodical, graceful way he established rapport with her and worked through his line of questioning. His sixty-plus years of state investigative and Bureau experience showed. His mind was as quick and penetrating as ever.

After dinner, Kelsey volunteered to do the dishes while Svetlana sat in the dining room with her laptop doing research. She and Kelsey were also going to piece together the sheets of notepaper I'd found in Conover's office. In the meantime, Frank and I went down to his basement gun room. His collection of WWII weaponry (American and German) had grown even larger in the year since I'd last been here.

The basement was divided into three long aisles with rifles standing on racks on each side of an aisle. There were maybe 200 rifles and machine guns in total: M1 Garands, Thompson sub-machine guns, Springfield rifles, MP 40 sub-machine guns, STG44s, and MG42s. All of them were locked to the racks by a steel cable threaded through the trigger guards. In locked glass cases underneath were dozens of pistols, including some very rare Lugers. And hanging over the furnace room doorway—a *panzerschreck*. Frank switched on more lights.

"Holy crap, Frank...when did you get a *panzerschreck*?"

"Oh, you mean the '*tank fright*'?" he said. "Few months ago, from a Texan. Private sale. Never fired, believe it or not. Never registered either. Most of the weapons down here aren't, but I think you know that."

"Damn, a *panzerschreck*." I shook my head in awe. "What about rockets for it?"

"That's the one problem," he said. "I could only get three. With some of these, the ammunition is rarer than the guns." He unlocked the cable at the end of a row of Thompsons and pulled it out of the trigger guards. "How're you fixed by the way?"

"Fixed?"

"Weaponry, son."

I told him I had two pistols, an AR, a sniper rifle, and a shotgun.

"Nothing full-auto?"

"No."

"Then take a Thompson at least. Hell, take three. I've got plenty, and I can give you a case of ammo for them."

"What am I going to do with three Thompsons, Frank?"

He pulled one out of the rack, locked back the bolt, and held it out to me. The infamous Tommy Gun. The Trench Sweeper. The Chicago Typewriter. I wrapped my fingers around the molded walnut hand grips. This machine gun was eleven pounds, almost twice as heavy as my semi-automatic AR-15, but it was an indisputably durable weapon.

"That's the thirty-round mag on there now," Frank said. "I've got the fifty-round drums for them, but they're for crap. We hated the damn things during the war. Rattled all the time. Krauts could hear us coming half a mile away."

"It's really nice, Frank, but—"

He nodded at the gun.

"Look, you've got two beautiful young women to protect, and you don't know what kind of resources you're up against. I'd take it if I were you."

I handed it back to him.

"Another time maybe. I can't afford to get locked up for possession of an illegal firearm."

"Okay." He raised his eyebrows and put the Thompson back in the rack. "But it's here if you need it."

I walked to the end of the aisle and sat on a stool in front of his workbench. This is where Frank repaired and cleaned the guns, and made his own ammunition. Once he'd locked up the guns again, he sat down on a second stool a few feet away.

"Frank, I'd like your thoughts on Kelsey's interview with the Bureau. Based on their line of questioning, what's their beef with Conover?"

"The national security angle, obviously," he said. "Which might be connected to this Terence Dalton they asked her about. You said the literary agent mentioned someone named Terence—as Conover's apparent source about the moon conspiracy. There might be a connection."

"Do you think the national security issue involves the moon somehow?" I asked.

"It could," Frank said. "Or it could be that Terence Dalton is the security issue."

"Good point," I said.

"No matter what, you need to find this Dalton guy."

"I will. Another thing bothers me, Frank—the questions Kelsey got about Philadelphia. She said she and Conover had been there for a sci-fi convention, but still…it seems an odd place to latch onto."

Frank straightened some tools on the workbench.

"If they're asking about a specific city, it usually means they suspect it's a meet or drop site. Remember, they also asked her if she'd seen any government documents. Classified or otherwise."

"What's the implication? That this nerdy science fiction author is doing cloak-and-dagger work on the side?"

"Don't rule it out," he said. "You don't know anything about him—only what his sister has told you. I conducted over a thousand interviews and interrogations during my career, Dakota, and I know when a person is lying. She's *not* lying. But it is possible her brother's living a life she knows nothing about."

I nodded and stood.

"Frank, it's like Sherlock Holmes said: 'Nothing clears up a case so much as stating it to another person.' Thank you."

"Anytime."

17

Über-Fans

Upstairs, Frank and I joined the women in the dining room. Svetlana was typing on her laptop, while Kelsey sat across from her staring at the wall.

"Kelsey, what's wrong?" I said.

She covered her eyes and began to cry. Svetlana grabbed a legal pad and gestured for me to follow her into the kitchen.

"Frank, would you...?" I glanced at Kelsey. He nodded.

In the kitchen, I dumped out my old coffee, poured a fresh cup, and stood across from Svetlana at the kitchen island.

"That is decaf," Svetlana said.

"Good." I lowered my voice, jutted my chin at the swinging double doors. "So what's that all about?"

"We assembled the scraps of paper you found."

"Yeah?"

"On the positive side," she said, "we now have three possible leads on where Conover went."

"Great. So, what's the negative?"

Svetlana looked at the ceiling for a second and took a long, deep breath.

"That bad?" I said.

"Yes. Among the pages we assembled, there are two chat transcripts. From different women."

"And the transcripts are…?"

"Quite explicit," she said. "It seems Conover has had relations with both of these women multiple times when they've been in Manhattan. They seem to be über-fans he met at conventions."

"*Relations*, Svetlana? Seriously?"

"Okay then—sex. Dirty, carnivorous, caveman–cavewoman *sex*."

"You're right," I said. "Let's stick with 'relations.'"

We smiled at each other.

"Any idea where the women are from? As if I even need to ask."

"I have already searched across Facebook and white pages listings and have tracked down two women who fit the profile," she said. "One woman is twenty-five, engaged, and lives in Naples, Florida. The other is forty-three, divorced, and lives on Nantucket."

I stooped over the kitchen island and rested my elbows on the counter.

"What about the other pages?"

"Most of them," Svetlana said, "are one long, sexually explicit email from a third woman."

"Just as graphic?"

"There are pictures."

"Uh-oh," I said. "And by pictures, you're not talking family portraits."

"That would be a no."

"The other kind," I said.

"Very much so."

"And where is this woman from?"

"Brace yourself," she said.

"I'm braced."

"Camden."

After a second, I stood up straight and sipped some coffee.

"And you know the woman is from Camden how?" I asked.

"Because it is a Camden, Maine library email address."

I spit my coffee on the floor. Svetlana calmly tore off a paper towel and handed it to me.

"She's a *librarian*?" I said.

"Yes," Svetlana said.

I wiped up the coffee. "What's her name?"

"Ginger Best. She is single, or at least unmarried."

"Ginger Best?" I said. "Sounds like a porn star."

"Having read her email, I believe that is a viable career option for her."

"She's not a redhead by any chance?"

"No," Svetlana said, "a brunette."

I shook my head. "A brunette Ginger. Somehow that doesn't seem right."

"Unlike the others, I could not find her home address in Camden anywhere. All I could find was an address in Boca Raton. I will continue to search however."

"The library," I said. "Who's the head librarian now?"

"Virginia McCourt."

"You're kidding. She was running things there when I was a kid. She scared me. I remember avoiding the library for a year because I lost a book."

She leaned across the kitchen island and patted my forearm.

"Well, I certainly hope you paid the fine. Otherwise, the interest could bankrupt us."

"Just go get the pages for me," I said. "All of them, please. Including the scraps."

Svetlana walked out. I cut myself a piece of Entenmann's walnut Danish and had just put a large forkful in my mouth when Svetlana slapped the pages down in front of me one by one, beginning with the email. Seeing the photos, I coughed and nearly choked.

There were eight "selfie" photos in all. Yes, Miss Best was an attractive woman of around 30, but it was her variety of bedroom poses and her lascivious facial expressions that most shocked me.

I put the photo pages aside face-down and skimmed Miss Best's email to Conover. In it, she described everything she would do to her favorite author if he came up to Camden sometime. The email was dated less than two weeks ago. The chat transcripts, on the other hand, were several months old.

"Of these three places," I said, "there's no doubt in my mind that he went to Camden."

"Hmm, I wonder why," Svetlana said.

"Kelsey did say it was one of his favorite places," I said. "How'd you make out with the other research—the North Dakota boys and Terence Dalton?"

"Well, I found nothing on the young men from North Dakota. I merely confirmed their address in Bismarck."

"Okay."

"Regarding the Terence, there is no Terence Dalton in Philadelphia or the surrounding area, but there is a 'T. Dalton' on East Seventy-third Street in Manhattan."

"It's worth checking out," I said. "Tomorrow, after we question the girlfriend, which we're doing early."

Svetlana pulled a pencil from behind her ear and consulted the legal pad.

"So…if Conover's project is about a conspiracy involving the moon…"

"Yes?"

"Is it not logical that the classified documents the FBI mentioned would have come from NASA? And that Terence Dalton works for NASA?"

"It's a leap in logic, actually," I said. "We don't know if the classified documents, Terence Dalton, *or* the moon are part of the case."

"Still," Svetlana said, "I would like to proceed under the hypothesis that the documents came from NASA and that a Terence Dalton of NASA is the one who leaked them to Conover."

I ate some more Danish. "Go ahead, see what you can dig up."

"Employee lists are easy to find. I'll start there."

"Take a break tonight. Play some chess with Frank."

"I would enjoy that," she said. "There is one final item. What shall we do about the car in Jersey? It is registered to a Vic Caprisi in Nutley."

"Stick a pin in it for now. He's not relevant to finding Conover."

I picked up the sheets of notepaper—the ones that hadn't been taped together—and skimmed them. Two of the sheets were from articles about moon colonization, and a third was a partial email from a professor of astrophysics and lunar science at MIT named Michael Rosetti. Svetlana pointed with her pencil.

"Conover mentions Professor Rosetti in the acknowledgments of several of his books."

I held up the scrap of Rosetti's email. "You know, MIT is—"

"Your alma mater. Yes, I am well aware of this."

"What was Rosetti's email about?"

"He is coming out with a book, and he wants Conover to write a foreword."

"What's the book?"

Svetlana read from the legal pad: "The title is, *Lunar Colonies: The Future Could Be Now.*"

"We might want to contact him," I said. "See if he's heard from Conover." I flapped the sheets at her. "What about these others that didn't match up?"

"They are partial Amazon order confirmations and web pages about grammar."

"What did he order from Amazon?"

She shifted to her most clinical tone.

"Condoms and spermicidal lubricant."

"Interesting," I said.

"Yes, a seventy-two condom economy pack."

"Damn. Someone planned on being busy," I said. "And do we know when he ordered them?"

"Yes, two weeks ago."

"And you didn't come across any condoms when you searched his bedroom and bathroom?"

"No," she said.

"Well, then, I think the quantity of condoms tells us something."

"Which is...?"

"If Conover went to Camden to visit Miss Best,"—I patted the pages containing her photos—"he planned on staying there for *quite* a while."

Svetlana smiled. "You can be very amusing sometimes, Holmes."

"You know my methods, Watson." I gave her a wink. "Hey, would you check in on Kelsey? I'm going to batten down the hatches."

"Yes."

While Svetlana went into the dining room, I walked room to room, making sure all of the windows and outside doors were locked. In the parlor, I shut out the lights, parted the front curtains and looked up and down the street. It was empty. A lone streetlamp shone onto the pavement, and the leaves of the big oaks stirred in a gentle breeze. I closed the curtains, checked the upstairs bedrooms, then went back downstairs.

In the parlor, Svetlana and Frank sat at the chess table while Kelsey slept on the sofa. Svetlana was playing Black. She and Frank were already several moves into the game, and she was up a pawn. Svetlana picked up one of her knights and set it down on a square in Frank's territory. Her knights both faced backward. This was one of Svetlana's signature maneuvers, designed to keep her opponents off-balance. I knew it worked because it distracted me (as did her beauty) every time we played. She spoke to me while staring at the board.

"What time will we be leaving in the morning to question the girlfriend?"

"About six thirty," I said.

"That early?"

"Have to," Frank said. "Traffic."

"Right," I said. "I also want to check on this 'T. Dalton' on East Seventy-third."

Svetlana nodded. "Frank and I will finish our game, and then I shall go to bed."

"All right, goodnight then." I roused Kelsey. "Time to hit the sack. Follow me."

"Give me a piggy-back?" She peeked at me sleepily with one eye.

"Aren't you a little old?"

"Please?"

I stooped, she climbed on my back, and I carried her upstairs.

18

My Observational Zeal

At seven fifteen the next morning, Svetlana, Kelsey and I stood at the threshold of Jennifer Lin's apartment on West 83rd Street, waiting for her to let us in. I estimated Jennifer was in her mid-20s—a conclusion I was helped to by the skimpy outfit she wore.

"This is ridiculous," she said in the doorway. "Do you know how early it is?"

I held up my watch. "Yup."

"You tricked me. On the intercom you said you were the FBI."

"No…I said the FBI might be coming to see you today."

"Jennifer," Kelsey said, "Conover's in a lot of trouble. We need your help."

"Who are these two?"

"Dakota Stevens, private detective." I showed her my license. She wasn't impressed. "And this is my associate, Svetlana Krüsh."

Jennifer stood there and huffed. You know how on some cool summer mornings you can tell it's going to be a hot day? Well, even though right now she had zero makeup on, I could tell that a dressed and made-up Jennifer Lin would be a scorcher. She had smooth tanned legs that descended strikingly from a diminutive sapphire kimono, and long black hair that shimmered like a jungle waterfall at night. *What was this Asian goddess doing with an unattractive sci-fi nerd?* It didn't make sense.

"Fine, come in," she said. "Before you wake my neighbors."

We followed her inside to a living room and kitchen, divided by a counter. A tan Michael Kors handbag lay on the counter with an open checkbook and stamped envelope beside it.

"One second." She wrote out a check, with her right hand I observed, stuffed the check in the envelope, and licked the flap the way some women licked chocolate syrup off naked skin. She noticed me watching her and smiled out of the corner of her mouth. I turned my attention to the living room, which was really a small gym.

It was packed with exercise equipment: Soloflex, treadmill and vertical climber. There were also dumbbells and an exercise ball in the corner. Crammed into the opposite corner was a love seat, where a repulsive seaweed-colored smoothie sat on a coffee table. She plopped down on the love seat, picked up the glass with her right hand, and crossed her legs. In my observational zeal, I ascertained she was wearing sapphire blue panties that matched her kimono.

"What a nice home gym you have," I said.

"My job requires me to stay fit." She sipped her smoothie. "Right now I need to work out, and then I have to leave for a shoot. So, what's this about the FBI?"

"Aren't you concerned about Conover?" Kelsey asked.

"No. Should I be?"

"He's been missing for over a week."

"I didn't know," Jennifer said. "I haven't seen him in a while."

"How long is a *while*?" I asked.

"I don't know...maybe three weeks ago."

"Where was this?" Svetlana asked.

"Here."

I glanced out the window facing the street. My car was double-parked down there. So far, no ticket that I could see.

"Did he talk about what he was working on?" I asked.

She leaned forward and looked straight at me. The woman had riveting dark brown eyes, and even more riveting décolletage.

"He didn't do much talking," she said.

"*Please*," Svetlana said under her breath.

"So, you don't know what he's working on," I said.

"That's right. No idea."

"Nothing about a conspiracy involving the moon."

I watched her eyes. They flicked laterally to her left. Since she had written out the check with her right hand, this meant she was accessing a real auditory memory. In other words, Conover *had* told her about what he was working on.

"No," she said, "nothing like that."

"So he did give you some idea of what he was working on."

"No, he didn't. He didn't tell me anything about it, whatever it is."

"You're his girlfriend," I said. "How can you not have some idea of what he's writing?"

"First of all, I'm not his girlfriend. We just hook up every once in a while. Second, he's always been secretive about his work. Kelsey'll tell you."

I nodded. "You should be glad you don't know what he's writing."

"Yeah?" she said. "Why?"

"Because the last person who probably knew—Kyle Foster, Conover's editor—was murdered yesterday." I let this fester for a moment. "You're sure you don't know anything?"

"I'm sure." She put her smoothie down. "Now, why is the FBI coming to see me today?"

"Because they're looking for Conover," Kelsey said. "Like we are."

"Yes, but *why* are they looking for him?" she asked.

Suddenly I wished Jennifer were a guy so I could cuff him in the mouth. But she wasn't. She was a supernaturally beautiful Asian woman looking at the three of us with a smug, feline expression on her face. We were getting nowhere. I took a deep breath and counted to three.

"All right," I said, "if you don't know what he was working on, and you haven't seen him, do you know where he might be?"

"Like in Manhattan, or somewhere else?"

"Someplace outside of the city," I said. "Where he might go to write."

"I don't know. Kelsey would know better than me."

"Guess," I said. "Maybe somewhere the two of you have been together."

"Hmm." She changed positions so she was sitting with her legs curled beneath her. "Somewhere we've been…Bermuda?"

"How about places within a day's drive of Manhattan?"

"I don't know." She ticked off possibilities with her fingers. "Montauk. The Cape. Atlantic City."

"Atlantic City?" Kelsey said. "Impossible. Conover doesn't gamble."

"Well, he did with me. He's a good poker player, your brother."

"What? Conover doesn't—"

"Jennifer, anyplace in Maine?" I asked.

"No."

"You're positive?"

"Positive."

I wasn't satisfied. I needed to poke around before I left.

"Okay, that about does it," I said. "Before we go, may I use your bathroom?"

She took a moment to answer, as if she were seriously considering sending me back into the street with a full bladder.

"Yeah, fine. It's down the hall. Just be quick about it."

"No problem." As soon as my back was to her, I looked at Svetlana and mouthed the words, "Stall her." She blinked in reply.

I walked down the hall, and when I reached the bathroom, I kept going until I reached her bedroom. A packed Rollaboard lay open on the bed. Glancing over my shoulder down the hall, I went to the bag and dug through it: makeup bags, toiletries, copies of *W* and

Vogue, jeans, blouse, stockings, blazer, three bras, and four pairs of panties. No cold- or wet-weather clothing. I was hoping to find a train or plane ticket, or some evidence she drove a car, but those were probably in her handbag in the kitchen.

I checked the hall again. Still clear. The bureau was bare, which I found odd. There wasn't a single photograph. In fact, I hadn't seen *any* photographs in the apartment. Quickly I searched the bureau drawers and made one discovery: the woman had enough titillating underwear to outfit a harem. Hardly a clue, but still. Even though a lot of people were looking for him, and my own search for him was proving to be a major pain in the ass, I envied him—Conover Wright, author of bestselling novels and bedder of exotic, lingerie-clad women.

Shifting my attention to the closet, I opened the louvered doors and scanned her wardrobe. Hanging next to some conservative pant suits were a lab coat and several uniforms, including those for a FedEx delivery person, hotel maid and cable TV repair person.

Did she do catalog modeling work, or were these bizarre role-play costumes?

I shut the closet doors and considered the contents of the room the way a museum-goer contemplates a painting. Speaking of paintings, the walls were bare except for a prosaic oil of San Francisco hanging over the headboard. Jennifer didn't strike me as an art lover. It was out of place.

I climbed onto the bed, started to pull it away from the wall with my jacket sleeve, and discovered that one side of it was attached to the wall by a hinge. And behind the painting, *voila!*—a wall safe.

Wall safe? What kind of young woman has a wall safe?

I tried the lever, but it was locked. I removed a pair of yellow panties from the Rollaboard. I wiped down the lever and the bureau, pushed the painting flush against the wall, smoothed out the bed, and put the panties back in the bag. Finally I hurried into the bathroom and flushed the toilet, then returned to the living room. Jennifer put down her drink and stood.

"Now, look—I have a gig out of town, and I need to get ready. I don't know where Conover is, I don't know what he's working on, and I need you to go."

We headed for the door. At the last second I spun around.

"In case you have an epiphany about Conover."

I jotted my cell phone number on a business card and tossed it to her. Maybe it was because I tossed it too high or too fast, or maybe it was because she didn't try to catch it until the last second, but either way it landed just below her neck and plummeted into her cleavage like a mountaineer down a crevasse. God forgive me, but it was the best three-pointer I'd ever made.

"Sorry about that," I said.

She fumbled with her kimono, trying to close the leaves with one hand and fish out the card with the other.

"Leave!"

Down on the street, I looked around for threats. Aside from a man walking a Great Dane, the sidewalks were empty. I unlocked the car and we got in.

"So…I think it's clear she knows what Conover's working on."

"What did you find when you went to the *bathroom*?" Svetlana asked.

"You mean besides a locked wall safe?"

"Wall safe?" Kelsey said. "What the heck does she need a wall safe for?"

"Exactly, my dear junior Watson."

I glanced at her in the rear-view. She smiled back at me.

"What else was there?" Svetlana asked.

"A half-packed bag. She's going out of town for a few days. Maybe straight to Conover. Kelsey, let me ask you, does she have a car?"

"I don't think so. Anytime she and my brother go someplace, they take trains and planes and stuff."

"Why does it matter?" Svetlana asked. "Were you considering following her?"

"Yes, briefly," I said. "But we've got stronger evidence that Conover went to Maine, so we're going to stick with that. Did you two learn anything else while you were stalling for me?"

"Yeah," Kelsey said. "Jennifer's a boring, selfish bitch. She doesn't give a crap that my brother is missing."

"She is both of those things," Svetlana said, "but she might have been trying to *appear* like she doesn't care about your brother. If she is going to rendezvous with him, she must appear cold and detached."

"Maybe you're right," Kelsey said. "But I still don't like her."

"Shall we check on 'T. Dalton'?" Svetlana asked.

"Absolutely," I said.

19

Butch, Sundance, and the Teenage Kid

The T. Dalton lead took us clear across town to East 73rd Street, an address that made me uncomfortable because it was a couple of doors down from Contessina Mallorca's gallery—a place I would forever associate with Shay. By the time I parked and we went inside, I was already on edge. Then the lead ended up being a bust. Only after Svetlana and Kelsey had smiled at the 20-something doorman, and only after I'd tipped him twenty bucks, did he tell us that the T. Dalton in the building wasn't a man named Terence, but a woman named Terry.

"Oh, sorry," he said. "Thought you said 'Terry.'"

He grinned. It was an affected grin made all the more annoying by an impeccably coiffed handlebar mustache. It took all of my self-control not to tweak it. I chuckled.

"Easy mistake. Hey, can I see the twenty I gave you?"

"Sure, why?"

He handed it to me. I tore it down the middle and stuffed half of the bill in his breast pocket.

"You jerk," he said.

I scrawled my cell number on a business card and shoved that in there.

"Stop it!"

I took out a stick of gum, popped it in my mouth, mock-glanced around for a wastebasket, and jammed the wrapper in his breast pocket. His jaw clenched. He puffed up his chest.

"Man, I'll kick your ass."

He was standing in front of a big leather couch.

"Kid," I said, stepping into his personal space, "while you've been busy grooming your mustache, I've been busy punching bad guys in the face."

I pushed him with two fingers and he collapsed onto the couch. Instantly he was half my height, glaring up at me.

"Look," I continued, "just call me if anybody else comes around looking for a Terence Dalton, okay? Do that and I'll give you the other half of the twenty, plus another fifty. Deal?"

"Another hundred and you got a deal."

"No...*fifty*. Seventy bucks should keep you in mustache wax for a long time."

"Fine, I'll call if anybody comes by."

As we started for the revolving door, Kelsey gave the doorman a dirty look.

"You'd better not flake."

"Easy, junior Watson." I guided her into the revolving door.

Back in the car, from 73rd Street I headed uptown on Madison Avenue. Once across the Harlem River, I made my way to the WWI minefield some comedian had named the Bruckner *Expressway*, and followed that to I-95 north. It was rush hour. The traffic heading south toward the city was bumper-to-bumper, but our lanes were wide open. We were on I-95 for all of five minutes before I glanced in the rear-view and saw a suspicious cherry red Range Rover. It was suspicious because it was maintaining a three-car buffer.

The Asians again. It had to be.

"Who are those guys?" I said.

"What guys?" Svetlana asked.

"The Asians. I think they're back."

"They must have been watching Jennifer's apartment," Kelsey said, looking out the back window.

"Or Terry Dalton's," I said. "I didn't see anyone, but then again, nobody's perfect."

"So, do we lose them?" Kelsey asked.

"Not yet. Svetlana, the binoculars in the glove compartment. Give them to Kelsey, would you?"

"Ah, yes." She handed them back. "The license plate."

"Yup. Kelsey, try to read the letters and numbers out to Svetlana."

"Everything's bouncing around."

I watched her in the rear-view for a second. After some difficulty, she got the binoculars focused and still.

"I can't—no, wait, I've got it. It's blue, white and red. Two-six-seven, C-N. And there's a big white 'D' on the right."

Svetlana jotted everything on her legal pad.

"That means they are diplomatic plates," she said. "Kelsey, can you see anything in the top right corner?"

"Hold on. Yeah, it says United something."

"United Nations," Svetlana said to me. "I cannot hack the U.S. State Department."

"Kelsey," I said. "Can you see the occupants?"

"Yeah. They're Asian. One of em's smoking."

"That's them," I said. "God, am I sick of these guys. All right, ladies, hold on."

As the next exit approached, I veered across two lanes and took the ramp for the Hutchinson River Parkway north. Once on the parkway, I put the hammer down. The women were plastered against their seats. That's what 469 hp and 0–60 in five seconds will do. I allowed myself a roguish smile.

I was roaring past cars from the right-hand lane, but I had to be careful. I couldn't afford to be pulled over—not with all the guns I had in the car. We crossed a drawbridge. City Island was the next exit. Following us on the Hutch was one thing, but good luck on the narrow streets of City Island. I took the exit, passed through the traffic circle, crossed the bridge onto the island, wended through the side streets, and backtracked to the Hutch. From there, I raced north to the pleasantly sylvan Merritt Parkway. Once we'd driven for a few miles with no sign of the Asians behind us, I eased off the gas and relaxed.

"I think we're in the clear."

Svetlana patted my arm. "Excellent driving."

"Nice stuntin', Dakota," Kelsey said.

"Pardon me?" I said. "'Stuntin'?'"

"Like showing off, you know? Driving fast in your expensive car?"

"Hey, I didn't do it to—"

"I'm just teasing," Kelsey said. "Dude, it's freakish how good you are. Have you done NASCAR or something?"

"No, they wouldn't let me. I don't have a mustache, and I refuse to make left turns all the time."

Kelsey giggled.

"The Bureau gave me some training, that's all."

I was being modest. My instructor at Quantico's TEVOC (Tactical and Emergency Vehicle Operations Center) said I was one of the best drivers he'd ever had—great vision, fast reflexes, coolness under pressure—and I had a gold medal on my fireplace mantle in Millbrook to prove it. Kelsey grabbed my seat headrest and spoke next to my ear.

"The Bureau," she said. "That's the FBI, right?"

"Right."

"What was it like?"

I shrugged. "There's not much to say. I worked for them for eleven years."

"Like a secret agent?"

"I was hardly a secret," I said. "Special Agent."

Svetlana pulled a copy of *Gotham* magazine from her purse and started flipping through it.

"And a forensic scientist," she said.

"Very briefly," I said. "And low on the totem pole."

"Ohmigod, Dakota!"

"What?"

Kelsey pointed between the seats at a billboard up ahead. It was for an apple orchard.

"I've always wanted to go to one of those," she said.

"You've never been apple picking?"

"No, I haven't."

I looked at Svetlana.

"I would not mind some hot cider," she said.

"I wouldn't mind some breakfast," I said.

When we got there, we spent half an hour picking a peck of Cortlands, Macouns and Romes. The grass in the orchard was wet with dew, and with one of the farm's yellow Labs loping alongside, the scene was quintessential autumn in New England. It was another cloudless, cool October day, but as I looked to the west, I noticed a bank of sinister gunmetal clouds on the horizon. I predicted an autumn blow in Maine tonight or tomorrow.

On our way back, a horse-drawn hay wagon passed us coming out of a barn. Kelsey grabbed me.

"Dakota, is that a hayride? Can we do it?"

"Hold it," I said. "Do you want to find your brother or not?"

She kicked at the gravel. "Yes."

We paid for the apples, and that's when I noticed the farm stand had a cafe attached. We sat on a sun-splashed terrace overlooking the still and empty orchard. On a ridge above the orchard, trailing into the distance, a stand of bright orange maples shone in the sun. We ate ham and egg croissants, sipped hot cider and admired the view. Across the terrace, a balding older man kept glancing up at Svetlana from his book, until he finally walked over with it.

"Miss Krüsh?" He held out the book and a pen. It was a copy of Svetlana's *Krüsh Your Opponents*. "I'm sorry to bother you, but would you mind?"

"Of course not," Svetlana said.

As she signed the book, I admired her perfect posture and the easy elegance with which she held the pen.

"I think your double rook sacrifice against Brigitte Klum is one of the greatest brilliancies ever."

"So do I," she said, handing the book back. "Thank you."

He smiled, walked off the terrace, got into a Mercedes convertible and drove away.

"Wow," Kelsey said. "Svetlana, you're like *famous*, aren't you?"

"I have many fans."

"She does, and not just for chess," I said. "Don't be surprised if some pervert with a Victoria's Secret catalog asks for an autograph. It's happened before. One of the models is her doppelgänger."

"Which means…?"

"Her double. Like her twin."

"Which model?" Kelsey asked.

I shook my head. "All I'll say is she's the one with the almond-shaped eyes and the pillows for lips."

Svetlana turned to me slowly, uncharacteristically wide-eyed.

"Do you sign them?" Kelsey asked Svetlana. "The catalogs?"

"Of course."

On our way out, I broke down and bought a dozen cider donuts hot out of the fryer, and we ate them as we rolled over the hills of I-91 with the panoply of color stretched out before us. By the time we reached the Mass Pike at Sturbridge, most of the donuts were gone.

My plan was for us to stop in Boston for lunch, and drive the final three hours to Camden in the afternoon. In the meantime, Kelsey and I battled over control of the XM radio. I was trying to get her to appreciate Frank Sinatra and the lyrics of "The Best is Yet to Come."

However, before the song finished she lurched forward and selected the hip-hop station. A young woman named Iggy came on. I couldn't understand three-quarters of the lyrics, and apparently Svetlana—who kept looking at me with a panicked expression on her face—couldn't either.

When I glanced in the rear-view mirror again, the cherry Range Rover was back.

"I can't believe it," I said.

"Believe what?" Svetlana asked.

"The Asians. They're back."

Svetlana lowered her Dolce & Gabbana sunglasses and stared out the back window.

"Who *are* those guys?" she said.

20

Tighty-Whities

"Well, unless they stole that vehicle," I said, "we know they're connected with the U.N. They're probably hoping we'll lead them straight to Conover."

Kelsey leaned forward. "But how are they following us, Dakota? You lost them like a hundred miles ago."

"I have an idea about that," I said.

This time I didn't bother trying to lose them. I stayed on the Mass Pike east toward Boston, and they followed us all the way in. I found a garage near Faneuil Hall Marketplace and parked in a secluded corner. The Range Rover didn't turn in with us. When we got out, I switched on my tactical flashlight and squatted by the car.

"What are you doing?" Kelsey asked.

"Looking for something."

I started with the wheel wells.

"He is looking for a GPS tracker," Svetlana said. "It is the only possible way the Range Rover could have continually located us."

"Svetlana's right."

The wheel wells were clean. I popped the engine hood, shone the light around in there as well, but there was nothing I could see. I closed the hood, lay on my side on the cement, and peered under the car. As I ran the light along the exhaust, the beam went over a black box about the size of my palm. It was attached to the fuel tank.

"Found it," I said, standing up.

"You're not going to take it off?" Kelsey said.

"Nope. Who wants clam chowder?"

We got chowder and lobster rolls at the Boston and Maine Fish Co. and walked to the restored waterfront. As we ate on a bench overlooking the harbor, Svetlana and I told Kelsey the story of how the two of us first met—on a case in Boston and Cambridge.

"Wow," she said when we finished. "And you've been together ever since?"

"You could say that," I said.

In fact, since then Svetlana had been my most constant female companion.

"Yes," Svetlana said, "it has been a chore at times, but Dakota can also be a lot of fun. My life was rather dull before I met him."

"Yeah, I can see that," Kelsey said. "The guys in chess—they aren't exciting like Dakota, are they?"

Svetlana stared out at the boats in the harbor. She twirled her crossed leg.

"Eat your lobster roll," she said.

Once more we got back on the road, heading north on I-95. With the foliage at its peak, the drive was spectacular. Within minutes of leaving Boston, the cherry Range Rover was behind us again and followed us steadily through Massachusetts and New Hampshire into Maine. As we approached the Kennebunk service plaza, I got an idea.

"Kelsey," I said. "Where's your messenger bag?"

"Right here."

"Still have the GPS tracker in there? I hope."

She dug inside the bag. "Yup. Got it."

"Good, give it to me." She handed it forward. "Svetlana, do you have your laptop?"

"Of course."

I held up the GPS tracker. "Same one we used last time, Svetlana. You remember—with Conover?"

"Yes."

"My brother?" Kelsey said.

"No, a *Mister* Conover," I said. "The philandering husband of a client. It was a divorce case—work I don't care for."

"Except when it pays well, as that one did," Svetlana said.

"Maybe. All right—hold on."

I slowed down abruptly and swerved onto the exit ramp. In the rear-view I watched the Range Rover follow.

"They're taking the bait," I said. "Now, as soon as we park, go straight to the restroom. Then, meet me in five minutes in the dining area."

I parked as close to the building as I could. The second I stopped, all three of us jumped out and rushed inside. I looked back. The Asians parked in the adjoining lot for tractor-trailers and jogged after us. Svetlana and Kelsey went into the ladies' restroom, but I split off, hustled through the service station convenience store, and went back outside. I circled the building.

The woods abutted the parking lot, so when I reached the corner of the building, I ran into the trees for cover. Then I wove through the dense spruce until I saw the Range Rover. It was flanked by tractor-trailers on both sides. Once I was shielded by one of the trucks, I switched on the GPS tracker and sprinted out of the woods. I crawled under the trailer, flipped on my back and reached underneath the Range Rover. The GPS was magnetic, so I just held it close to the undercarriage until it found a part to clamp onto. When it clunked into place, I gave it a gentle tug to make sure it was solidly affixed, then sprinted back into the woods and returned inside to the service plaza.

I used the bathroom, and when I came out, Svetlana and Kelsey were at a table in the dining area. They looked up from the laptop.

"You may tell him," Svetlana said to Kelsey.

"We have a signal, Holmes."

"Nice," I said. "Let's move. I don't want them getting suspicious."

After gassing up, we continued north through Maine and exited the interstate at Route 1 in Brunswick. It was four thirty and the sun was low in the sky. When we reached Bath, I rolled down the windows to let in the lovely salt air—a smell that evoked my early childhood and teenage summers. Sadly, Red's Eats in Wiscasset was closed when we passed the little hut and crossed the bridge.

We reached the Downeaster Hotel and Resort, a few miles south of Camden, around five thirty. I was concerned about not having a reservation during the height of leaf-peeping season. Concerned, that is, until Svetlana took charge.

"Watch this," I said to Kelsey.

In one fluid motion Svetlana shrugged off the wool sweater coat she'd been wearing all day, revealing a deep V-neck cream silk blouse with her aristocratic curves beneath. As she homed in on the front desk, the clerk, a genteel man in his early sixties, clutched the countertop and looked around for help that wasn't there. I held back a laugh. Downeast Maine doesn't see many like Svetlana. She leaned across the counter, spoke to him in a comically heightened Ukrainian accent, and in about seven seconds got us a three-bedroom suite with an ocean view and hot tub. The poor guy didn't stand a chance.

Once we got settled, we ate dinner in the hotel restaurant, and afterwards played gin-rummy in the room until eight o'clock. Svetlana checked the GPS tracker online. The Range Rover signal was now stationary a few miles south of us, at the Sea View Motor Court on Route 1.

"Good," I said. "Let's go."

Outside, I removed the Asians' GPS from the Cadillac, made sure it was still on, and tossed it in the bushes.

"See 'ya," I said, dusting my hands.

Not surprisingly, the "Sea View" Motor Court was nowhere near the ocean. In fact, the only view it boasted was of a cement plant across the road. As soon as I saw the motor court sign flickering in the darkness, I switched off the headlights and crept into the parking lot. The cherry Range Rover was parked in front of an end unit—number 15, the farthest one from the dimly lit office. There were three other cars in the lot, and I wondered why so few until I noticed that half of the windows were boarded up. Svetlana pointed.

"Oh, but look," she said. "They have gnomes."

I parked in the shadows and shut the engine off. We got out.

"Stay close to me, both of you," I said. "And if we have to talk, make sure to whisper, okay?"

"Shout at the top of our lungs," Svetlana said. "Understood."

Kelsey snickered.

The window shades in number 15 were down, but I could see through the cracks that there were lights on inside. I put my ear against the glass. The voices inside sounded like the two Asians, but I couldn't tell if the language was Japanese, Chinese, Korean or something else. Also, the TV was on and fairly loud. I waved Svetlana over to the window and whispered to her.

"What language are they speaking?"

She pushed her hair back and pressed an ear to the glass. After a second, she whispered, "Mandarin."

I leaned next to her so she could continue to eavesdrop.

"That's a Chinese dialect, right?"

"Correct."

"I thought you didn't know Chinese."

"I have been taking lessons from Eric Chen. I decided that if a quarter of the world's population speaks a language, I can no longer avoid it."

"What are they saying?" I asked. "Can you make out any of it?"

"They are laughing about how stupid that American detective is—that he hasn't figured out how they're tracking him."

"Hmm...seems you've learned quite a *bit* of Mandarin."

"Eric says I am an excellent student," Svetlana said. "Wait...now they are talking about bringing Conover back into the fold. Sort of. The idiom does not translate well."

"Interesting," I said. "That's what I want to question them about."

I put my ear to the glass as well. Our faces were less than a foot apart.

"Now they are speaking gibberish," she said. "They sound as if they are eating between words."

The theme to the TV show *Magnum, P.I.* began to blare against the glass. I stood up.

"Ladies, that's my cue. Stand over there and wait for me to call you inside." I pulled my Sig Sauer, flicked off the safety, and backed up thirty feet from the door.

In the movies, cops are able to break down doors with a single swift kick from two feet away. I have found this to be bullshit. Breaking down most doors requires mass times acceleration, otherwise known as force. I licked my teeth. To say I was looking forward to this was an understatement.

Starting slow, I ran toward the door, increasing my speed as I drew closer. When I reached the walkway, I jumped and drove a forward kick into it. The instant my boot planted against the wood near the knob, I knew the door was going down. I could feel the entire latch assembly snap, and the chain was ripped out of the doorframe. The door flew open, banged against the air conditioning unit. I landed on my feet inside the entryway.

"Howdy, boys!"

The two Asians sat bolt upright in separate double beds. They stared at me. They wore nothing but tighty-whities and were eating Kentucky Fried Chicken from buckets between their legs. Their hands froze with drumsticks on the way to their mouths.

On the TV, Tom Selleck wagged his eyebrows at the camera just as the theme song ended. I closed the door as far as it would go; I'd shattered the poor thing.

"Guys," I said, directing my attention to the Asians again, "it's time to talk."

21

Little Piggy

I walked between the beds and pointed the Sig Sauer at each of them. "Is either of these Original Recipe?"

The older Asian held up his bucket.

"This one?" I said. "Thanks."

I plucked a meaty breast out of the bucket and took a bite. I turned to the younger Asian.

"Hate to break it to you, buddy, but Extra Crispy is just day-old Original dipped in batter again and re-fried. Old friend of mine, Jeremy Stone, told me that."

He looked at his drumstick with disgust and dropped it back in the bucket. I called out to Svetlana and Kelsey.

"You can come in now."

The men looked at each other. As the women walked in, they shoved their buckets of chicken aside. Each covered himself with a pillow.

"That's it, cover up," I said. "Ladies, why don't you sit at the table." I raised the gun to remind the Asians I still had it. "Gentlemen, let's start with your names. And don't try that, 'We no understand Ingwish' crap. With the exception of Junior here screwing up '*I'll be back*,' I have a feeling you two speak better English than my lawyer."

"Do not call me 'Junior,'" he said.

The older Asian held up a hand at the younger one.

"I am James Zhang, and this is Peter Wu."

I took another bite of the chicken. It wasn't as tasty as I remembered.

"Where are your wallets, Jimbo?"

"Excuse me?"

"American nickname for James. Jim, Jimmy, Jimbo—you get the idea."

James blinked. "In our suit jackets. In the closet."

"Svetlana, get them would you?"

She crossed the room, fished through the inside pockets and found them.

"They are telling the truth about their names," Svetlana said. "They both have UN IDs and…oh, this is interesting."

"What?" Kelsey said.

"They also have identification from the Chinese Ministry of Science and Technology. It seems they are part of China's National High-Tech R&D—or Eight-Six-Three—Program."

"Score." I sat on the credenza facing the beds. "Well, how about it, guys? What's the deal with this Eight-Six-Three program?"

Peter clutched his pillow.

"I am not telling this man anything, James. He can… what is the expression? Yes, he can *blow me*. Or better still"—his eyes lingered over Svetlana and Kelsey—"*they* can blow me."

"Eww, disgusting," Kelsey said.

James barked at him in Chinese. Svetlana followed up with some Chinese of her own, which caused Peter to glower at her. I smiled, put the chicken down and sauntered over to Peter.

"No, Dakota, don't," Svetlana said.

"Don't what?" Kelsey said.

I gave Peter a brisk left jab between the eyes with some horseradish on it, hammering his head into the headboard. I doubted I broke his nose, but I did manage to leave a nice red indentation of my fist on his forehead. I wiped my greasy hand on the bedsheet.

"Smarten up, Junior." I turned to James. "You two brought this on yourselves."

"Please understand, our government expects results. We must find Mister Wright and question him."

"Question him about *what*?" Kelsey said. "Who the hell are you guys? Why are you after my brother?"

"Kelsey, I'm working on it," I said.

"Sorry," she said.

"James," I said, "what is your government's interest in Conover?"

"Mister Stevens, if we divulge anything that compromises our government, we will be executed and our families charged for the cost of the bullet."

"They really do that?"

"Execute traitors? Certainly."

"No," I said. "Bill the family for the bullet."

"Yes." James reached for a pack of cigarettes on the nightstand.

"Please don't smoke," I said.

He withdrew his hand.

"Look," I said. "I don't care what your government does with you. Tell me why you're after Conover."

"Or…?"

"Or I'll take your chicken away. Or, I have this big gun and might decide to shoot one of Junior's toes off. And hurry up. I'm getting sick of seeing you two in your skivvies."

Peter spoke Chinese to James.

"What'd he say, Svetlana?" I asked.

"I think he said, 'Do not say anything.'"

James took a deep breath and stared at a spot on the wall.

"I will tell you what I can that will not endanger Peter and myself, or betray my government."

"Go on," I said.

"Mister Wright has been providing us with certain information."

"What kind of information?"

"I cannot tell you that," James said.

"Providing information?" Kelsey said. "You mean like *spying*? My brother would never do anything like that."

"I am sorry you must learn of it this way," James said.

"Again," I said, "what information was he giving you?"

They were both tight-lipped. Svetlana leaned back in the chair and crossed her legs.

"Is it information about the moon?" she said.

I watched James. The question seemed to have made him anxious, which can cause dryness and discomfort in the mouth and throat. He swallowed. Whatever he said next would most likely be a lie.

"No," he said.

"Nothing about a conspiracy involving the moon?"

"He told you no," Peter said.

"This information," I said. "Was it classified documents from NASA or another U.S. agency?"

James swallowed again. "We know nothing of classified documents."

"Who was supplying Conover with the documents?" Svetlana asked. "Terence Dalton?"

"We do not know," James said.

"So there *were* classified documents," I said, "but you just don't know who's been supplying them."

"I have nothing more to say," James said.

"Okay, let's go," I said, standing up. "These guys aren't giving us anything else."

"Can I ask them a question?" Kelsey said.

"Sure."

She gazed imploringly at the two men.

"Are you forcing Conover to do it? Or did he come to you guys and say, like, 'Hey I've got all these cool classified documents. You want 'em?' Which is it?"

They didn't say anything. Kelsey started to cry.

I noticed Peter roll his eyes, and I lost it. I grabbed his foot, thumbed back the hammer on the .45 and pressed it against his big toe.

"Answer her, *right now*, or this little piggy ain't makin' it to market!"

"Don't!" Peter yelled. "He came to us! He came to us!"

Kelsey began to weep. She hunched over in her chair clutching her stomach. Svetlana put her hand on Kelsey's back.

"How long?" I said, still pressing the gun against Peter's big toe. "How long has he been providing you with information?"

"Only a few months! Please, stop!"

"Was he paid for the information?"

"No, no! He give us, free."

I uncocked the gun hammer and let go of his foot.

"All right, I'm done with you. But if I catch you following us again, I'm going to do a lot worse than shoot off your toes. Svetlana, Kelsey—ready?"

We were leaving when I thought of one last thing. With my free hand, I grabbed both buckets of chicken.

"What is this?" James said. "We are hungry, and the KFC in Rockland is closed by now."

"Tough. You don't deserve it."

Outside, I threw the chicken in a dumpster while Svetlana guided Kelsey into the car. Across the road, the cement plant was lit up like a Broadway musical destined to flop, but Route 1 was dark and desolate in both directions. I pulled out and took the car up to speed.

"By the way," I said to Svetlana. "About Peter, Peter chicken-eater back there."

"Yes?"

"When you spoke to him—what'd you say?"

She gazed out her window into the darkness.

"I intimated that 'Junior' could perhaps be applied to certain parts of his anatomy."

Kelsey suddenly stopped weeping.

"Ohmigod," she said, "Svetlana, you are awesome!"

I shook my head in admiration. "She is, isn't she?"

In the light of the dashboard instrumentation, I caught a glimpse of Svetlana. She was as beautiful as I'd ever seen her, and, perhaps because she thought I couldn't see her, she was smiling full-out.

22

Autumn Blow

It was after ten o'clock when we got back to the hotel, and even though we had a suite I wanted to give the women some time and space to get ready for bed. I also wanted to make sure we hadn't been tailed up here by somebody else. For the past three days, I'd been surprised over and over again. I wasn't taking any more chances.

"I'm going out to look around," I said to Kelsey. "I'll be right back."

She sprang off the sofa. "Dakota, where're you going?"

"Out for a walk. Ten minutes, tops."

"I really need to talk to you."

"Sure," I said. "As soon as I get back."

Outside, I stepped into a driving rain. A sharp wind made the rain slice across my face. The autumn blow I'd predicted that morning had begun.

Bent double, I dashed into the parking lot, found my car and grabbed the umbrella from the trunk. With it turned into the wind, I switched on my tactical flashlight and walked the rows of cars. There were no gold Cadillacs or cherry red Range Rovers, or any cars from New Jersey.

I finished my inspection of the parking lot and was on my way back inside when a beam of light swung past me in the darkness. It was the lighthouse at the end of the breakwater, which was a short walk across the 18th hole on the golf course. Rain or no, I needed the fresh air, and I had always relished autumn storms—especially here in Maine. The fresh salt air and the wet would clear my head.

I reached the edge of the putting green, and below saw the jagged edge of the breakwater trailing into the darkness. I heard the rough waves crashing on the rocks. The lighthouse beam swept past again. The rain pounded on the umbrella. I stared out at the dark sea and pondered the events of the last 72 hours.

It was clear that whatever Conover was into, it was more than shady—it was probably illegal and possibly treasonous. I didn't know what information he had given the Chinese. Secrets from the Apollo missions? What?

And where was he getting this information? From the mysterious Terence Dalton?

The real stumper was this: What did the Mob and a couple of North Dakota quasi-tough guys have to do with this? Where did the moon angle fit in with them? Was the Mob getting into the space freight business? The idea was ridiculous. No, they and the North Dakota boys had to be involved for other reasons.

The wind pushed against the umbrella, and I had to hold it at a 45° angle to avoid getting soaked. I quelled a sudden impulse to race up to Camden, find Conover, and kick him in the shins for abandoning his sister. I wanted to be done with this case already.

But the fact was, I couldn't go up there tonight. I didn't know where Ginger Best lived—if Conover was with her at all. Besides, the fierce storm would make searching difficult. And if I did find Conover in Camden, I might not be the only one to find him, so I had to be ready for anything.

To get a handle on the case, I needed a working hypothesis. I considered what I knew:

The FBI, the Mob, two Chinese scientist-diplomats, and two thugs from North Dakota were looking for Conover.

The FBI wanted Conover on a matter of national security.

Two apartments had been searched.

Conover's editor, Kyle Foster, had been murdered.

Those were the only solid facts. I also had some unconfirmed pieces of data, which, if true, could support a hypothesis:

Conover was allegedly working on a book about a conspiracy involving the moon.

Conover had an "inside source" furnishing him with information about this conspiracy.

The Bureau's interest in Conover involved someone named Terence Dalton.

Conover allegedly approached the Chinese and supplied them with information.

I closed my eyes, listened to the crashing surf, and let a hypothesis coalesce.

Okay, what if Conover is working on a book that will expose a conspiracy involving the moon? What if he has access to classified documents from an inside source and has been providing said documents to the Chinese? Domestic counterintelligence is under the Bureau's purview, so they need to find Conover. The Chinese want to continue receiving information, so they're looking for him, too.

As far as the Mob was concerned, the moon wouldn't matter to them. But it might matter a great deal to someone who had hired them—an outside entity. The Mob might not even know why the outside entity wants to find Conover. Heck, they might not even know who they're working for.

But why would the outsider want to find him?

To shut him up.

Why shut him up?

Because the outsider stands to lose by what Conover is writing.

So, who is the outsider? And how do the two brutes from North Dakota fit into this?

I opened my eyes and walked back to the hotel. On my way inside, I checked my watch. I'd told Kelsey I would be gone for ten minutes, and half an hour had passed. The front desk clerk, a young woman with a sharp jawline and cat-eye glasses, scrutinized me as I crossed the lobby. Must have been the fact that I looked like Edmond Dantes just escaped from the Château d'If. She was frowning at me as the elevator doors closed.

I got back to the suite and was setting the umbrella in the corner to dry when Svetlana walked into the room. She was wearing purple and black plaid pajama bottoms and a T-shirt that read, "CHESS DIVA."

"Where's Kelsey?" I asked.

"In her room, I think."

Before I could take my jacket off, my intuition told me to check the rest of the suite. She was gone. A vague sense of dread came over me.

"She's not here," I said to Svetlana.

"She may have gone to the vending machines."

"I'll go check."

Beginning with our floor, I worked my way downstairs, searching the hallways, the stairwells, the vending and ice machine alcoves, until I reached the ground floor and still hadn't seen any sign of her. The worry must have shown on my face, because when I went to the clerk, her expression changed to one of concern.

"Is something wrong, sir?"

"A teenage girl—black hair, Cleopatra bangs—have you seen her?"

"Yes," she said.

"Well? Where'd she go?"

"Toward the pool."

"It's still open?" I asked.

"Yes, sir. Twenty-four hours. At your own risk, of course."

"How long?"

Her brow scrunched up. "How long?"

"Since you saw her," I said.

"I don't know, maybe ten minutes."

"Which way?"

"End of this hall."

She pointed down a long corridor. I started walking. A few strides in, I found myself walking faster and faster until I was jogging and then I shifted into a full-blown sprint. I didn't know why I was running, I just was.

As I neared the end of the hall and the glittering light from the pool shone through the glass doors, I heard watery yells for help. I yanked the door open and saw her, flailing in the deep end of the pool, her head barely above water. Then the yells stopped.

No!

I ran down the poolside and dove in—jacket, gun, shoes and all—and swam underwater to her as fast as I could.

She had tied one sleeve of a light sweater to her ankle and the other end to a metal lounge chair, which sat on the bottom of the pool. Her eyes and mouth were open, an expression of terror fixed on her face. Her hair was splayed out around her. I dug into my pocket, pulled out my Buck knife and cut the sweater sleeve tied to her ankle. I dropped the knife in the water and swam keeping her head above water to the shallow end. When I was able to stand, I picked up her limp body and climbed out of the pool with her.

I laid Kelsey flat on the cement and checked her pulse. It was faint, but she wasn't breathing. I tipped her head to the side and some water drained out. Tilting her head back, I pinched her nose shut, made sure I had a tight seal on her mouth, and exhaled into her four times. I checked her pulse again. Still there, but even fainter this time. I listened for breath and looked to see if her chest was moving.

I put another four breaths into Kelsey, repeated my checks, then another four breaths and repeated the process all over again. I was losing hope. Adrenaline-fueled panic was about to take over.

I straddled her at the hips and rammed my hands against the base of her diaphragm. Pounding with all of my strength, I worried I might crush one of her organs. A geyser of water flew out of her mouth. I returned to the resuscitation position, exhaled four sharp breaths into her, and she began to cough. I tilted her head to the side as she coughed out the water.

After she had stopped coughing and I was sure she was breathing on her own, I sat up and spat. The adrenaline had left me with nausea, and my legs were trembling.

A minute passed before she sat up and said, "Are you okay?"

"Me? You nearly drowned. Damn, Kelsey, why? You could have talked to me."

I leaned back against the wall. She leaned against me.

"My brother's a traitor and—"

"But to kill yourself, Kelsey? It's a permanent solution to a temporary problem." I stared across the pool. "Believe me, I know how you feel. Not too long ago, I lost someone, and when it happened, I considered taking my own life."

"But Dakota, if he's dead or goes to jail, what will I do? He's all I have. What will I do without my big brother?"

I nudged her. "Hey, I can be your big brother."

"What?" She sniffled.

"I'm an only child. We're going to hope for the best with Conover, but whatever happens, I can be a big brother to you."

She rested her head on my shoulder. "Dakota...I didn't want to die."

"I know," I said, "but when we get back to New York, I want you to see a therapist."

She nodded.

"I'm getting cold in these wet clothes," I said. "Let's go upstairs, change and get some sleep, what do you say?"

"All right," she said.

I helped her up, and as we staggered to the door together I glanced at the pool. The sweater, still attached to the lounge chair, swayed beneath the water.

23

The Game is Afoot

Shortly after five o'clock in the morning, I awoke without an alarm, eager to start the day. I was hopeful that today was the day I'd find Conover Wright and finish this case.

After the pool incident I had stayed up late cleaning and oiling my handguns. Now, despite operating on five hours' sleep, my body craved exercise. Outside, the autumn blow continued, so a run wasn't an option. I slipped on a pair of gym shorts and took my heavy resistance band with me out to the kitchen area, where I drank a bottle of Poland Spring water and started the coffeemaker. Motivated by the smell of brewing coffee, I crossed to the living area and launched into my calisthenics routine: 100 push-ups, 100 incline push-ups, 200 crunches, 100 triceps dips, 100 bicep curls, and 25 burpees (a bitch).

I was cooling down with some stretches, and taking sips from a cup of coffee, when Kelsey walked into the room in a pair of Hello Kitty pajamas. I stood up with my coffee.

"Good morning."

Her eyes sprang open. "*Damn* you're in good shape! Can I punch you in the stomach?"

"I don't know, can you?"

She rolled her eyes. "*May* I punch you in the stomach?"

"If you want."

I put down my coffee and flexed my abs. She drew her arm back and—

"Forget it," she said. "I'll break my hand on that stomach." She pointed. "Ouch. What are the bruises from?"

"Oh, I don't know," I said. "Maybe from the three fistfights I've been in since I took your case."

"Sorry. Sorry I'm so much trouble."

"It's all right." I smiled. "Trouble is my business."

"'*Trouble is my business*'—that's good," she said. "Hey, please don't tell Svetlana about last night, okay?"

"I won't, if you promise not to pull another stunt like that."

"I promise." She glanced at Svetlana's closed bedroom door. "You like her, don't you?"

"Of course I like her," I said. "We work well together. She's indispensable to me."

"That's not what I mean and you know it," she said. "I see the way you look at each other."

"Sounds like you've got it all figured out."

"Yeah? What if Svetlana told me she likes you?"

I stared at her for a second. She had an excellent poker face—until it cracked.

"Nice try," I said.

"Well, she likes *you*. I can tell."

Miraculously I was able to rouse Svetlana at seven o'clock by knocking on her door and saying, "Come, Watson, come! The game is afoot!" She replied from behind the door in typical Svetlana fashion—with a growl and a muffled insult.

The Camden Memorial Library, a brick Colonial with tall paned windows, sits on a knoll at the top of Main Street, commanding a view of the harbor below. My parents had sailed out of that harbor one afternoon over 30 years ago bound for the Caribbean, got caught in a freak storm, and disappeared at sea. I tried not to think about it now, but it was difficult. From our current vantage point in the library parking lot, I could see the exact spot on the dock where I'd stood with my grandparents waving them goodbye.

We still had a few minutes before the library opened at nine o'clock, and with the rain and wind still howling, I kept the car running and the wipers going. Outside, the wind stripped leaves from a fiery red sugar maple towering over the library. It was a beautiful moment.

"Ladies, look," I said. "Gorgeous, isn't it?"

"Thrilling," Kelsey said.

"I second that," Svetlana said.

I shook my head. "A couple of jaded city girls, that's what you are. The wonders of nature are lost on people like you."

"Yes," Svetlana said, "and your point is…?"

Despite extensive searching, Svetlana had been unable to find Ginger Best's home address, which is why we were here. Hopefully we'd be able to question Ginger directly. If we couldn't, we'd have to improvise. The wipers swept across the windshield.

"By the way," Svetlana said, "I found some interesting information about our Terence Dalton."

"Which is?"

"I will tell you later so you are not distracted."

"Just tell me this: the information—is it good interesting or bad interesting?"

She raised an eyebrow. "Good."

"Nice. I need some good news."

A pair of cars pulled into the lot and two women got out clutching pumpkins to their chests. They rushed down the walkway to the back entrance. One of them was Mrs. McCourt. Her hair was now short and gray, but it was her, I was sure of it.

"There's Mrs. McCourt," I said.

"I think you can call her Virginia now," Svetlana said.

"Seriously, dude," Kelsey said.

I shut the car off.

"Okay, I'll go in first. Wait five minutes, then you two come in. Svetlana, if I scratch my head, it means I need you to improvise."

Her eyes narrowed, like she was visualizing a moment in the distant past.

"No, you should scratch your neck," she said. "You are often confused."

Kelsey laughed. "Do you want the umbrella?"

"Are you kidding?" I said. "There's only one, and if I take it, Svetlana will quit." I looked at her. "Wish me luck?"

"What is luck to trained detective?" she said. "Now go."

I got out, dashed to the back entrance and went inside. I'd been in the storm for all of ten seconds and I was certain I looked like a sea otter. I swept the wet hair off my forehead.

Mrs. McCourt and the other woman were chatting in front of the checkout desk. Two large pumpkins sat on the floor. Mrs. McCourt was still tall and slender, and she still had the same high cheekbones and impassive mouth that suggested she was perpetually displeased with the state of the world. The other woman, around 30, had glossy deep chestnut hair, and sparkling gray-green eyes that bespoke a dreamy intelligence behind them.

"Good morning," the young woman said. "Can we help you?"

Mrs. McCourt squinted at me and walked closer.

"Dakota Stevens," she said.

"Hi, Mrs. McCourt."

"Handsome as ever."

She hugged me. This I hadn't expected, and it was strangely thrilling. As she let go, she spoke over her shoulder to the other woman.

"Michelle, I've known Dakota since he was a baby."

Michelle shook my hand. She locked eyes with me and let her hand go submissive in mine.

"A pleasure."

She wore a silky green and gold dress. The dress had the perfect amount of cling, in all the right places.

"Taught himself to read, Michelle—when he was three years old."

"Amazing."

I grinned. "And it's been all downhill since, Mrs. McCourt."

"You can call me Ginny now, Dakota."

She led me over to the checkout desk. On a credenza behind the desk, a coffeemaker hissed and sputtered. To the side of the credenza was an office with the lights on. The sign next to the open door read, "Ginny McCourt, Library Director." Michelle touched my arm.

"Can I get you some coffee, Dakota?"

"No thanks," I said.

"How about a towel to wipe yourself off?"

"That would be great. Thanks."

Michelle walked away—a gentle swing in her hips, an ambrosial trace of perfume in her wake. She glanced over her shoulder at me. I watched her go and mused about how nice it would be to experience those eyes of hers horizontally from six inches away. I watched her until she disappeared somewhere into the stacks.

"Michelle is an attractive young woman," Ginny said.

"Yes, she is."

"A *married* attractive young woman. With two small children."

"Married? I didn't notice."

"Mm-hmm."

"What can I say, Ginny? I'm incorrigible."

She gave me a flicker of a smile. "So, what brings you? All the way from New York City, is it?"

"Yes. I'm trying to find one of your employees—Ginger Best."

"Oh, her."

"Not your employee of the month, I take it."

"Hardly. Hasn't shown up to work in over a week. Why are you looking for her?"

I decided to go with my "class action suit" cover story. People tended not to question its veracity.

"Well, I'm still a private detective," I said.

"I figured as much."

"And I've been hired by a Manhattan law firm to locate a number of people, Ginger Best among them. She's due a settlement from a class action suit. I need to locate her so they can issue a check."

"Some people have all the luck," Ginny said. "Already has plenty of money in her family. Doesn't need more."

"Maybe," I said, "but it's my job to find her. Do you know where she lives?"

She looked around and lowered her voice. "The girl's a sail bum. Lives on her boat."

"Where's her boat?"

"Down in the harbor. That's where her paychecks get mailed anyway."

"You wouldn't happen to know the name of the boat, would you?"

She shook her head. "Honestly, I try not to allow Ginger Best to take up space in my head. The only reason I keep her on staff is because her stepfather's given the library a lot of money."

Michelle returned, slightly winded, and handed me a terrycloth towel.

"Here you go, Dakota."

"Thanks, Michelle."

I patted my face dry. Maybe it was my imagination, but when I put down the towel, she seemed to be gazing at me the way a little girl does a dizzying amusement park ride. Behind me, the door opened. Ginny leaned around my shoulder.

"Can I help you, ladies?"

Svetlana and Kelsey stood at the entrance.

"My niece is looking for your science fiction section," Svetlana said, collapsing the umbrella.

"We use the Dewey Decimal System," Ginny said. "Number eight-oh-eight." She waved a hand. "Straight back, take a left. It's in the far corner."

"Thank you. Run along, Jane."

Jane? Seriously, Svetlana—you couldn't come up with something better than Jane? I glanced at her and scratched my neck.

"Ladies," I said to Michelle and Ginny, "maybe you'd give me the grand tour? It's been such a long time, and I have so many wonderful memories of this place."

"Of course," Michelle said, touching my arm again. "I'd love to."

Ginny gave me a knowing look.

"We'll *both* show you around, starting with the new addition. This way."

As they led me into the stacks, I glimpsed Svetlana heading toward Ginny's office.

24

Crash and Smash

By the time we made it down to the harbor, it was late in the morning and the storm had stopped. The pavement around the public landing was dappled with wet leaves, and when the sun peeked through the passing clouds, the leaves twinkled scarlet, gold and pumpkin. I peered over the wharf edge at the water. The metal docks floated five feet below. It was somewhere between high and low tide, but I couldn't tell whether the tide was coming in or going out. A few dozen yachts, cabin cruisers, lobster boats and rubber dinghies bobbed in their slips.

"I have no idea which boat is hers," I said. "Mrs. McCourt called Ginger a 'sail bum,' so I'm assuming it's a sailboat. If she's living on it, I imagine it's one with a sleeping cabin and a head, which would make it a yacht."

"Head?" Kelsey said.

"Toilet."

Kelsey shoved her hands in her coat pockets.

"Conover better be here. I want answers."

"I know," I said. "We all do. I guess we'll just have to walk around until we—"

"Allow *me*," Svetlana said.

She was staring in the direction of the harbormaster's office: a small gray shed with lobster buoys hanging on the side and a chalkboard showing the tide times propped in the window. Her eyes were fixed on something ahead like a tiger's on a tethered goat. The subject of her predatory stare was a weathered old-timer, short in stature, with white hair and a green quilted coat. He was sitting on a bench against the shed, whittling. With her quarry in her sights, Svetlana handed me her handbag, yanked the snaps of her raincoat open, and flipped her hair over her shoulders.

"Hey," I said, "get the tide times while you're at it."

With a nod, she strode toward the hut. Today's outfit, or bait for information, was the red hip-length raincoat, a black sweater, form-fitting jeans and her omnipresent tall black leather boots. I hoped she didn't make the old guy slice his hand open with that jackknife.

"There she goes," Kelsey said. "Gosh, I'd love to look like her."

"What? You don't need to look like Svetlana. You're beautiful. Be yourself."

"Thanks, Dakota."

She bumped me with her shoulder. I bumped her back.

The old-timer looked up from his whittling, saw Svetlana and rose to his feet. They spoke for a minute, the man pointing into the harbor with his knife, and then she nodded and started back toward us. Watching her leave, the man was frozen. I could identify with him; Svetlana had magnificent posture and an utterly feminine gait. No matter how many times I saw it—and I'd seen it thousands of times—Svetlana's walk hypnotized me.

"Take a picture," Kelsey said beside me, "it'll last longer."

I didn't say anything.

"Dakota," she said, "you need to tell her how you feel. I bet she feels the same way."

"*You* need to mind your own business."

When Svetlana was almost on top of us, Kelsey spoke up beside me.

"Hey, Svetlana, Dakota thinks you look nice in that outfit."

"Ignore her," I said, holding out her handbag. "She's being a brat."

Svetlana took the bag. "Dakota thinks I look nice in every outfit. That and the fact that he lets me do whatever I want, are the main reasons I work for him."

"So," I said, "what'd you find out?"

"That was Cal, the deputy harbor master. I told him Ginger and I are old friends."

Down the dock, Cal waved. Svetlana waved back.

"And?" I said.

"Ginger's boat is named...are you ready for this?"

"No."

"The *Lady Conover*."

"Jesus."

"Ugh," Kelsey said. "Creepy."

"All right, let's go see it," I said.

"The boat is not here. Apparently Ginger took it out a week ago."

"Which is when she stopped going to work," I said. "Does Cal have any idea where she went with it, and whether Conover was with her?"

"No and no," Svetlana said. "Cal is not very aware of what goes on around here, and the harbormaster is on vacation." She gestured at a dock with several sailboats tied to it. "You were right about its size though. Cal called it a small sailing yacht—a thirty-eight footer."

"Does she live on the boat?" I asked.

"She does, but she sometimes stays on land."

"Where?"

"In Camden. He was uncertain where, but I have an idea."

We went back to the car, and Svetlana had me drive up to the library parking lot again. There, she took out her laptop and connected with the free WiFi signal.

"What are you doing?" Kelsey asked.

"A reverse phone lookup of Ginger's emergency contacts. One is a Camden number, the other is Boca Raton."

"Where'd you find them?" I asked.

"On Mrs. McCourt's computer. She had already logged in, so I had unfettered access."

Svetlana typed on the keys, then after a pause said, "Interesting."

"What is it?" Kelsey said.

"Ginger's emergency contact in Camden is a man named Hamilton Savage."

"You're kidding," I said. "Mr. Savage is one of the wealthiest people in Camden. Let me guess—he's Ginger's stepfather."

"Correct," Svetlana said. "How did you know?"

"Because Mrs. McCourt said Ginger's stepfather has given a lot of money to the library."

Kelsey tapped my shoulder. "Are you thinking she might be at the stepfather's? With Conover?"

"I don't know," I said, "but we're going to find out."

Svetlana closed her laptop. "He lives—"

"—out on Dillingham Point. I know. Anybody who's spent any time here knows where he lives. It's a five-minute drive."

And it was a pretty one. The road out to Dillingham Point was rainswept, and the sun was coming out again. A long driveway terminated in a cul-de-sac. The place looked empty. We parked and got out.

"Wow," Kelsey said.

The Savage mansion is a rambling Colonial that looks like several Colonial homes of various sizes joined together. The place had ten second-story dormer windows, and that was only on this side of the house—the side *not* facing the ocean.

From the moment we got out of the car and I saw the leaves banked up high and wet against the doorstep, I knew no one was home, but I rang the doorbell over and over anyway. No one answered. I rang again, waited a minute, and when there was still no answer, I turned to Svetlana and sulked.

"Disappointed!"

"Now what?" Kelsey said. "This is getting annoying."

"*You're* getting annoying." I pinched her cheek. "We switch to Plan B."

"What's Plan B?"

Svetlana and I smiled at each other.

"We break in," Svetlana said coldly.

"Wait a second while I check things out."

I walked along the side of the house, peering in the windows. All of them had magnetic alarm sensors on the window frames, and the last one had the name and phone number of a Bangor security company. When I got back to the doorstep, Svetlana and Kelsey already had latex gloves on. Svetlana handed me a pair.

"Alarmed," I said.

"So we're not breaking in, right?" Kelsey said.

"Negative. We are."

"But if we do this, won't it make me an accessory?"

"Yes," Svetlana said.

I spied a grapefruit-sized rock in the bushes.

"Kelsey," I said, pointing, "get that rock and hold on to it."

I took out my lock picking set and went to work. With practice over the past year, I had become a lot faster, reducing my average time from around twenty minutes to five. Once the last pin in the lock had set, and before I turned the torsion wrench to open the door, I glanced at Kelsey.

"When I tell you to, hand me the rock."

She nodded. I turned the wrench, and the door opened. Immediately I heard beeping from somewhere inside. I shoved the tools in my pocket and held out a hand to Kelsey.

"Rock."

The second she put it in my hand, I ran inside toward the beeping sound. I passed a staircase, went down a short hallway to the alarm panel, and pounded it with the rock. I kept pounding until it was nothing but shattered plastic and electronics parts on the wood floor. By the time I was finished, only the wiring remained. Called the "crash and smash," it took all of 15 seconds to disable the alarm this way—long before the alarm had a chance to alert the security company. I returned to the foyer. Svetlana shut the door behind us.

"Okay, Kelsey," I said, "your job is to keep watch. If anyone comes, call out for us."

"All right. It's a sucky job, but I'll do it."

"But first"—I handed her my car keys—"there's a black satchel in the trunk. Get it, would you?"

"Sure."

"Svetlana, you take upstairs," I said.

"And what are we looking for?" she asked.

"Evidence Ginger has been here, hopefully with Conover. Let's go."

Svetlana went up the stairs while I went down the hall.

In no time at all, besides photos of Ginger with Mr. Savage and a 50-something woman I assumed was her mother, I found compelling (and somewhat disturbing) evidence suggesting Ginger had indeed been here with Conover. Of the fourteen rooms on the first floor, in seven of them—the living room, study, library, TV room, solarium, dining room, and kitchen—I found multiple condom wrappers.

"Damn, buddy," I said out loud.

It was the same brand of condom that Conover had ordered online weeks earlier. I left each room without disturbing anything, and moved on.

In the kitchen, there were two condom wrappers on a chair, a slew of wine bottles on the table, and an assortment of glasses on the counter. I pulled out my magnifying lens and examined the glasses. There were lots of distinct fingerprints.

Excellent.

I went back out to the foyer, winked at Kelsey and took the satchel from her.

"Hey," she said, "find anything?"

"Yes. Keep watching."

Back at the kitchen sink, I opened the satchel. I'd assembled this mobile CSI case a few months ago, and it was about to prove itself indispensable. Pulling out the fingerprint kit, I picked three glasses at random and dusted them with powder. I focused on the larger thumb prints first and compared those prints to the ones I'd lifted from Conover's DVD cases and playing cards.

Tented arches again.

Because tented arches comprise less than five percent of the population, the odds were good that Conover had been here. Especially when I factored in the brand and quantity of the condoms present.

I scrubbed the glasses and washed the fingerprint powder down the sink, then packed up the satchel and returned to the foyer. Svetlana and Kelsey were talking.

"What'd you find?" I asked Svetlana. "Condom wrappers?"

"Many. In four rooms at least."

"Seven down here."

Svetlana opened her mouth to speak and promptly closed it.

"So?" Kelsey tapped me on the elbow. "What's the deal?"

"Your brother was here," I said. "I can't be a hundred percent sure, but I found fingerprints that reasonably match the ones from your apartment." I handed the satchel to Kelsey. "The question now is, where did they go? I think I saw a clue in the library. You two wait in the car, and I'll be right out."

Returning to the library, I stood in the doorway and scanned the room. It was a replica of a 19th century English club, complete with mahogany walls and bookcases, leather-bound books, club chairs, a standing globe, and a glass case filled with sailing trophies. Framed paintings of ocean scenes, and photos of sailboats including the *Lady Conover*, hung between the bookcases. Other photos featured a teenage or 20-something Ginger posing with trophies.

In a corner alcove was a grid of deep pigeon holes with cylinder tubes jutting out. One of the holes was empty. I crossed the room. The one with the missing tube was labeled "Vinalhaven." I pulled the "Rockland" tube, removed the rolled plastic inside, and spread it out on the table. It was a waterproof nautical chart of Rockland harbor. I put it back and inspected every photo of the *Lady Conover*. She had a white hull with regal purple and gold sails. In several photos she leaned with the wind and crashed through waves, but one in particular caught my attention. The boat was moored in a small cove surrounded by spruce trees. In the background, a massive A-frame log home with a front bank of windows stood on a point.

I was certain I'd seen this house and cove before. It was on Coombs Neck, a spit of land on the extreme eastern side of Vinalhaven Island. With only a couple of dirt roads in or out of there, it was the perfect hideout for Conover.

But how the hell would I get over there? If I took the ferry, the instant I drove onto the island in my conspicuous Cadillac, word would spread that old Al Stevens's grandson was on the island. And with Svetlana and Kelsey along? Forget it.

I had to find another way over there. Several of the photos showed a 25- or 30-foot cabin cruiser, *Belle*. The boat had to belong to the Savages, and if it did, and if it was docked in Camden…

The kitchen.

I followed the maze of rooms back there. Next to the pantry door hung keys to a number of expensive cars—Mercedes, Hummer, Mercedes, Ferrari. There were also what looked like spare sets of house keys, and one of the hooks was empty. But what really caught my eye were the two sets of keys with floating key chains. I grabbed the one with the tag that read, "Belle," and hurried out of the house.

25

An Eerie Stillness

Vinalhaven is about 15 miles from Camden, so even in the choppy water we reached the eastern side of the island in an hour and a half. But crossing the deep water of Penobscot Bay and passing through the Thoroughfare between North Haven and Vinalhaven was the easy part. Now we had to navigate dangerous shoals to find the cove I was certain I'd seen before.

While I piloted the boat, Svetlana sat on the port side watching the sonar unit and consulting the Vinalhaven depth chart on her laptop. Kelsey stood at the windshield between us, sweeping binoculars along the shoreline, looking for the log home or the *Lady Conover*. At the moment, there was nothing in sight but water, rocky shoreline and dense spruce trees. A cold wind flapped our hair around. It had been much warmer on the mainland.

After leaving the Savage mansion, we'd had to kill time while waiting for high tide. We ate a big lunch at Cappy's Chowder House, parked the car in a public lot and made our way down to the harbor, where, with binoculars, I located *Belle*. In a small stroke of luck, Cal wasn't around when we hurried down the gangway to the boat. Before we boarded, I made sure we were all wearing latex gloves, and then we threw off the lines, put on life vests, and crept out of the harbor. Still, we monitored the radio as we crossed the bay; I wanted to make sure the boat wasn't reported as stolen. However, by the time we reached Vinalhaven, I wasn't worried about the Coast Guard anymore; I was worried about rocks.

"How are we doing for depth?" I asked Svetlana.

"Twenty feet in this area."

"The draft on these boats is about three or four feet. We should be all right."

"*Should* be?" she said. "This is not encouraging."

"We'll be fine," I said. "Kelsey, see anything yet?"

"No."

"Keep looking."

Chugging along, weaving between lobster buoys, keeping the speed to 5 knots, I reached the mouths of two coves, one on the left, one on the right. They both looked familiar. This was the general area, but I had to choose the correct cove. We didn't have much time to search; sunset was in only three hours or so. I steered into the one on the right.

"Two coves," Svetlana said.

"Yup."

"How do you know this is the correct one?"

"Instinct, my dear. Instinct."

"You mean guessing," she said.

"You say tomato…"

"Wait," Kelsey said. "I see something. It's a sailboat."

"What color sails?" I asked.

"They're down, I can't tell. No…wait…they look purple. Yeah, they're purple."

"Look for a log house, a big A-frame."

Kelsey swiveled with the binoculars, then stopped.

"Got it," she said.

"You do?"

"Yes. Straight ahead."

"Let me see," I said.

I took the binoculars, and sure enough, there was the giant A-frame log home I'd seen in the photo. A sailboat with purple sails—I couldn't see the stern to read its name—rolled in the light chop about 100 yards offshore. It was on a mooring. There was a floating metal dock near the house, but I didn't see any kind of dinghy to take somebody between the shore and the sailboat. The dock extended a good hundred feet into the cove, far enough out that, even at lowest tide, the water would be more than six feet deep (I hoped). I handed the binoculars back to Kelsey.

"We're going to the dock," I said. "Svetlana, keep a sharp eye on that sonar."

"Yes, captain."

I reduced the speed and took us around the sailboat to read the stern. There it was, the *Lady Conover*. When we neared the dock, I turned the boat and backed in stern-first. Svetlana tossed out the rubber fenders, and once I got the boat steady, I gave her the wheel, jumped out and fastened the lines to the cleats. Svetlana cut the engine, then she and Kelsey disembarked. We stood on the dock with the chop slapping the side of the boat, and stared at the house.

"I hope he's here," Kelsey said.

We took off our life vests and tossed them in the boat. The women grabbed their bags.

"I'll lead," I said.

Maybe it was the metallic echo our shoes made on the dock, or the fact that the woods around the house were silent, but whatever it was, there was an eerie stillness about the place. We went up a set of stairs to a porch at the front of the house. There were several Adirondack chairs and a small pile of wood in front of a big picture window. We cupped our hands and peered inside.

"See anything?" I asked.

"No," Kelsey said.

"It is too dark," Svetlana said.

Kelsey went to the door and knocked.

"Conover? Open up, it's me." She waited, tried the knob, then pounded on the door. "Goddamn it, Conover, open up! I've had enough!"

"Clearly," Svetlana said, "no one is here."

"They might have gone out with the dinghy somewhere." I walked down the deck stairs.

"Where are you going?" Kelsey said.

"Around back, to see if they left a door open. I don't feel like picking another lock right now."

I walked around the side of house, rounded the back corner and stopped short, nearly tripping over something in the process.

26

The Letter "H"

"Girls, stop!" I called over my shoulder.

"What is it?" Kelsey said.

"Ginger Best…I think," I said. "She's dead. I don't want either of you seeing this."

There was panic in Kelsey's voice: "Dead?"

"Yes."

"Is Conover with her?"

"No. Stay where you are."

Ginger was barefoot, but fully clothed and on her side in a fetal position. I got on my knees and examined the body without touching it. She had been shot in the back of the head at close range, execution-style, with a large-caliber weapon. It was a noticeably larger entry hole than the ones in Kyle Foster's head.

The shot to Ginger's skull was close enough that the muzzle blast had scorched her hair and caused stippling on the scalp around the entry wound. The exit wound on her face was so gruesome, I couldn't bear to look at it for more than a few seconds. The grass and spruce needles around her face were spattered with tissue. It looked to me as though her killer had made her kneel, and when she was shot, her body went into cadaveric spasm—an instantaneous stiffening of the entire body. Although rare, under extreme emotional and violent situations, it was known to happen, freezing the victim's last bodily position. In Ginger's case, if I was correct, she had frozen in a kneeling position, and then fell over on her side.

I got to my feet and paused. To think that this woman—this admittedly sexy woman, if her photos were accurate—was now as dead as a fallen log. I shook my head. That's the thing about this business: You see the absolute worst that human beings are capable of. It was a miracle I'd been able to maintain a sense of humor over the years.

Getting back on my hands and knees, careful to avoid the areas spattered with tissue, I spiraled in toward the body from six feet away. There were a few faint impressions from Ginger's bare feet, leading in random directions as if she were being chased, and several boot prints. The boot prints were all the same size and tread. I pulled out my phone and snapped some close-ups. I searched for shell casings, but when I didn't find any, I decided to follow the boot prints.

"Ladies," I said, "don't come over here. I'll be right back."

About twenty feet from the area where Ginger was killed, I picked up a trail of the boot prints in the driveway. In fact, there were two sets: one coming in, another going out. The ones coming in were less distinct than the ones going out; it might have been raining when Ginger's killer came in, and it might have stopped when he left. I followed the prints 100 yards down the driveway until they faded and I lost the trail, at which point I went back. It appeared the killer had walked in from the road and gone out the same way. I returned to the body and examined it up close.

While I wasn't an expert on establishing time of death, I estimated Ginger had been killed sometime the previous day. Her hair was matted and damp, and there was no blood on the ground near her head, which meant it had been raining when she was shot and it got washed away, or it started to rain while she bled out. There were no flies; there were no fly eggs visible in the wounds, or her mouth or nose; and there were no signs that animals had been feeding on the corpse.

Finally, I lifted her blouse and saw the green putrefaction caused by decay; it was beginning to appear on her stomach—an indicator that she'd been killed in the past 24 hours. I wanted to look at the side of her against the ground to get an idea of the *livor mortis*, or settling of the blood, but I couldn't do it without moving her body. I got up and went to the front of the house, where Svetlana and Kelsey were waiting.

"Bad?" Svetlana said.

I swallowed. "Yeah. We'll call the state police once we're back on the mainland. I want to look inside the house first. Go up on the porch and I'll let you in."

I found the door in back. No time today for niceties like picking locks. I was wearing my leather jacket, so I thrust an elbow through the window above the doorknob. I went inside and hit a light switch.

Like Kelsey's apartment, the place had been thoroughly ransacked. Before the destruction, it had been the prototypical expensive log home: chalet fireplace, vaulted ceiling, stainless steel kitchen, and of course an unobstructed view of the cove through a massive bank of windows. There were more condom wrappers lying around. I let the women inside.

"Everyone's still wearing gloves?" I asked.

"Yes," Svetlana said.

"Any sign of my brother?" Kelsey said.

"Only condom wrappers so far," I said.

"Cripes, Conover." She clutched the strap of her messenger bag.

"Let's do a search," I said. "Anything that might give us an idea of his whereabouts."

We split up. I went to the front windows, where a small desk faced the view. The desktop was empty, so if there had been a computer here, it was gone now. The drawers had been rifled through. I pushed the desk away from the windows and found a sheet of paper on the floor. Skimming it, I gleaned it was about nuclear fission. I folded up the paper and put it in my pocket.

I heard the chortle of boat engines out in the cove. Two long, black Rigid Inflatable Boats (RIBs)—like the ones the Navy Seals use—coasted up to the dock. I counted eight men in black private security uniforms. Several of them had their tactical jackets open, and I saw lightweight bulletproof vests underneath. I couldn't be certain without the binoculars, but most of them looked to be carrying AR-15s—the same rifle as mine, which I had left in the boat.

"Svetlana, Kelsey. We have to go. Now."

"What is wrong, Dakota?"

Svetlana glanced out the front window. Her face fell.

Kelsey came out of the other room. I grabbed her by the elbow and steered her straight toward the back door.

"What are you doing?"

"We're leaving," I said. "Into the woods. Don't say a word. There are armed men here."

I pulled my Sig Sauer, flicked off the safety and led us outside. As we passed Ginger's dead body, Kelsey froze in her tracks.

"Ohmigod, ohmigod, ohmigod."

"Shhh."

With Svetlana in the lead, I pulled Kelsey across the driveway and into the woods. Twigs and fallen leaves rustled and snapped beneath our feet. We needed to find some kind of cover, fast.

"That woman," Kelsey said, "I can't believe it."

"Quiet, Kelsey," I said.

"We should run," she said.

I gripped her elbow tighter. "We're not running. Do *not* run, Kelsey."

About 200 yards from the house, the ground sloped upwards, and I found the best cover we could ask for: a small group of boulders concealed by underbrush, with a rocky slope at our backs. I made Kelsey and Svetlana sit at my feet. I got down on one knee and aimed around the side of a boulder. Through gaps in the spruce trees, I glimpsed the clearing behind the house. Six men—I didn't know where the other two were—had gathered near Ginger's body.

A wave of nausea washed over me. I had screwed up. By not taking the AR-15 out of the boat when we got here, I'd screwed up but good.

Our best chance was to stay hidden. The boulders and underbrush provided excellent cover, and there was a chance that if we stayed as still as fawns, they would walk right past us. I looked at the women. Svetlana seemed calm to me until I saw beads of sweat trickling down her cheek, which was disconcerting because Svetlana never sweat. As for Kelsey, she was sitting with her knees clutched to her chest, shaking. I laid a hand on her shoulder to comfort her. It didn't seem to help.

I looked at the clearing again. The woods were deathly quiet. I could hear the men talking to each other, although I couldn't make out what they were saying. They moved carefully and methodically, like soldiers. One of them walked to the edge of the clearing and squatted near the spot where we'd entered the woods. Then he stood, waved the others over, and pointed in our direction.

Damn it. I leveled the Sig at a gap in the trees. Eleven shots. I had two more 10-shot magazines in my jacket pocket, and the 5-shot .357 Magnum on my ankle. Thirty-six rounds total, or about as many as *one* of their rifle magazines. Even with this cover, the only way we stood a chance was if they came straight toward us.

Which they didn't. They spread out to flank us. Now I really regretted leaving the rifle in the boat.

One of them called out, "Give it up, Wright! You're done!"

The sounds of swishing tree limbs and snapping twigs grew louder. I whispered in Kelsey's ear.

"No matter what happens, stay down and be absolutely still. Okay?"

I waited for her to nod, but she didn't. She stared at the ground and shook.

Peering around the boulder again, I noticed that the three men who'd been following our trail had stopped. They were trying to decide which direction to go in. There was a chance they'd move away from us.

"Go on, leave," I whispered to myself. "Leave."

Then, behind me: Svetlana whispering loudly, "Dakota!" and a clattering sound—like small stones. I turned around and Kelsey was scrabbling up the slope, hyperventilating, clawing at the earth with her fingernails. Svetlana and I tried to grab her, but she got to the top just as my hand caught her boot, and she slipped away. She ran out of sight. The men shouted from below.

"It's the girl! The sister! Get her!"

I grabbed a sapling high up on the slope, and hauled myself up with it. I pulled Svetlana up and when we reached the top, I saw Kelsey, about 50 yards ahead, trying to run in those clodhopping Doc Martens. Svetlana and I went after her, hurdling logs, dodging rocks, weaving through the trees.

At this point, all we could do was try to outrun our pursuers. The ground was flat, but Kelsey was running precariously close to a cliff edge, with a fifty-foot fall to the rocks in the cove below. When I caught up to her, I grabbed her arm.

"Kelsey, this way!"

Svetlana took hold of her other arm, and we jogged together away from the cliff. Our one chance was to return to the boat. If we could get back there and disable their faster boats, we might make it.

We circled back toward the dock. The underbrush was dense, some of it thorns, and getting through it without making a lot of noise proved tricky. When we emerged into a small clearing, two of the men were waiting for us with their rifles leveled.

"All right, drop the gun," one of them said.

I noticed that neither had his finger on the trigger. They were either really dumb, or they had no intention of shooting us. Bulletproof vests or no, they would be incapacitated if I shot them. The blunt force trauma from my .45 rounds would see to that.

"We just want the girl," the other one said.

Habitually my gun flew up and aimed for their center masses, and I popped three rapid shots into each of their chests. They went down. Svetlana and Kelsey gaped at me.

"Let's go!" I said.

On the other side of the clearing, we ducked back into the woods. It was dim here. We kept going. The house and the dock appeared through a break in the trees.

"All right, let's—"

Three men came up the hillside about 50 feet away.

"Svetlana, Kelsey, go! Get out of here!"

The men started to raise their guns at me, but I already had the Sig up and aimed. I fired twice as one of them moved, and put a bullet through his hand. He yelled and his rifle fell into the brush. I swiveled with the gun and fired three at the next guy. Two hit him in the chest and the third caught him in the shoulder. He went down. I dropped to one knee, changed out the magazine. Standing behind the other two, the third one sighted through his scope at Kelsey and Svetlana.

Adrenaline pulsed through me. *Svetlana!*

Instinctively I aimed for his head and fired. He crumpled to the ground. Then the one with the mangled hand reached for his sidearm. I shot him twice in the chest, knocking him over into the brush. I ran out of the woods for the dock.

Svetlana and Kelsey had paused at the front corner of the house. I halted beside them. They were panting, and Kelsey's eyes were huge—the adrenaline. Down on the dock, one of the uniformed men stood with his gun at the ready. He was smoking a cigarette.

I made a mental note: I had seven rounds left until I needed to use my final magazine. After that, I only had five rounds in the .357 Magnum.

There was shouting from the woods. The others would soon figure out where we were. I gave us two minutes.

"I'm going down there," I said.

Svetlana put her gloved hand on mine. "Dakota, be careful."

"I'll be fine, Champ. Fifteen seconds. Time me."

I took a few deep breaths and watched the man on the dock. The second he turned his back to us and raised his cigarette hand, I sprinted from the house. He was facing the water when I reached the dock and ran straight toward him. I was halfway to him before he started to turn. I shot at him twice, hit him once in the chest, and dove onto the dock on my elbows. The shot staggered him, but hadn't put him down. I fired two more times. One shot grazed his arm, and blood sprayed into the water. He dropped his gun. I got to my feet and aimed straight at his head.

He raised his hands. Waving over my shoulder for the women, I walked toward him. The dock resounded with running footsteps, and then Svetlana and Kelsey were beside me.

Keeping the gun steady on him, I reached out with my free hand, pulled his sidearm and threw it in the water. On the chest of his jacket I noticed an embroidered black letter "H."

"So," I said, "I guess today's paramilitary operation is brought to us by the letter 'H.' What's the 'H' stand for?"

He didn't answer.

"Doesn't matter. You're coming with us." I motioned to Svetlana and Kelsey. "Quick, untie the lines."

As I moved to let them scamper by, I was distracted for a split second. The man grabbed my wrist and twisted my gun hand. The gun went off. A scalding sensation flared up in my left thigh. My leg buckled and I stumbled backward. I fell, whacked my head on the dock, and splashed into the water.

In the muffled distance I heard Svetlana and Kelsey shouting my name. They were afraid.

The coldness of the water was my last sensation before the darkness smothered me.

27

Consider Yourself Lucky

Shivering. A burning sensation in my thigh. A hard object digging into my back. The smell of salt air and the sound of water lapping nearby. The feel of something crinkly against my skin.

I opened my eyes and saw gray-blue sky. Dawn or dusk—I couldn't tell which. I lay on a rocky beach above the tide high-water mark. I was wrapped in a Mylar emergency blanket. I sat up. Something slid off the blanket. A cell phone. I stuck my arm out from underneath and grabbed it.

I snapped the blanket off and felt my body heat dissipate in an instant. I was stripped to the skin except for my shorts. Even the latex gloves I'd been wearing were gone. My left leg was propped up with a black jacket, and a heavy bandage was taped tightly to the outside of my thigh.

I looked around. Ginger Best's house and the dock were behind me. The *Belle* was still at the dock.

"Svetlana? Kelsey?"

No answer. Just the ceaseless lapping of water.

The cell phone in my hand wasn't mine. I pressed a button and the screen lit up. There were eight text messages and a photo waiting. Once I figured out how to do it, I read the messages in the order in which they'd arrived:

> *Not bad, Mr. Stevens. You almost got away. Almost.*
>
> *Consider yourself lucky. The bullet went clean through your outer thigh. No major blood vessels.*
>
> *We have taken the women. If you want them back, you WILL find Conover Wright. Do NOT contact us until you have him.*
>
> *Do NOT contact the FBI. We know you have connections there, but if you want to see the women alive again, be smart and find the writer.*
>
> *If you're thinking of searching the body of the man you killed, forget it—we took him with us.*
>
> *You need to move fast. My men haven't been laid in weeks, and this partner of yours is one juicy piece of ass.*
>
> *The girl is pretty sweet, too, and some of us like them young.*
>
> *Get moving, Mr. Stevens. Our employer is waiting.*

My throat got tight. I clutched the phone so hard, the plastic started to give in my hand.

I let go. I needed this phone.

The photo was of Svetlana and Kelsey in one of the RIB boats. They were seated on the floor, and their hair was being tossed around in the wind. Svetlana, a defiant expression on her face, had her arm around a terrified Kelsey.

Even as I shivered uncontrollably, I had enough presence of mind to know that I needed to get the hell out of here. Yes, I was on an isolated part of the island, but gunshots carried, and gunshots attracted attention. I also didn't know how long I'd been unconscious. The Coast Guard or Maine State Police may already be on their way to the scene. It was getting dark and I had to navigate the shoals again—this time alone.

I staggered to my feet, hugging the Mylar blanket to my chest. A jolt of pain shot through my leg that almost caused me to vomit. I stopped and breathed until the nausea passed, and was about to leave when I glanced at the tactical jacket they'd left behind. I needed clues about who the mysterious H-Men were working for. I grabbed it, put the phone in one of its pockets and headed for the dock.

The overwhelming reality of the situation—that Svetlana and Kelsey were gone and in danger of being harmed, or worse—was creeping in on me, but I focused on my walking. Every time I put weight on my leg, the pain flared up like gasoline was being poured on the wound. I broke out in a cold sweat from the exertion.

There were no signs of anyone. The shoreline and surrounding woods were still.

When I reached the dock, it occurred to me that both of my guns were gone. The Sig Sauer was somewhere down in the water, and the .357 surely was, too. At least the boat was still here. Hobbling down the dock, I saw some objects scattered near the boat. They were Svetlana's Gucci bag and Kelsey's messenger bag. The can of grizzly repellent lay alone, rolling back and forth on the undulating dock. And that's when it hit me: Svetlana and Kelsey were gone, and it was my fault. My eyes clenched shut and held back tears.

Once I'd pulled myself together, I picked up the bags and the repellent, wrapped everything in the Mylar blanket, and tossed it on board. I untied the lines, then took hold of the boat at the stern. I threw my good leg over the side and rolled into the boat.

I managed to land on my hands and knees, but even so the pain was intense, and I had to catch my breath before trying to stand up again. I thought I might pass out. When I finally got to my feet and steadied myself, I found my things and got dressed.

28

THE HIPPOCRATIC OATH

The next twelve hours felt like days.

Heading out of the cove, I was sick with worry about Svetlana and Kelsey, but I had to put it out of my mind. Navigating the shoals alone at near low tide and piloting a boat across open water in the gloaming took all of my concentration. There were some close calls with shallow ledges that came out of nowhere, but I managed to avoid them. After an hour, I made it through the shoals and the Thoroughfare, and gained time in the open bay.

The bay was placid as I sped across it in the gathering darkness. There was chatter over the radio from fishermen about gunfire coming from somewhere on Vinalhaven. However no one had seen anything, and gunshots are notoriously difficult to pinpoint. Thankfully no one had reported *Belle* as stolen.

Still I wasn't taking any chances, and when I approached Camden, instead of going into the inner harbor, I killed the pilot lights and steered toward Eaton Point. I found a dimly lit, empty dock and coasted in. Once I'd secured the boat, I stuffed all of our belongings in my large duffel, wiped everything down, and limped a painful half-mile to the car.

I had to get to New York. My leg required medical attention, but I couldn't go to a hospital. At a 24-hour service station in Rockland, I gassed up and bought a large coffee and a bottle of the strongest painkillers I could get. From a payphone I called the Maine State Police and reported Ginger's murder, then I headed out.

The drive took nine hours. It should have taken seven, but when I reached Massachusetts, I was exhausted and had to nap for two hours in a rest area. I lay in the back seat with my wounded leg propped up, and stared at the fabric ceiling. I was debating whether to elicit the help of Svetlana's father, Oleksander Krush, a powerful boss in the Ukrainian Mob. He had tremendous resources, but he had also once told me that if I ever let anything happen to his daughter, he would hold me responsible, and by "hold responsible" I was pretty sure he meant "kill." No, until I found her and Kelsey, I wouldn't talk to Oleksander. And I didn't have to worry about him contacting her; he and Svetlana were on the outs again.

I was back in the city by 5:00 a.m. and drove straight to a garage on East 89th Street and limped over to Clarissa's apartment building. Now that I was up and moving again, my thigh was throbbing. Upon first seeing me, what with a large bloodstain on my jeans, her doorman refused to call upstairs. Eventually I was able to persuade him, and when I stepped off the elevator, Clarissa was there.

"You don't answer any of my texts," she said. "I worry about you and then you show up at five o'clock in the morning and…" Her eyes sprang open at the sight of the bloodstain. "My God, are you okay?"

"Please get your ex-husband over here, pronto."

"What happened?"

"I'll explain inside," I said.

She got under my arm and helped me into the apartment.

"Hope you don't mind blood on your sheets," I said.

"Shhh, Lainey's asleep," she said. "I'll put you in the maid's room. I don't have a live-in anymore."

"Poor darling. How will you ever manage?"

She smiled at me with a curtain of hair obscuring half her face. In the maid's room, she eased me onto a twin bed and put pillows under my wounded leg.

"Now, what's going on?"

"I've been shot."

"What?! We need to get you to a hospital!"

"No, I just need your ex-husband to patch me up."

"He's a *plastic* surgeon, Dakota. He can't do anything for you."

"A surgeon's a surgeon. Call him and tell him a friend needs medical attention right away."

She scoffed. "A *friend*. You've got to be kidding. When he sees you, he's going to flip."

"Occupational hazard, beautiful. Sometimes we PIs get involved with our clients. Especially when they're as adoring and pretty as you." I touched her cheek. "Now go, call him. And tell him to bring his doctor bag—with everything he needs for minor surgery."

"Okay." She bent down and kissed me on the mouth. "My God, those lips. It's wonderful to see you, Dakota. It always is."

"Even shot?"

"Even shot."

"Go." I patted her on the behind.

And with that, I lost consciousness.

When I came to, Clarissa's stocky and hirsute ex-husband, Dr. David Coleman, was sitting on a chair, leaning over my leg, wearing a surgical mask and gloves. I was still on the bed in the maid's room, and it was getting light outside. While I was passed out, someone had cut the leg off my jeans. He grabbed the tape around the bandage and pulled it off slowly, as if to yank every last hair off my leg in the process.

"Oh, Mr. Stevens, you're awake," he said.

"Doctor Coleman."

"Don't mind me. I need a better look at the wound. By the way, if it's a gunshot wound, I'm required by law to report it."

"No need," I said. "It was an accidental discharge."

"Well, I have to report it anyway."

"Then I'll have to report to the court that you're still having your wife followed."

"That's ridiculous," he said. "I wouldn't—"

"You would, you still are, and you did—the entire seven years you were married. The iPhone, the GPS tracker, the PIs. I don't think you want your settlement agreement reopened, do you?"

He set his jaw and stared at a spot on the wall.

"No."

He pulled the bandage off and some blood leaked out. He probed around and inside the entry and exit holes with his fingers. I wanted to scream.

"Is that necessary?" I said.

"Yes."

After an agonizing minute, he stopped.

"You know," he said, "you're very fortunate."

"Yeah? How's that?"

"Well, had the bullet hit your femoral artery, you would have bled out in two minutes. In your case, it didn't go anywhere near major blood vessels."

"That's good," I said.

"It entered and exited your outer thigh causing little cavitation, and there's no internal bleeding. The bullet also doesn't appear to have fragmented."

"Makes sense," I said. "My rounds have full metal jackets."

"Yes, whatever," he said. "There was no damage from muzzle blast either. The wound is largely superficial. Once I treat it, as long as you change the bandage every day and stay off your feet for a week, you—"

"Hold it, Doctor, I can't lie in bed for a week."

He scowled at me in the surgical mask. "I should think you'd like that prospect. You and my wife could—"

"Ex-wife," I said. "And I know what we could do. But I'm dealing with something life and death right now, Doctor, so I can do without the sarcasm."

"Fine. Then perhaps I won't treat you."

"You will."

"Oh, and why is that?"

"The Hippocratic oath. You're still a doctor and a damn good one, and you're not going to turn your back on a person who needs your help."

"All right," Coleman said, "two days. I'll clean up the wound and insert a drain today, then I'll come back to stitch you up. If you agree to stay in bed for two days, I'll treat you. Otherwise, I go straight to the police."

"Okay, deal," I said. "I'd shake your hand, but there's blood all over that glove."

He went to work. Half an hour later, he was finished. He wrote me two prescriptions—one for an antibiotic, and a second one for Percocet—and began packing up. Clarissa came in, put all of the bloody things in a garbage bag, and took them away.

"Nice work, doctor," I said. "Thanks."

"Day after tomorrow, I'll come back to stitch you up. I'll bring you my bill then."

"Of course. Do you need my insurance card?"

"I don't do insurance," he said.

"Great."

He grinned, grabbed his bag and left.

A few minutes later, Clarissa returned, holding her cell phone so casually I could have sworn it was glued to her hand. She was in her workout clothes, about to get on the treadmill. I was in the middle of thinking about Svetlana and Kelsey, fending off a crushing feeling in my chest. I wasn't having a heart attack, but I couldn't breathe.

Clarissa sat beside me on the edge of the bed. She pulled her hair around her neck so it draped down her chest. The gesture reminded me of Svetlana for some reason.

"What's wrong?" she asked.

"My partner and client are missing. But don't tell anyone."

"I won't. That's awful. I'm so sorry, Dakota." She gestured at the bandage. "Did this have anything to do with it?"

"It had everything to do with it."

She laid a hand on my heart. "I'm under strict orders from David not to allow you to leave for two days. I'm afraid you're mine, baby. *All* mine."

"Hmm…hardly chaste, Clarissa." I forced a smile. "I'm not up for that right now, but if you could help me get some work done while I lie here, I promise to make it up to—"

She put a finger on my lips to shush me. "I'll help you." She smiled and dragged her fingertip across my lips. "And I know *exactly* how you'll repay me."

29

TO HELL WITH CONOVER

I slept the entire morning. When I awoke at noon, Clarissa had retrieved my duffel from the Cadillac and procured chicken soup from Hale & Hearty and bagels from H&H. I didn't feel much like eating, but I forced myself to. I wouldn't be able to focus on finding Svetlana and Kelsey until I stabilized, and food would ostensibly speed my recovery. After I ate, Clarissa brought my medication.

"Here you go." She handed me pills and a glass of water.

"Thanks. Just the antibiotic."

I swallowed it and handed back the Percocet. Clarissa winced at the bandage on my leg.

"It's gonna hurt, Dakota."

"I know, but I need to be able to think, and Percocet makes me loopy. Get me three ibuprofen, would you, doll?"

"Only because you called me 'doll.' Anything else?"

"A phone, please."

She pouted.

"What's wrong?" I said.

"I was hoping you wanted...*you know*..."

"Clarissa, my partner and client are missing, their lives are in danger, and my leg has a bullet hole in it. This isn't the time."

"You're right." She nodded decisively. "One phone coming up."

Late last night, I had made a decision. To hell with Conover. Even though the H-Men text message said that finding him was how I would get the women back alive, I wasn't wasting any more time on him. With the dinghy gone but the sailboat still there, it stood to reason that he'd left at some point and never returned. He might be dead, he might have fled to Canada, or he might have been taken by somebody else. I had no idea, and I didn't care. All I cared about was finding Svetlana and Kelsey, and to do that, I needed to figure out who was pulling the strings behind all of this.

In his final text message, the H-Men leader mentioned his "employer." I had already determined that any information (even classified information) about the moon wouldn't matter to the Mob or the brutes from North Dakota. As I'd reasoned earlier, if Conover was writing about a moon conspiracy, then the third party must be someone who would be affected by the book becoming public. Up to now, I had assumed that the groups looking for Conover were all separate, but...what if the *same employer* had hired all three groups: the H-Men, the Mob, and the North Dakota brutes?

I was getting warmer, I was sure of it. I needed to find out who the employer was, and I knew exactly where to start—with the Mob guy from New Jersey, Vic Caprisi. I'd need some help, but I was sure Falcone would be eager to lend a hand.

When I came out of my reverie, a cordless phone stood on the nightstand. I called Falcone.

"About friggen time," he said. "I thought we were doing tit for tat."

"What, you have something new?" I said.

"No. You?"

"Yes. I know the name and address of one of the guys who's been operating in your territory."

"Well? Let's have it."

"No, this is serious, Falcone. I need to question this guy, not send him a wrapped-up fish. How soon can you get over here?"

"Where's here?"

"Eighty-ninth, around the corner from the Guggenheim," I said.

"Why can't you come over here?"

"I'm incapacitated."

"What," he said, "you mean like a broad?"

I took a breath.

"No...that would be *indisposed.* I've been shot. I'm bedridden."

"Rough, but it happens," he said. "Let's just talk now. I've got a thing way the hell out in Rockaway later and—"

"Damn it, Falcone, get your ass over here! I can't discuss this on an open line. It's Svetlana. She's in trouble. She's in trouble and I need your help."

"Say no more. What's the address?"

I gave it to him.

"Leaving right now," he said, and hung up.

While I waited for Falcone, I decided to check Svetlana's things for clues. She had mentioned something about Terence Dalton. There might be other clues in her Gucci bag as well.

I pulled out Svetlana's laptop and legal pad. I leafed through the legal pad first, and upon seeing her precise and elegant handwriting, I was ambushed by that crushing sensation in my chest again. I breathed through it and read her notes. With the exception of the information about Vic Caprisi, there was nothing I hadn't heard from her or Kelsey.

Between her notes on the case, the legal pad also contained a number of surprising scribbles, including beautiful drawings of chess pieces (I never knew she could draw), mathematical formulae I didn't understand (e.g., $e^{i\pi}+1=0$), and the notations of moves from complete chess games, evidently written down from memory, like this one:

"Morphy's Immortal/The Opera Game"
1. e4 e5 2. Nf3 d6 3. d4 Bg4 4. dxe5 Bxf3 5. Qxf3 dxe5 6. Bc4 Nf6 7. Qb3 Qe7 8.Nc3 c6 9. Bg5 b5 10. Nxb5 cxb5 11. Bxb5+ Nbd7 12. O-O-O Rd8 13. Rxd7 Rxd7 14.Rd1 Qe6 15. Bxd7+ Nxd7 16. Qb8+ Nxb8 17. Rd8# 1-0.

I felt as if I were seeing a side of Svetlana I'd never fully appreciated or understood. Suddenly a dark thought, a thought that made my entire body ache, encroached on my consciousness: *I might never see her again.* A similar feeling came to me when I thought about Kelsey, my new little sister, and I had to push my feelings aside. I couldn't entertain the idea of never seeing them again. Success was the only option. I didn't care what it took, what illegal things I might have to do, what scumbags I might have to kill—I was getting them back safe.

Setting the legal pad aside, I opened Svetlana's laptop. It awoke out of sleep mode on the login page. There were two accounts: "Dakota Stevens Investigations" and "Chess Goddess." I wanted the business account, but I couldn't remember the password.

Damn it, Svetlana gave this to you sometime in the past year. When was it? Where were we?

I lay back against the pillows and closed my eyes. I thought about our cases of the past year and the witty Watson-esque sobriquets she had given each of them: "A Study in Harlot," "The Adventure of the Free Range Archivist," "The Thomas Kinkade Affair," and "The Adventure of the Heckled Band."

Yes, the rock band—Rich Citizens. It was during that case. The lead vocalist, Brett Shayne, a trust fund kid, financed the band himself. Heckled at every club they played. Started getting email death threats, and we joined them in Austin for a six-city tour. Svetlana, ever the chameleon, met them in a groupie's ensemble: ruby sequin V-neck top, black leather miniskirt and skyscraper stilettos. Then, in Vale, ski bunny attire. That's where she told me. In the lodge, in front of the chalet fireplace. She sat in a rocking chair, typing on her laptop, while I paced around. With an impish smile on her face, she waved me over and said, "In case you ever need to log in to my computer, the password is…"

I entered it, and it worked. There were several windows open, including a word processing file titled "Dalton Dossier," which I looked at first. Somehow Svetlana had found a photo of Terence Dalton—a clean-cut man of retirement age—as well as his Social Security number, home and work contact info, education and work history. Currently he worked not for NASA, but for the Department of Energy (DOE), Office of Nuclear Energy, as Deputy Assistant Secretary for Science and Technology Innovation. In fact, Dalton had spent his entire career with the DOE, including 12 years in the DOE's Office of Intelligence and Counterintelligence. But this raised a question: Where was a DOE bureaucrat getting access to classified information about the *moon*?

I needed to talk to him. I needed to know about the material he'd been feeding Conover, and who might stand to lose by it. I had a hunch the answers would lead me to the employer, and from there to Svetlana and Kelsey.

I dialed Dalton's Washington, D.C. work number, got his voicemail and hung up without leaving a message. Then I called his home in Bethesda, Maryland. It rang and rang. I was about to hang up when a woman answered. Her voice was shaky and loud.

"Who is this? Why won't you people leave me alone? I don't know anything! Stop calling me!"

"Mrs. Dalton," I said, "my name is Dakota Stevens. I'm a private investigator based in Manhattan, and I'm working on a case that involves your husband. I need to talk to you."

"I have nothing to say, Mr. Stevens. Goodbye."

She hung up.

I put down the phone and did a web search on Terence Dalton. Several hits for news articles came up, including a *Washington Post* piece published this morning titled, "DOE Assistant Secretary Slain, Motive Sought."

"Son of a bitch," I said aloud.

Clarissa popped her head into the room.

"Something wrong, sweetie?"

"Everything's wrong, but not with you," I said.

"Get you anything?"

"Maybe coffee and Danish? I'm expecting a visitor—a guy named Falcone—in a few minutes."

"There's a nice bakery on Madison," she said. "I'll have some delivered."

"Thanks, beautiful."

I clicked through to the *Post* article. Dalton had been found shot dead in a Maryland motel the day before. There were no witnesses.

I decided to call a detective I knew on the D.C. Metropolitan Police. Andrea Martin was rare among women I'd known in that she couldn't stand me—a fact I used to my advantage. She was often willing to give me scraps of information to make me go away.

"Detective Martin," she said.

"Andrea, it's Dakota Stevens."

"Oh, God. What do you want?"

"One question, Andrea, I promise."

She let out a groan that rattled the line.

"You've got thirty seconds," she said.

"The DOE Secretary found dead in Maryland yesterday. Some guy named Terence Dalton."

"That's not my jurisdiction."

"I know, but I figured you'd at least know the scuttlebutt. I just need the MO. I know he was shot, but—"

"Two shots with a small-caliber weapon," she said. "Close range, back of the head. No signs of a struggle in the motel room. No eyewitnesses to the slaying, or the assailant. Evidence that a woman had been there with him earlier. Unknown whether said woman was a prostitute or not. His wallet contained less than a hundred bucks and was left untouched. And that's your thirty seconds."

"Wait, what was the evidence?"

"Goodbye, Stevens."

She hung up, but I got what I needed—the MO. Two shots to the back of the head with a small-caliber weapon. The exact same MO as Kyle Foster's murder.

Both men were connected to Conover. Both might have known the details of what he was working on, and therefore both might have been silenced for the same reason. And *silenced* was the operative word; both murders were professional.

Then I read another article, this one on the *New York Times* website, that didn't surprise me at all. Stoddart Prince, Conover's literary agent, died in a fall yesterday from his 11th floor balcony on Central Park West. Authorities deemed it an accident, but I knew better. Someone was cleaning up loose ends. And if that someone thought Svetlana and Kelsey knew anything, they might be next.

What else could I search for? Right. The letter "H" on the jacket.

I googled "private security" and "H." There were 1.3 million results. I scanned the first few pages, but it was all junk. I clapped the computer shut.

My head spun with names and images—Vic Caprisi, Terence Dalton, Kyle Foster, Stoddart Prince, Professor Michael Rosetti (I needed to contact him), James and Peter of the 863 Program, Ginger Best, Jennifer Lin, H-Men,

Conover, a moon conspiracy, and gunshot wounds—and I didn't notice Falcone until he was already in the room snapping his fingers.

"Hey, numb nuts!" He pulled a chair up to the bedside. "I'm here. Now what's this about Triple-X? What kind of trouble are we talking about?"

"She's been kidnapped. She and my client both."

"Come on, this is a joke, right?"

"No, Francis, it's not," I said. "It's life or death. Hers and my client's."

"Holy shit." He stood and went to a window that faced the back alley. "Well, who took her? I'll unload my entire friggen crew on the sonovabitch!"

"If I knew, don't you think I'd already be doing that? I don't know. But you can help me find out."

"Anything for Triple-X, you know that," he said.

"Her name is Svetlana, Falcone. She's not a goddamn Bond girl, all right?"

He turned from the window and nodded. "You're right. How can I help? You said you know who's been operating in my territory. They have something to do with this?"

"I think so. Whoever kidnapped Svetlana and Kelsey—"

"Wait, who's Kelsey?" he asked.

"My client."

"Gotcha. Go ahead."

"I think whoever kidnapped them also hired a Jersey crew to find my client's brother."

"What? Who?" He waved a hand as though to halt his thinking. "Never mind that. Jersey eggs? That's who's been working in my territory?"

"Sure looks that way," I said.

Clarissa came in with a tray bearing coffee service and a plate of Danishes, and set it on the nightstand. With only a bed, nightstand and chair, the room looked like a nun's cell.

"There you go, boys. Enjoy."

"Thanks, Clarissa," I said.

As soon as she had left the room and her footsteps faded down the hallway, Falcone said, "How'd you score her, Stevens? Whatever. Who's the prick whose license plate you got?"

I shook my head. "No way. I don't want him having some kind of accident before I can talk to him. I need to know who hired him, and then I need to know who hired that guy."

"Then what do you need me for?" Falcone asked.

I took a cherry Danish and had a bite. I pointed at the bandage on my leg.

"Backup. Maybe you and Dominick?"

He exhaled out his nose. "And you really think this prick's connected to Trip…Svetlana's kidnapping?"

"I do."

"Then I'm in. And so's Dominick. And six or seven other guys if we need 'em. When?"

"Day after tomorrow."

"Why not today?" He grabbed a Danish.

"Again, bullet hole. I can't move—doctor's orders."

"All right. Call me."

"I'll pick you up. You and Dominick."

He broke off a piece of Danish and gesticulated with it.

"Look, you think you're gonna need to get information out of this guy?"

"I might."

"Maybe I oughta call Sick Vinny," he said.

I felt the anger smoldering inside myself and said, "No, I got this one. By the way, you know I can't pay you."

"Screw money," he said. "I'm doing this for Svetlana. She's the classiest broad I've ever met, and I plan on getting a date out of her someday."

"Ah, Falcone," I said. "'If wishes were horses, beggars would ride.'"

"What the hell is that?"

"Nursery rhyme. Means keep dreaming, pal."

30

That Would Be Scanned

I slept through the rest of that afternoon and night, changed the bandage on my leg, and stayed in bed all through the following day. Dr. Coleman came back that second evening, stitched up the wound and said it was healing well. After feeding me more soup and bagels that evening, Clarissa persuaded me to sleep in her bed, promising she wouldn't start any hanky-panky. Surprisingly, she kept her word.

As we went to sleep she snuggled against me, and truth be told, I needed it. I needed some affection to stave off the feelings of guilt and loss, anger and sadness, that rose up in me whenever I thought of Svetlana and Kelsey. Thinking about them wasn't going to help me rescue them any sooner. I had to focus on finding a trail of clues that led to the employer.

Sometime in the night, I awoke to a man and a woman arguing in hushed tones in the other room. Clarissa's side of the bed was empty, and the woman's voice sounded like hers. At first I thought the man might be her ex-husband, but the voice sounded higher-pitched than his. They argued for a good five minutes. I was about to go see what the problem was when a door slammed out in the hallway and Clarissa came back to bed.

"Is everything okay?" I asked. "Who was that?"

"It was nothing," she said. "Go back to sleep."

"Was it your ex?"

"Please, sweetie." She kissed me. "Forget it."

Some hours later, my eyes flickered open again and I found myself in that unsettling state between sleep and consciousness with the image of a wall safe in my mind. Clarissa's arm was across my chest. A cool breeze wafted in the window from 89th Street, and with it a thought came to me, a thought startling in its clarity:

Something about Jennifer Lin isn't kosher.

That wall safe.

What kind of young woman has a wall safe?

There was also the lack of personal photos. And those uniforms. What was the deal there?

And what was she doing with a sci-fi nerd anyway? Sure, Conover had money, but he wasn't much to look at, and she could do much better. That an attractive young librarian from Maine, a librarian who adored Conover's fiction, would want to have sex with him (*many* times)—that made sense. Same with the other über-fans. But a model with a body and face that could launch a thousand ships? No way.

In the immortal words of Hamlet, *that would be scanned.*

Gingerly I lifted Clarissa's arm and slid out from beneath it. My bad leg was stiff, and a lightning bolt of pain went through it when I stood up. I caught my breath, went to the window. The windowsill was wet, and gusts tossed the trees outside. A *New York Times* delivery truck whisked by, splashing through puddles.

I walked out to the kitchen, chugged a glass of orange juice and checked the time. It was quarter past four. Too early to be showing up at Jennifer Lin's apartment.

But not too early to do some investigating.

After a quick sponge bath and a fresh bandage, I got dressed, left Clarissa a note and hobbled down the street to my car. Two days of solid rest had made the hitch in my step almost bearable.

When I got to my apartment, I checked the cell phone the H-Men had left me. There were no new texts. I had no idea what was happening to Svetlana and Kelsey, and speculating made me sick. I had to block it out.

I carefully spread out the Mylar blanket on the dining room table, and took the H-Men jacket over to my computer. I snapped a decent-quality photo of the embroidered "H" and uploaded it to a reverse image search engine. While the site did its work, I put on a pot of Jamaican Blue Mountain and shaved while it brewed. I was looking pretty ragged, and I always thought better when I was clean-shaven—or at least I imagined so.

I changed into clean clothes, strapped on a new shoulder holster, and plunged my .45 Colt revolver into it. When the coffee was ready I poured a mug and went to the front hall closet. There I pulled out my old compound microscope. I set the microscope on the dining table, plugged in a gooseneck lamp and aimed it at the slide stage. Lastly, with an X-Acto knife and tweezers, I sat down at the table and examined the jacket.

The jacket was noticeably dirty, and I identified a dozen distinct stains on the fabric. I knew at least one of the stains was blood—my blood—but I was hoping one of them would be unique enough to tell me where the H-Men came from.

I pulled out a dozen blank slides and laid them on the Mylar beside the jacket. Using the X-Acto knife, I scraped tiny bits from each jacket stain onto separate slides. I selected the lowest-power objective lens on the microscope, then studied each sample.

The ideal instrument for viewing solid samples is a stereo zoom microscope because it uses reflected light instead of light transmitted through the sample. I had one in my mini-laboratory up in Millbrook, but not here. Still, my compound microscope setup was proving effective. Within an hour and three cups of coffee, I had identified seven of the stains: sea salt crystals, coffee, blood, sand, ketchup, maple syrup and gunshot residue. And I'd only had to check my microscopy reference books once. All of the hours I had spent over the years peering into a microscope were now paying off.

However, I couldn't be certain about the remaining five stains. They were big blotches that had soaked into the fabric. I saw tiny bits of sedimentary rock—mostly shale—but I couldn't identify the substance that had caused the blotchy stains. I picked up the jacket and sniffed. There was the faint odor of WD-40 or gun oil, which made sense because the H-Men would clean and oil their weapons regularly.

Finished, I wrapped up the jacket in the Mylar again, put the bundle in a black garbage bag, and hid it deep in the hall closet. I needed access to real testing equipment. I needed to contact my mentor at the FBI Laboratory,

Lily Wang, and ask for her help. There was more evidence on the jacket than my simple examination could reveal.

From a forensic science standpoint, the one thing of value I'd managed to establish was this: the owner of this jacket had been in a place (possibly recently) where he was exposed to bits of sedimentary rock. A mine or quarry, perhaps?

Were Svetlana and Kelsey being held in a mine?

I dumped out the samples. I put the microscope and everything else away, and shut off the coffeemaker. It was six thirty.

I checked the computer, but the image search had yielded zero matches. Zero. I shut it off.

Out of nervous habit, I checked the H-Men phone again. Still nothing. It occurred to me that if I wasn't looking for Conover anymore, I shouldn't be carrying it. They might be monitoring my movements. I removed the battery and put the phone and battery in a dresser drawer. Then I threw on my trench coat and left.

31

Bathsheba Level of Temptation

It was still too early to drop in on Jennifer Lin, so I got breakfast at City Diner on Broadway. I didn't have much of an appetite, but once again I forced myself to eat. The food was fuel, plain and simple. Fuel to keep me going so I could find Svetlana and Kelsey.

Normally I enjoyed flirting with Lexie and Elaine, two musical theatre actresses who waited tables on the morning shift. I enjoyed hearing about their latest auditions and vicariously living the artist's life through them. But today, I wasn't in the mood. Today, between the kidnapping, the gunshot wound, and the nausea brought on by worry, I was feeling my age. I told them to break a leg at their next auditions and left them my usual avuncular cash tip.

The lights were on in Jennifer's front window when I arrived. I got a parking spot this time, plodded up the brownstone doorstep stairs and swiped my finger down all of the intercom buttons except Jennifer's. In moments the outside door buzzed open, and I continued upstairs. Of course Jennifer had to live on the third floor of a walk-up building. By the time I reached her apartment door, the troll in my leg had awakened, and I was perspiring from the pain. I opened my trench coat. There were faint sounds of exercise equipment coming from inside. I knocked.

There was no answer. I knocked again, harder this time, and heard stomping toward the door. The peephole darkened, and the door flew open.

"What do *you* want? How'd you get up here?"

Jennifer wore a red sports bra and shorts, and sneakers with ankle socks. She was panting and sweating. I hadn't noticed the other day with her in the kimono, but the woman was *ripped*—arms, shoulders, abdominals, legs. Scant and tight, the exercise clothes left absolutely no mysteries about her anatomy, like whether or not she kept certain areas streamlined.

"I need to ask you a few more questions," I said.

"About?"

"They'll just take a minute. You can do your workout while I ask. Fair enough?"

"I should make you leave, but…oh, whatever. Come in if you're coming."

She left the door open and I followed her inside. I watched her as she crossed the living room. Her hair, in a ponytail, swayed along her shoulder blades, and when she mounted the vertical climber, her glutes flexed.

Dear Lord, the things were harder than Brazil nuts.

I leaned against the kitchen divider so I was facing her from the side. It was the ideal vantage point for savoring her bodily profile, but in this case I was watching her face. I wanted to see how she reacted to my questions.

"All right, ask away," she said. "I'll even let you stare at my ass while you do it."

"Nah, I've seen better."

"Like hell you have." She glared at me. "I work out three hours a day."

"Interesting. You know, there's this new psychological condition. It's called narcissism."

"It's not narcissism if it's the truth," she said. "Whatever. Ask your questions and get out of here."

She gripped the handles and began climbing up a cliff side only she could see. With each thrust of her arms and legs, the machine made noises like sawing wood.

"Okay," I said, "do you know who Kyle Foster is?"

"I do now. The other day you said he was Conover's editor."

"Right, I guess I did," I said. "How about Terence Dalton?"

Her rhythm on the vertical climber faltered slightly, but her face showed surprise.

"No. Who's he?"

"Worked for the Department of Energy. He was killed day before yesterday, in the same way as Kyle Foster—shot in the back of the head with a small-caliber gun."

"Gross, but no…I don't know who he is either."

"How about Stoddart Prince?" I asked.

"Conover's agent, right? I've heard of him. Never met him or anything."

"That's good, because he was also killed the other day. Pushed off his balcony and fell eleven floors to his death." I tilted my head to watch her face. "Sure you don't know anything about it?"

"Of course not."

"Not even from the papers?"

As she continued to climb, her face crinkled in disgust, like I'd just told an off-color joke.

"The *papers*?" she said. "Really? What is this, 1940? I don't read newspapers. I don't even have a TV."

"Tsk-tsk—how do you keep up with current events?"

"I don't care about current events," she said.

Just when I thought she was climbing as fast as a person possibly could, her pace on the machine doubled. The woman was in incredible shape. If she were climbing K2, she would have summited in about thirty seconds. I crossed my arms.

"Well, here's a piece of current events you might be interested in," I said. "The other day I met two men who work for the Chinese Ministry of Science and Technology—in their Eight-Six-Three program. Their names are James Zhang and Peter Wu. Ring any bells?"

She slowed to a cool-down pace. When she caught her breath, she eyed me unflinchingly.

"What, you think all Asians know each other? As for this Eight-Six-Three program, I have no idea what you're talking about."

"Last question. Do you own a gun?"

"No, all right? This is ridiculous. And I'm done answering your questions."

She got down from the machine, grabbed a towel from the counter beside me, and proceeded to wipe herself off. Her entire body glistened. A musky, piquant scent, redolent of jasmine incense, surrounded her. She removed her sneakers and socks.

"Hey, where's Kelsey and the other one today?"

"You mean Svetlana," I said. "They couldn't make it."

"I'm glad." She patted her face dry with the towel and handed it to me. "Would you get my neck?"

"Get it yourself."

"Please?"

She turned and lifted her ponytail out of the way. I wiped her neck off.

"There," I said.

No sooner had I finished than Jennifer spun around and shucked her bra over her head. The sudden and unexpected exposure to such beauty made me reel back a step. She couldn't have seemed any more nonchalant. While gazing into my eyes, she dragged the towel out of my dumbfounded fingers and dried her breasts. Then, in one quick motion that displayed remarkable flexibility, she hinged over and peeled off her shorts.

Yes, I thought as she stood back up, *the woman keeps things streamlined. Very streamlined.*

She held the shorts up high by her fingertips, released them, and stared at me as they plummeted to the carpet. Taking my hand, she laid it in the hollow where her lower back and glutes met. It was smoother than polished aluminum; it was the smoothest thing I'd ever touched. I shivered a little.

"So," she said in almost a whisper, "I have nowhere to go today. Nowhere to go and nothing to do. How about you join me in the shower, and we have a little workout of our own? Huh?"

Hot tar filled my throat. I had to swallow to create an airway.

"What is this?" I said. "Five minutes ago, you wanted me out of here."

Jennifer shrugged. "What can I say? You've grown on me." She parted the leaves of my trench coat and cast her eyes down at my groin. "Oh yes, you most definitely have…grown on me."

I kept my eyes on her face. "I think you're lying. I think you're involved in this thing with Conover somehow. And if you know anything about Svetlana and Kelsey, you'd better tell me. I'm not in the mood to be jerked around."

"Well, I think you're nuts," she said. "But I also think you're hot and that I want to be fucked silly." She compressed her breasts against my stomach and laid her palms on my chest. "Can you do that for me—fuck me silly? If you can, I'll be in the shower."

She brushed past me. Her muscles—in her shoulders, her back, and especially her buttocks—rippled and gleamed. Indeed, her callipygian assets rivaled the buttocks of a Greek nymph I'd once seen in the Louvre, and that statue was made of marble. I watched her disappear down the hall. Then I heard the water start and the shower door slide closed.

Despite the Bathsheba level of temptation she presented, I wouldn't be joining her. But I wanted to get a look at some things while she was occupied. I scanned the room for her handbag. It wasn't here. Maybe in the bedroom. I limped as fast as I could down the hall and peeked in the bathroom. The shower hissed, and the room was filling up with steam, but I couldn't see her through the glass. I leaned farther inside, and as I did, a shadow moved across the mirror. I spun around.

Jennifer, nude and stone-faced, raised a pistol from her hip. There was a silencer on the end. Reflexively my hand seized the gun barrel and twisted it. The gun went off with a high-pitched puff, and the toilet tank shattered. I kept twisting the gun away. She yelped. With my free hand I threw a punch at her jaw, but she slipped it and landed a sharp chop against my windpipe. It staggered me. I coughed for air. My grip on her gun hand loosened. I punched her in the breast. She grunted, her face flushed. Then, before I realized what was happening, she had her other hand inside my trench coat on the handle of my revolver. I grabbed that hand as well.

Now she had both guns in her hands and all I could do was keep her from getting a firm hold on either of them. She tried to knee me in the groin, but I turned my hip into it, and when she tried again, I brought the heel of my shoe down on her bare instep. She cried out and threw her head back. This was my chance. With a firm grip on both of her hands, I yanked her toward me and head-butted her on the nose. She yelled again and swore in Chinese. Blood gushed. She began to thrash. She was 110 pounds of solid muscle. I couldn't control her much longer. This became clear when she went up on one leg, yanked on *me* this time, and delivered two swift roundhouse knee strikes to my hip that made my entire skeleton shudder. As she attempted a third knee strike, her gun went off again, this time penetrating the doorjamb inches from her. When her eyes flicked in that direction, I used the temporary distraction to put an end to this. Taking a chance, I let go of her hand holding my gun and gave her a brutal elbow to the jaw. This dazed her. With my other hand I pounded her gun hand against the doorjamb until she grunted. The gun fell. Her eyes sprang open and she lunged at my face with her nails bared. She was bleeding from the nose, huffing through her mouth, glaring at me. *Enough of this shit.* I shoved her away and thrust a forward kick into her stomach that made her backpedal ten feet into the bedroom.

She smashed into the bureau and went still.

Her breasts rose and fell. She wasn't dead. Good. I pulled my gun, grabbed her by the hair, and hauled her to her feet.

"You're opening your safe," I said. "Right now."

Her head was limp. She nodded. I shoved her onto the bed and planted my gun barrel against the back of her head.

"Don't even *think* of pulling some surprise out of there, got me?"

"Yes."

She moved the painting away from the wall, dialed in the combination and opened it.

"Good," I said, stepping off the bed. "Now take everything out—slowly. Then I want you to sit in that chair facing me."

Several folders, passports, ID badges and bundles of currency—dollars, Euros, and yuan—landed on the bed. I tossed her the sapphire kimono.

"Put it on," I said.

She did and sat with her legs crossed. I kept the gun on her while I thumbed through the items. The folders contained dossiers on Kyle Foster, Terence Dalton, Stoddart Prince, and Conover and Kelsey Wright. The photo of Kelsey was taken at a distance with a zoom lens, and seeing it once again reminded me that she and Svetlana were in serious danger, and that the urgency couldn't be greater.

"With all the noise," I said, "I'm sure somebody called the cops, so we don't have much time. If you give me the truth, and fast, I'll leave."

She nodded and wiped some blood off her face with the back of her hand. I tossed the folders aside.

"Foster and Dalton—did you kill them?"

She nodded.

"Did you kill the agent?"

"No."

"Were you supposed to kill the agent?"

"Yes."

"So, someone else got to him first," I said.

"Correct."

"Any idea who?"

"No."

"Are you working with James and Peter from the Eight-Six-Three program?"

"Yes."

"Explain your connection to them."

"I was brought in to clean up," she said. "To eliminate anyone who might know that Conover was providing our government with classified information."

"What kind of classified information? What was Terence Dalton giving Conover?"

"The only material I saw was on James's desk at the UN. It was about moon colonization. That's all I know."

"I don't believe you, but we don't have time to get into it," I said. "Kelsey and Conover—were you supposed to kill them?"

"Conover, no. I was just supposed to monitor him. Kelsey, only if she learned too much."

"Are you behind her and Svetlana's kidnapping?"

"What?" she said. "I don't know about any kidnapping."

"Who else wanted these people dead?"

"I don't know."

"Did you kill Ginger Best?" I asked.

Her brow crinkled up. "Who?"

"Another person shot in the back of the head—your specialty, it seems."

"Do you see a file there about her?"

I stared at the smear of blood on her face, then pointed the gun at the closet doors.

"The uniforms in there. Are they part of your work? How you gain entry to places?"

"Correct," she said.

"Here's the deal, Jennifer. I'd hand you over to the cops, but justice doesn't concern me right now. All I care about is getting Svetlana and Kelsey back. But you're out of business in the U.S., honey. I want you out of Dodge. Got me?"

"By 'out of Dodge,' do you mean out of the country? Back to China?"

"Yes," I said.

"How do I explain this to my superiors? I could be executed for this."

"Like I told your buddies, Peter and James—that's your problem." I holstered my gun. "You're a beautiful young woman, Jennifer. But if I were you, I'd get out of the assassin business. One day it's going to catch up with you." I backed out of the room. "Sorry about your nose."

I stopped at the bathroom to wipe down her gun with a towel, then left the building and drove back to Clarissa's to take a nap. After fighting Jennifer, I needed one.

32

ACME Vending, Inc.

It was one o'clock in the afternoon and raining. I was driving across the Verrazano Bridge in stop-and-go traffic with Falcone and his heavyset partner, Dominick. When I'd picked them up at Falcone's lair in Williamsburg, I told them we were going to see Vic Caprisi, whom I had nicknamed the Linebacker for his ridiculous size. I put him at 6'6" tall, 270 pounds to my 6 feet, 200. According to Falcone, Caprisi was a soldier in the North Jersey Mob, but neither he nor Dominick had any idea of which crew he was with or who his boss was. There had been a lot of changes in the Mob hierarchy across the river. The one thing Falcone knew for certain was that Caprisi lived alone and did not have a Junior League demeanor.

"Look, Stevens," Falcone said, "I've heard of this guy, okay? Not only is he an animal capable of ripping your entire head off, he's a *made* animal, so if you kill him—even by accident—your life is over, you hear me?"

"I get it," I said. "But I spoke on the phone to the guy he was working for, and I need to know if that guy's the one who kidnapped Kelsey and Svetlana. And if not,

I need to know who hired *him*. I'm trying to find a trail that will lead me to the kidnappers, *kapeesh*?"

"*Kapeesh*," Falcone said. "Dom, will 'ya listen to this guy?"

"Stevens," Dominick said from the back seat, "whaddaya need us to do?"

"Find out where he is, and if possible who his boss is, so we can pay them a visit."

Ahead, in the middle of the bridge, a tractor-trailer had broken down in the right lane. I signaled and merged in with traffic to go around it.

"All right," Falcone said. "But I want to be clear—we're doing this for Svetlana, not you. *Kapeesh*?"

"Understood," I said.

They began working the phones. They must have made twenty calls in ten minutes. It was fun to hear them work. Especially Falcone, who seemed to speak in a prearranged code. He was an artist, and gathering information over the phone was his medium.

"Hey, Vin, our friend on the Jets, lives in Nutley," Falcone said. "You know, that brick wall they've got for a linebacker?...Uh-huh, that's him. Yeah, right, fuhgeddaboudit. You know what gym he uses?...Yeah?...And when's he like to work out?...How about the guy that owns the gym? He independent or part of a chain?...Gotcha. And what kind of equipment they got over there?...I see. That free weights or cardio?...Okay, thanks. Bye."

Falcone shut off his phone and turned to Dominick in the back seat.

"What'd you get?"

"Ate breakfast at the diner there in Nutley. Couple of pretty boys and a fat SOB with him."

"That's him," I said.

"What else?" Falcone asked.

"Did some collections at a pool hall and a pizza joint in Newark. Last anybody seen of him today."

"Nice work, Dom," Falcone said.

"What about you?" I said to Falcone.

"He's in a crew working out of Elizabeth. Capo's name is Sammy Carrozza. Been running the crew for a year or so. Nervous type, trying not to screw up. The crew's main front is a vending machine business—get this…ACME Vending, Inc."

"Wile E. Coyote fan?" I said.

Falcone snorted. "Right? Place is in that burned-out factory area over there, close to Newark. This time of day, should be seven or eight guys there. Our linebacker friend usually shows up around two."

"Damn you guys are good," I said.

"Best in the Tri-State Area," Falcone said.

"Maybe best in the *underworld*," I said, "but we both know who the best legitimate guy is."

"Whatever you gotta tell yourself," Falcone said. "All I know is, I can't wait to have a little chat with this Carrozza jerkoff. Everybody knows—New York, New Jersey, Connecticut, you want to find *anything*, you call Falcone, not some friggen Jersey egg."

"Put the address in the GPS and we'll go right now," I said.

At a few minutes before two o'clock, we found the street where ACME Vending was supposedly located. Huge crumbling brick factories and warehouses with burned-out windows lined the street. The lots were overgrown with sumac, and weeds sprouted through cracks in the road.

We approached a less behemoth white brick building with an "ACME Vending, Inc." sign over the entrance. The front had a single steel door and one window. It looked like the kind of place a guy walked into but didn't walk out of. I drove past it.

"What are you doing?" Falcone said. "This is the place."

"We're finding another way in," I said.

I took the next turn and pulled into a vacant lot adjacent to ACME Vending. I shut off the engine, removed the binoculars from the glove compartment and studied the layout. The two lots were separated by thick undergrowth and a leaning chain link fence. There were two loading bay doors open behind the building, and the doorways glowed dimly through the rainy gloom. Three company box trucks were parked to the side of the loading bays, along with a few cars.

"Somebody else is pulling in," Falcone said.

It was Vic Caprisi's gold Cadillac.

"Bingo," I said. "That's his car."

"Lemme see," Falcone said.

I handed him the binoculars. The car parked and the Linebacker got out. He went up the stairs.

"Damn, he's a big sonovabitch," Falcone said. "The Jets could really use this guy."

"With Dominick at nose guard," I said.

"Nah," Dominick said from the back seat. "Only thing I like about football is Monday morning collections."

Falcone put the binoculars away. "So how you want to play this, Stevens?"

"Simple," I said. "Walk in there and ask Carrozza who hired him, or who hired the guy who hired him."

"Not for nothin', but you think it's gonna be that easy?" Falcone said. "Walk in there and this capo's going to spill everything to you?"

"What choice do I have? This is one of the best leads I have to find Svetlana and Kelsey, and I'm doing whatever it takes."

"You sure you're up for this?" Dominick asked. "With your bad leg and all?"

"It hurts, which is why I'm going to avoid a physical altercation as much as possible. I already had a fight with a Chinese woman assassin this morning."

"Yeah, lotsa luck," Falcone said.

"Fine, don't believe me."

I pulled the stun gun out of my coat pocket and tested it. It made a sharp crackling pop. Falcone jumped.

"What the hell, Stevens?"

"Yeah, Christ," Dominick said.

An acrid scent filled the car.

"Stun gun," I said. "For non-lethal persuasion if necessary."

"And if it comes to lethal?"

I opened my coat and showed him the .45 revolver.

"I'm prepared for that contingency as well. Ready?"

Falcone and Dominick checked their gun magazines and slipped the guns back into their belts. The three of us got out and jogged through the rain to the fence.

"I don't like the look of these weeds," Dominick said. "There'd better not be any of that poison shit in here, Stevens."

I glanced at the undergrowth. "You'll be fine."

"How the hell would you know?" Falcone said.

"Because I was an Eagle Scout and Order of the Arrow." I smiled. "I'm also one-sixteenth Native American."

Falcone shook his head. "Always the friggen joker."

Dominick pushed on the leaning fence with his shoe and flattened it so it formed a makeshift bridge across a drainage ditch. Once in the parking lot, we climbed the stairs to the loading bays. It wasn't until I heard men's raucous voices coming from inside that I realized how foolish—possibly reckless—this was. But I had no choice. All I could think about was Svetlana and Kelsey in captivity somewhere, and if I had to risk my life to find them, so be it.

We walked through the loading bay door toward the light inside. A row of vending machines lined the wall.

"Will 'ya look at these prices?" Dominick said.

"Ridiculous," I said.

Farther in, machines stood in two long rows, forming a wide corridor between them. We walked toward the light deep inside the building. The sounds of men joking and laughing grew louder. A pair of men in delivery uniforms smoked in the shadows. We kept going.

We emerged from the vending machine corridor into a wide open space beneath high fluorescent lights. A pair of forklifts sat against one wall. Spread out around the rest of the space were La-Z-Boy chairs, a desk, couches, an HDTV, a pool table, and a poker table.

Six men, including Fatso, the Linebacker and the two models, were playing poker. The one dealing cards, whom I hadn't seen before, was telling a story when we walked in. He had a flattop haircut. By his grating voice and vocabulary, I recognized him as the one I'd heard on Fatso's phone.

"Best blow job I ever got was in a fuckin' rocking chair," he said.

The others chuckled.

"I'm not kiddin'. We're in this dump of a motel, and I'm just rockin' back and forth, sippin' a cold one and she's blowin' me. I've got my beer in one hand, and her long hair in—"

He stopped and stared at the three of us.

"Who the fuck are you? Vic, Vito—you know these fuckin' guys?"

They turned around.

"It's that PI prick," Fatso said. "The one that shot up Vic's car. Other two, I got no idea."

I nodded at the dealer. "Mr. *You*, I presume?"

"What'd you call me?" he said.

"Aren't you Mr. F. You? We spoke on the telephone. I advised restraint in your use of the F-word, remember?"

"Why don't you shut the fuck up and tell me what you want."

"How can I shut up *and* tell you what I want?" I said.

His face got red. "What do you want?"

"Well, for starters, my colleagues and I lost some money in one of your machines." I thumbed over my shoulder. "Two dollars for a Snickers bar? You should be ashamed of yourself."

He slammed the deck of cards down on the table.

"Vic, show these guys out. Bounce 'em on the pavement some while you're at it."

"You got it, Sammy."

His chair screeched on the cement. He wore a navy blue polo shirt that fit him like it was purchased in the boys' department. He stood and walked over.

"Stevens," Falcone said, "I hope you know what you're doing."

"So do I."

Vic was a sequoia with legs. I kept my hands in my coat pockets.

"Hi there," I said.

The man's upper arms made my thighs feel inadequate. He grabbed me by the coat lapels and lifted me off the ground.

"Careful," I said. "It's an antique."

Any other trench coat would have ripped, but this was my grandfather's London Fog, back from when they still made things to last. When my eyes were level with his, Vic held me steady.

"You owe me three grand for my car," he said. "Bodywork, radiator and two new tires."

"Hey, can I ask you something?"

He jutted his chin. "What?"

"Do you shock easily?"

As he processed my query, I pulled out my 500,000-volt stun gun, rammed it into his neck and pressed the button. The air popped. Vic's knees buckled and he collapsed on himself like an imploded Vegas casino. I landed on my feet and drew my gun. Falcone and Dominick already had theirs out. Over at the table, five shocked faces stared in our direction.

"What the fuck is this? You know who you're fuckin' with?"

"Please stop talking," I said. "You're hurting my ears."

Falcone stepped forward. "You're Sammy Carrozza, right?"

"Yeah."

"You know the job you got—the one to find the writer and his sister?"

"Yeah, I know the one."

"Well, I'm Francis Falcone and this is my partner Dominick. That's our territory you were working in."

Carrozza groped behind himself on the poker table and got a pack of cigarettes. He lit one.

"So you've heard of me," Falcone said.

"Sure, you're a made guy, well-connected," Carrozza said. "Look, I didn't mean to step on any toes. What's the big deal?"

"How dense are you? That was my job. You never should've taken it in the first place."

"Look, all I know is, I got orders. But tell me something."

"What?" Falcone said.

"You and Dominick"—he gestured with his cigarette—"what are you two doing with this PI prick?"

"His partner and client were kidnapped," Falcone said. "We're helping him find them."

"Which is where you come in." I walked toward the table with my gun covering them. "You're going to tell us who hired you."

"Hired us?" Carrozza said. "We were given orders."

"From whom?"

"*From whom?* From somewhere high the fuck in the fucking food chain. Who the fuck knows?"

"Well, *somebody* put out the contract," I said. "Who was it?"

Carrozza picked up the cards and shuffled them. "I might know about that."

"Well?" I said.

"We only got paid half for the job. Now, if I was to get the second half promised me, I might be willing to share what I know."

"How much?"

"Twenty-five grand."

I slipped my free hand in my coat pocket then patted my torso, as if looking for the money.

"Nope, don't have it on me. But if your information is solid and it helps me find my partner and client, I'll pay it."

"After Carrozza here gives me a taste," Falcone said. "Since it should have been my job to begin with."

"All right," Carrozza said. "But I tell you when I see the money."

"No," I said. "You tell us now, and you'll have to trust me for the money."

He looked at Falcone.

"He's good for it," Falcone said.

Carrozza shuffled the cards one more time and put them down.

"Alls I know is, my boss kept saying the guy was a Mr. Big type from the Midwest. Called him 'Mr. H.' a few times."

"The Midwest?" I said. "Big area. Nothing more specific?"

"No, the Midwest. That's it. That's what I got. Now when can I expect my twenty-five?"

"That's pretty lame information for twenty-five grand, but I'll pay it," I said. "I'll have it here in a couple of days."

Carrozza shrugged. "That's okay, 'cause the vig starts the second you walk out of here anyway."

"Screw you the vig starts," Falcone said. "And I'll be taking my taste out of the twenty-five, so don't blame Stevens here when the envelope's light."

"Two days then, Stevens," Carrozza said. "But don't make us come looking for you."

"Relax, I keep my word."

I backed away from them, and when I reached Vic's inert body, I made a production of stepping over it.

"By the way, I'm not sure how long the effects of a stun gun last." I holstered my revolver. "But you should probably get him some electrolytes or something."

"Get the fuck outta here."

33

Return to Zanclus

Later that afternoon, at rush hour, I stood at the windows in my office. Rain raked the glass. Across the street in Madison Square Park, the trees that recently had been so full and vibrant were now stripped of their leaves, and the entire park was rainswept and dreary. Sodden piles of leaves covered the sidewalks while a river of umbrellas flowed up and down Fifth Avenue in the waning daylight.

The scene was a far cry from the clear and crisp morning a week ago when Kelsey came in and I took her case. Not only was the weather now rotten, but she and Svetlana had been kidnapped. I shook my head to force it out of my mind.

My bad leg was throbbing from the day's activity. I lay on the couch with my leg propped up with pillows, and tried to think things through.

At this point, I had to assume Conover was dead or he had left the country. Therefore, any information I gathered was for one purpose: locating Svetlana and Kelsey. The problem was, the few clues I had were feeble at best. I had a tactical jacket with several mysterious stains and traces of shale on it. I had the dubious word of a Mob capo—that the person who hired his crew was a "Mr. Big type," nicknamed "Mr. H.," from the Midwest. Meanwhile, for all I knew, "Mr. H." was a Chicago heroin dealer. Finally, I knew that Jennifer Lin was behind the murders of Foster and Dalton, and that the Chinese government had been getting classified documents from Conover.

Were there leads I hadn't followed up on yet? Well, I had Terence Dalton's widow to interview, if I could. She might know more about the classified documents, which might tell me who was so keen to shut up Conover. I had a hunch that whoever was trying to shut up Conover was also behind Svetlana and Kelsey's kidnapping.

I needed to put the tactical jacket in Lily Wang's hands so she could perform some conclusive analytical tests. It was a long shot, but those traces of shale might be unique enough to pinpoint where the owner of the jacket had been.

And I had that sheet of paper about the downsides of nuclear fission. I'd been over it and over it, and it made no mention of the moon. I needed to show it to Professor Rosetti—the astrophysicist and lunar scientist Conover often acknowledged in his books, most recently in *Return to Zanclus*.

Lily was at work and Mrs. Dalton wasn't talking, but I could at least call Professor Rosetti. The problem was, the office phone wasn't hooked up yet. I didn't want to use my regular smart phone, and I'd lost the disposable cell. I also didn't have the professor's contact information, and the office was still without WiFi. I had to go out.

I grabbed my laptop and held onto it under my trench coat. Then I put on a Sam Spade fedora I kept on the hat rack for days like this—rainy days when I didn't want my hands encumbered by an umbrella—and went down in the elevator.

Even though it was in the opposite direction, I strolled through the park in the rain before circling back to Broadway. There I bought and activated a new disposable cell phone, then continued to the Starbucks at Broadway and 26th. From the street the windows were steamed up like a Parisian cafe's in the cold, and inside the place was full with commuters grabbing drinks on their way home. I got a *large* latte (I refused to use their pretentious names for drink sizes), found an empty table and pulled out the laptop.

Professor Rosetti's contact information was easy to find, but when I called his office, his voicemail said he would be in Baltimore all week for the International Congress of Astrophysicists. I checked their website. Professor Rosetti was one of the speakers, and he was scheduled to speak at eleven o'clock tomorrow morning.

I sat up from the computer and sipped my latte. The place was loud with hissing steam and customers placing orders. The cacophony mirrored my mental state: I had several leads vying for my attention, all while two words—*"Find them!"*—played over and over in my mind. If I was ever going to find them, I had to be able to follow up on every lead as soon as possible. Right now I needed to be in Baltimore, Bethesda, and Washington, D.C., and if the tip about a "Mr. H." in the Midwest was true, I would need to be able to cover thousands of miles at the drop of a hat.

And wherever the trail led me, I needed to bring a gun, possibly several—which isn't possible when you fly commercial. Then, if I got a line on Svetlana and Kelsey's whereabouts, I had to be able to follow it immediately.

All of this pointed to one conclusion: I needed a private jet. I needed a private jet and twenty-five thousand dollars in cash, and there was only one person—a grateful former client—that I could ask: Vivian Vaillancourt.

Return to Zanclus indeed.

34

The Macallan 1939

I hadn't driven my nemesis, the Long Island Expressway, at rush hour in many months, and I'd forgotten what an arduous journey it can be—especially in a rainstorm. Between the snarled traffic and the driving rain, the trip from Manhattan to Sands Point took twice as long as usual, so I didn't reach Vivian's gate with the giant "V" crest until eight thirty. It was dark, the gate was closed, and I had to roll down my window in the cold rain and stare into a camera before the gate deigned to open.

As I crept up the curving, tree-lined drive, the wind stripped swarms of leaves from the trees. Clumps of them stuck to the windshield and side windows. The foul and ominous weather made me think about Svetlana and Kelsey. I prayed they were okay. I also prayed that Vivian Vaillancourt would be sympathetic to my plight and loan me the resources I needed to find them. When I emerged from the gauntlet of trees, however, and saw her mansion looming ahead in the storm, my confidence that she would help me began to wane.

I parked under the porte-cochère, but the wind was so strong that the rain blew in sideways beneath the overhang. I hobbled to the front door and rang. Vivian's latest houseboy, a bronzed man of indiscriminate age, let me in. He took my wet trench coat and hat and brought me into a massive great room I hadn't seen the last time I was here, over a year ago, during the case of who killed Vivian's twin brother.

At the far end of the darkened room, a fireplace large enough to roast a steer crackled and sputtered. Vivian Vaillancourt sat in an Eames chair with her feet up on a matching ottoman, and an omnipresent highball in her hand. She was still trim and had pewter hair, but the darkness and the firelight softened her imperious features, making her look ten years younger than her actual 60-something.

"Ah, Dakota Stevens," she said, gesturing with her glass. "The prodigal detective returns. And injured, I see. Sit down, put your feet up, have a drink with me."

I sat on the sofa across from her and slid an ottoman under my bad leg. We were ten feet from the fireplace. The heat radiated from it like a steel smelter.

"Thank you, Vivian, but I don't drink while I'm on a case."

"On the phone you said you were coming out to ask for a favor. The least you can do is have a libation or two with your former client."

Her jaw was set. If I were to say no, I feared she would send me packing.

"All right, *one*," I said. "Do you have any really good single-malt?"

"Is a Macallan 1939 good enough for you?"

I coughed. "Jesus, isn't that like ten thousand dollars a bottle?"

"Yes, but I keep a few on hand for emergencies." Vivian winked, picked up a cell phone and dialed a number. "A new experiment I'm trying instead of yelling." She sipped her drink and spoke into the phone. "Yes, John. Bring in the Macallan 1939 and two glasses." She hung up. "On its way."

"I can't wait," I said.

She regarded the fire. She wore jodhpurs and shiny brown riding boots that shone in the firelight. It was the same outfit she wore the summer day I first met her. She was shooting skeet at the time.

"Still shooting skeet?" I asked.

"Every day, weather allowing. Couldn't today obviously."

"Obviously."

John arrived with the bottle of scotch and two glasses. He placed them on the coffee table in front of me and nodded to Vivian.

"Will there be anything else?"

"A corned beef sandwich," Vivian said. "Mr. Stevens, a corned beef sandwich?"

"No, thanks."

As I poured the Macallan, I calculated the cost per shot and concluded that this was by far the most expensive drink I would ever have—a $500 glass of Scotch whisky.

"Bring two sandwiches, John."

"Yes, Vivian."

He left the room. Vivian tilted her glass in my direction.

"You need to keep up your strength, Mr. Stevens. You're looking less robust than I recall."

Her formality—calling me "Mr. Stevens" over and over—was disconcerting.

I took a sip of the scotch. There was no harsh bite to the liquor whatsoever. It was so peaty and smooth, it was as if I were drinking not liquid but smoky time in a bottle.

"How's the Macallan?" Vivian asked.

"Transcendent."

I took a deeper sip this time. The liquor was entrancing. I almost forgot why I'd come here.

I wasn't sure how to segue into asking for what I needed. Her contented posture said she had no intention of going anywhere. Despite the urgency of the situation, I decided to take my time, and was about to discuss an activity precious to her—sailing—when she initiated the conversation.

"So, tell me, Mr. Stevens—how is the detecting business?"

"Honestly?"

"Of course."

"Not great." I pointed at my bulging pant leg.

"I see," she said. "What is it?"

"Gunshot wound," I said.

"Goodness. But I can't say I'm surprised. You *are* a bit quick to resort to violence, aren't you?"

"Maybe. But this time it was absolutely necessary."

"The case you're working on now," she said, "can you tell me about it?"

"Not really. When you were my client, you wouldn't have liked me telling other people about *your* case."

"As I recall, when I was your client, you told me very little about my case."

I drank some more scotch. "I was remiss in reporting to you. Sorry. It's a shortcoming of mine, one I'm working on."

John returned with pair of sandwiches on a tray. He handed me a plate with a tower of corned beef on rye, a dill pickle spear and a small ramekin of mustard. The sandwich was so high, it was in danger of tipping over at any moment. John put the tray with the second sandwich on Vivian's lap. He left the room.

"Eat, Mr. Stevens," she said.

I wondered if Svetlana and Kelsey had eaten. I wondered if they might be tied up and blindfolded in a room someplace. The fire popped, snapping me back to reality. I had to stop. I had to stop thinking about them before my imagination ran away with me.

"Thanks," I said.

The next half hour dragged like I was stuffing envelopes. We sipped our drinks, ate our sandwiches, said nothing. The fire crackled. A log settled. Vivian spread mustard on her sandwich, I spread mustard on mine. As we continued to eat and the wind howled against the windows, I realized something: Vivian was a lonely woman who wanted company. A poor little rich girl. But I refused to feel sorry for her, nor was I going to let this realization divert me from my purpose. When I finished half of the sandwich, I laid the plate on the coffee table.

"Well, Vivian, I should get to why I'm here."

"Are you in a rush?"

"As a matter of fact, yes."

"Is it a matter of life and death?" She put her tray on the floor but retained her highball glass.

"Yes."

"And does it involve the case you're working on?"

"It does," I said.

"Which you can't tell me about."

"Right."

She clenched her jaw. "What do you need? Money, I presume."

"Yes, that's part of it."

"How much?"

"Thirty thousand," I said. "Cash."

"Well, I have to say, Dakota Stevens—I'm disappointed in you. You burned through your reward fast enough."

"I haven't *burned through* anything. I just don't have time to deal with banks right now."

She stared at the fire. "You said that was part of your request. What is the other part?"

"You have a private jet, right?"

"I do. A Challenger 350. I keep it at Farmingdale. Why?"

"I need to borrow it."

"Borrow it?" she said.

"Charter it, I mean. Don't worry, I wouldn't be flying it."

She crossed her boots. "Pour me some of the Macallan."

I did and handed it to her. She closed one eye and swirled the liquor in the glass. I felt my temper rising because not only did I sense a "no" coming on, but a lecture as well.

"I am not in the habit of loaning my private jet," she said. "Especially when I don't know what it will be used for. It would be different if—"

I pounded on the armrest. "Goddamn it, Vivian, Svetlana and my client have been kidnapped!"

My reaction shocked both of us. She stopped herself in mid-sip and put down her glass. I poured myself a second Macallan. Staring straight at her, I downed the entire $500 drink in one swallow, then poured myself a third, took a $250 slug of it, and stared at my leg. Vivian studied me intently.

"Doesn't your former employer handle kidnappings?" she asked.

"Yes, but I can't inform them. For a couple of reasons I'm not going to get into."

"I'm not saying no," she said, "but tell me—why can't you fly commercial?"

"Because if I get another lead, I need to be able to follow up on it immediately," I said. "Because this gunshot wound slows me down. And because I need to bring a gun. Several actually."

"I see."

"I'll tell you right now, the guns won't be legal," I said. "If I were caught with them on your plane, you could get into trouble."

Vivian scoffed. "That is what lawyers are for, my dear."

She sipped her drink. I continued.

"The people I'm pursuing can't know I'm coming. If the plane is in your name, they'll have no way of tracking me. And I've got to be honest with you—I don't know how long this is going to take. It could be a couple of days, or it could be weeks."

Vivian nodded. "When would you need to leave?"

"Tomorrow morning. Before dawn if possible."

She put down her drink and picked up her phone. Five seconds later, she was making arrangements with someone named Brian. She cupped the mouthpiece.

"Where are you going first?"

"Washington, D.C.," I said.

"Washington, D.C.," she said into the phone. "And from there you should be prepared to fly anywhere at a moment's notice." She paused. "Correct. And one other thing...only I should be listed on the manifest. A Mr. Dakota Stevens will be flying in my stead, but as far as any official records are concerned, *I'm* the passenger. Is that clear? Excellent. Goodbye then." She hung up and looked at me. "There you go—one private jet, at your service. Now the cash."

She called John and told him to bring thirty thousand dollars from the safe.

When she hung up, I said, "Vivian, I can't thank you enough for this."

She poured more Macallan in both of our glasses and raised hers.

"Here's to your finding them, Dakota. Safe and sound."

"I'll drink to that."

35

A Lily and an Iris

At seven thirty the next morning, I was at my mentor Lily Wang's house in the suburbs outside of D.C. Actually, I was in her leaf-blanketed backyard, stealing up to the deck off her kitchen.

Inside, she was seated at a kitchen island in a blouse and slacks. She sipped from a mug and read the *Washington Post*. I rapped on the sliding glass door. I was holding the garbage bag containing the black tactical jacket, and it was only after I'd knocked that I realized I looked like a low-end burglar. When she saw me, she gave a start and almost fell off her barstool. I could hear her through the glass.

"Dakota? What are you doing here?" She got up and opened the door. "Dakota, I have a front door, you know. Come in." She closed the door behind me. "Coffee? It'll have to be fast. I'm leaving for work in a few minutes."

"No thanks, Lily."

She laid a hand on my arm and looked up at me.

"Are you okay, dear? You look awful."

"Haven't been sleeping. I need your help, Lily. More than ever."

"Help with what's in the bag?" she said.

"Exactly."

"What's going on?"

"Lily, you can't breathe a word of this to *anyone*. The lives of two people are on the line."

"Tell me."

I gave her an abridged account of the case, finishing with my gunshot wound and Svetlana and Kelsey's kidnapping. She looked at me like I'd spoken to her in Russian.

"You haven't informed the Bureau of this?"

"No."

"Why not?" she asked.

"Because I was warned by her kidnappers not to. Which is why I snuck into your backyard from the development up the hill. Also, my partner's father is a boss in the Ukrainian Mob, and he's already made it clear that if anything ever happened to her, he'd hold me responsible."

"Mmm, and I can imagine what that means." She rinsed out her mug and put it in the dishwasher. "So what's in the bag?"

I placed it on the counter.

"It's a jacket worn by one of the kidnappers. There are a number of stains on it, including some that I think are petroleum-based with traces of shale in them."

"And you know this how?"

"A cursory examination with a microscope."

"I see," she said. "And ideally, from the stains on this jacket you would like to figure out where its owner has been."

"Right."

"Because you're hoping one of those places is where your partner and client are being held."

"Yes," I said. "Can you do it for me?"

"How soon do you need it?"

"Tonight."

"Hmm." She considered the bag with a hand on her cheek. "This could be tricky. I have a backlog of tests right now."

"There's no one else I can ask, Lily."

She nodded. "I should be able to swing it. Worst case, I'll have to do it after-hours."

"Thank you. And remember, it can't be logged into evidence anywhere, okay?"

"I'll do it, Dakota," she said. "But there's something I want you to do for me."

"Anything. Name it."

"Get some rest. I've never seen you so haggard."

"I'll rest once I've found them," I said. "Where should we meet later? Here? Or would you like me to take you to dinner?"

"No, I think we should keep this more on the Q-T, don't you?"

"You're right."

"Tell you what," she said. "Do you know where the Takoma Park library is?"

"Takoma Park?"

She smiled. "I stop there sometimes on my way home. Meet me in the mysteries section."

"How Jake Gittes of you."

"Who?"

"The detective in *Chinatown*," I said. "Forget it. When tonight?"

"I'll call you later with a time. Give me your number."

I did, and once she'd entered it into her phone, I took her hand and squeezed it.

"Thank you, Lily."

She shook her head. "Don't thank me yet. I haven't seen the evidence. I might not be able to do anything for you."

"Don't sell yourself short, Lily," I said. "We both know you're the best."

From Lily's house it was a short drive to Iris Dalton's place in Bethesda. She lived in a luxury apartment high-rise, one of those built in the 1980s with boutiques and services in the basement. One of the services was a coffee shop, and I killed time eating breakfast before going upstairs to the apartment lobby.

Given Mrs. Dalton's reaction on the phone the other day, when the doorman called her and announced me, I expected to be turned away. Instead I was ushered upstairs to the 17th floor.

Iris Dalton answered the door wearing a bathrobe and slippers. It was difficult to tell her age (mid-50s maybe?) because her hair was unkempt and she wasn't wearing any makeup. Her eyes and nose were red, and she clutched a handkerchief in her hand.

"Mr. Stevens?"

"Yes."

"Come in."

She led me into the living room and waved at a sofa. I sat down.

"Coffee? Tea? Sparkling water?" she asked.

"No, thank you," I said.

"I looked you up online after you called. I know you're legitimate, Mr. Stevens, but could you please show me some identification?"

"Sure." I produced my private investigator's license. "I'm also a former FBI agent."

"So I read. Thank you. Now, suppose you tell me what you know about my Terence's death."

"Excuse me?" I said.

"On the phone you said you were investigating a case related to Terence's death."

"Yes."

"So I assume you have leads on his killer."

I felt bad about lying to her, but my priority was getting information that would help me find Svetlana and Kelsey, not giving her information about Terence's killer. Her husband was dead, and as tragic as that was, I couldn't afford to get sidetracked by revealing what I knew about Jennifer Lin.

"I'm sorry if I gave you that impression," I said. "At present I have no leads. But I was hoping you might know something that would help me."

She took a pack of cigarettes and lighter out of her bathrobe pocket and lit one.

"Like what?" she said. "What could I possibly know that would help you find his killer?"

"Do you know if your husband and Conover Wright, the science fiction novelist, were friendly?"

"Yes, Terence was a big fan. He has all of Mr. Wright's books in the other room."

"Do you know where and how they met?" I asked.

She took a drag on the cigarette and blew it out toward the ceiling.

"It was a sci-fi convention in Philadelphia a year or so ago."

"And after this convention, do you know whether Conover and your husband stayed in touch?"

"Yes, I'm fairly certain they did," she said.

"Do you know what they talked or corresponded about?"

"No, but I have my theories."

"Such as…?"

"Classified reports." She flicked an ash into an ashtray. "I think Terence was providing Mr. Wright with classified reports to aid him in book research. Or at least that's probably how he rationalized it to himself."

"What gave you this idea?"

"Before he was killed, the FBI was questioning him about a certain report."

"Did the FBI question you?" I asked.

"No."

"This report—do you know what it was about?"

"When I asked him, Terence told me two things," she said. "First, he said it was a joint report between the DOE and NASA."

"NASA? You're sure?"

"Yes."

"And the second thing?"

"He said he did what he did because he wanted the truth to get out. That's all he told me."

"And you don't know any of the report's specifics?" I said. "Like whether it has to do with the moon?"

"No. But whatever it was, the FBI said it was a threat to national security. So I want to know—who killed my Terence? I think the FBI did it because he knew too much."

"The FBI did *not* kill your husband," I said. "If he hadn't been killed, they might have prosecuted him, but the FBI isn't in the assassination business."

"How do you know?"

"Because I'm a former Special Agent, and I'm telling you the FBI was not involved."

She stared at me.

"I'm going to choose to trust you on that."

36

The Cliffs Notes Version

From Bethesda, I continued my information-gathering odyssey north to the Mount Washington Conference Center outside of Baltimore. A network of brick buildings on a sprawling green campus, the place looked like a celebrity detox resort.

The lobby was airy and bright, and stationed right in the center, at the registration table, was a Rubenesque young woman in a navy blue dress. She wore glasses and a name tag that read, "Mindy." Attendee badges covered the table. There were no photos on the badges.

"Good morning, Mindy." I pointed at a badge. "I'm Professor Scott Hilkert, University of Chicago."

"A pleasure to meet you, Professor."

"Please excuse my appearance. I just flew in."

"It's no problem, Professor, but could you show me some—"

"You know, I was thinking about Newton's gravitational constant during the flight." I picked up Dr. Hilkert's badge and pinned it on. "We can quantify gravity, but we still don't know precisely what it is. We still don't know exactly what causes two objects to be attracted to each other." I stared at her. "You have such lovely eyes, Mindy. Are they violet?"

"Yes, a few people have described them that way. Thank you."

"You have a good day, my dear."

"Enjoy the conference, Professor."

"I shall."

I found Professor Rosetti in a small auditorium. He was alone, writing equations on a whiteboard down at the front. Equations that, despite my bachelor's degree in chemistry, I didn't understand. It was hard to tell how old he was because he had a youthful face and a full head of jet black hair. I guessed he was in his late forties. I waited until I reached the bottom of the stairs before interrupting him.

"Professor Rosetti?"

"Yes?"

"I'm Dakota Stevens, a private investigator from New York, and I could really use your help."

"Are you an attendee of the conference?" he asked.

"Oh, this?" I said, touching the badge. "No, I used this to get in. Let me explain why I'm here."

"Fine, but I hope you won't mind if I multitask," he said. "My lecture starts soon. How can I help you?"

"Well, my case involves the disappearance of Conover Wright, the science fiction writer. You're mentioned in the acknowledgments in several of his books."

"Yes, Conover, of course," he said. "He's missing?"

"He is. When was the last time you saw him or had contact with him?"

"I saw him two months ago. We had lunch in Manhattan, at the Penn Club."

"Have you had any communication with him since?"

"No, nothing."

"When you saw him," I said, "did he mention what he was working on?"

"He said he couldn't discuss it, but that I would be interested. I expected to hear from him again when he wanted my help."

"I'd like you to take a look at something."

I pulled out the sheet of paper with the passage about nuclear fission. He read it quickly and handed it back.

"An intermediate discussion on the drawbacks of nuclear fission," he said. "I fail to see its significance."

"It's the only clue I have about what Conover might have been working on. Based on this, can you think of what his book might be about?"

"Based strictly on this, no. But if I had to guess, I would say some aspect of his book discusses either the drawbacks of nuclear fission or the benefits of nuclear fusion."

"And what if I told you he was allegedly writing about a conspiracy involving the moon?"

Rosetti stopped writing on the board and sat on a stool behind the lectern with his chin in his hand.

"I don't know about any conspiracy involving the moon, but nuclear fusion and the moon do have something in common, and that's helium-3."

"Helium-3?"

"An isotope of helium missing one neutron." He squinted at me. "I should probably start with the basics."

"Please do," I said.

"This will be extremely simplified, but here goes. There are two types of nuclear reactions: fission and fusion. Fission splits matter, and fusion combines it. Fission is the process used in our nuclear reactor plants. The main problem with fission is that it produces nuclear waste. On the other hand, a fusion reaction with helium-3 produces a lot more energy with no nuclear waste. And here's the best part: helium-3 fusion produces a *direct* conversion to electricity, without the need for an intervening steam conversion process. It involves the fusion plasma and the various forms of radiation emitted, but you don't need to know any of that. The bottom line is, with steam conversion methods over sixty percent of the energy is *lost* in the conversion process. Electricity from helium-3 is nearly twice as efficient."

He jumped off the stool and started drawing molecules on the whiteboard.

"You see, when helium-3 is combined with deuterium—also known as 'heavy hydrogen'—it produces massive quantities of energy. It also produces two safe byproducts: a hydrogen nucleus and a common helium molecule. No radioactive byproducts. No neutrons are emitted, and—"

"I don't mean to seem impatient, Professor, but what does any of this have to do with the moon?"

"Okay, that's where it gets a bit more involved," Rosetti said. "Helium-3 has been produced by our sun for billions of years, and it gets carried in the solar winds. The thing is, our magnetic field repels it, so it's extremely rare on Earth.

"However…the moon's magnetic field is negligible, so helium-3 gets imbedded in the lunar regolith, or soil. Helium-3 could be extracted from the soil, brought back to Earth, and used in fusion reactors to produce energy. As I said a moment ago, it's much more efficient than fossil fuels, and it doesn't produce radioactive waste like fission reactors do. It also doesn't produce carbon dioxide, which is contributing to the greenhouse effect and climate change."

"So, if you were in the fission reactor or fossil fuels industries," I said, "I take it you wouldn't like the notion of helium-3 at all."

"No, I would be scared to death of it. Besides being clean and efficient, it's abundant. It's been estimated there are five million tons of helium-3 on the moon. That would be enough to meet the entire world's energy needs for the next ten thousand years."

"Incredible."

"It's also theorized that helium-3 will make interstellar travel possible someday."

"So it would change a lot of things," I said.

"Yes. The downside, of course, is its impracticality." The professor sat down again. "It would require tremendous investment to establish a mining colony, and the mining of helium-3 would consume a lot of energy itself. Then there are the costs of transporting it back to Earth and building reactors."

He reached in his bag, removed a bottle of water and drank some.

"But...if those obstacles could be overcome, think of it...clean energy for ten thousand years."

Attendees trickled into the hall and sat down. Professor Rosetti stood and erased the helium-3 diagram he'd drawn.

"I'm sorry I don't have more time. Feel free to contact me again if you have further questions."

"I may do that, Professor. Thank you."

When I got back in the car, I thought about Professor Rosetti's mini-lecture on helium-3, and the fog in my head dissipated. My investigative instincts told me I had just found the key to this case. Instead of overthinking it, though, I wanted to do something mindless for a while to allow my subconscious to process everything I'd learned. I had to wait for Lily to call with a meeting time anyway, so I spent the afternoon at the National Zoo.

She called while I was at the Giant Panda exhibit, watching a panda ingest bamboo. I was glad for the interruption. "Five thirty," she said, and hung up. It was already four thirty. I left the zoo and headed for Takoma Park.

The mysteries section in the Takoma Park Library resided in the back of the building. There were no patrons around. I saw Raymond Chandler's *The Little Sister* on the shelf. I thought of Kelsey. I opened to a random page and read: *"She smelled the way the Taj Mahal looked by moonlight."* This made me think of Svetlana. I immediately shut the book and shoved it back on the shelf. Lily arrived. She was poker-faced as she handed me the garbage bag.

"Well?" I said softly.

"Is it good? Tell me."

"Okay," she said. "Besides examining the stains with a stereomicroscope, I snipped out swatches and subjected them to GC-MS analysis. I imagine you've forgotten how gas chromatography–mass spectroscopy works."

"Give me a break, Lily. I've been out of the lab for a long time, but I know enough. I know it breaks down samples into ions and then analyzes the spectrum."

"Umm, something like that."

I glanced over my shoulder. We were alone.

"All right, what about the stains?"

"Most of them don't tell us where the jacket has been. Those stains include—"

"Yes, I know—sea salt crystals, coffee, blood, sand, ketchup, maple syrup and gunshot residue."

"Right," she said. "But your query was really about the other stains, right? The ones you thought were petroleum-based."

"Yes, but now I'm sure they're petroleum-based."

"How do you know this?"

"Intuition," I said. "Based on something I heard today."

"Well, your intuition is correct. The stains are from crude oil."

"Wait a minute—crude oil's black. Those stains are pretty light."

"Not all crude is black," Lily said. "You see, my young apprentice, crude oil varies in weight and color. Some has the consistency of gasoline, which is what we've got here."

"Does this help us pinpoint where the jacket has been?" I asked.

"It does," she said. "But the results from the analysis are even more telling."

"Such as…?"

"The oil stains also contained traces of dozens of toxic chemicals, including benzene, toluene, naphthalene, methanol, ethylene glycol and hydrochloric acid. These chemicals are used in hydraulic fracturing. Are you familiar with fracking?"

"The basics. It's where gas and oil companies fracture rock—generally shale—with water, sand and chemicals to release fossil fuels."

"That would be the Cliffs Notes version," she said, "but—"

I motioned for Lily to stop talking. A woman wandered by at the end of the aisle. Once she had circled back to the front of the library, I nodded to Lily.

"What were the other results?" I asked.

"Well, the type of shale in the stains was telling. I had one of our senior forensic geologists take a look."

"Lily, I asked you—"

"Don't worry, he's an old friend and I trust him," she said. "Besides, I needed his expertise. According to him, the samples contained fragments of black, organic-rich shale, along with siltstone and sandstone. This geology is consistent with the Bakken Formation."

Deep in my gut, I felt the click of several disparate pieces fitting together. I leaned against the stack.

"Hold it—that's the big oil field in North Dakota, right?"

"Yes," she said. "It's also natural gas, and some of it extends to Montana and Saskatchewan."

For a moment I was euphoric and didn't feel the pain in my leg at all.

"Excellent," I said. "Did any other results point to the Bakken Formation?"

"Yes, the low flash point of this particular crude. In other words—"

"It's explosive."

"Exactly," she said. "Of course, crude oil is flammable, but light, *explosive* crude is fairly rare. There have been several railway tanker explosions in North Dakota and Montana because the crude coming out of the ground there is so explosive. It seems the Bureau has assisted the NTSB with the lab work on their investigations, so we have a lot of data on this particular crude."

"This is fantastic, Lily," I said. "You have no idea. Two of my suspects are from Bismarck. Now I finally have a solid lead to follow."

"Slow down, Dakota." She touched my forearm. "Don't get your hopes up, okay? The Bakken Formation is huge—we're talking over twenty-five thousand square miles—with dozens of companies that own dozens of fracking facilities. Dozens of them. The best we can say is that the jacket was recently in the Bakken Formation somewhere. It's impossible to be more specific."

"Lily, this is already a lot more than what I had. I can't tell you how grateful I am. How can I repay you?"

"Find your partner and your client, and then, if you were so inclined, a bouquet of roses might be nice."

"Done," I said.

37

Autumn in Bismarck

Early the next morning, I flew back to New York to make preparations. I brought the twenty-five thousand to Falcone, who agreed to deliver it to Carrozza. I stopped by the office and rifled through boxes until I found my audio surveillance kit, portable GPS, and DSLR camera. I called Johnny Quinn and told him he could pick up his truck at my garage. Then, not knowing how long I would be gone, I went back to my apartment and packed enough clothes and cold weather gear to last me two weeks. I put the bags in the car, along with my guns and ammunition, and returned to Clarissa's, where she changed my bandage, packed up a first aid kit that included my antibiotics, and made lunch. Afterwards, she walked me out to the elevator foyer and gave me a long kiss.

I pressed the button for the elevator. "Thanks, beautiful—for everything."

"Anytime." She stroked my cheek.

"You're sure? Because the other night I got the impression you're seeing another guy. Are you?"

"Yes. Why, you thought we were exclusive?"

"Yeah, I did," I said. "I mean, you acted like—"

"Oh, come on, Dakota." She put her hands on her hips. "You're never around. You make plans and cancel them with no notice, you don't answer my texts for days, and then you show up in the middle of the night with a friggen *gunshot wound.* You are not what any woman would consider stable boyfriend material."

"I do my best. So if I'm not your boyfriend, what am I?"

"You want to know what you are, Dakota?" she said. "You're exciting. You're funny, strong, and—well…I'll just say it—you're gifted in bed. Listen…we met when I was married to David, and we had a good time together, right? What's wrong with us continuing that way?"

"Hold it…are you *marrying* this other guy?"

"As a matter of fact—"

"Do you love him?" I asked.

"He's an older man, a corporate lawyer." She crossed her arms. "I have to be practical."

"How much older?"

She didn't answer.

"He's fifty-one," she finally said.

"Pardon me?"

"Hey, don't judge. He has two adult children, so he knows about raising kids. I have Lainey to think about. Besides, do you have any idea how expensive this building is?" She looked around and lowered her voice. "I had to get rid of my *live-in*, Dakota. David's alimony isn't cutting it."

I'd been in this building at least two dozen times and never noticed how opulent it was. A giant gold-leafed mirror hung across from the elevator. A marble-topped table held a tall vase overflowing with calla lilies. The cream carpet was deep enough to lose coins in. At that moment, I knew Clarissa could never give up this lifestyle, and that she could never be without a man to take care of her. The elevator dinged. I picked up my duffel.

"Clarissa, I care about you and I want you to be happy..."

"But?"

I stepped into the elevator. "But being a lonely woman's plaything isn't enough for me anymore."

"Wait." Her eyes got teary. "So...this is goodbye?"

"I think it has to be. Take care of yourself, sweetheart."

I pushed the button for the lobby.

At the airport, I parked in a sequestered lot for private jet passengers, grabbed my bags and guns, and boarded the plane from the tarmac. It was a cold, overcast day, but once we took off, in minutes we were cruising above the clouds. I lay on a firm leather sofa with my leg propped up and stared out the oval window at the view. Nothing but clear blue sky. I'd be in Bismarck in three hours. I tried to nap, but I couldn't stop thinking about the poor conditions Svetlana and Kelsey might be in. My chest constricted and my temper flared.

And God help their kidnappers if Svetlana and Kelsey were dead.

It made sense that I was having these feelings about Svetlana, but why Kelsey? I hadn't known her very long. I suppose that when I rescued her from drowning, she ceased to be solely a client, and truly became my little sister. I looked around. The luxurious seats made the empty cabin seem even emptier, reminding me just how desperate this mission was. I closed my eyes and fell asleep.

When we landed, it was dusk and snowing.

Snowing.

In October.

Guess this is autumn in Bismarck.

Vivian had arranged to have an SUV waiting for me when I landed. By the time I drove from the airport to downtown Bismarck, it was dark and the snow had begun to stick. I passed a large mall and drove a broad avenue lined with early 20th century brick buildings housing shops and restaurants. Traffic on the road was light, and I kept waiting for the city skyline to appear in my windshield. What I discovered was, rather than a dramatic cityscape, Bismarck is composed of collections of low buildings, few taller than three stories, as if the entire city were perpetually hunched over, bracing itself against the inevitable cold and wind.

I checked into the Radisson, changed into warmer clothes, and ate a palatable steak and baked potato in the hotel restaurant. Then, with my .45 revolver and a pocketful of extra cartridges, I set out to find the Bishop brothers.

By now there were a couple inches of snow on the ground, making it tricky to maneuver with my bad leg. When I finally made it to the SUV, I entered their address into the GPS and navigated my way through the quiet streets to Prairie View Apartments. I parked in a visitor's spot a few doors down from their unit. I shut off my lights but kept the engine running and the windshield wipers on. The snow was steady now and melted as soon as it hit the glass. I cracked the window for some cold fresh air and stared across the parking lot.

Part of me wanted to go up there, ring the bell, and get answers out of them with the gun. The trouble was, if that gambit failed, I had nothing else. Unfortunately, the situation called for patience and prudence—two things I was short on right now. I gritted my teeth and settled in to watch.

Stakeouts are boring no matter what, but doing one alone and in the snow is the worst. You'd think the snow would make it more exciting somehow. It doesn't. I waited for someone to come out, or someone to arrive, but nothing happened. The wipers, set to intermittent, pulsed hypnotically as I watched the apartment. My eyes got heavy. I checked the clock on the dashboard. It had been an hour, and I didn't even know if they were inside. If I was going to follow these two clowns, I needed to verify they were home.

Their unit was on the end of the building. If this place was like many other apartment complexes I'd seen, there would be patios and sliding glass doors behind each unit, where I could peek inside. I shut off the engine and got out. The snowfall had slowed, but there were now three or four inches on the ground. The building was ten units across. I didn't want it to be obvious that someone had been looking only in the Bishop brothers' apartment, so I decided to start on the opposite end and walk the entire length of the building.

As I'd predicted, each unit had a patio with a sliding glass door, and although a couple units were dark inside, most were lit up by lamps and TVs, and I could see clear into the living rooms because the curtains were open. Clearly none of them expected some jerk to be skulking around at night in their backyards. Disliking it myself, I stayed far out of the patches of light on the snow, and made a point of not looking inside.

Besides the patches near the windows, the only thing resembling light was a grayish gleam coming off the snow. I couldn't see the contours of the ground and slipped a couple of times. The sudden weight on my wounded leg sent jolts of pain through me.

Ahead, the unit at the end blazed with light. I walked to the edge of the light patch, where I was still in the darkness, and looked in the sliding glass door.

At first all I could tell was that two men were sitting next to each other in recliners watching TV. Then I saw they had the same dark hair and beefy builds, and I knew it was the twins. One of them had a cast on his wrist. Must have been Dickies, whose wrist I'd smashed with the baton. To see them, twins, in the exact same position on the chairs, with the TV flashing on their faces, was disturbing. I took a final glance and hobbled back to the SUV.

Tomorrow, the real work would begin.

38

The Most Slender of Hopes

Not knowing when (or if) the Bishop brothers would leave for work, I had set a wake-up call for four o'clock in the morning. When the call came, I washed up, changed my bandage, got dressed, and left by four thirty.

After picking up an extra-large coffee and somebody's blasphemous idea of a bagel, I drove to Prairie View apartments and parked in the same spot as the night before. It was a few minutes past five o'clock. The snow had stopped, but a few more inches had accumulated overnight—enough to cover the tracks I had left behind the building. Sipping the coffee and struggling to chew the bagel, I kept an eye on their door and settled in for what could be a long wait.

Sitting there in the darkness with a weary body and a wounded leg, I was forced once again to face the possibility that I would never see Svetlana or Kelsey again. I refused to accept it. Even if I had no leads at all, I would keep searching for them. Fortunately I now had a decent one: the black tactical jacket had recently been somewhere in the Bakken Formation.

Right now my entire investigation hinged on the most slender of hopes: that the Bishop brothers were connected to "Mr. H." The one Midwest location I had was this address, and since they had been looking for Conover and Kelsey, it was possible that "Mr. H." was the one who had hired them.

As it began to get light out, a few people shoveled their walks, cleaned the snow off their cars and drove away. None of them noticed me. I choked down the rest of the bagel and kept watch. At five thirty, lights went on in the brothers' upstairs window. At last—activity. More people left. A plow truck made a few passes. I watched it drive away, and when I looked back, the two brothers were shoveling their walkway. Minutes later, I was following their red pickup out of the complex. I let another car get between us as they headed out of town.

They'd driven for fifteen minutes when they pulled into the Round Tuit Cafe and went inside. I went a good 100 yards past the cafe and pulled onto the shoulder. I angled the side mirror so I could keep an eye on the cafe entrance. It was quarter-past six, and there were several pickups and tractor-trailers outside. Steam rose from the cafe's chimney. I tortured myself imagining all of the good things the Bishop brothers were eating right now—pancakes, sausage patties, hash browns, Western omelets. Cars hissed by. Tanker trucks roared past, shaking my SUV in their wakes.

Half an hour later, the brothers emerged again. When they pulled onto the road and came up behind me, I put my back to the window and pretended to study a map. They drove by, continuing north out of Bismarck on US-83.

The farther we went, the less snow there was on the ground. As a guy who had grown up in the Northeast, what I was most struck by in this part of the country was the lack of trees. Along the road were continuous barbed wire fences, beyond which stretched vast swaths of rolling prairie. I went miles and miles without seeing a single tree, and when I did they were huddled together in small copses, as if they subscribed to the maxim of safety in numbers.

After a while, the monotony got to me, and I switched on the radio. It was nothing but static, so I shut it off. I monitored my distance from their truck, making sure I always had at least one car between us. I looked right and left, hoping to see some kind of scenery, but it was desolate. Once in a while, a farmhouse and barn appeared on the horizon. A few horsehead oil pump jacks churned by the roadside. And along some stretches, giant wind turbines dotted the landscape in the distance.

With nothing else to occupy my mind, my thoughts went to Svetlana. I marveled at how a woman could be so impossibly beautiful and brilliant at the same time. And I thought about Kelsey. Funny and remarkably mature for her age—and controlled by her brother. At first I had pitied the guy, but now I felt only contempt for him. For getting his kid sister mixed up in his *cause célèbre.* For treating her like a slave and not caring about her safety. I didn't care what conspiracy Conover was writing about; nothing was worth his sister's life.

They drove for two hours, and then, at the town of Minot, they peeled off into a gas station. I slowed down. They parked at a pump. Filling that truck would take a while. I was fine on gas, but I needed to use the bathroom, so I pulled into a fast food restaurant two buildings down, used their facilities, and got back in the SUV. While I waited at the exit to begin tailing them again, I wished I'd had time to buy some food, but I couldn't take the chance of losing them.

When they pulled out, instead of continuing north, they went west. A tanker truck was between us. We drove on.

We drove for another two hours over mostly barren country, punctuated by oil rigs and more pumps. The highlight of the drive was stopping to let a small herd of bison cross the road. Otherwise it was nothing but tedium, a sore leg, and nothing to eat or drink.

A few miles past the entrance to Willstown International Airport, we came over a crest in the road, and I was awed by the view. There in a shallow valley was a flood of towering rigs, pumps, storage tanks, trailers, Quonset huts, tanker trucks, and long lines of train tanker cars. As we headed downhill into the valley, both the tanker truck and the red pickup signaled right and slowed. They went down an access road that led into the center of the compound. I didn't dare follow. I had no idea what kind of security checkpoint I might encounter.

About a quarter-mile back, I had passed a dirt road that went up an incline and appeared to run along a ridge with a view of the compound. I did a U-turn, raced back and drove up the dirt road. There, I pulled over and took out my high-power binoculars. I searched for the red pickup and spotted it parked outside a construction trailer. The two brothers emerged a few minutes later wearing coveralls and hard hats. Back in the pickup, they drove to the far edge of the compound, maybe half a mile away, where they parked again and disappeared into a big red building. I waited for a while, didn't see them, and swept the binoculars across the entire facility.

The place teemed with men and tanker trucks—indeed, I'd never seen so many trucks in one place in my whole life. The entire opposite side of the compound was a giant rail yard. Train tanker cars filled multiple siding tracks, and the sidings connected to a main track that led out of the facility and faded into the prairie. A switch engine moved a pair of tanker cars from the storage tank area to a siding near the main track.

I looked for the name of the company, but all I saw was "HES" in giant letters on some of the storage tanks. It seemed that everybody who worked here knew who they worked for.

When I swept the binoculars back to the big red building, the Bishop brothers were standing outside talking to a stout man in a sport coat and cowboy boots. He had a full head of silver hair and was obviously an executive because two uniformed guards with sidearms stood near him. Their uniforms looked the same as those of the H-Men who had kidnapped Svetlana and Kelsey. *This could be it*, I told myself. I wished I could hear what they were saying, but my audio surveillance equipment didn't have this kind of range.

The stout man talked with the twins for a while, and then the group of them went into a construction trailer across the yard and didn't come out.

I surveyed the place one more time and put away the binoculars. Decision time. I could continue to follow the Bishop brothers, but I'd have to stay parked on the highway, totally exposed, where I might arouse suspicion. Or, I could drop the brothers and look into this company instead. There was a town on the horizon. I would go there and find out more about this massive operation.

Once beyond the facility, I passed housing developments under construction and a shiny new sign—"Willstown, North Dakota: America's 21st Century Boomtown"—then acres of trailers, RVs and campers on flat dirt parcels that stretched to the edges of superstore parking lots. I entered the town proper. A wide main drag was flanked by two- and three-story brick buildings. "Help Wanted" signs hung in every window. The buildings all had a gray and dusty pallor, giving me the sense that Willstown had seen boom and bust times before.

Once through the town, I crossed the Missouri River, where more RVs and campers were parked near the riverbanks. Seeing nothing ahead but empty prairie, I turned around.

In small communities, the most reliable sources of local general information are newspapers and libraries. Cafes or diners are good, too, if you want the town scuttlebutt or access to old-timers who know everyone. But I needed hard information—the name of the oil company outside of town ("HES" had to be an acronym), as well as the name of the owner.

I was hungry and my thinking wasn't exactly trenchant at the moment. It was a few minutes past noon, and ahead was the Prairie Dog Cafe. I pulled into a parking space as someone pulled out, and went inside.

39

Nothing to Lose

After breakfast I stood at the register debating whether to go to the town newspaper or the library first. As it turned out, I didn't need to go to either.

Behind the cafe register was a wall of photos—of sports teams, town fairs and other events—and in every photo, one company appeared as the event or team sponsor: Harlan Energy Solutions.

One photo showed a Little League team called the Harlan Oilers. Their uniforms had a graphic of a derrick gushing oil. Posing with the team was a stout, silver-haired man named Jack Harlan. He resembled the man I had seen at the compound, but I couldn't be certain; that had been through binoculars from half a mile away. But assuming he was the same man, this connected the Bishop brothers with the owner of a major oil operation—a Midwest "Mr. H." I paid my check, left a tip and went out to the SUV.

Ordinarily I would tail Harlan for a day or two, break into his house or place of business, and gather clues surreptitiously, but I didn't have time for any of that. All I cared about was finding Svetlana and Kelsey as soon as possible. I would confront Harlan and gauge what he knew. I'd be as conciliatory as possible, and make it sound as if I was doing his bidding. But I'd have to do it unarmed, because there was no way Harlan's security people were going to let me waltz in there with a .45 revolver under my coat.

After I put the gun and shoulder holster under the front seat, I slid my coat back on and started the engine. I caught a glance of myself in the rear-view mirror. With the dark circles under my eyes and a burgeoning beard, I looked like I'd ridden into town on a boxcar. I tried to reassure myself with a smile, but it was forced, and the part of me craving reassurance knew it.

I drove out of town the way I'd come in, and pulled into the compound access road. Ahead the road divided, and on the spur road was a long line of tanker trucks. I continued on the main road until I reached a gate. A guard stepped out of the booth with a clipboard.

"Name?" he said.

"Dakota Stevens. I'm a private detective from New York here to see Mr. Harlan."

He checked the clipboard.

"I don't have an appointment," I said.

"Well, then we've got ourselves a problem," he said. "Can't let you in without an appointment."

I pointed at the wall phone in his booth.

"Call Mr. Harlan. He'll want to see me."

"I'm not supposed to—"

"Look, you get on the phone and tell him Dakota Stevens is here and wants to talk to him. Got it?"

He stared at me for a second and reached for the phone. He retreated into the booth, spoke for a minute, then hung up.

"Turns out Mr. Harlan will see you after all."

"I bet he will," I said. "Where do I go?"

"Straight ahead, then take your second right. It's the red building down at the end."

I passed through the gate and drove by what looked like barracks, equipment sheds and other outbuildings. At the red building, I parked and got out.

The first thing I noticed was the smell: the air was thick with the stench of petroleum. Next I noticed the noise: machinery running, men shouting, a PA unit blaring.

This was the same building I'd seen from the ridge above. I casually looked up and scanned the length of the ridgeline outside the fence. It was bare except for an area a couple hundred yards away, where a copse of trees stood. *A good spot to set up with my equipment.* The Bishop brothers' pickup was nowhere in sight. Limping toward the door, I was aware of the empty space under my arm, where my gun normally was. I ignored the naked feeling and went inside.

Several men in suits were sitting on chairs reading magazines. The receptionist, a wizened woman easily in her eighties, eyed me fiercely. If her job was to scare visitors, she was very good at it. She hung up the phone.

"You must be Dakota Stevens, the detective," she said.

"The man, the myth, the legend," I said. "At least that's what it says on my coffee mug."

She narrowed her stare. "What's this regarding?"

"Mr. Harlan knows."

"All right, take a seat. Mr. Brace'll be out soon to escort you."

"Great."

I stood by the window, looking out on the work site. Taking in the scope of this operation from up close—the dozens of pumps, rigs, trucks, and workers everywhere—I instantly knew what a wealthy and powerful man this Jack Harlan was. I have to admit, I felt a little intimidated.

The office door opened and a man in his fifties, very tall—maybe five inches taller than my six feet—stepped into the room. He was lanky in build, but his ramrod posture said he was ex-military, and the unwavering blue eyes said Special Forces.

"Mr. Stevens, I'm Bill Brace, head of security for HES."

We shook hands. His grip was unnecessarily firm. As a rule, I ignored pissing contests, but today I was in no mood to be challenged. I squeezed back so hard, his hand practically folded in half. His eye twitched. He pulled away.

"Please follow me."

I went into the next room. Two guards stood in the corner. The room was empty except for a row of plastic chairs and two wooden ones beside another door. Brace held out a hand.

"First I need to see your credentials."

I took out my license and showed it to him.

"All right. Now I need to frisk you."

"Fine."

I assumed the position against the wall. The paint was smudged with other hand prints. He frisked me.

"This way, Mr. Stevens."

The guards watched me as I followed Brace through the second door. He closed it behind us.

The silver-haired man I'd seen from the ridge stood at a giant standing desk in the middle of the room. He was stocky and wore a sport coat and cowboy boots. Behind him was a long table, also standing height, covered with a laptop, reference books and unfurled blueprints held down by stones. Across the room, a row of hard hats hung beside a door. There were no frills in the room of any kind. No pictures on the walls, no books, not even chairs. Just a massive window looking out on the work site. This was hardly the lair of a nefarious kidnapper.

I was beginning to wonder if I'd jumped to conclusions about the situation when Brace moved to the side, revealing a chess table behind him. There were no chairs with the table, but the table matched the two wooden chairs in the other room. Several White pieces stood on the sidelines of the playing area; whoever was playing Black was crushing White.

I studied the black pieces. The knights both faced backward. *Just like in Svetlana's game with Frank.* Adrenaline surged through me. It couldn't be a coincidence. She had to be here.

I wanted to leap across the room and strangle Harlan. My legs quivered from restraining myself.

Harlan put down his pen, walked over and shook my hand. He had the solid body of a man who had done a lot of heavy physical labor in his youth.

"Jack Harlan. So, Mr. Brace tells me you're a detective from New York."

"*Private* detective," I said. "But you already knew that."

"Please forgive the lack of chairs," he said. "I happen to believe the things make you lazy. Started out as a wildcatter thirty-five years ago—got used to the long hours on my feet. I find I'm a heck of a lot more productive standing up. Better for your posture, too. But you know what the best benefit is?"

"No."

"It makes people you're dealing with get to the point faster."

He stared at me. He had hard, gray eyes.

"Okay," I said, "you want me to get to the point? I know you have Svetlana and Kelsey."

"Who?"

"Spare me the bullshit," I said. "Svetlana Krüsh and Kelsey Wright. Your men kidnapped them in Maine and left me with orders to find Conover Wright. I came here to tell you I'm playing ball—I'm working on finding him—but I need more time."

"I don't know a damn thing about any kidnapping," Harlan said.

His eyes didn't waver. Either he was telling the truth, or he was an excellent liar. I forged ahead as if he hadn't said anything.

"I want you to know—the phone your men gave me," I said. "I took the battery out and left it in New York. I'm not going to have your men track me, and when I finally find Conover, swoop in and snatch him away. He's my one piece of leverage."

I considered questioning him about the chess game in progress, but I didn't want to tip him off. If he thought I suspected Svetlana was here, he might move her.

"I'm getting tired of this conversation," Harlan said. "I don't know a damn thing about any kidnapping."

"Keep it up and I'm going to get angry," I said.

"Young man, I'd be careful if I were you. Trust me when I say, you don't want to get on Mr. Brace's bad side."

Brace had his hands on his hips. I locked eyes with him.

"*Fuck* Mr. Brace. Here's the deal. If anybody has hurt Svetlana or Kelsey, they're going to die, plain and simple." I laughed. "I don't think you get it…I have nothing to lose."

"Don't threaten me," Harlan said. "I don't like the idea of anybody being kidnapped, but I can't help you."

I wasn't sure what I'd expected—to confront him and get him to instantly confess, I suppose—but this wasn't working. I felt like an attacker against an aikido master: my every move was being used against me, and I was getting exhausted. I was also running out of questions.

"So, is this facility the extent of your drilling operations?" I asked.

"I'm not discussing my business with you," Harlan said. "You came here asking about a kidnapping, I've told you I know nothing about it, and now you need to leave. Goodbye, Mr. Stevens."

Brace went to the far door and opened it. He gave me the hard stare as I stepped outside. The second my boot landed in the mud at the foot of the stairs, the door slammed behind me.

40

My Internal Geiger Counter

When I left the compound, I drove back to the ridge and followed the dirt road until I saw the copse of trees I had spied from outside Harlan's office. The trees were some distance below the road. I parked the SUV in a turnout, strapped on my gun, grabbed my gear, and hiked down to the trees. There, I crept beneath the russet canopy to the edge of the tree line facing the compound. The red building, an equipment hangar, several Quonset hut barracks and outbuildings were a couple hundred yards away.

I found some undergrowth for cover, opened the case and set up the tripod and parabolic dish. I scanned the area with the binoculars until I saw workers or guards chatting. Then I aimed the dish at them and put on the headphones.

Parabolic microphones are notorious for being unable to pick up bass frequencies, so everyone sounded like a space alien. A group of men discussed a new female rig worker. They weren't keen on her. Big surprise. Next I saw two men in lab coats walking between trailers, talking about what they each brought for lunch. I kept locating men, then aiming the dish at them and listening, but all of their conversations were irrelevant to my cause. Every few minutes, I trained the binoculars on the red building, hoping Harlan and Brace would come outside, but they didn't, and the yard around the building remained empty.

I was about to write off my surveillance as what Kelsey would call a "hashtag fail" when I spotted an SUV stopping in front of an Army green Quonset hut at the extreme corner of the compound. A guard with a rifle slung over his shoulder stood at the hut entrance—a black steel door. Another guard exited the SUV's passenger side, removed a covered crate from the back seat and went to the door. He nodded at the crate in his arms.

"Lunchtime," he said. "Shit, wish we ate this good."

"What's today's?"

"Prime rib. Crazy, right?"

The guard unlocked the door and the man carrying the crate disappeared inside. The driver's door on the SUV opened and a guard got out and stretched. One of his arms was in a sling, and his hand was bandaged. My internal Geiger counter went berserk. This was the guy I'd shot in the hand. I was sure of it. He walked over to the guard at the door.

"How goes it?"

"Oh, you know—another day in paradise. Boring shit."

The guard spun around and unlocked the door again. The crate-bearer emerged.

"Get this," he said. "Guess what the hot one said to me."

"What?"

"She says, 'This is not rare enough—send it back.' I tell her that's all there is, and she goes, 'You are dismissed.' Can you believe the balls on that chick?"

Svetlana. It could be no one else.

I closed my eyes and gave thanks.

"Bitch," the driver said. "Wouldn't I like to get my hands on her."

"Yeah," the guard said. "What's the deal with the girl? How old's she anyway?"

"Old enough," the driver said.

They laughed.

"She barely eats. Sleeps all the time far as I can tell."

The driver checked his watch. "We'd better go. Harlan's waiting for an update."

"See 'ya."

"Yeah, later."

The driver and the one with the crate got in the SUV and drove away. I removed the headphones.

I was dizzy with relief to know that Svetlana and Kelsey were here, but now the question was, how would I bust them out? While scanning the compound I'd counted no fewer than thirty H-Men on patrol. They also manned the gate, guarded buildings and protected Harlan. There was no way I could mount a rescue alone. To do it, I would have to climb down the steep hill, cut through the fence, subdue the guard, pick the lock, and get Svetlana and Kelsey back up the hill—all without being detected or setting off alarms. The best approach to the Quonset hut was from behind the red building—Harlan's office—but that was a couple hundred yards from the hut and over open ground.

I switched the DSLR to auto and snapped fifty or so photos of the entire compound. I got close-ups of the Quonset hut, Harlan's office and the barracks. Then I left the cover of the trees and crawled along the ridge through the tall weeds, snapping photos from other angles. When I reached the rear of the compound, I focused on the rail yard and all of those oil tanker cars—a major vulnerability.

By the time I finished, it was early evening and starting to snow. I packed up all of the gear and limped back to the SUV.

41

The Magnificent Seven

Flying back to New York that evening, I was tormented by the idea that I had been so close to Svetlana and Kelsey, but couldn't rescue them yet. I needed to act fast, before they were moved to another location. There was no way I could put together a team of 30, or even a dozen, men to mount a rescue, but I could cobble together a handful of tough, skilled A-players, starting with Falcone and Dominick.

This rescue required military planning and execution far beyond my expertise. Frank was a WWII vet who'd led a platoon and seen a lot of action. He had also been the lead tactical ops trainer at Quantico. And, he was the one person I knew with an arsenal in his basement. I picked up the phone beside my seat and called him. He answered on the second ring.

"Roma."

"Frank, it's Dakota."

"Hey, kid, how are you?"

"Not good, Frank."

I told him about everything that had happened after we left New York: the confrontation with the Asians, the shootout on Vinalhaven, the kidnapping, and finding Svetlana and Kelsey.

"What do you need?" he said. "Anything."

"Weapons, Frank. Thompsons, MG42s, and the *panzerschreck*. With plenty of ammo."

"I've got plenty for everything except the *panzerschreck*. What else?"

"You, Frank. I'm putting together a team to get them out of there, and I need your experience."

"Dakota, listen, I might act like I'm fifty, but I'm no spring chicken."

"I need your help planning this thing," I said. "I figure a guy who was in Normandy and Operation Market Garden can handle this. I've got photos of the layout."

"I can do that."

"Great. A guy named Francis Falcone and his—"

"Wait," he said. "This isn't the same Francis Falcone that runs a Mob crew in Brooklyn, is it?"

"The same. He's going to be helping us. He'll be at your place tomorrow morning with his number-two, Dominick."

Frank grumbled. "I don't like the idea of working with mobsters, but we're talking about Svetlana and that sweet girl, so I'm in."

"Thanks."

"Let me go, so I can get things organized."

"Okay," I said. "We'll meet at the airport in Farmingdale tomorrow. Private jet departure area. I'll call you with an exact time."

"Good enough," Frank said. "Bye."

The second he hung up, I called Falcone.

"Falcone, it's Dakota. I found her."

"Svetlana? Great, she with you?"

"No. I'm going to need your and Dominick's help. What are you guys doing for the next couple days?"

"For Svetlana? Whatever you need us to do."

"Good. Tomorrow morning, I need you to go see a guy in Dyker Heights. His name is Frank Roma and he's a former FBI colleague of mine. He has the weapons we're going to need."

I gave him Frank's address and phone number.

"Don't let him carry too much," I said. "He looks like he's in his seventies, but he's actually ninety years old."

"Don't worry, me and Dom'll do the lugging."

"Meet me tomorrow at Farmingdale Airport. The private jet area. I'll call you with a time. And wear all black."

"No problem," he said. "My whole wardrobe is black."

"Hey, Falcone?"

"Yeah?"

"Thanks."

"I'm doing it for Svetlana, Stevens, not you."

In the morning, I called Vivian and asked her to arrange for two black Suburban SUVs to be waiting for us in Willstown that afternoon. Then I drove to the East Village to do the thing I'd been dreading: tell Svetlana's father she'd been kidnapped, and that I needed his help.

I found a parking spot across from his restaurant, shut off the car and looked at the building. There was a possibility, however slight, that once I walked through those dark glass doors and gave him the bad news, I wouldn't be walking out.

No. He'd realize that he needed me. I knew where Svetlana was being held, and I'd assembled the resources to rescue her. I nodded at myself in the rear-view mirror and got out.

It was clear in Manhattan today, and I savored the cool air on my way inside. At the front of the restaurant was a bar, and Svetlana's beautiful younger cousin Anya stood behind the counter, drying glasses. Looking up, she recognized me. Her intense eyes narrowed.

"Dakota Stevens, when you marry Svetlana, eh?"

"Hello, Anya. Is your uncle in?"

"He go to church, pray. St. George, Seventh Street. You go. Good you should ask for her hand in church."

"Thanks, Anya. I'll see you later."

I left my car parked and walked the few blocks to St. George's Ukrainian Catholic Church. The architecture was Byzantine, I think, with a big dome on top. Although I'd passed this place many times (my old office was on East 10th), I'd never been inside.

Stepping into the nave, I was struck by the high vaulted ceilings and the gleaming gold leaf paint. All of the pews, except two near the front, were empty. I swallowed. Even from behind I recognized Oleksander Krush by his thick, steel-gray hair. Behind him, on the other side of the aisle, his two hulkingly muscular bodyguards, Yuri and Viktor, couldn't be missed either. The two looked as though they'd been coarsely chiseled out of granite. They stared at me then nodded as I passed.

I tended to address him as "Mr. Krush," but the situation was dire and I needed to appear confident. He was sitting up with his eyes closed and his hands folded in his lap when I rapped on the pew.

"Oleksander?"

His eyes opened. "Ah, Montana Stevens."

"Dakota. May I sit down?"

He shrugged. "Is free country, yes? If you see me about place on Tenth Street, I already rent it."

"That's not why I'm here."

I sat down and looked into his black eyes, eyes that seemed to contain the souls of men who had crossed him.

"It's about Svetlana," I said.

"Yes?"

"She's been kidnapped."

Somewhere in the church, a door banged shut. The sound echoed in the empty nave.

"But I know where she is," I said. "And I have reason to believe that she hasn't been harmed."

Oleksander stared at me. For a long, uncomfortable moment—the most nerve-wracking moment of my life—he didn't move, didn't blink. Then he reached inside his coat, pulled out a cigarette and lighted it. He stared at the altar.

"This happen when?"

"A week ago," I said.

"A week?" He exhaled smoke through his nose. "A week and you not come to me?"

"I wanted to find her first. I'm ninety percent sure I've found her and—"

"Ninety percent? You are not certain?"

"I'm as certain as I can be, and I have a plan to get her out. Her and my client, a young woman. She was also taken."

"Your client I do not care about. Only Svetlana. Where is she?"

"An oil drilling facility in North Dakota."

He faced me with his jaw set. "Oil? Is this one of your *cases*?"

"It was, but now it's just about Svetlana and my client. And I need your help."

"For you I have news, Dakota Stevens. You will have my help whether you like or not. Now tell me this plan."

I didn't have the details down yet, so I painted some broad strokes: a small group of us would assault the compound that night, get Svetlana and Kelsey out, and fly back on the private jet. Oleksander flicked his ash on the floor.

"Your plan is joke. Not enough men. We do my way. I send fifty men. People will die for this."

"Damn it, Oleksander, if you do that, you're going to get them both killed. This requires stealth. Stealth and surprise. Fifty men will turn this into a war. All we care about is getting Svetlana and my client out."

He stared at me again, took a drag on the cigarette and looked up pensively at the stained glass windows. He blew smoke at the ceiling.

"Perhaps you are right. We bring Yuri and Viktor."

"We? You mean you're coming?"

"Of course. My little girl is kidnapped. You think I not come?"

"You're right, sir."

"Yes I am right." Oleksander dropped the cigarette and crushed it under his heel. "Tonight I personally kill every man I see. Now we go."

There were seven of us: Frank, Oleksander, Falcone, Dominick, Yuri, Viktor, and me. We were the closest to The Magnificent Seven as I was going to get on such short notice.

For the first hour of the flight, Frank and I studied the photos of the compound on the HDTV mounted on the cabin wall. I pulled up Google Earth images, and we discussed the layout. The situation, he said, was similar to a hostage case he'd handled in the 80s.

Once we had the plan roughed out, Frank and I sat in swivel chairs next to the TV while the rest of the team crammed onto the long couch across the aisle. Everyone but Frank wore black tactical clothing.

"Okay, guys," I said, "the objective is simple: to rescue Svetlana and my client Kelsey Wright. Frank Roma here has put together a plan. Frank was the lead trainer at the FBI Academy in tactical assaults and hostage rescue ops. During his career, he led over fifty such operations, so he knows what he's talking about. He was also a platoon leader in World War Two, and a training officer for the Army reserves. Tonight, Frank will stay behind the lines and give the orders. Frank?"

He held the TV remote and clicked through the photos as he talked about each location.

"All right, gentlemen, the compound is a huge oil fracking facility. As you can see, there are drilling rigs, storage tanks, a rail yard, trailer offices, barracks, a gatehouse, and a small network of roads. The entire facility is surrounded by high chain-link fence with razor wire on top. However, the fence does not appear to be electrified."

Frank brought up a photo of the Army green Quonset hut.

"This is the building Dakota believes Svetlana and Kelsey are being held in. There's a guard at the door, and there may be others inside. Once the fun starts, it will fall on Dakota to get inside, get the girls, and get them out. The hill directly behind this building is too steep, so he'll have to cross open ground with them to here." He switched to a photo of the red building—Harlan's office. "A hole will be pre-cut in the fence. They'll duck through it and climb the hill to the SUVs while the rest of you provide covering fire."

"Wait a second," Falcone said. "Dakota said there are like thirty guards in this place, right?"

"Correct," Frank said.

"So, what kind of covering fire can we give against thirty guns?"

"We have two MG42s, Mr. Falcone. They fire twelve hundred rounds per minute and have a range of eleven hundred yards. If well placed, two of these guns will produce more than enough suppressing fire to keep their guards out of the action."

Dominick whistled. "Do we get to keep one afterwards?"

"No," Frank said.

"Please continue, Frank," I said.

"You're going to be executing a basic SBF—Support by Fire—maneuver. Two teams will set up in fixed positions with the MG42s to provide suppressing fire, while the rescue team penetrates the compound and secures the hostages. Is everyone on board so far?"

"Who is rescue team?" Oleksander asked.

"Dakota and Mr. Falcone," Frank said.

"No. Me and Dakota. I am Svetlana's father. I fight in Afghanistan many years ago and do similar missions."

"Dakota?" Frank said. "Okay by you?"

The prospect of having an armed and seething Oleksander at my back during the rescue made me nervous, but I had to show him I wasn't afraid. I looked him in the eyes and nodded.

"Absolutely."

"Then one support team will be Falcone and Dominick, and the other Yuri and Viktor."

"Why two guys to one gun?" Falcone asked. "Wouldn't it be better if we were spread out with more guns?"

"No," Frank said. "The MG42s need to be operated by two men. One man fires while the other one feeds the ammunition belt. And the barrels may need to be changed out. Also, don't lay on the triggers. Short bursts of no more than five seconds, okay? I'll give you a short lesson on the guns when we get there. But right now let's review positions and timing."

I passed around copies of my hand-drawn map as Frank talked and showed photos on the TV.

"Both MG42 teams will set up in a copse of trees. Team One will provide suppressing fire down this road through the compound. Team Two will create cross-fire by aiming at the barracks. This is to prevent the guards from approaching the escape point in the fence. Everyone clear?"

The men nodded.

"One other thing. The MG42 teams *must* maintain fire discipline. If one of those large storage tanks gets hit, the entire facility could explode."

"Got it," Falcone said.

Oleksander spoke to Yuri and Viktor in Ukrainian. They nodded and crossed their arms.

"Good. Now the timing," Frank said. "Dakota and Oleksander will create a diversion at the rail yard. One minute after the diversion, on my radio command, the two support teams will provide suppressing fire.

"Dakota and Oleksander will then make their way to the Quonset hut, neutralize the guards and secure Svetlana and Kelsey. Once Dakota confirms he has them, I will say, 'Cease fire.' The support teams must stop firing immediately because their line of fire is along the escape route. Then, once Dakota and Oleksander reach the hole in the fence, one of them will lead the women out, while the other stays behind to cover their escape.

"In the meantime, support Team Two will move to a ditch near the main highway, lay a spike strip across the eastbound lane, and direct suppressing fire at the gatehouse on the access road. This is to prevent anyone from coming after us. Everyone else will rendezvous at the SUVs and drive to the end of the dirt road, where we'll pick up Team Two. Finally, we have to get back to the airport A-sap. When we pull out, I'll call the pilot and tell him to be ready for immediate takeoff. Any questions?"

The cabin was silent. For the first time since leaving New York I could hear the hum of the engines, the whoosh of the air against the fuselage.

I checked my watch. One hour until we landed.

"Okay, guys," I said, "let's do this."

42

Everything Fell Away

When we landed, Frank drove into Willstown and picked up some last-minute supplies, including a handheld spotlight, bolt cutters, and thin rubber work gloves for everyone. He also bought dinner, and we ate it on the plane. By eight o'clock, it was cave dark with an overcast sky. Cool, but not cold, with a light breeze. As we headed out for the ridge above the compound, I prayed Svetlana and Kelsey hadn't been moved.

The side of the compound nearest us—with offices, trailers, barracks and the Quonset hut—was well-lit, as was each tall drilling rig scattered around the facility. But the storage tank area and rail yard lay in shadow.

While Frank led the two MG42 support teams down to the copse of trees, Oleksander and I carried a heavy duffel of weapons and equipment to the fence near the red building. The window shades inside Harlan's office were drawn, but there were lights on inside. We hid in the weeds until a guard passed, and then I cut the fence links from the ground to five feet up. I marked the spot by jamming some weeds through the holes. We circled to the rear of the compound behind the rail yard, cut another hole in the fence and crawled inside with the duffel. We took cover behind the end boxcar and lay in a prone position.

About 100 yards away, on the siding nearest the main track, was my chosen target: a lone tanker car in the shadows. Yesterday I'd seen that this was where the filled tanker cars were staged. I unzipped the duffel. Oleksander and I slung Thompsons over our shoulders, and then I pulled out the *panzerschreck.* Once Oleksander loaded the rocket, I spoke into my radio headset.

"Rescue team in place," I said.

"Roger that," Frank said. "Support teams, remember—do *not* fire until I give the order. Acknowledge."

"Got it," Falcone said.

"Yes," Yuri or Viktor said.

Beside me, Oleksander held the spotlight. I covered my headset and spoke to him.

"When I say, 'Now!' you hit it with the light."

"Good," he said.

I got the *panzerschreck* barrel balanced on my shoulder with my head behind the blast shield and looked through the little window. I lined up the sights with the center of the tanker car, took a deep breath and exhaled slowly.

"Now!"

The spotlight cast a bright beam on the side of the tanker car, and I fired. There was a sharp crack and a hiss, and the bright rocket trail slashing through the darkness. Then there was a gong and the rocket flew in erratic loops and landed somewhere in the distance without exploding.

It had glanced off the rounded hull of the car. My stomach sank.

"You miss," Oleskander said.

"Never mind that," I said. "Get us reloaded."

He did.

"You stay and keep the light on it," I said. "I'm going over there, where I can shoot more straight-on."

I hustled over to a space between two boxcars and took direct aim at the tanker car. I squeezed the trigger. Nothing happened. The rocket didn't ignite.

Carefully I removed the rocket and hurled it across the rail yard. It hit the gravel with a dull thud.

"Rescue team," Frank said. "What's your status?"

"One shot glanced off," I said. "Second was a dud."

"Roger that. Make the third one count."

I went back to the duffel and loaded the *panzerschreck* again.

"Final rocket," Oleksander said.

"I know."

"You ever fire RPG?"

"No."

"I should fire."

"I've got it," I said.

This had better work. If it doesn't, we won't have a diversion.

I went back to my space between the boxcars and stood so the tanker car was perpendicular to me. Floodlights flashed on around the rail yard. The sudden brightness made me squint, but I kept the sights trained on the center of the car.

I squeezed the trigger.

In an eyeblink—before anything had a chance to register—the rocket shot out of the tube and the tanker car exploded. I was flattened to the ground. An orange fireball rose and swelled skyward into a tremendous mushroom cloud. Metal clanged against the boxcars, and I felt the scorching heat. Black smoke began to fill the rail yard. My ears were ringing, but in the distance I heard alarm sirens. Oleksander ran over yelling.

"We get Svetlana! Now!"

He helped me up. I took the Thompson off my shoulder, switched off the safety and ran as fast as I could along the fence line. We passed behind a drilling rig. The workers stood dumbfounded staring at the explosion. We continued along the fence and ran through the barracks area.

"Hey!" someone shouted. "Stop those guys!"

Gunfire rang out behind us. While Oleksander ran ahead, I paused behind a Caterpillar bulldozer with the Thompson ready. Three guards ran into the open, and I emptied a magazine into them. They stopped short and fell backward like they'd hit a brick wall. I changed out the magazine, caught up to Oleksander, and we plunged into the shadows between two buildings. Once in the open again, we circled a yawning equipment hangar.

"We're clear of the barracks," I said on the radio. "Let 'em have it."

"Support teams, fire!" Frank said.

Several hundred yards ahead and to our right, the MG42s opened up, the sound like snare drums being played inhumanly fast. As we ran, bright tracers flashed down the road and across the open ground behind us. Oleksander and I ran flat-out for the Quonset hut. A guard stood in front of the door beneath a light. By the time he saw us, we were already on top of him. Oleksander leveled his Thompson.

"Open door," he said. "Now."

The guard did as ordered.

"Keys," Oleksander said.

The guard handed him the keys.

Oleksander stepped back a few feet and fired a burst into the guard's head. The guard crumpled to the ground so his body held the door open. Oleksander rushed inside ahead of me. I heard a man shouting and then the *RAT-A-TAT-TAT!* of the Thompson. When I got inside, a guard lay face-down on a desk with a puddle of blood around him. In the background behind the desk were two rows of metal-frame beds and foot lockers. The place was empty, except for the rear of the hut, where Kelsey sat alone on a bed. She saw me.

"Dakota!"

Oleksander and I ran over. Kelsey was handcuffed to the bed. She threw her free arm around me.

"Dakota, you're here!"

"Where Svetlana?" Oleksander asked.

"She…she's playing chess," Kelsey said. "With that man Harlan."

"Oleksander," I said, "she's handcuffed here."

He thumbed through the key ring, found the handcuff key and unlocked Kelsey. We headed for the door.

"Can you run?" I asked Kelsey.

"I'll try."

"I get Svetlana," Oleksander said.

"No, you get Kelsey out."

"But—"

"I know where she is," I said. "You don't. Please, Mr. Krush."

He glared at me. "Shoot anyone gets in your way. Do not screw up, Dakota Stevens."

I nodded. "Frank," I said into the headset, "cease fire. We have Kelsey."

"What about Svetlana?"

"Negative," I said. "I'm going to get her."

"Hurry up," Frank said. "The police will be here soon."

"Roger that."

"Cease fire!" Frank said. "Cease fire!"

Outside, the MG42s went silent.

"Young lady, we go," Oleksander said to Kelsey.

"But, Dakota..."

"Go," I said. "I'll be right behind you."

They exited the building, Oleksander shining the spotlight at the fence as they ran. I cut across the open ground toward Harlan's office. I was hobbling badly now, and when I got to the office door, I was sweating and my leg throbbed. The door was locked. I banged on it.

"Mr. Harlan, sir? We need you to see this."

I knocked again, and as the door opened, I leveled the Thompson. Wonder Woman stood silhouetted in the doorway.

What? I closed my eyes and quickly opened them.

It was Svetlana, in a Wonder Woman costume. She was stooped over with one arm behind the door.

"I'm handcuffed, Dakota."

I squeezed through the doorway, unavoidably brushing against her. She was shackled to the chess table. Most of the pieces lay on the floor.

"Any keys around?" I asked.

"No."

"Harlan and Brace—where are they?"

"I don't know. Harlan left a few minutes ago. Brace I have not seen."

"I'll have to pick the lock," I said. "Sit down."

She sat on the table and crossed her legs. Steeling myself against her magnetic aura, I laid down the Thompson, got out my lock-picking set and went to work. There was distant gunfire outside.

"A week, Dakota?" she said. "I thought you would be here much sooner."

"What do you want from me? I was shot."

"I know. I was worried. Are you okay?"

"Barely." I worked on the lock. "Your father is here."

"My *father*?"

"I couldn't stop him from coming. Frank's here, too. And Falcone and Dominick."

"*Layno*," she said. "Now I might have to give Francis a date."

I looked up at her and shook my head. She smiled.

The handcuff lock should have taken me seconds to pick, but with Svetlana leaning over in the corset inches from my face, my attention was somewhat divided.

"So," I said, nodding at her costume, "do I want to know?"

I jiggered the lock.

"Is not what you think," she said. "Every night he makes me play him in chess and wear a different outfit. Black gown one night, Little Bo Peep costume the next night. I had to wear the outfits and insult him while we played."

"Whoa...talk about in your wheelhouse."

"Ha, ha. I had to do it. He threatened to let the guards harm Kelsey if I didn't."

"There." I removed the cuff and rubbed her wrist. "Better?"

"Much."

We stood. In the red knee-high boots, Svetlana stood as tall as me. We studied each other's faces. And then everything else—the sirens and gunfire outside, the harshly lit office, the smell of oil smoke—everything fell away and there was only the two of us. I saw her eyes dilate, and she reached for me a split second before I did for her. Our lips touched, and I swear an electrical current pulsed through me. I closed my eyes and held her. Her arms were draped around my neck; my hands caressed her willowy rib cage. We kissed gently until she whimpered. In all the years I'd known her, I'd never heard the always cool Svetlana make such a sound. I yanked her torso into mine so her curves compacted against my chest. Her breath was hot on my cheek. I had never been in such physical proximity to this woman. Her scent this close—warm and floral—was a headier form of the aroma that surrounded her always. Her fingertips caressed the nape of my neck. Then our tongues touched and I thought my mouth would spontaneously combust. An "Mmmm" came from deep in her throat and vibrated up her tongue. She backed me against the wall. I kissed her some more on the mouth, then uncoupled and nibbled my way up her neck to her ear.

"Wonder Woman is my favorite superhero," I whispered.

"*Zadnitza*. Stop talking, Holmes."

As she leaned in to kiss me again, I heard a door slam in the outer office. I eased her away and grabbed the Thompson.

"We have to go."

Taking hold of her hand, I led us to the outside door. At the bottom of the steps, we ran across the open ground toward the fence.

"I've got Svetlana," I said into the radio.

"We know," Frank said. "Tell Wonder Woman we heard everything. *Holmes*."

"Wonderful."

A few yards from the fence, my bad leg gave out. I fell. Svetlana crouched, got under my arm, helped me to my feet.

"You know," I said, "you're a lot stronger than you look."

Even in the darkness I could feel her predatory eyes on me.

"And you are somewhat smarter than *you* look."

We ducked through the hole in the fence and tottered up the hill together. The light from the distant flames was at our backs.

"*Layno*," she said, looking at her hand. "I think I broke a nail."

"Deal with it, Wonder Woman."

43

Are You Ready to be Wowed?

We were back in New York late that night, and the next morning I sent Lily and Vivian big bouquets of American Beauties. Kelsey was understandably traumatized, so I put her up at my place and took her to a therapist who specialized in treating post-traumatic stress. Svetlana allowed Yuri and Viktor to guard her, and for the next couple of days, we rested.

Besides being exhausted from the case, I was confused about where things stood between Svetlana and me. Did we kiss because we were both swept away by adrenaline, or was the kiss the culmination of a long-smoldering passion? When all of us ate dinner at Svetlana's one night, Svetlana and I, for the first time ever, stumbled trying to talk to each other. It didn't help that the monolithic Yuri and Viktor were there.

The three of us could have laid low for a month, but fate intervened. Kelsey and I were watching TV in my apartment when there was a knock at the door. Gun in hand, I checked the peephole. It was NYPD Detective Ellis Carter. She was carrying a Fairway grocery bag. I put the gun away and opened the door.

"Detective Carter, what a nice surprise," I said. "You finally decided to come over and cook for me."

"Oh, Dakota Stevens—always trying to score a date." She gave me a grim smile. "I've been looking for Kelsey Wright. Did she end up hiring you to find her brother?"

"Yes, and she's here as a matter of fact."

"I have news about him," she said.

By her tone, I knew what the news was.

"Yeah. Come in."

I led her into the living room. When Kelsey saw the detective, she shut off the TV and sat up.

"What's going on? Is this about my brother?"

"Yes," Ellis said.

"He's dead, isn't he?" Kelsey said.

"Yes, I'm afraid so."

"I knew it. Was he murdered?"

"It doesn't appear so." Ellis put down the bag and sat beside Kelsey. "These are his personal effects. His body is at the city morgue."

"So, what happened?" Kelsey asked.

Ellis explained. Conover's body had been found in the rocks on the Vinalhaven shore. A rubber dinghy was found capsized in a nearby cove. The Maine State Police believed Conover had been in the boat during a storm, and when the boat capsized, he drowned. They contacted Detective Ellis when his missing persons report came up.

"So the report was useful after all," Kelsey said.

"Yes," Ellis said. "I've been trying to find you for a few days. I had your brother's body transported back to New York. You'll need to make arrangements as soon as possible."

"Okay, thanks for coming," Kelsey said.

Ellis gave me a quizzical look.

"I'll have her call if she has questions," I said.

"Goodbye, Kelsey," Ellis said. "I truly am sorry."

Kelsey grabbed the grocery bag and went into the second bedroom. I walked Ellis to the door.

"This has been stressful on her," I said.

"I understand." She went to the elevator and punched the button. "By the way, this probably has nothing to do with Conover or Kelsey, but his girlfriend, Jennifer Lin, was found murdered the other day. Did you question her?"

"Yes. Where was she found?"

"In an alley near her apartment," she said. "Speaking of apartments—nice one by the way. Love that Swingin' Sixties look."

"Thanks."

The elevator arrived and she boarded it and disappeared. I went to Kelsey's bedroom. The door was open. She was going through Conover's effects on the bed.

"Are you all right?" I asked. "Do you need to talk?"

"No." She looked at a sweater and folded it up.

"I'm sorry about Conover," I said.

"You know what? I'm kind of relieved. Not knowing what happened to him was worse. Way worse."

"I can understand that."

"And you know what else?" she said. "When they were holding me hostage, I thought about him a lot. He was so selfish. He just expected me to take care of him, and he didn't give a crap about what I wanted. And all of his secrets. He never trusted me enough to tell me the truth about his life. Then he gets involved in this whole mess, never thinking about how it might affect *me*."

"I know, but you don't have to remember him that way. You can remember him for the good things."

"I suppose."

"Do you want to start making arrangements for him?" I asked.

"Not today."

She picked up a pair of jeans, felt inside the pockets, and tossed them on the bed.

"Looking for something?" I asked.

She dug into the bag, pulled out a yellow foul-weather jacket, and kept rummaging through the bag.

"As a matter of fact…ah, here we go." She removed a belt with a thick buckle. "Are you ready to be wowed?"

"What do you mean?"

Pinching and twisting on the buckle, she made a hatch slide open in the back. Something dropped into her hand. She clenched her fist so I couldn't see what it was.

"Remember when I said Conover always kept a copy of his work on him?"

"Are you saying what I think you're saying?"

She opened her palm, revealing a small plastic baggie with a flash drive inside.

"Well done, junior Watson."

She beamed.

"Let's take a look," I said.

Kelsey grabbed her messenger bag, laid her laptop on the bureau and turned it on. She inserted the flash drive. It contained eight PDF files and a word processing document titled "Helium-3 Conspiracy."

"Open one of the PDFs first," I said.

It was a scanned image of a printed report, with the words "CLASSIFIED — TOP SECRET" at the top of every page. Logos for the Department of Energy and NASA appeared on the cover page along with the title: "LUNAR HELIUM-3 FEASIBILITY: A JOINT STUDY."

"Jackpot," Kelsey said.

"This is incredible," I said. "Now open the—"

She clicked on the word processing file:

The Helium-3 Conspiracy: An Exposé
by
E. Conover Wright

I patted Kelsey on the shoulder. "There's somebody who needs to see these."

"Who?"

"Professor Rosetti at MIT. I spoke to him a few days ago. Let's go down to the office and print them out."

"Should I back them up first? Put them on my hard drive?"

"No. We don't want copies of these files floating around. Eject the drive and give it to me."

On our way down to the office, I called Svetlana, told her what we'd found, and asked her to meet us. By the time she arrived, we had already printed the eight PDFs and the 237-page book manuscript.

"Hey, Champ," I said. "Could you call your manager friend at the Taj in Boston and book us a suite for tonight and tomorrow?"

"Certainly. Are we going to see Professor Rosetti?"

"I'd prefer it if he came to see us. Please call and ask him to come to our room tomorrow morning."

She swiveled in her chair to face me.

"And when he asks why, what shall I tell him?"

"Tell him about Conover," I said, "and that we have startling information about his last book. Tell him that we need his expertise. I'm pretty sure he'll come."

She gestured at the door to the hallway, where Yuri and Viktor were standing guard.

"And what about my mute musclemen?"

"They should come too."

I thought about this prospect.

"But get them their own room."

44

The Good Guys Don't Always Win

After breakfast the next morning, the five of us including Yuri and Viktor sat in our suite at the Taj waiting for the professor to arrive. I looked out the window at the Public Garden. It was a bright but cold and blustery day. Pedestrians walked through the park hunched over as leaves swirled around them. Behind me, Svetlana and Kelsey sat on a sofa, typing away on their laptops. I checked my watch. It was eight thirty.

The night before, I had read the eight classified documents and parts of Conover's book. Much of the science went over my head, but the common conclusion of all of the materials was clear and convincing: that adoption of helium-3 as the world's primary energy source would be revolutionary, making fossil fuels irrelevant. No wonder Harlan was so desperate to prevent the documents from getting out.

At nine o'clock, there were three knocks on the door, followed by two more. I had my gun out as I answered it.

"Who is it?"

"Doctor Rosetti."

Holstering my gun, I let him in and checked the hallway. It was clear. Back inside, I locked and chained the door.

"Thank you for coming, Professor," I said. "This is my associate, Svetlana Krüsh—you two spoke on the phone. And our client, Kelsey Wright—Conover's sister."

"Yes," he said, shaking her hand, "my condolences, Miss Wright. I admired your brother a great deal."

"Thanks, Professor," she said. "He felt the same about you."

Rosetti turned to me and frowned. "Now, Mr. Stevens, why all of the clandestine maneuvering?"

"I'm sorry about that, Professor. Did you change cabs?"

"Yes, as instructed I took one to the Copley Plaza and a second one here. I assume this has to do with the sensitive material Ms. Krüsh mentioned."

"Extremely sensitive," Svetlana said.

I sat in an armchair and waved at the one across from me.

"Please, Professor, sit down."

After a moment's hesitation, he eased into the chair. On the coffee table between us were two manila envelopes. I pointed to them.

"We need your opinion on these documents."

"Okay." He started to reach for the envelopes.

"Wait," I said. "Before you start, there's something you should know. People have been murdered over this information."

He sat back in his chair. "What are the documents?"

"One envelope contains classified reports by the Department of Energy and NASA. The other is the manuscript of Conover's last book. It's about helium-3. More than anything, I need to know if Conover's conclusions are accurate."

"What are the classified reports?" he asked.

"They're also about helium-3. There are eight of them, but the most detailed one is a feasibility study."

He eyed the envelopes and tapped the chair arm with his fingers.

"If you choose to read them," I said, "you'll have to read them here. We can't have these leaked."

"Are these your only copies?"

"Physical copies, yes. The electronic files are on a flash drive locked up in a safe place."

He continued to tap the chair arm.

"Should I be worried about my own safety, or my family's?"

"Well, let me ask you—does anyone know that we met in Baltimore?"

"No."

"Does anyone know you're here today?"

"No."

"Then you're fine," I said.

"Famous last words." The professor nodded at Yuri and Viktor, who sat across the room playing with their smart phones. "Who are they?"

"Protection," I said.

The professor raked a hand through his hair.

"Which one has the reports?" he asked.

"On your left."

He picked it up and opened it.

"If you need anything, Professor," I said, "let us know."

"Just let me read."

He put on a pair of glasses, crossed his legs and rested the reports on his knee.

"Svetlana," I said. "I'm going out for a walk. Remind Yuri and Viktor that the code for the door is three knocks, then two, okay?"

"Yuri, Viktor," she said.

They looked up from their phones.

"Dakota pryymaye na prohulyanku. Pam'yatayte-try stukaye u dveri, potim dva. Zrozumiv?"

They nodded.

"Good." I slipped on my coat.

"Dakota," Kelsey said. "Can I come with you?"

"Not right now. I need to think. Don't worry—you're safe here."

Out on Arlington Street, I waved off a doorman who offered me a cab, then crossed the street and went into the Public Garden. Even though I wore a sweater and overcoat, the cold wind cut through me. I tucked my hands in my pockets and breathed deeply of the fresh air to clear my head.

In almost every respect, this case had been a failure. Yes, I'd gotten Svetlana and Kelsey back, which I was profoundly grateful for, but Harlan Energy Solutions was going to get away with kidnapping and murder.

I crossed the street and walked into Boston Common. The park was empty except for a smiling young woman adroitly walking a dozen dogs in a bizarre, tangled ballet. I marveled at her as she turned uphill with the dogs toward the gold-domed statehouse. I went to a coffee cart, bought a hot chocolate and sat at the top of some bleachers overlooking the baseball diamond. A group of college kids, male and female, played touch football in the outfield.

Up to now I had an undefeated record in private practice. But in this business, as in life, the good guys don't always win. The best I could hope for was to eke out a draw. I wouldn't be able to nail Harlan and his people for the murders, but I could make sure the victims hadn't died in vain.

Sipping the hot chocolate, I knew what I had to do. One, release Conover's book. And two, release the reports most damaging to Harlan, but least damaging to U.S. national security. I would ask the professor which reports met those criteria. Clearly Harlan knew this material could harm his business, which was why he'd tried so hard to stop Conover. Maybe Harlan couldn't be prosecuted for what he did, but I wanted him to know that at least one other person knew the truth. To accomplish this, I would have to confront him face-to-face. How I would do that, I had no idea yet.

With thoughts of the documents and Harlan temporarily off my mind, questions about the situation with Svetlana crept in. Could we continue to work together? How did she feel about me? How did I feel about her?

I put up my coat collar against the wind. I sipped the hot chocolate and stared at the leaves blowing across the baseball diamond. I sipped, stared, and waited for answers. None came. In the outfield, the football game broke up. The college kids shambled by below me and disappeared down the path. I took one last sip of my hot chocolate. Finding it cold, I climbed down from the bleachers, threw it away and continued my walk.

When I returned to the hotel, the professor was engrossed in his reading. Svetlana worked on her laptop while Kelsey slept in her bedroom. I got Svetlana's attention and asked her to join me in the adjoining bedroom. I shut the door behind us.

"I wanted us to talk alone for a few minutes."

"I assume you did some thinking during your walk," she said.

"I did."

She settled into an armchair and crossed her legs. "And what are your conclusions?"

I sat in the other armchair.

"I want to do two things—confront Harlan, and release the documents. Conover's book at least. Harlan has been trying to prevent the truth from getting out, and I want him to see that no matter how powerful he is, he's powerless to stop this."

"Won't this put Kelsey and us in more danger?"

"No," I said. "Harlan's going to keep searching for Conover's work—that keeps us danger. But if we expose what he's been trying to keep secret, then everyone will know and the fact that *we* know won't matter anymore. The question is, how can we release the documents without getting caught?"

"Leave that to me." She plucked some lint off her sweater. "I know some people who are capable of putting these materials on the web and covering their tracks. The information will go viral in a matter of hours."

"Good. Now I have to figure out how to meet face-to-face with Harlan. It's not like I can make an appointment."

"I think confronting him is foolish, Dakota. This is your ego talking. You should let it go."

"I'm not letting it go, Svetlana. It may be my ego, but I've got to make things a *little* uncomfortable for him. What if I did it in public?"

"Fine, if you insist," she said. "I will look into it."

The room was quiet. Sitting in the armchair, with Svetlana in hers six feet away, I realized this was the first time we'd been alone since the kiss. I then became aware of the king-sized bed in front of us. I thought of the kiss and stared at the bed. I stared at the bed for several seconds, and when I looked at Svetlana again, I saw that she, too, was staring at the bed. She turned to me. Her chest rose and fell. We gazed at each other until she heaved out a breath and rose to her feet.

"We should see how the professor is doing," she said.

"Yes. Yes, we should."

I stood and opened the door for her.

"Thank you." She went out.

Finished with the reports, the professor had moved on to Conover's book, which he appeared to be a third of the way through. With Yuri and Viktor in tow, Svetlana went shopping on Newbury Street while Kelsey and I stayed behind and played cards. When Svetlana returned, we ordered room service, and the professor continued reading as he ate. After lunch, Kelsey and I strolled over to Trinity Church in Copley Square, where Kelsey lit a candle for her brother. When we got back to the hotel, Kelsey went into her bedroom for a nap. Svetlana approached me as I hung up my coat.

"He finished," she said.

"Incredible material," Rosetti said.

I sat down across from him.

"In your opinion, Professor, do any of the documents contain any state secrets? In other words, is there anything that might harm the United States if it got out?"

He slipped the printouts into their manila envelopes and sat back in his chair.

"Not that I can see. The most revealing thing is that NASA and the Department of Energy conducted a feasibility study on lunar mining and extraction of helium-3. They determined that while the initial investment would be astronomical—in the order of a trillion dollars—a mining colony on the moon could be paying for itself within a decade. Within two decades, ninety percent of our energy could be coming from helium-3."

He sipped his soda, put it down and continued.

"One of the reports includes formulas on energy production and gives concrete examples. I've read one of its examples elsewhere—that twenty-five tons of helium-3, enough to fill a space shuttle, would power the entire United States for a year."

"Amazing," I said.

"The other secret—although I wouldn't consider it a *state* secret—is in Conover's book. He states unequivocally that for twenty-five years Harlan Energy Solutions has exerted influence on Department of Energy and NASA officials, as well as influential members of Congress, to have multiple reports suppressed."

"Does Conover substantiate that claim?" I asked.

"Absolutely." The professor gestured with his glasses. "He cites an interview with a DOE secretary named Terence Dalton. He also tracks Harlan's campaign contributions, and he documents an intricate, forty-year misinformation campaign conducted by the fossil fuels lobby. Among their many tactics, they have convinced Congress and scientists that obtaining energy from helium-3 is impossible, that it's science fiction."

"So, Professor, personally, what do you think of Conover's book? Does it have scientific merit, or is it the ramblings of a nut?"

"This book most certainly has scientific merit, and as a fan who has read all of Conover's work, I think it's meticulously researched, and that this is the best writing he's ever done. But what I admire most about it is Conover's ability to visualize the future and explain the implications. He comes to three conclusions in the book."

"Which are?" Svetlana said.

"One, that helium-3 is a viable alternative to fossil fuels that produces no carbon dioxide emissions, and can supply the Earth's energy needs for ten thousand years."

"*Incroyable*," Svetlana said.

"Two, that to make helium-3 the world's energy source would require international business and government cooperation on a scale not seen since World War Two. And since Harlan and other companies have been investing in fracking technology for decades, and it's finally beginning to pay off, they are going to be highly resistant to cooperating on helium-3 energy projects."

"That makes sense," I said.

The professor nodded.

"But Conover's third conclusion is by far the most illuminating," he said. "Conover predicts that a clean, abundant, inexpensive energy source like helium-3 would revolutionize the world's economic system. For starters, with electricity so cheap, all cars would be one hundred percent electric. Fossil fuels would take an incalculable hit. But here's a more concrete example that speaks to the economics. Today the cost of energy puts close to one hundred billion dollars into the U.S. economy every year. However, with helium-3 as the energy source, that figure would drop to an estimated three billion per year. Obviously this is a huge economic threat to Harlan and the entire fossil fuels industry."

I stood and paced around the room.

"If helium-3 is the solution to the world's energy problems, why aren't we doing it yet? I mean, besides because of the greed of the fossil fuels industry."

The professor tented his fingers.

"As I think I mentioned to you the last time we spoke, one of the major obstacles with helium-3 is the difficulty of mining it and returning it to Earth. For example, extremely large amounts of lunar soil would need to be processed to extract the helium-3. However"—he nodded at the envelopes—"these reports indicate that that obstacle can be overcome."

"What are the other obstacles?" Svetlana asked.

"Well, the others are mainly financial in nature," he said. "To build the first helium-3 fusion power plant would cost an estimated six billion dollars. Then, before power companies could break even, they would need to have five such plants on line. So it would require tremendous investment before they would see any payoff."

"But in the long run," I said, "it would probably be more profitable for them, wouldn't it?"

"Almost certainly," he said.

"One final question, Professor, and we'll let you go."

"Yes?"

"If this information got out to the public at large, what do you think the repercussions would be?"

He folded his arms across his chest and gazed at the blank HDTV screen.

"Well, I imagine there would be Congressional hearings—particularly about the reports. The Justice Department would probably investigate, and the media would be interested in Harlan's influence on congressmen."

Svetlana looked at me. "If I may."

"Of course."

"Do you think this could create a change in U.S. energy policy?" she asked.

His brow furrowed. "I'd like to think so, but it's doubtful. It might spark a debate, but eventually the controversy would die down."

"Thank you, Professor." I shook his hand. "Needless to say, you never read these documents, and this meeting never happened."

"Agreed."

I walked him to the door, shook his hand again and let him out. When I returned to the sitting area, Svetlana was putting the envelopes in her bag.

"Wow, right?" I said.

"Yes," she said. "Very much so."

A door opened. Kelsey emerged from her bedroom rubbing her eyes.

"So he's gone?"

"Yes," I said.

"What happens next?"

"We release the documents," I said.

"When?" Kelsey asked.

"As soon as I confront Harlan."

45

Espionage Personified

At nine o'clock the next morning, we were all in the office back in New York. While I unpacked banker's boxes and put file folders in filing cabinets, Svetlana sat at her desk doing research. With the Internet hooked up—finally—the first thing she did that morning was set up the WiFi. She also had several gallons of paint and painting supplies delivered and put Yuri and Viktor to work. I think they welcomed the activity. Kelsey slept on the couch, covered by a blanket.

"So." Svetlana laid her computer on her lap. "I have three options for where you could confront Harlan."

"Great."

She removed her glasses and rolled toward me in her chair.

"It seems he is on an East Coast tour. Tonight he attends a political fundraiser in D.C., and—"

"Exerting more influence."

"Yes," she said. "Anyhow, there are still tickets available."

"How much?"

"Ten thousand dollars a plate."

I snorted. "As Falcone would say, 'Lotsa luck.' What else?"

"Tomorrow morning he is giving testimony in Albany to a Senate fracking committee," Svetlana said. "He is expected to discuss a recent DOE report that says fracking does not contaminate ground water. According to an article in the *Times*, he has been trying to extend his operations into New York for years."

"Albany won't work either," I said. "I'd never get close enough to him."

"Well, *Goldilocks*, perhaps this one will be *just right*." She adjusted an earring. "Tomorrow afternoon he is supposed to join a pheasant shoot at the Pawling Sporting Club. Apparently it is quite exclusive."

"It's exclusive all right. A lot of wealthy people fly up in helicopters to hunt there. It's close to my place in Millbrook, too."

"How would you get in?" she asked.

"By showing up in my Cadillac wearing shooting clothes and carrying a Beretta over-under shotgun."

"Looking like you belong there," she said.

"Exactly."

Svetlana glanced at her computer screen.

"While researching Harlan's schedule, I discovered something interesting."

"What?"

"Half of his board of directors served in the Department of Energy for a decade or more, and the current Secretary of Energy was an HES vice president immediately preceding his Cabinet position."

"Big surprise. It's that private sector–public sector revolving door again. This explains how Harlan got reports shelved, and how he learned about Terence Dalton's leaks. Nice catch, Svetlana."

"Möchten Sie etwas weniger von mir erwarten?"

"German, right?" I said. "Translation?"

"'Would you expect any less from me?'"

"Never."

She nodded and rolled back to her desk.

"We should get going. Kelsey has her appointment soon."

"Right," I said. "What time are we meeting the hacker?"

"Four o'clock. At the Cloisters, in the courtyard with the quince trees."

"Weird, but okay," I said.

"He will do what I ask, without any questions. I wake Kelsey now."

I watched her as she went to the couch, stooped and whispered in Kelsey's ear. It was the most motherly thing I'd ever seen Svetlana do.

With Yuri and Viktor following in their SUV, we took Kelsey to her therapy appointment, then to a funeral director where she arranged for her brother's cremation, then to an attorney to settle his estate. After a late lunch, we drove up to the northern tip of Manhattan, to the Cloisters—a rebuilt French monastery overlooking the Hudson River.

A heavy fog had rolled up the island, and it was misting when we got out of the car. The inside had a collection of medieval art, but behind its high walls were also a number of courtyards with covered walkways around the perimeter (cloisters).

At four o'clock, we went outside into the Cuxa Cloister—the one with the quince trees. The leaves were a deep russet red. Aside from an elderly couple sitting on the low walls beneath the columned arches, the courtyard was empty. Svetlana, Kelsey and I stood by the fountain near the trees, while Yuri and Viktor leaned against an archway across the courtyard. When fifteen minutes had passed, I started to wonder if this guy would show.

Then a young man wearing a newsboy cap and sunglasses walked into the courtyard. He had his hands in his pockets. As he drew nearer, I noticed he had sandy blonde hair and a wispy, wishful attempt at mutton chops. He didn't look much older than Kelsey. He walked around the courtyard once, then sidled up to Svetlana. In her belted trench coat and a rakish olive fedora, she was espionage personified.

"You are late," she said.

"Sorry. Missed the bus."

I flashed Svetlana my "You Sure Can Pick 'Em" face and turned to the kid.

"Forget it," I said. "I don't know who you are—and I don't want to know—but before Svetlana gives you the files, I want to be clear about a few things. First, are you certain you can release them so they can't be traced back to you?"

"Of course," he said. "Do I need to explain how?"

"No. And obviously you will *not* copy the files onto your hard drive."

"I won't."

"And you know to destroy the flash drive once you've uploaded the files?"

"Yes," he moaned.

Svetlana jabbed a finger at him. "This is serious. Some dangerous people do not want these files released. You will destroy the flash drive as soon as the files are uploaded."

"All right, Svetlana, I'm sorry," he said. "Jeez."

"Last thing," I said. "Don't release them until you hear from Svetlana, got it?"

He nodded meekly. Svetlana handed him the flash drive, and held onto it.

"Do not lose it."

Kelsey said, "We went through a lot for that."

"Relax," he said, tucking it in his pocket. "It's under control."

"When are you going to release the files?" I asked.

"When Svetlana contacts me."

"Buy a burner with cash and text me with the number," she said. "After I call you, destroy the burner."

"All right."

"And make sure the files are distributed widely," I said. "To the major media outlets most of all."

"Don't worry. An hour after Svetlana calls, they'll be viral, I guarantee it. Can I go now?"

"Take off your sunglasses for a second."

He did. He had a serious face for a young man.

"All right, go ahead," I said.

He put the sunglasses back on and disappeared into the museum. I tapped Svetlana on the arm.

"How do you know him anyway?"

"From a blindfold chess exhibition I did three years ago. He was one of my vanquished opponents. Now he worships me."

"Who doesn't?" I said.

She batted her eyelashes.

46

A Fresh Bouquet of Pheasants

It was one thirty on the day of the pheasant shoot, and I stood in my Millbrook dressing room checking out my shooting ensemble in the mirror. I wore a wool flat cap, a tweed shooting coat I'd picked up in Scotland years ago, and wool trousers tucked into olive green wellies. I had a leather cartridge bag filled with 12-gauge bird shot over my shoulder and a .45 Glock under my arm.

The men at the shoot would be dressed like English manor lords, and while I didn't look exactly like them, I would pass for a loader—the guy who stood behind the manor lord and loaded his shotguns. I picked up my shotgun in its leather case and went upstairs.

I passed Yuri and Viktor sitting in the library, and when I went into the living room, Svetlana was on the sofa in front of the fire, playing through a chess game on the big slab coffee table. She looked up with an amused expression.

"Not a word," I said.

She rose and followed me to the back door.

"Off to shoot some poor defenseless birds," she said.

"I won't be shooting any, I promise."

"Aiding and abetting at least."

"Harsh, but true," I said. "Where's Kelsey?"

"Taking a nap."

I nodded and checked my watch.

"Remember, in forty minutes—"

"Yes," she said, "call the lodge and ask for Mr. Brace. Consider it done."

I put my hand on the doorknob.

"Wish me luck?"

"I still think this is unnecessary and foolish."

"Maybe, but I need to do it."

Without a word, she stepped up to me, appraised my outfit and adjusted my cap. We were frozen looking at each other when a floorboard creaked and Viktor passed behind her into the kitchen.

"Okay, I'm off." I opened the door.

"Dakota?"

"Yes, Champ?"

"Be careful."

Right then I wanted to kiss her and I sensed that she did me, but with Viktor peering in the refrigerator ten feet away, it didn't seem right.

"I will," I said as I closed the door.

I sped along the serpentine roads, reveling in the bright sky and the colorful leaves swirling in the car's wake. Once through the club gate, I roared up the mountainside, passed a pond with duck blinds in the reeds, and parked my Cadillac in front of the big lodge among fifty Range Rovers. I got out carrying the shotgun. Wood smoke and the piquant smell of leaf tannin were thick in the air. A young man driving an all-terrain golf cart approached. I waved him down.

"Help you, sir?" he said.

"Yes, I'm one of the loaders. Which way to the shoot?"

"Heading down there myself. I'll give you a ride."

"Appreciate it."

I got in and we bumped down a rutted gravel road, then turned onto a grass-striped lane flanked by full maples and oaks.

"You're in luck," the young man said. "They haven't started the first drive yet. Who're you loading for?"

"Mr. Harlan."

"Really? I thought that other guy—Brace—was his loader."

"Nope. He was just filling in until I got here."

"Gotcha. Well, here we are."

"Thanks."

He pulled into a broad field. I got out. Women in fitted tweed suits and feathered felt hats lounged at tables sipping from teacups. Under any other circumstances one of the wives, a forest fire redhead, would have rendered me helpless. But today was different. Today I was thinking about what I was going to say to Harlan.

Across the field, facing a tree line whose color had already peaked, were ten pairs of men spread out in a long row. In the center I spotted Brace, towering over Harlan. I checked my watch. Svetlana would call any minute.

Pheasants heading in all directions flew over the tree line. Shotguns boomed. One pheasant's wings ceased flapping, and the bird plummeted out of the sky like a badly thrown football. Svetlana's comment about the "poor defenseless birds" came to mind. The pheasant landed in the grass a few yards from me. A golden retriever streaked across the field, picked up the bird in its jaws and trotted back to a group of dog handlers.

A club attendant near me spoke into a walkie-talkie and crossed the field to Harlan and Brace. That would be Svetlana—right on time. The young man spoke to Brace, who handed over a shotgun and walked out of the field. When I was sure he was gone, I inserted ear plugs and marched over to Harlan.

Harlan aimed at a pheasant passing overhead, and missed with both shots.

"You missed," I said loudly.

Harlan spun around glaring at me. "You? What the hell are *you* doing here?"

I tapped my cartridge bag. "Here to load for you." I put down my shotgun in its case. "I thought we could catch up."

Harlan stared at me. I stared back. After three seconds, he figured out that he was outmatched in a staring contest. He glanced at the attendant and jerked his head to the side. The attendant handed me the second shotgun and walked away. Once I'd loaded it and traded guns with Harlan, he faced the tree line again.

"You know, Mr. Stevens, I could easily have an accident with this. The former Vice President had one."

He grinned at me over his shoulder. I held my coat open and showed him the Glock.

"So could I."

He turned away from me.

"What do you want?"

"A chat," I said. "I'll talk. You'll listen."

"Fine. Start talking."

A new wave of pheasants flapped madly over the tree line. I opened the empty shotgun at the breech, inserted two fresh shells and snapped it shut. Harlan fired both of his shots, and we traded guns again—the empty one for the loaded one. I reloaded the empty one. Harlan faced away from me as we waited for the next bouquet of pheasants to fly overhead.

"I'll keep this brief," I said. "Believe me, I don't want to spend any more time with you than I have to. It's clear you're going to get away with your crimes, but I wanted you to know that I know the truth."

"And what is the truth, Mr. Stevens?"

"Well, first of all, I know you got those DOE–NASA classified reports shelved."

"I have no idea what you're talking about."

"Sure you don't," I said. "You couldn't afford to have information about helium-3 in the hands of environmental crusaders, or members of Congress pushing alternative energy reform. Those reports explicitly state that helium-3 is a viable energy source. This is not information that a multi-billionaire from the oil and gas fracking industry wants the general public to find out about."

More pheasants flew overhead. Shotgun blasts rang out along the row of shooters. Again Harlan missed with both shots. I handed him the freshly loaded gun and took the empty one.

"Through your contacts at the DOE—a bunch of former executives of HES; nice revolving door you've got there by the way—you learned there was a leak in the department: Deputy Assistant Secretary Terence Dalton. Not only had he *not* shelved the reports, but he'd passed them to a writer named E. Conover Wright."

I reloaded the shotgun in my hands and snapped it shut.

"But it didn't stop there," I continued. "Unbeknownst to Dalton, Conover was sharing the information with the Chinese Science Ministry. He couldn't stand that industry and government were preventing the development of a viable energy solution."

"This is highly imaginative," Harlan said. "Go on."

"Getting back to you," I said. "You knew about Dalton, Wright and the Chinese, so you tipped off the FBI. You figured their investigation would shut down whatever Dalton and Conover were working on. The problem was, the meetings between them had stopped, Conover disappeared, and that's when you started to worry.

"You sent those knucklehead Bishop brothers to New York, who were useless. Next, you called in some wiseguys from Jersey—also ineffective. I'm guessing that's when Mr. Brace and his security team got involved. Or should I say killing squad? Because that's what they did—kill people. People like Ginger Best, an innocent fan and Conover's lover. I still don't know how your men found them on Vinalhaven, but it doesn't matter now."

Harlan fired, hit a pheasant, and traded guns with me. I didn't reload the empty one.

"You had other people killed for what they might know—people including Stoddart Prince and Conover's girlfriend Jennifer Lin. However, I suspect Brace did those, not your security team. I bet you wanted Dalton and the editor Kyle Foster dead too, but someone beat you to it. Any guesses as to who it was? No? Jennifer Lin. She wasn't the girlfriend—she was a Chinese assassin sent to clean up. The Chinese didn't want his book getting out either."

Harlan was looking at the sky above the tree line with his gun poised. He lowered his head.

"Interesting," he said. "Continue, Mr. Stevens."

"I plan to," I said. "What really pissed me off was your people kidnapping Svetlana and Kelsey to make me find Conover. He was already dead, of course, but neither of us knew it at the time. My hunch is Conover took his laptop with him when he escaped, so it's probably at the bottom of the Atlantic now."

Harlan fired his two shots, missed, and handed back the empty gun. Both guns were empty now, and I held onto them.

"Gun, Mr. Stevens."

"Of course the truth won't come out now," I said, "and you and your fracking pals will continue to make billions."

"A shame, isn't it?"

"Well, fortunes can change, Mr. Harlan. A lot faster than you might think."

He crossed his arms. "A fascinating tale."

A fresh bouquet of pheasants rushed over the tree line. He nodded at them.

"Care to try your hand, Mr. Stevens?"

"No, thanks," I said. "The pheasants haven't given me any reason to kill them. Unlike some humans I know."

I shoved both empty shotguns into his hands.

"By the way, I have to thank you," I said.

"For what?"

"For giving me the chance to blow up a tanker car," I said. "I'd always wanted to do that."

Harlan's face turned red. A vein along his temple bulged.

"Easy, Harlan. Don't have a stroke. It's just a tanker car."

I picked up my shotgun case and headed back across the field. On my way out I grabbed a chicken salad sandwich from the refreshments table. As I turned up the grassy lane, a golf cart passed me. Brace glared at me from the passenger seat. I ignored him, gnashed into the sandwich and hiked to my car.

When I got home, the place was alive for the first time since my grandparents died. The smells of roast beef and pumpkin pie wafted through the warm house. Sinatra singing "The Good Life" filled the living room. Kelsey and Johnny Quinn, wearing aprons, cooked in the kitchen while Yuri and Viktor watched. I hung up my coat and went into the living room. The fireplace crackled softly. The chessboard was still on the coffee table, but Svetlana wasn't around.

I put the shotgun and shooting things away and changed into jeans and my favorite cashmere sweater. When I returned, Svetlana met me in front of the fire. She held a glass of red wine in one lissome hand, a highball of dark liquor in the other.

"Two-fisting it, Svetlana?" I said. "Tsk-tsk. I thought we didn't drink when we're on a case."

"*Zadnitza*. The scotch is for you."

"I'm intrigued. Macallan?"

"Yes. Eighteen-year. A double." She handed it to me. "And the *case* is over."

"You're right." I took a long, deep breath. "Finally."

"Shall I release the hounds?"

"Do it, Watson."

Pulling out her cell phone, she dialed a number and said, "Go." She hung up and sipped her wine. I made a grand gesture with my arms.

"What's all this?"

She closed her eyes and shrugged minutely.

"What," I said, "no pipe and slippers?"

I smiled and went to the sofa. Svetlana sat down beside me. We were watching the fire when "Strangers in the Night" came on. We glanced at each other and chuckled. Our bodies weren't touching, but I could feel the warmth from her. I sipped my scotch.

"Hey," I said, "let me ask you...that Wonder Woman costume—what ever became of it?"

"I kept it," she said.

"*Really...*"

She gave me her patented half-smile with hooded eyes.

47

The Word Was Out

After dinner, we gathered around the TV in the sunroom to see what traction the Harlan–Helium-3 story had gained. Svetlana and Kelsey sat on either side of me with their laptops on TV tray tables.

The first media outlets to pick up the story were the political websites, but by ten o'clock, all of the cable news channels were doing segments about helium-3, fracking and Harlan Energy Solutions.

"You know, it's funny," Kelsey said.

"What?" I said.

"This case with my brother. It's so *out there*. I mean, helium-3, fusion, fracking, kidnapping, murder, the moon, secret government reports, Chinese spies, scary guys with guns, and a creepy billionaire—"

I winked at Svetlana. "Who likes strong women to dress in sexy costumes and insult him."

She sighed.

"Yeah," Kelsey said. "It's all so weird. Of all the books my brother wrote, none of them are this weird."

I thought about this for a second.

"I guess it's like Mark Twain said"—I tapped the small tattoo on her wrist—"'The *truth* is stranger than fiction.'"

"That's for sure."

"We should get some sleep," I said. "This will still be here in the morning."

"It most certainly will." Svetlana stared at her computer screen. "I am predicting a media firestorm."

Before hitting the sack, I went out to the living room and threw the hard copies of the reports and Conover's book on the fire. I stood there with my nightcap, watching them burn to cinders, then stepped out on the front deck for some air. It was the coldest night of the fall yet. I gazed across the neighboring horse fields at the distant ridgeline, where a full moon had risen. Wispy clouds drifted across it, and then it was unobscured, lighting up the sky around it a dusty midnight blue. The moon itself glowed a ghostly shade of blue, and in that moment I realized something: because of what I now knew, I would never look at the moon the same way again.

There was enough helium-3 up there to power the Earth for ten thousand years.

I looked at it for a while, until a thick layer of clouds moved in and covered it. Then I went to bed.

I was back in front of the television by seven o'clock. The morning news programs featured various scientific experts, talking heads, politicians and bureaucrats arguing over Conover's revelations. I was glad not to see Professor Rosetti among them. Officials from NASA and the DOE made conflicting statements about the reports and the viability of lunar helium-3 as an energy source. NASA said they could get the helium-3, but that the DOE didn't have the ability to make helium-3 fusion work. The DOE said they could make it work, but that

NASA couldn't get the helium-3. Suddenly helium-3, an obscure isotope, was a celebrity.

Then an enterprising reporter got some outstanding footage: Harlan shoving a cameraman while trying to sneak out of the St. Regis in Manhattan, and calling the cover-up allegations "nothing but scurrilous libels" as he ducked into a gas-guzzling, monstrous SUV. After all of the grief the man had put us through, it was wonderful to see him squirm.

Later that morning, three senators held a press conference on Capitol Hill and called for hearings. Jack Harlan and his revolving door of corporate executives/ bureaucrats were to be the focus of the investigation. As for Conover, no one seemed to care that he had disclosed classified material. In fact, in one op-ed piece mourning his death, he was referred to as "a bold visionary and patriot." None of Conover's dealings with the Chinese were mentioned, and it was doubtful they ever would be. The Bureau, having skin in the game now, would see to that.

After a late breakfast, I talked Kelsey into raking leaves with me while Svetlana watched from the deck up the hill. Kelsey had never raked before, so I had to teach her how. We covered a tarpaulin with leaves, dragged it to the edge of the woods and dumped the leaves down a steep embankment.

"How are you feeling?" I asked her.

"A little better. How's your leg?"

"Much better. I heal fast."

We dragged the empty tarp back toward the pool.

"Is the therapist helping at all?" I asked.

"A little bit, like with the trauma, but knowing my brother was a traitor really hurts—even if no one's calling him a traitor yet."

"I think you need to look at this from your brother's perspective. It's not about loyalty to the United States. His loyalty was to *humanity*. I think he gave the classified documents to the Chinese to spur competition, hoping it would eventually turn into cooperation. Your brother was seeing twenty years into the future." I dropped the tarp and picked up my rake. "And while we're talking about the future…what do you think you'll do now?"

"I don't know, travel maybe," she said. "Sell the apartment. I can't live there anymore, that's for sure. Too many memories of Conover."

"Well, I'm always available if you need me."

"Thanks, Dakota. I can't tell you how much that means to me."

I waved a hand at the remaining leaves. "Help me finish?"

"I'd love to."

In the mid-afternoon, Svetlana and Kelsey went into the village with Yuri and Viktor to buy provisions for one more overnight. As soon as they left, I took a few minutes to clean and lock up my guns, and put a load of laundry in the washer.

It had been cold the night before, and with another cold night forecasted, I decided to build a fire. I wanted it roaring by the time everyone got back. The only logs left in the woodshed were gargantuan, so I was going to have to split some. I took off my shoulder holster with the Glock, hung it on the fireplace mantle and went outside.

Besides solving crimes, there are a couple of things I'm very good at, and splitting wood is one of them. I picked up my baby, an Iltis Oxhead splitting maul: premium hickory shaft, seven-pound hand-forged head, and a blade sharpened to a paper-fine edge. I could see my breath in the afternoon air. Choosing a mammoth section of maple as my first victim, I placed the log on the chopping block and stepped back to admire the foliage on Chestnut Ridge. The sky was cloudless, the air cool and resplendent. I took in deep lungfuls of it tinged with horse manure from my neighbor's boarding farm, and that unique sour scent of autumn in the country. Then, lining up my feet at a slight diagonal, I focused on the center rings, began my windup with the maul, and cleaved the first section neatly in two.

All told, I split ten of the mammoth logs before I was through. I wanted enough wood to last the night, and I wanted to make as few trips as possible, so my first armload was huge—a dozen thick pieces of maple. I almost couldn't open the back door. The storm door closed behind me, I started into the living room and a string of gunshots went off. There were several thuds against the wood, and my upper arm instantly burned. The wood toppled out of my arms. I fell into the kitchen.

I was bleeding onto the floor. My Glock was in the living room. All of my other guns were in the safe. And the shooter was between me and both places. I had to get out of the house. I grabbed a dishtowel and pressed it against my arm.

Bent double, I crossed the kitchen and opened the door to the basement. Two more shots went off, the bullets splintering the doorjamb above my head. I hurried downstairs. The washing machine was in its spin cycle. I continued down a second set of stairs into the original dirt and stone basement, and hid behind a wall.

I couldn't hear anything over the washing machine. I removed the dishtowel from my arm and looked at the wound. Fortunately, this bullet had only grazed me, but even so it had cut a two-inch gash in my skin and was bleeding steadily. I ripped the dishtowel lengthwise and wrapped one half of it tight around the wound.

The shooter had to be Brace. I hadn't seen him on TV with Harlan this morning.

The floorboards beneath the basement door creaked. The shooter was coming down here. I needed a weapon. The Glock and my gun safe were upstairs, so those were out. I didn't keep guns in the garage or guesthouse. But there *was* one other gun on the property.

After the art forgery case a year and a half ago, I realized that bad guys knew about this place, so I planted a gun in the old Scout 4x4. It was abandoned in the woods behind the guesthouse. I figured if I ever found myself outside and unarmed when bad guys showed up, I'd still have access to a gun.

But to get that gun, I first had to escape from the basement. There was one other exit—a pair of storm cellar doors on the back of the house.

I groped in the dark while avoiding the low floor beams, and finally reached the doors. A sliver of light shone through the crack. I felt around, found the bolt. It was rusty. I tugged on it. It squeaked. From another part of the basement, I heard a bucket being knocked over. I yanked on the bolt again and it opened. Bracing my feet on the steps, I rammed the doors open. Light flooded in, and I bounded blindly up the steps as another gunshot went off behind me.

I slammed the doors shut and sprinted behind the house. When I reached the orchard, two more shots went off behind me. I didn't look back, but I sensed I had a good 100-yard lead on the shooter.

From here, I could either follow the fork in the driveway that led to the guesthouse, or take a shortcut through a patch of woods. I chose the woods. When I reached the grass on the other side, my leg was throbbing. My breath was rasping and I felt as if I were floating from the adrenaline. I passed the guesthouse, and as I plunged back into the woods, there were several sharp reports behind me. Sounded like an assault rifle. I ran in the direction where I thought the Scout was, realized I'd gone the wrong way, and ran back.

Finally I found it—in a clearing beneath a walnut tree. The ground was covered with walnuts still in their green husks. I went to the passenger side, wrenched the door open and felt around under the seat.

My hand brushed springs and foam, and then I touched something smooth—a plastic bag. I yanked it out, opened it and removed the oiled cloth covering the gun. It was a 5-shot Smith & Wesson .357 Magnum revolver with a three-inch barrel. Virtually useless beyond 50 yards, and laughably outgunned by an assault rifle, but it was better than nothing. I opened the cylinder to make sure it was loaded, snapped it shut and pocketed the extra speed-loader.

The woods were loud with stillness—leaves and nuts falling, a distant woodpecker drumming on a log. It was cold, and the sweat on my skin had chilled. Shivering, I strained my ears to hear footsteps. There was a faint rustling of leaves to my right. Gently I picked up a heavy stick and threw it in the direction of the noise. The rustling stopped. I eased down on one knee and closed my eyes to focus on sounds. The rustling started again. It was heading for the other side of the truck.

I pivoted around the front bumper and sighted down the gun barrel. About 50 yards ahead, a tall, dark shape moved forward, dipping beneath the tree limbs. It was Brace, carrying an AR-15. He wore a bulletproof vest over a sweater. My shot, when I took it, would have to be a head shot.

As I steadied the gun, a walnut fell on the truck roof. Brace swiveled and sprayed a burst of shots through the windows. I ducked behind the fender. Glass got in my hair. There was a brief pause, and then another string of gunshots went off and suddenly stopped. His magazine was empty. I scrabbled into the trees, got to my feet and ran.

I needed a place where I could nullify his long-range shooting advantage, and where I'd have cover so I could ambush him. The hunting tree stand was too far away. Running along the tree line, I passed the bass pond, the tennis court, the trout pond, and finally reached the brook that ran under the driveway. The culvert pipe was a good four feet in diameter. The woods on both ends of the pipe were dim and dense with undergrowth. This was the best possible spot I could hope for. I crawled inside and squatted in the middle of the pipe, the revolver out and ready.

Brook sounds resonated in the pipe, and I couldn't hear anything from outside. I looked down the left half of the pipe, then the right. I waited there, squatting in water up to my shins, for what felt like an hour. Meanwhile, I had no idea if Brace was still on my trail. I wanted to go outside and check. But I didn't. I waited.

As I was peering down one end of the pipe, the light from the other end was suddenly blocked out. I turned and saw Brace crossing the brook. He was about 30 feet away, facing away from me, scanning the woods. Still stooped over, I crept up the pipe toward him. My feet were numb from the cold. The running water masked my footsteps and I was able to get outside and stand up before he sensed I was behind him. He started to turn around when I put his head in my sights and thumbed back the hammer on the .357 Magnum. At the sound of the click, he stopped.

"The pipe," he said. "Shit."

"Drop the gun."

He lowered it but continued to hold it in one hand by the grip, like it was a giant pistol.

"You don't want to shoot me." He spoke half over his shoulder, with his face in profile. "Shooting me will complicate your life. Shoot me, and Mr. Harlan will have a dozen men over here tomorrow." He slowly turned to face me.

"No, he won't," I said. "You don't matter enough to him."

He stared straight at me. "You know, I almost let my men loose on your partner and the girl. Now I wish I had. I would have watched."

On top of the adrenaline buzz and the pain in my leg, a flash of rage went through me. It was one of those rare instances in life when I knew exactly what I had to do. Even if Brace dropped the rifle, I had to kill him. If I didn't, I would spend the rest of my days looking over my shoulder and worrying that he'd try something against Svetlana.

"What's it like?" I asked.

"What's *what* like?" He started to raise the rifle.

"Knowing you're about to die."

His eyes opened wide and the rifle came up fast. But it was too late. His head was square in my sights, and I fired through it. He pitched backward. I fired two more times as he was falling, putting both of those shots through his neck. He collapsed into the brook.

I knew he was finished, but even so, I waited a moment before approaching him and feeling his neck for a pulse.

He was quite dead. His skin was already cool from the brook water eddying around him.

I stood there, not sure what to do.

And then a solution came to me. I hiked up to the house and called Oleksander.

"Yes, Dakota," he said. "What is it you want?"

"I need to make something disappear. Can Yuri and Viktor help me with this?"

"If I tell them to, yes. What is it you wish to disappear?"

As vaguely as I could, I told him it had to do with Svetlana's kidnapping.

"You know, Dakota, you might be disappeared, but Svetlana defend you. My daughter was harmed by your detective foolishness. It must never happen again."

"It won't."

"But that is not my biggest concern. My daughter is fond of you. Too fond. Far worse for you would be to break her heart. This would be unforgivable. *Zrozumiv*?"

"Yes, sir."

"Good. I call Yuri and Viktor now. Show them problem and they disappear it for you."

"Thank you, Mr. Krush."

"I am watching TV about billionaire. He is very impressed with his power and believes he is untouchable. I am thinking he will meet with unfortunate accident. We shall see. Goodbye."

The line went dead. I hung up and started thinking.

Where would Brace have parked his car before sneaking in here?

The Middlemiss house.

I went outside, down the hill, past the pool, and crossed the bridge to the old Middlemiss place. A Mercedes sedan was parked in the driveway. I checked the registration on the window. It was a rental car. I walked back up to the house thinking about how I could no longer consider this place my private retreat. Clearly, the word was out about my so-called *sanctum sanctorum*.

I cleaned and bandaged the bullet wound on my arm, then changed my clothes and picked up the wood in the living room. I was mopping the kitchen floor when Svetlana, Kelsey, Yuri and Viktor returned. I asked Svetlana to join me in my office and closed the door.

"Something happened while you were out."

"What?"

I told her about the shootout with Brace.

"Your father is cleaning it up," I said.

"Hmm." She wandered across the room and gazed out the window. "I wish you had not involved him, but I understand. We cannot have ties to Brace."

"I think we should get out of town for a while. You, me and Kelsey."

She turned around. "Where?"

"Let's ask her," I said. "But first I need Yuri and Viktor to do what they do."

Oleksander had already called them, so once I showed them Brace's body and car, they took care of the rest. Within twenty minutes, it was as if Brace had never been here. I poured myself a Macallan, swilled it down, and poured myself another. Then I poured Svetlana and Kelsey each a glass of wine and the three of us sat in the living room.

"Kelsey," I said, "I think we all need to get out of town for a while."

"Why?"

"Don't panic, okay?"

"Okay."

I explained what had happened. She took a deep drink of wine.

"Will there be more of them?" she asked.

"I don't think so, but I can't be certain," I said. "You said you wanted to travel. Where would you want to go?"

"Really?"

"We will come with you," Svetlana said, "wherever it is."

"Paris," she said. "I'd like to see if I can get into the American University. No matter what, it'd be nice to spend some time there."

Svetlana and I looked at each other. She gave me her "Absolutely" nod.

"Paris it is," I said.

"When will we go?" Kelsey asked.

"Do you have a passport?"

"Yes."

"Then tomorrow."

48

Hemingway's Ghost

It was late in the morning of our second day in Paris, and we stood on the sidewalk in front of the giant wooden doors to the American University. We'd just finished the tour.

"I love it," Kelsey said. "What do you guys think?"

"It's terrific," I said. "But remember, for spring admission you need to start your application right away."

"I will—tonight. Svetlana?"

"I have two thoughts," she said. "First, it is several months before the spring semester and you need to learn French. We should enroll you in an immersion course."

"Okay," Kelsey said. "And second?"

"You will require an apartment. I know an agent. I will call her, and we will start looking this afternoon."

"There's something else," Kelsey said.

"What?" I asked.

"My wardrobe. I feel so out of place. I want to look good. Like you, Svetlana."

Svetlana didn't look good. She looked *breathtaking*—brown suede jacket, rust orange ribbed turtleneck, pleated miniskirt and high-heel boots. Between the tops of her boots and the hem of her skirt were ten inches of bare leg—enough to cause any passing admirers to walk into lampposts.

"That can be arranged," Svetlana said. "We will see some apartments, then go shopping."

I jammed my hands in my pockets.

"Apartment hunting? Clothes shopping? Sorry, ladies, but I'll be having no part in this."

"Oh," Svetlana said, "and what makes you think we want you along?"

"Thanks," I said.

A Parisian woman rode by on a bicycle. She pedaled in high heels with her hair in an updo. I shook my head in amused awe.

"Wait," Kelsey said. "I forgot to ask them something."

She ran back inside. Svetlana and I stood under a tree with the buses roaring by on Avenue Bosquet.

"So," I said, "how serious were you about shopping?"

"Deadly."

"Well, while we're on the issue of money, I haven't discussed payment with Kelsey. Maybe you—"

"I already submitted a bill to her lawyer, and the funds were deposited yesterday."

"Well, *lah-dee-dah*," I said.

An elderly man strolled past us with his hands clasped behind his back. He leered at Svetlana's legs on his way by and tripped on a crack in the sidewalk. Just like back in New York.

"Okay," I said, "so you and Kelsey do your thing, and I'll see the sights. But for dinner, let's make it me and you. Kelsey can stay at the hotel and work on her application."

"Oh?" Svetlana said with a jaunty eyebrow. "Where?"

"How about *La Closerie des Lilas*? Seven o'clock?"

"Fine."

"Should I book us a table?" I asked.

She swung a new Louis Vuitton handbag in front of her like a pendulum.

"Dakota, I speak fluent French and know several of the waiters. If you are as smartly dressed later as you are now, we will not have a problem."

"Hmm…was that a compliment or not? I can never tell with you."

She leaned in, planted a lingering kiss on my cheek and spoke in my ear.

"Dakota chérie, je suis impatient de ce soir, plus que vous savez."

Her naturally predatory eyes were soft when she pulled away. I could still feel the warmth of her lipstick on my cheek. My heart pounded.

"Svetlana, that was the hottest thing I've ever heard. Say it again."

"Later perhaps." She raised her chin. "Are you sure you can get around on your own? This *is* only your second time to Paris."

"Hey, I know a little French. *J'ai besoin d'une fourchette*."

She smirked. "A handy phrase to know…*if* you need a fork."

"I'll be fine."

Kelsey emerged from the building and joined us beneath the tree.

"All set?" I asked.

"Yup."

Svetlana pulled out her phone, dialed a number and started speaking in French.

"Have fun today," I said to Kelsey.

"You, too. I can't believe I'm here!"

Her cobalt eyes were wide as she took in the autumnal scene around us. Svetlana hung up and fixed her eyes on Kelsey.

"The agent has three places to show us in the Saint-Germain-des-Prés area. Ready?"

"This is so exciting," Kelsey said. "Later, Dakota."

"*À tout à l'heure*, Dakota," Svetlana said.

"Mind your spending," I said.

They started down the sidewalk. I watched them go. And then Svetlana did something she'd never done before.

She looked back.

The look said she wanted one last glimpse of me until tonight. The look said she would be thinking about me today. But most of all the look said that the earth had shifted permanently beneath us and that she was both nervous and delighted about what the future held. It only lasted a couple of seconds, and when the corners of her mouth rose just before she turned away, I knew what she felt in her heart.

I watched them disappear up the avenue, then crossed the street and headed for the Eiffel Tower. It was as impressive as I remembered, and after circling the base, drinking it in from every angle, I walked to the Rodin Museum, where I lost track of time studying *The Thinker*. There was an anguish in the statue's eyes that is visible only in person. I wandered through the gardens, admired the statuary and had a buttery, pillowy *pain au chocolat* outdoors at the museum café. Although it was late October and brisk, many people were sitting outside. One of them—a young Parisian woman, black bolero hat, wide red-lipsticked mouth—smiled at me over her book.

Then I saw three burly American-looking men in leather jackets. They were conspicuously not looking in my direction. The thought raced through my mind that they might be H-Men, but when they got up and left without incident, I dismissed the thought as paranoia.

The case was over. Harlan was beaten. Brace was dead.

I finished my pastry.

From the Rodin Museum I took the Metro to the Latin Quarter, strolled the cobblestoned quay along the Seine, and, with my leg feeling back to normal, hiked up a long hill to Ernest Hemingway's flat at 74 Rue de Cardinal Lemoine. There was nothing to see there except a plaque beside the entrance, so I continued up the hill to the intimate Place Contrescarpe, where people at a café sat outside beneath a heated awning. I got a table facing the plaza, ordered a *café crème* and people-watched for a while.

A middle-aged man with a youthful face, wavy silver hair and striking eyes looked around the café and wrote in a notebook. I pegged him as a fellow American. Sitting across from him was a woman with dark curly hair and pale blue eyes. She had the same spark behind those eyes that Svetlana had, a spark that radiated inner beauty and brilliance.

Waiters wove between the tables. At the table next to mine, a woman fed a lapdog—a silky Maltese wearing a rhinestone collar—from her plate. Her male companion read a newspaper with the headline *"Milliardaire du pétrole américain en hélium-3 scandale."* I nodded contentedly to myself. Harlan's plight was now world news.

A pair of seasoned Frenchmen leaned back in their chairs, holding cigarettes in their fingertips and studying a backgammon board. Women of all ages with beautiful legs abounded, sipping wine and chatting. None of them, however, had the legs of Svetlana.

I fantasized about quitting our practice in New York and Svetlana and I setting up as private investigators in Paris. Complications with citizenship, visas or the language didn't matter. Our adventures would take us around the Continent: Brussels, Zurich, Munich, Monaco, Venice. When not in school, Kelsey would join us.

Then I wondered if I would miss the States. I probably would.

When my *café crème* was gone, I left a few Euros and headed west out of the Place Contrescarpe, following narrow, shop-lined streets to the splendid Jardin du Luxembourg. The gravel paths were full with bundled-up people ambling in the sunshine. I bought a bag of roasted chestnuts from a cart and swished through the fallen leaves, watching the men play chess and the nannies push strollers. I took a seat on a bench between two rows of trees. The bag of chestnuts was still warm, and I held it in my hands.

I crossed my legs and gazed out at the fountain and the still-radiant flower gardens. This was our second day in Paris, and I didn't know how long Svetlana and I would stay. A week? Two? We hadn't discussed it. Perhaps we would over dinner. A wave of pleasure, like settling into a warm tub, cascaded over me as I thought of her, and of her sitting across from me in the restaurant. Every man in the place, right down to Hemingway's ghost, would be envious.

I was far away in these thoughts when two of the burly men I'd seen earlier walked over and leaned against trees ten yards away. Then I heard someone sit down on the bench behind me and open a newspaper.

"Don't turn around," a man said.

I recognized the voice. It was Marty Paulsen, Deputy Director of Operations for the CIA. He'd been peripherally involved in our art forgery case a year and a half ago.

"Pretend you don't notice me," he said.

"Well, that's easy, since I can't see you," I said.

"Mr. Stevens, do you remember when we last saw each other? I said that one day I'd come asking for a favor."

"Yes, I remember." I groaned inwardly.

"And do you recall what else I said?"

"You said, 'And when I contact you, don't say no.'"

"Correct. I have a case for you, Mr. Stevens. For you and Miss Krüsh."

If Paulsen is involved, it's sure to be Big Trouble.

But...then again...trouble is my business.

"Mr. Stevens?" he said.

"Go ahead. I'm listening."

About the Author

Chris Orcutt has written professionally for over 20 years as a fiction writer, journalist, scriptwriter, playwright, technical writer and speechwriter.

Orcutt is the creator of the critically acclaimed Dakota Stevens Mystery Series, including *A Real Piece of Work* (#1), *The Rich Are Different* (#2) and *A Truth Stranger Than Fiction* (#3). Orcutt's short story collection, *The Man, The Myth, The Legend*, was voted by IndieReader as one of the best books of 2013. And his modern pastoral novel *One Hundred Miles from Manhattan* (an IndieReader Best Book for 2014) prompted *Kirkus Reviews* to favorably compare Orcutt to Pulitzer Prize-winning author John Cheever.

As a newspaper reporter Orcutt received a New York Press Association award, and while an adjunct lecturer in writing for the City University of New York, he received the Distinguished Teaching Award.

If you would like to contact Chris, you can email him at corcutt007@yahoo.com or tweet him @chrisorcutt. For more information about Orcutt and his writing, or to follow his blog, visit his website: www.orcutt.net.

Excerpt from *A Real Piece of Work*

Book 1 in Chris Orcutt's Dakota Stevens Mystery Series is also available. *A Real Piece of Work*, the 1st novel in the series, delves into a world of art forgery, secret identities and murder. Following is the opening of *A Real Piece of Work*.

Back in my FBI days, during soporific stakeouts when I dreamed about the life I might lead as a private detective, I never imagined the job would one day require me to scuba-dive across a half-mile of ocean brimming with sharks.

Basically, anything capable of eating me was absent from my business plan.

Right now, despite the Caribbean sun on my face and the piquant salt air in my nose, I wished I were back in snowy Manhattan, safe behind my desk, listening like Sam Spade to some elegant dame tell me her troubles. Instead I had a 20-year-old scuba bum and my bikini-clad associate, Svetlana Krüsh, all but shoving me into the water. They stood silently beside me as wave after wave spanked the hull. Under my wetsuit, the heat began to rise.

"You're positive they're both on there," I said, nodding at the 80-foot motor yacht in the distance.

"According to the chambermaid," Svetlana said, "they left together this morning."

"And we're sure they're, ah, busy?"

"I am told they never leave the room."

She adjusted her bikini strap. After three days down here, Svetlana had only a whisper of a tan, but the way the leopard print hugged her aristocratic curves, you didn't care. Kyle, our alleged guide, leered at her. I grabbed him by the mouth and pinched his cheeks together.

"How about it, *dude*?"

"Wha?"

"Our friend on the yacht."

"Already told you—guy runs their slip says they put out every morning, come back around one."

"What time we got?"

With a flourish, Svetlana held out her watch. High noon.

"How long to get over there?" I asked.

"Half an hour, tops." Kyle scratched in his ear. "Quit stalling, man. I've gotta meet somebody at Sloppy Joe's soon."

I looked over our stern. Key West was a purple mist on the horizon. I turned back to the yacht.

"Let me see, one more time."

Svetlana passed the binoculars. While the captain and his mate read newspapers on the bridge, three bodyguards sunned themselves on the bow. Conover and his mistress had to be inside, doing what mistresses and CEOs of financial services companies did.

"*Moneta*?" Kyle said. "What the hell kind of name for a boat is that?"

"Goddess of money," I said. "Greek, I think."

"Roman," Svetlana said.

"There you go—Roman. We know what he worships anyway."

To the south dark clouds were creeping in, and the mounting wind flapped Svetlana's hair across my cheek. Between their boat and ours was a gulf of iridescent blue-green water that looked like it would take a week to cross. I wanted to call it off, but if I chickened-out now, in two weeks my business would shrivel up. Besides, Mrs. Conover was counting on us. I handed the binoculars back.

"Ready, Mr. Stevens?" Kyle said.

"Stop with the 'Mister' already. It's Dakota." I strapped on the flippers. "Why am I doing this again?"

Why? Because Mrs. Conover had made it sound so simple—snap a few photos, collect a big check. "I'll cover any expenses," she said. "Consider it a vacation...take a week, a month—I don't care. Just catch the bastard."

Svetlana nudged me. "Because you are sucker for jilted women. Especially when they are rich." She handed me a mask. "And don't forget, a blizzard is starting in New York, so we must catch six o'clock out of Miami."

I spit in the mask, rubbed it around and put it on.

"Sharks?" I said to Kyle.

"Sure. Blacktips, a few bulls maybe. No big deal."

I squatted down and slipped into the vest with the scuba tank. Kyle showed me the buttons for the buoyancy compensator.

"So, Miss Krüsh," I said, "while I'm risking life and *limb*, what will you be doing?"

She donned a pair of Dolce & Gabbana sunglasses and tied a mocha sarong around her waist so it hung fetchingly off one hip.

"Wave when you finish, and I swoop in like cavalry." She plopped down behind the wheel, crossed her runway legs and rubbed sunblock on her shoulders. Kyle jammed the regulator in my mouth.

"Remember what Nietzsche said, man—the shit that doesn't kill you makes you stronger. Trust me, you're gonna love it." He tipped backward into the deep.

I patted the vest's waterproof pouch to check for the camera and plunged in…

CPSIA information can be obtained at www.ICGtesting.com
Printed in the USA
LVOW06s1619100915

453651LV00011B/717/P